MEASURE

BOOK TWO

OF
SECRETS
AND
SPIRITS

LYNN PEREZ-HEWITT

PAGE PUBLISHING
Conneaut Lake, PA

First originally published by Page Publishing 2022

ISBN 978-1-6624-7767-6 (pbk)
ISBN 978-1-6624-7768-3 (digital)

Printed in the United States of America

For Diamond Jim,
original believer, first fan, and the best husband a writer could have

CONTENTS

MAPS OF SKYRIDGE RANCH

Skyridge Valley

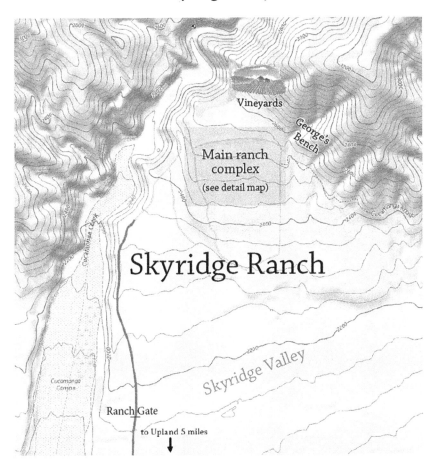

Skyridge Ranch

The Bunk Houses:
VV-Vineyard View   The Casitas: Other Living
MV-Mountain View   B - Bonita   Quarters:
SV-Sky View   D -Dulce   H - Head of School
RV-Ridge View

CAST OF CHARACTERS

Donald "Don" Sullivan Grant, b. 1946, retired high school science teacher, father of Ben and Charlie, Vento Junction, AZ

Benjamin "Ben" Sullivan Grant, b. 1974, history teacher, Vento Junction Community College

Charles "Charlie" Sullivan Grant, PhD, b. 1978, physicist

Nicholas "Nick" (a.k.a. Brown) Nishimura, PhD, b. 1920, physicist, Pasadena, CA

Grace Nishimura Acevedo, b. 1928 Pasadena, California, sister of Nick, currently living in Indio, CA

Hector Acevedo, b. 1925 New Mexico, husband of Grace, married 1946, deceased 2006

Daniel Acevedo, b. 1947, attorney, son of Grace and Hector, father of Nicola

Victory "Vic" Acevedo, b. 1948, actress, daughter of Grace and Hector

Nicola Acevedo, b. 1977, graduate student in physics at UCLA, daughter of Daniel, granddaughter of Grace

Richard "Dick" Stanton, PhD, b. 1918, physicist, best friend of Nick Nishimura

Elizabeth "Betsy" Baldwin Stanton, b. 1920, teacher, wife of Dick, mother of Rick and Rosemary

Richard "Rick" Stanton, PhD, b. 1947, teaches physics at UCLA, advisor to Nicola Acevedo, husband of Jane MacLane, son of Dick and Betsy Stanton

Patrick "Mac" MacLane, b. 1918, colonel, stationed at Los Alamos (1943–1944), founder of The Institute

Martha O'Hara MacLane PhD, b. 1922, teacher of math and physics at Stanford, wife of Mac MacLane, mother of Jane and Robert

Jane MacLane Stanton, b. 1947, daughter of Mac and Martha, married to Rick, director of The Institute

Mitchell "Mitch" Stans, b. 1978, head of security at The Institute, adopted son of Rick and Jane Stanton

Suzanne Brown, PhD, b. 1978, biomedical engineering researcher at The Institute

Nicholas G. Fabian III, PhD, b. 1982 in County Sligo, Republic of Ireland, cybersecurity specialist at The Institute, former geologist

Clary McGonigal, b. 1990 in County Sligo, Republic of Ireland, geology prodigy at The Institute

Theresa Cisneros-Johnson, b. 1928 in Los Alamos, NM, teacher, mother of Aurelia "Lia" Gonzales-Thompson, grandmother of Elizabeta and Mercedes

Aurelia Johnson Gonzalez Thompson, b. 1949, daughter of Theresa Cisneros-Johnson, mother of Elizabeta and Mercedes, married Sergio Gonzales in 1983 (who died in 1986), married George Thompson in 1988 (whom she divorced in 2000), currently living near Los Alamos, NM

Elizabeta "Beta" Gonzales-Thompson, b. 1984, daughter of Lia Gonzalez-Thompson, granddaughter of Theresa Cisneros-Johnson, twin sister of Mercedes

Mercedes "Mercy" Gonzales-Thompson, b. 1984, daughter of Lia Gonzalez-Thompson, granddaughter of Theresa Cisneros-Johnson, twin sister of Elizabeta

Michelle Matthews, b. 1978 in Chicago, IL, journalist, currently living in Phoenix, AZ

Henry Cisneros, b. 1926, brother of Theresa and Tommy Cisneros, lives near Los Alamos, NM

Albert Ortiz, b. 1927, friend of Theresa and classmate of Tommy Cisneros, lives near Los Alamos, NM

Oscar Bunelos, b. 1927, friend of Theresa and classmate of Tommy Cisneros, lives near Los Alamos, NM

Braulio "Butch" Ontiveros, b. 1926, grandfather of John Henry, friend of Theresa and classmate of Tommy Cisneros, lives near Los Alamos, NM

Manuel Ordonez, b. 1926, friend of Theresa and classmate of Tommy Cisneros, lives near Los Alamos, NM

John Henry Ontiveros, b. 1978, grandson of Butch, former student at Skyridge Ranch School, archaeologist turned general contractor, lives near Los Alamos, NM

Gail Kincaid Gustafson Hickson, b. 1921, married Dave Gustafson (July 30, 1944), married Reginald "Reg" Hickson (January 1945), currently living near Pasadena, CA

Darrin "D-man" Hickson, PhD, b. June 1945, son of Gail and David Gustafson, raised by Gail and Reg Hickson

Reginald "Reg" Hickson, PhD (1919–2002), physicist and former team member for the Trick at Los Alamos

Paul E. Sanchez, MD, b. 1973, neurologist currently at The Institute doing mind-body research

Gordon "Gordy" Chambers, b. 1978, classmate of Mitchell Stans, owns a communication corporation with top secret clearance.

Tommy Cisneros, b. 1927, brother of Theresa, disappeared from Los Alamos on September 8, 1944

Rosemary Stanton Edwards, b. 1950, daughter of Dick and Betsy and sister of Rick Stanton, popular author of science fiction novels, currently interim head of school at Skyridge Ranch

Darcy Gail Hickson, b. 1971, daughter of Darren Hickson, community college professor of American literature of the twentieth century

Robert P. MacLane, b. 1949, colonel of the US Army, son of Patrick and Martha MacLane, younger brother of Jane MacLane Stanton

Feynman, male Irish wolfhound, belongs to Rick and Jane Stanton, b. 2004

Samantha Jane, female miniature Australian shepherd, belongs to Don Grant, b. 2002.

Rose, female standard border collie, belongs to Lia Thompson, b. 2000

Amy June, female miniature Australian shepherd, belongs to Grace Acevedo, b. 2002, littermate of Samantha Jane

PROLOGUE

On September 8, 2008, twenty-four-year-old Japanese American physicist Nick Nishimura became the first but not the only person teleported via an experiment nicknamed the Trick from Los Alamos, New Mexico, 1944. When he opened his eyes, he was stunned to realize that not only his *where* but his *when* had changed.

He met and trusted Don Grant, a retired Southern Arizona High School science teacher. This connected him to Don's sons, Ben, a history teacher, and Charlie, a physicist and student of time travel who had followed Nick's work.

They helped Nick reach out to his sister, Grace, now eighty years old and living in nearby California. A quick road trip to meet not only Grace but her granddaughter Nicola, Nick's grandniece, led to Nicola's graduate advisor at UCLA. He is revealed to be the son of Nick's best friend, Dick Stanton. On the road again, they are soon in a Southern California living room greeting the now ninety-year-old scientist who wept upon learning he had not killed his best friend after all.

Dick Stanton's daughter-in-law, Jane, is the director of The Institute, a private think tank founded by her father Mac MacLane, the military leader of the civilian science team that designed the Trick. Jane opens positions at The Institute to the three young physicists.

Two and a half months later, it's Thanksgiving Day at The Institute. Nick has just embraced a special guest, the Native American woman who long ago befriended him at Los Alamos. Theresa's reassurance that spirits were watching him has stayed with him.

Theresa's older brother Tommy disappeared at the same time as Nick. But when he arrived, the teens he met thought he was on drugs or crazy when he told them where he was from. Only weeks ago, he was rescued from a juvenile facility in Arizona. Now safe in Southern California, he was at the Thanksgiving dinner, but before Tommy could reunite with his sister, Nick collapsed in her arms.

CHAPTER 1

THURSDAY, NOVEMBER 27, 2008, THANKSGIVING DAY PUMPKIN PIE INTERRUPTED, THE INSTITUTE, LOS ANGELES, CALIFORNIA

Jane Stanton glanced over her shoulder at the people leaving the dining room to gather in the lobby as she spoke into her earpiece, standard comm equipment for the director of The Institute during events.

"Mitch, I need a gurney in 1-A near the infirmary. Theresa collapsed."

"On it." Her adopted son was the calm, competent presence she relied on as her security director, exactly what was needed now.

Mitch spoke into his earpiece to his longtime friend and colleague. "Foot, I need you to cover the Dining Room. Calm the crowd and get them out of the lobby. I have another emergency."

Gordy Chambers, a.k.a. Foot, replied, "You mean being the biggest, blackest man in the room isn't enough to quiet a crowd?"

"Dude, these people are pretty freaked out. Former football player is not the credential needed right now." Mitch was grinning but serious.

"Then my skinny self is at your service, Hands. Gotcha covered." The nicknames acquired during their UCLA football days had stuck through the years, Gordy as kicker and his best friend's because he couldn't catch a damn thing.

Father Joe Perez had joined the trio of women guarding the young man, now on the gurney, who had moments earlier crumpled to the dining room floor. Father Joe had been at Theresa Cisneros-Johnson's side when she collapsed. His EMT training kicked in as he protected her head and began to check her pulse.

Jane surveyed the group around the gurney. "Mercy, come with me. We can get this gurney into the treatment room. Father, you're right where we need you. Mitch will be here in a minute with one for her. I'll leave the door open so you can roll right in." Mercy, granddaughter of the motionless woman, moved quickly to help.

As they began to walk, Jane spoke again to her son. "Mitch, find Paul Sanchez. He should be here now, and we could use him."

"Okay, Mom. Don't worry, and Gordy's managing the dining room and lobby."

"Thank you, good thinking." Her relief was felt through the comm system. Gordy Chambers was another bright light from her son's college football days.

Moments later, Mitch and the gurney arrived in the hallway. He and Father Joe gently lifted the still quiet older woman and finished the trip to the treatment room. Mercy Thompson pulled a chair between the two patients and took their hands. Stretched out on one side was her grandmother, with a history of speaking to her spirits through trances. On the other side was a young man she had only met an hour ago, yet his connection to her grandmother must be powerful.

With the hubbub everywhere, no one noticed the two dogs followed by two teenage boys walking purposefully down the hallway. They were in the infirmary and at the door of the treatment room before they were noticed by the occupants.

Clary McGonigle, the tall Irish teen, spoke first. "Dr. Jane, Feynman was about being wild in the courtyard, so we were thinking it best to be letting him in."

His fellow teenager, Tommy Cisneros, joined in. "And Sam was frantic. It's not like her. I agreed with Clary here to let them in."

Dr. Jane smiled to reassure them. "It's okay, boys, they can stay. They appear to have settled down, yes?" She surveyed her own canine, Feynman, an Irish wolfhound, and his new friend Samantha Jane, a miniature Australian shepherd. She continued. "Now you can help me by going back to the dining room and helping Gordy to keep people calm."

They looked at each other, shrugged, and nodded. As they left, a harried man in a white lab coat brushed by them to enter the treatment room.

Glancing around the small room, Jane announced, "I'm going to step out for a few minutes. Father, I suggest at this point we proceed on a need-to-know basis."

He nodded his understanding. What he knew about the young Asian man on the gurney was a closely held secret. As soon as she exited the infirmary, Jane activated her earpiece again. "Mitch, we need Suzanne Brown's help at the infirmary. Would you find her and get her here, please?"

Instantly she heard. "Will do, Mom. How's it going there?"

"Better now that Paul is here. I'm not at all sure what's going on medically, but having biofeedback available for Paul might be valuable. Suzanne's bound to have something in her lab that she can rig up quickly. Oh, and Sam and Feynman are here as well, if anyone's looking for them."

Mitch chuckled. "Of course, they are." The unlikely was often the norm around The Institute.

"You might let your dad know when you fill him in on the status. Father Joe just left to return to the dining hall. I have Paul Sanchez, Mercy Thompson, and two patients in treatment room A. No change."

"Got it." Mitch was walking into the lobby of the building to begin his search for the biomedical engineer in a souped-up electric wheelchair.

He heard her machine before he saw her. "Wheels, I need you."

A stunning young woman with short spiked blond hair spun her motorized chair and stopped in front of him. "What up, big man?"

3

"Mom needs some biofeedback gear for the two people who collapsed. They're in the infirmary."

"Two? I only saw the guy go down. Now we got two? What the hell?"

Mitch continued. "And if you haven't met Paul Sanchez yet, this is your chance. Oh, and it's Dr. Paul Sanchez, medical doctor. He's doing some research that you'll want to follow. Your biomedical escapades have made the rounds, the good kind." Mitch was heading back to the dining room.

"Okay, Big Man. You got my attention. I'm on it." She began to roll toward the elevators. Just then, the glass doors of the main entrance swung open to admit a tanned, graying man in shorts, flip-flops, and a long ponytail. Suzanne grinned. "D-man, late as usual. Follow me. I'll fill you in while you help me out."

Dr. Darren Hickson, the D-man himself, eyed the crowd, heard some shouts from the dining room, and decided to take her offer. "Deal, Wheels. Where we headed?"

CHAPTER 2

THANKSGIVING 2008,
ON THE WAY TO THE BIOMEDICAL
LAB INSIDE THE INSTITUTE

"I'll fill you in on what I know, and no guarantees that I know enough to make sense of it, but let's get away from this crowd." Suzanne was on the move.

"No argument from me. I just spent three months studying waves on the Oregon Coast. No crowds. Not really even many people. Lots of quiet. Between LAX and this, I need to put some space between this noise and my chi."

As they proceeded toward the elevator, he continued. "While I was watching the waves, I got this idea. Of course, having ideas, that's why I went, but anyway. A quantum tsunami. I started with collapsing wave theory and watching those waves day after day, it just came to me. Why couldn't the action of waves be applied to that theory? But more than just waves, what about bigger wave action? That's when I knew it was time to come back. Anyway, it's Thanksgiving, and I want to be here."

They moved into the spacious elevator with the clear window facing the atrium of the deceptively spacious building. In less than a minute, they were on the second floor, and Suzanne was speeding up.

"Whoa there, Wheels. I'm not equipped with a motor. Let me catch up. I don't have my badge to get access, so leave the door open. Okay?"

"Did I speed up, or did you slow down while you were gone, old man?" Suzanne was busting his chops a bit.

"So you're saying I've been gone so long that you've undergone a personality change. Have you?" D-man could give as good as he got.

Suzanne whirled around to face him, or at least look up at him. "I'm still ornery and brilliant if that's what you mean. Nothing's changed. I'm holding up my end of the duo. Oh yeah, the duo. But I've been solo for how many months? Wheels my rolling butt."

D-man was sheepish. "Okay, I didn't call. I didn't write. I didn't email. But damn, Wheels, it was remote, and I was into it and making progress."

"Yeah, yeah, all you science bros are the same. Science always comes first. Well, maybe I'll just keep what I think I know to my own self." She turned away and privately grinned. This would kill him.

"So now I'm just a science bro. That hurts, little girl. That hurts." D-man was trying to angle back into her good graces.

"I'll make you a deal, but if you don't come through, I'm done." Suzanne got serious.

"Whoa, when did you get so serious?" D-man backed up a foot.

"When you left me to fend for myself and things started to get weirder than normal." Suzanne set her jaw.

"I thought we talked about this before I left, and you were cool with my sabbatical." Darren was not entirely clear.

"And I thought you agreed to be in touch regularly. That means weekly. Not monthly and definitely not *never*." This last statement was a little heated.

Darren sat down in a chair nearby so he could look her in the eye." You're right. 100 percent. I lost my sense of time and found my selfish self. Pretty quickly, in fact. I do way too well all alone. At least that's what I tell myself when I start to feel guilty."

"Look, we're colleagues and friends. I deserve at least the respect you give to the others."

"If it's any comfort, I didn't even send messages to my kids, and boy, are they torqued." Darren was trying for a light tone.

"Nope. Nobody's really happy with you, D-man. You've got a lot of fences to mend." Suzanne began to rummage in drawers and pull out wires.

"Can I help you there?" Darren tried to change the subject.

"You can get me a rolling box. In the closet over there."

"What's the hurry, and what are you building?" He sounded genuinely curious.

"Well, if you must know, we have two people in the infirmary who just collapsed before pumpkin pie, and Dr. Jane asked me to rig up a biofeedback contraption with my spare parts." Suzanne was borderline exasperated.

"That's why it was chaos when I got here. People collapsed? Something they ate, something contagious?" She had his attention now.

"Dr. Jane just asked for biofeedback gear, so I don't think so. It was kinda tense, and I didn't stick around to ask why, you know?"

"Well, who are they? Do you know that much?"

"I know one of them, kind of. He's part of what you've been missing. His name is Nick Brown, but I think it's phony. He got here in mid-September, and two other newbies came too. The girl, Nicola, is nice enough. Pretty in an exotic kinda way. She sticks to him like a Siamese twin. The other dude is Charlie. He's a wiry bundle of energy. Seems smart. Always has something to munch on in his hand. I like him, but he sticks with Nick and Nicola, so it's been hard to get a read on him. And lately, they expanded their circle to include Fabian."

"So you know the Siamese twin thing isn't cool. And the big Irish dude? The cyber guy?" D-man was trying to absorb this data.

"And you mistook me for someone who was PC? You've been breathing salt air too long, D-man."

"Okay, okay. So three new people, one who may not be who he says he is. And now the annoying Irishman is with them. I still don't get it. Why does it matter?"

"Because Mr. Nick Brown is one of the people lying in a coma, or whatever state it is they're in." Suzanne had started pulling together her soldering torch and pulled on her eye protection.

"So out of the four, we have mystery man down. Who's the other person? Do we know?" D-man liked a mystery.

"The other collapsed person is an older Native American woman. Just before Nick collapsed, they had hugged each other. Then he went down like a bag of rocks. She was walking along beside him on the gurney and collapsed. I had started to kind of follow them while everyone else had their hair on fire." Suzanne had lit the soldering torch.

"Okay, still not connecting dots here." He was wrinkling his forehead, trying to put the limited bits of information into a hypothesis, to no avail.

"Oh, and two more new scientists arrived today. Twin sisters. And the woman who collapsed is their grandmother."

"How do you know they're scientists?"

"We were talking about them at the table. And I think there are two more connected dudes, and I can't entirely figure out how they're connected."

"And they would be?" Not as serene as watching waves hit the shore, but Suzanne never failed to be interesting.

"One is a history teacher from Arizona. He's Charlie's brother. Kinda cute in a dusty way. The other. Whoa. You will *never* guess. Okay, I'll tell you." Her head was down as she created a second contraption.

"So tell me already." D-man was into the game now.

"Daniel Acevedo. *The* Daniel Acevedo, attorney at righteous f——ing law. That's who."

"I think I need a whiteboard or a scorecard. Three new scientists. Then add the Irishman. Twin scientists whose grandmother collapses after hugging the mystery guy. A dusty history teacher and a righteous lawyer. Tell me any of this makes sense. Please." He was shaking his head.

"The dusty guy is Charlie's brother, remember? So he has a direct connection. The righteous lawyer is Dad to Nicola, part of the threesome now four. Again, a connection, but not clearing up the collapsing people. Not at all sure how the science twins came to be here or their grandma." She sat up straight to look at him through her goggles. "You know it's actually more confusing saying it out loud. How does *that* happen?"

"Here's what my yoga teacher says."

"*Yoga* teacher? Damn, D-man, when did *that* happen?" Suzanne was shaking her head and grinning at him.

"Oregon Coast. You gotta try it. Anyway. First, take a deep cleansing breath." He closed his eyes and did just that.

"Okay, that would be a no. I'll just keep my breaths nice and shallow, thank you very much. Is it clearing any of this up for you?"

"Let me try to unpack this a little. New guy, who may or may not be who he says he is, collapses today after hugging an older Native American woman." He was ticking items off on the fingers of his left hand.

"Two new sister scientists arrive today, and their grandmother just happens to be here, who collapses after hugging mystery man. Have I got it?" Second finger ticked off on his sun-burned hand.

"Oh, and security Mitch grabbed the remaining mystery group along with dusty brother and his squeeze and took them off for a huddle right after the collapses." Suzanne was remembering more of the melee.

"Security Mitch is part of it. Okay. That's probably important."

"And Dr. Jane's husband, Rick, knows all these people. He doesn't usually, does he? Know the new scientists? And his *dad* knows the grandma who collapsed." Suzanne closed her eyes to see the room again before the chaos started.

"Whoa, did you know that their dads knew my dad? Jane's dad and Rick's dad, I mean. They all worked together during the War. The Second World War. Not my war. I wonder if that's a connecting factor?" D-man was thinking.

"And mystery scientist dude is like Asian or something."

"Or something? Chinese, Korean, Japanese? Can you narrow it any?"

"I think Japanese. Maybe. I heard Nicola saying something about her grandparents being in one of those camps during that war."

D-man Hickson sat back to absorb what he just heard. A Japanese American mystery scientist who knew an older Native

American woman. This had bits of stories his dad used to tell him. And they were secret stories. No one was supposed to know.

"Suzanne, honey, this could be big. You know my dad was at Los Alamos. He used to tell me stories, secret stories, about what they were working on at Los Alamos. It was Jane's dad, Rick's dad, and this other scientist. A Japanese American guy. Really smart. Oppie pulled him from one of those camps. They were working on a project, and the Japanese American dude disappeared. That's all my dad knew. And then all the scientists on the project got transferred to other places until the end of the war." D-man had leaned forward.

Suzanne was staring at him. "Do you think the collapsed mystery dude is that guy? From Los Alamos? That would be impossible. What were they working on? Did your dad tell you?"

D-man nodded slowly. "Before he died, he told me they had been working on teleportation. For military intelligence, but he didn't think it worked. I mean, the guy disappeared."

"Oh my God, oh my God, oh my God. It's him. It's got to be him. It explains so much!" Suzanne almost spun around in her chair.

D-man looked at the rig on her lab table. "Is it ready to go?"

"It's ready and so am I. Coming, Wave Man?"

CHAPTER 3

THANKSGIVING 2008, MOMENTS EARLIER AT THE INSTITUTE INFIRMARY

Dr. Paul Sanchez was still shaking his head when he saw the infirmary door open. He felt a little guilty for not being on hand when this emergency, or whatever it was, erupted. But volunteering at the clinic nearby was a balm for his soul. Helping people healed him, and sometimes the hours evaporated just like water in hot fields. That reminded him of his family near Fresno and brutal days picking crops. The sweat turning into salt crystals on his father's shirt. Those were the days that started his road to the studies that brought him to this amazing place. That and meeting Mitch Stans.

Mitch had said that there was a collapse and then another and that he doubted it was food poisoning. Then he said something that increased Paul's pace. *I think this one is right up your alley.* That grabbed his attention as his pulse raced.

Suzanne sped by and turned her head to shout. "You must be the doc. Get in there. I'll be back with some biofeedback gear as soon as I can."

He dodged the engineer nicknamed Wheels, stepped through the open door, and heard Jane Stanton. "I'm texting Paul Sanchez. He should be back by now."

"Someone say my name?"

"Good to see you, Paul." Jane greeted him with relief. To Mercy and Father Joe, she said, "This is Paul Sanchez. He just joined The Institute, and his research is uniquely qualified for this situation." Turning to him, "Paul, the man in this bed is Nick Brown. The woman in the other bed is Theresa Johnson. At the door is Father Joe Perez, an EMT, and yes, also a priest. He was with us when Theresa collapsed. Between Nick and Theresa is Mercedes, Theresa's grand-daughter. More importantly, she's joining The Institute to study quantum consciousness."

Surveying the situation while preparing to listen to chests with his stethoscope, Paul asked, "What have we got?"

Father Joe spoke, "Native American female, age eighty."

Mercy looked up, holding the hands of the two still figures. "Hi, Dr. Sanchez. I think if I understand your studies correctly, you'll find what's happening compelling. My grandmother and Nick are psychically connected and are currently in a quantum state. She has a history of trances, but this is unusual."

Paul pulled up a short stool. "A quantum state. I need a bit more. Dr. Stanton, do you want me to check vitals or do you have a diagnosis?"

Jane smiled. "Yes, and the diagnosis is very preliminary. This is a new episode for Nick, a familiar one for Theresa, and so vitals will be valuable as their situation unfolds."

"How did they present?" Paul shifted into clinical mode. Father Joe looked over the room. "I think you're in good hands. I'll head back to my friends and give them a status."

"Yes, thank you, Father. I'll talk with you later, I'm sure." Jane smiled her gratitude as he left and returned to the conversation in the room.

Mercy spoke. "They had both finished their meals. Nick came over to greet G-Ma. She knew he would be there, but he didn't know he would be seeing her. They knew each other years ago. As they embraced, I heard Nick groan like he was in pain, and then he crumpled to the floor. Mitch got a gurney. We were walking by Nick's side, almost here when she just collapsed. We caught her before she hit the floor. They've been here for fifteen minutes or so. Does that help?"

"Does your grandmother have a history of collapsing?"

Mercy smiled ruefully. "She has a history of semi-trancelike states when she gets visits from her spirits. This is the first time I've seen her collapse. But then again, this is the first time she's seen someone like Nick."

"Someone like Nick?" Paul raised his eyebrows.

"Yes, someone she knew sixty-four years ago."

"So she knew him as a spirit, and now he's here?" Paul tied to make sense of what he heard.

Jane spoke. "It's a bit more complicated than that. We're going to fill you in on something utterly confidential, but as the medical professional of record here, you'll need to know. Nick's true name is Nishimura, and a couple of months ago, he traveled through time from 1944, arriving in present-day Southern Arizona."

Paul stared at her. "I knew strange stuff happened here. Mitch alluded to as much when he suggested this was the best place for me to pursue my research. But this…"

"Yes, this is even stranger than usual for us. But trust me when I say that we have verified that he is who he says he is and was. And sixty-four years ago, when Theresa was sixteen years old, she was his maid at Los Alamos where he was a research scientist." Jane continued.

"What was their relationship sixty-four years ago?"

Mercy replied, "According to G-Ma, she befriended him and that was all. Her spirits told her that he would travel and that he would be safe. Nothing else."

"And you say they had not seen each other for sixty-four years until today. And when they embraced, he collapsed first."

Mercy nodded. "Yes. And then it was about five minutes later while we were walking here, she was still holding his hand that she collapsed."

"You said he made a groan like he was in pain. Did she make any similar sound?"

Jane and Mercy looked at each other." It was more of a sigh, wasn't it, Mercy? At least that's what I thought I heard." Jane was frowning, trying to recall.

Mercy nodded. "Yes, I do recall a soft sound. Not at all like she was in pain. More like she let go of something."

"Have you been around her when she goes into her trancelike state?" Paul embraced this new diagnostic challenge.

"Not often, but enough to know that it's silent. But then again, she's often sitting and has a warning or a hint that a visit is coming."

"What do those warnings sound or look like? Does she report any pain or discomfort?"

"The last time I was with her when a visit happened, she just kind of tilted her head and said that she'd better lie down. I went with her to her bedroom, where she did lie down. Her eyes closed, and she was in her trace for about an hour. She's never said anything about pain."

"Is that how long they usually last?"

"It varies, but the longest I've heard from her is several hours. Of course, there isn't always someone around when they happen, so I don't really know."

"Has she ever had blood pressure or any other check done during or after a trance?"

"She's usually at home when they happen, so no. It's pretty remote there, so no one has ever either had the inclination or the equipment before."

Paul straightened his shoulders. "What you're telling me is that I have a woman with a history of trances, a young man with no history of same, who saw each other after sixty-four years and then instant trance."

Jane interjected, "For Nick, it's only been a few months."

"Oh yeah, the time travel thing."

Mercy nodded." You should know that I feel something kind of flowing between them."

"You feel something. Something through your hands?" Paul stared at those hands as they connected his two newest patients.

"Yes. It's not exactly a current, but it's a flow of some sort."

"Have you ever held your grandmother's hand during a trance?"

"Yes, a couple of times. I didn't feel what I'm feeling now."

Jane spoke. "Suzanne will be back as soon as she can with some biofeedback gear. She thought she could re-rig some equipment in her lab."

Paul nodded. "That should be helpful. In the meantime, I'm going to get my blood pressure cuff and pulse oximeter, basic stuff, and start charts on both of them. Mercy, can you fill me in on any family history that could help? Dr. Stanton, what do you have on Nick?"

"He had baseline tests done shortly after he arrived in Arizona. I have those records electronically. I'll call them up and text you." She left the room to go to her office.

Paul looked at Mercy. "Tell me more about your work."

"I study quantum consciousness. And trust me, nothing like this has ever happened during my studies, at least not so far. I'm in unknown territory."

"Well, that makes two of us. Glad to have you with me."

Meanwhile in the Second-Floor Private Conference Room at The Institute

Nicola Acevedo, Beta Gonzalez-Thompson, Nicholas Fabian III, and Charlie Grant looked up as Mitch Stans opened the conference room door. Beta spoke quietly. "We didn't know where else to go to be away from the crowd and we didn't want to go to the Commons either."

"Good move. Things are settling a little, but it's better that you moved out of sight before anyone could question or track you. It's time to make plans."

Charlie spoke first. "Okay, big man, what have you got in mind?"

Nicola didn't give him a chance to open his mouth. "Beta and I think we should go to Los Alamos, like right now."

Fabian leaned back. "Good God. It's a breather he needs. It's been chaos and the man's the head of fecking security. He's had a bit on his plate."

Nicola was chagrinned. Lightly punching Nicholas, she pointed out, "Your Irish is showing." Looking to Mitch, she grimaced. "Of course. I'm sorry, Mitch. It's just we're all afraid for Nick and Theresa and figure the sooner we can find answers, the sooner we can help them both."

"I understand." Mitch had pulled out a chair at the head of the oval table. "For your information, they are both stable. Mercy is with them. Father Joe was at Theresa's side when she collapsed, and they are all with Dr. Paul Sanchez now."

Beta spoke up. "Good. My sister can help. What about Jane? And there's a...what kind of doctor there?"

"It's all good. Mercy is sitting between Nick and your grand-mother holding their hands. Jane is right there, and Paul Sanchez is a man I've known for more than ten years. He's a medical doctor and a good friend."

"That's all good to know, but why is a medical doctor here today? Do people usually collapse on Thanksgiving at The Institute?" Charlie was not at ease with the update.

Mitch grinned. "Skepticism is expected among scientists, even ones who study time travel. Dr. Paul Sanchez is a neurologist special-izing in integrated medicine. His area of research is the mind-body connection."

Nicola and Beta locked eyes and turned to Mitch as Nicola gasped. "You gotta be kidding! What kind of luck is this?"

Fabian spoke. "It's never luck here, lasses. It just happens this way. We get, find, or are given what we need when we need it. Why do ye think scientists from the world over be here."

Beta smiled. "My sister would tell you that the energies in the quantum realm were drawn to the place and the people."

"Whatever you be calling it. I'll be knowing what I see, and what I know. What happens here won't be such as anything you've ever seen before." Fabian rested his case.

Mitch continued. "The good news is that our patients are sta-ble, and we can return to the original topic of conversation. The plan for our next step."

Charlie leaned forward. "Does everyone agree that Los Alamos is where we need to start?"

They all nodded. Beta spoke. "You'll want to meet with some of the men who were around when it happened."

Charlie raised his eyebrows. "Are there still guys around from back then?"

Beta grinned. "Not only still around, they meet every day to have coffee and talk about the old days, the problems of the world, and baseball."

Mitch leaned in. "And just where do they meet every day for coffee and conversation?"

"The coffee shop in the center of the old section of town. Almost across the street from Fuller Lodge."

Nicola almost leaped up. "You mean where it all happened?"

Charlie raised his palms. "Not exactly where it *all* happened. Where they ate and slept sure, but the science happened in an old building on the edge of the Hill."

Nicola dismissed him. "Picky, picky. It's there. They're there. We need to be there. Yes?"

Mitch chuckled. "Well said, Nicola. Beta, do you have suggestions about where we fly into, stay, contacts on the ground?"

"It's where I grew up. So yes, I do. Let me make a call and I'll have answers for you in a few minutes."

While Beta moved to a corner of the room with her phone, the others moved closer. Mitch lowered his voice. "The Institute has a corporate jet available, and I can fly it."

Charlie had to ask. "With a license?"

"Yes, funny man, with a license. I can file a flight plan this evening, and we can leave early if Beta can get us set up."

Nicola and Fabian shared a glance. She spoke. "How do we explain our departure?"

Fabian grimaced. "No one cares, lass."

Mitch reassured them. "Mom will cover for all of us. Besides, I'm sure she's up to something. Trust me. This is not a woman without a plan A, B, C, all the way through Z."

Nicola nodded, "Of course, you're right. Jane will smooth the way."

Beta returned. "I spoke with my mom. First, she was alarmed to hear about G-Ma, but I filled her in, and now she's okay, especially hearing that we're coming. We can stay at the house. It's plenty big enough for all of us. That way, we won't leave more of a trail than we need to. And the Los Alamos air strip can handle a small jet. Lots of government types still fly in and out, so it won't be unusual."

Mitch smiled at the newcomer with growing appreciation. "Thank you for that consideration. Much appreciated. While you were on the phone, we all agreed to fly out in the morning if your call was successful. We'll take The Institute's private jet."

Charlie stood up. "Then it's back to the fray. Where do we meet in the morning? How do we get to the plane? And has anybody seen my dad and my brother, oh, and, Michelle?"

Mitch stood to stand next to him. "Your dad is with my dad, and Ben and Michelle are helping Gordy in the dining room." Shifting gears, he thought out loud. "Pack light for a couple of days. Charlie, Fabian maybe some testing gear for soils and rocks. Nicola, a laptop will be important. Meet me at 6:00 a.m. in the lobby. We can take the corporate van."

The group began to disperse. Mitch and Beta lingered. He gently took her hand. "Thank you for your help. It can't be easy seeing your grandmother like that. I appreciate your calm and levelheaded response to the situation."

She gave him a wise and slightly weary smile. "With a family known for seeing spirits, somebody needs to be levelheaded, and that falls to me. But thank you for noticing."

"Oh, I noticed. I noticed." The big man smiled as they headed out to face the unknown.

CHAPTER 4

AUGUST 1997, UCLA LOCKER ROOM

Mitchell Stans was curious about the visitor hanging around the football practice field and now in the weight room. He hadn't said anything to him. Just watched. He looked fit, but not like an athlete kind of fit. He figured if the guy was supposed to be here, somebody would say something.

When Coach finally explained, Mitch decided to challenge this doctor here to study the athletes. "So what do you think there is to learn between the mind and the body, Doc. Isn't it obvious they're connected?"

Paul Sanchez was surprised that it was the oversize black lineman who spoke first, but in his line of research, being surprised was pretty common. He held out his hand. "I'm Paul Sanchez, and thank you for asking the question. The answer is 'yes, and.' Yes, we know a lot about the connection, the obvious one, between the mind and the body. The 'and' comes in because we're learning more about that connection all the time."

Mitch shook Paul's hand, slung his towel around his impressive neck, and sat on a weight bench. "Mitchell Stans. You can call me Mitch, and for example, what *more* are you learning, Doc?"

Paul sat on a nearby bench. "When I was a kid in Fresno, I watched my dad and my uncles working in the fields all day, every day. They just kept working, almost like machines. I asked them how they did it. What they told me then was what started me studying the connection. It was more than a brain telling a hand to pull a stalk. They didn't have scientific words to describe it, but I started to write down what they said. I dated the entries and noted the weather too."

Mitch looked at the intense young man. "You're quite a way from Fresno, Doc. Wanna connect the dots for me?"

Paul continued. "My family wanted me to follow a different path. Not go into the fields. I was good in science, did well in school. Got scholarships. Then biology and medicine really drew me in. I saw a way I could give back to my family. So I kept studying, kept getting scholarships. Finally, I was in medical school. It was time to choose what kind of medicine. I picked family practice. During my residency, somebody passed me an article about integrative medicine. I shifted to neurology, and it all clicked. I could help my family by learning more about this mind-body thing."

Mitch smiled. "So you're really from the lettuce fields?"

Paul grinned. "Lots of fields. My family immigrated a few generations ago, but they have deep roots, pun intended, in Fresno."

Mitch looked around. "I like you, Doc. A few of the guys are going to study together tonight. You want to meet us and get to know them, too?"

Paul perked up. "That would be great. I hate to intrude, but I'm eager to start collecting data."

Mitch reached into the pocket of his sweatpants. "Hang on a minute, I'll clear it with my mom."

"Your mom?"

"Yeah, I live at home, and the guys come to the house to study. Dad teaches physics, and Mom is a scientist."

Mitch pushed a number to speed dial. "Hey, Mom, the guys are coming over tonight to study, and there's a doctor here studying us, a mind-body connection research thing. I invited him to come over. Is that okay? Cool. Thank you. I'll give him directions."

Mitch looked at Paul. "Want me to text you, or do you have paper?"

"Both." Paul pulled out a small notepad as well as his phone. They exchanged info. "See you at six?"

"Better make it five thirty. If you come at six, the pizza will be long gone."

"Got it. Good to know. Can I bring anything?"

"Just be prepared for the third degree. My folks are great, but they ask a lot of questions. It makes them good scientists, but kind of different if you know what I mean." Mitch was heading for the showers.

When the doorbell rang at the sprawling Ranch-style house, Dr. Rick Stanton opened the door. "You must be Paul the doctor. Come on in. The guys are on the patio, and there are still a few slices left. And the dog is friendly, just big. His name is Enrico."

Paul headed toward the sounds of laughter. The house was nice, kind of sprawling, comfortable, even lived in. When he opened the door to the backyard patio, a very large, very furry beast waddled happily over to sniff him. "Well, who are you, my large friend?"

Mitch looked up from the pizza. "That's Enrico. I told you my folks are scientists. Even a Saint Bernard gets to be named for somebody famous."

"Ah, Fermi! That's cool. I take it he's friendly?" Paul was petting a very happy new friend.

Rick came up to join the newcomer. "Very friendly. He'll slobber all over you if you let him. Let's get you some food. Beer?"

"That would be much appreciated. I am of age, just in case you wanted to know." Paul grinned.

Rick opened a bottle and handed it to him. "Thank you. As a faculty member, I have to be careful not to encourage any infractions, if you get my drift. These young men are all twenty years old and are allowed to have a drink here and only here. And only two. They are supposed to study after dinner."

Paul grabbed the beer and sat down to grab a slice of pizza. "What are you studying tonight?"

Mitch swallowed and was the first to answer. "We're all computer science majors. Not everybody goes pro. You have to have something you can do after graduation."

Paul raised his eyebrows. "Any of you able to build a database?"

"Gotta be more specific, man. There's lots of ways to build a database, and it depends on what kind of queries you're thinking about." This came from Gordy, a wiry, heavily tanned guy at the end of the table.

Paul was about to set his pizza down. The guys all looked at him and together said, "*Don't do that!*" Enrico had his slobbering jaw treacherously near the tempting morsel. Then they all cracked up.

Gordy said, "We've all learned the hard way. Mr. Enrico is a hoover when it comes to people food. Especially pizza."

Paul took his last bite. "Thank you. It's too good to let even a dog I like have it. And thank you for that question. What's your name?"

"I'm Gordy Chambers. I'm a kicker, if you want to know what I do on the team. And like Mitch said, there are only so many spots in the NFL. I'm planning a career with a keyboard. Which means I'm very interested in what kind of data will go into the database and then what kind of reports you're going to want to pull."

Rick was paying close attention. He broke into the conversation. "Mitch, I think your mom just got home. Would you like to make the introductions?"

Jane Stanton, Dr. Jane MacLane Stanton, surveyed the patio and scratched Enrico's lolling head. "Well, most of you I know already. Nice to see you all." She turned to Paul. "You must be the young Dr. Mitch called about. I'm Dr. Jane Stanton. Lots of doctors in this house, but none in medicine. I'm curious about your research."

Paul grinned. This group was a total find. He sensed it would lead him to new questions and many new answers.

CHAPTER 5

THANKSGIVING, 2008, HEADING BACK TO THE ACTION INSIDE THE INSTITUTE

D-man Hickson still had more questions than answers as they reached the lobby. He spied his lifelong friend Rick Stanton and left Suzanne's side. Talking with Rick always helped him think through the tough stuff. He wove his way through the shifting bodies. Before he could speak, Rick said, "Yo D-man, good to see you, bad time to talk. Later? Coffee in the morning, your lab?"

"I'll hold you to that, bring bagels, and I want the low down, the full-tilt-boogie lowdown. This is more than the usual Institute uproar. Be prepared to spill." D-man was grinning and completely serious. The Institute was his semipermanent home, whatever that meant now. He needed to know what the hell had changed while he was on sabbatical. Yes, he had needed a break, and Jane had nudged him for his own sanity. Now turnabout would be fair play.

Across the dining room, Don Grant had stuck close to Nicola's grandmother, Grace, her son Daniel, and especially her daughter Victory, or Vic, a new special friend of his, as the dining room had erupted. Rather than try to move, they all huddled at a table near the middle of the melee. He raised his eyebrows. "Do you think it's a physics phenomenon that all the action found the edges of the room?"

Daniel smiled. "I'm not sure about a physics phenomenon, but it looks like people who know this place have gathered with their small groups. I'm guessing they are trying to work out what the hell just happened."

"And we know more than they do, and even we don't know what happened." Vic squeezed Don's hand.

Grace looked around. "I have faith that Jane and her people are doing what needs to be done. I'm sure she will find us if we can be helpful or if there is news. Let us sit and watch for now."

D-man looked around the room and saw the table of people he didn't recognize. Could they be related to some of the new people Suzanne talked about? Fair game indeed. He pulled up a chair and introduced himself. "Hi, my name is Dr. Darren Hickson, or Dr. D-man to the locals."

Vic grinned at him and squeezed Don's knee under the table. "Okay, Dr. D-man, I give. Where does that name come from?"

"Only if you tell me yours, pretty lady."

"I'm crushed that you don't recognize me from my film days. My name is Victory Acevedo, or just Victory then." She raised an eyebrow.

Before D-man could speak, Daniel stepped into the fray. "And I'm her brother, Daniel. And this is our mother, Grace."

Then Grace took his hand. "You look very confused. My grand-daughter is a scientist here. Daniel is her father, Victory is her aunt, and this calm gentleman next to her is Don Grant, the father of yet another new scientist here. Oh, and Father Joe over there taking care of someone with their head between their knees, he's one of ours as well. He's been busy this afternoon. Not because he's a priest, he's also an EMT."

D-man cocked his head to the side. "I think you all are the missing puzzle pieces for me. Or maybe just more of them. I was upstairs with Suzanne as she was rigging up some biofeedback gear, and she filled me in. Well, that's not exactly true. She blew a whole of lot of names and speculation at me, but I remember snatches that might link to you all."

Don smiled. "I find that not a stretch of the imagination at all. Let me connect a few more names and scientists for you. My youngest son is Dr. Charlie Grant, a physicist. Nicola Acevedo, almost PhD, is Daniel's daughter, and one of the people who collapsed is a relative of theirs, and he's also a physicist. The young woman who went with them, Mercedes, is also a new scientist here and the granddaughter of the other person who collapsed."

"Remember that old line 'you can't tell the players without a program'? Well, I need that program. I think you both helped and muddied the picture." D-man was shaking his head and grinning at the same time. "To add to my confusion, I just today arrived back from three months on sabbatical."

Don asked, "What did you do on your sabbatical, if I may ask?"

"You may, and I'm happy to tell you that I watched waves for three months. Ocean waves, lake waves, waves in creeks and rivers. I study collapsing wave theory, and Jane thought maybe I should get out of my head and into the out-of-doors to make progress."

"Did you? Make progress, that is?" Daniel was enjoying this.

"Yes, I think I did. It's a confounding thing, and the waves are all so different, but I'm distilling a notion. I have to run it by Rick tomorrow."

"Rick Stanton?" Daniel wondered.

"The same. Why?"

"He's my daughter's advisor, and she has changed her thesis topic *three* times now. We're hoping the quest that brought her here will be the final topic. So is he."

"And what is her new, and you hope, final topic?"

"Good thing you're sitting down, although you are a scientist at The Institute, so you may have a higher tolerance than most, Time travel." Daniel shook his head and gazed at the crumpled napkin in front of him.

"Far out! I want to work with her. Where is she? I need to meet her." D-man was excited.

Don added, "Then you'll want to meet my Charlie as well. He's been researching the topic for most of his career."

"Wait a minute. Charlie is Charles Grant. Dr. Charles Grant. I think you said that, but wow, Charlie Grant? He's your son?" D-man was even more excited. "I've followed, as much as I can, his work for the past few years. He's wicked smart. And he's here now too? Well hell! I leave for three months, and things get interesting. Damn."

D-man Hickson shook his head and surveyed the chaos and made his decision. "Folks, it was great to meet you, and I'm hoping we'll meet again soon. I just got back a little while ago, and I need to get my gear, unpack and maybe unwind, even eat something. So I'll say goodbye for now." He smiled as he rose then headed for the kitchen.

Vic, Daniel, and Don looked for Jane and Rick. Vic gave a sly smile. "Folks, I think it's time to make like Elvis and leave the building.

The hubbub was lessening. At a table across the room, Dick Stanton looked at his wife, Betsy, who was serenely surveying the nearly empty dining room. She spoke first. "I think it's time for us to take our leave."

He took her hand. "I quite agree. Got a plan?"

She pointed toward the center of the room where their son was headed for a huddle of four familiar visitors. "I think I want to go where they're going. How about you?"

He chuckled. "Good catch. They look like they're planning an escape and soon. What have you got in mind?"

"We move quite a bit more slowly. That will give them time to sort out their next step. You can text Rick, and he'll spill to you. That's when we turn on the ignition. Until then, I think we just gather ourselves together and move gracefully toward the exit as people of our vintage are allowed to do."

"Have I told you lately how much I love you?"

"It's always nice to hear." She leaned her head toward his and pecked his cheek.

"You were right, as usual. They're walking toward the exit as we speak. And by the time we get to the car, what do you want to bet they'll be at Rick and Jane's?"

"I presume the same. It's close, and if they need to return, it's easy. It gives them a place to go and lay low while they sort out what the heck just happened."

Dick raised his eyebrow. "Do you think *you* know what just happened?"

"I have a few thoughts, but I think I want to save them until we're with the youngsters."

"Not gonna even give me a hint?"

"Well, let's just say you won't find my conjectures in any of your physics textbooks."

Dick moved slowly to his feet, standing for a few seconds to be sure of his balance. "That's fair, and I have to agree with your statement." He held out his hand.

Betsy rose and stood as her husband had. Experience had taught them that moving too quickly was unwise after having sat for more than an hour. "I'm ready and steady. How about you, old man?"

"Old man? That's an honor. Why, thank you, my good woman." And they began the slow walk to the front door and then the parking lot.

One of the young servers noticed the elderly couple moving slowly and went to assist them. Before the vintage couple accepted the help, Dick watched a pair of the remaining visitors nearby.

As the younger set had edged out the door of the still buzzing dining room, Grace stayed behind to wait for her oldest and dearest friend. She motioned for him to join her. "A penny for your thoughts."

Father Joe Perez slyly glanced around the emptying room before replying. "For my money, of which you know there is precious little, I say we head for the hills."

Grace chuckled. "My thoughts exactly. I see Betsy and Dick moving slowly toward the door. Victory and friends are leaving now. Do we want to join ranks?"

Her question was answered when Dick Stanton walked back to them and said, "We're not sure what's going on or might go on here, but we think we have a plan. Want to take a chance with us?"

Joe stood and held out his hand to Grace. "Best offer since pumpkin pie. Don't mind if we do. We're in unfamiliar territory, and we appreciate the invitation."

Grace narrowed her eyes at the aging scientist. "And just what might you be up to?"

"Oh, it's not so much me. It's my better half or two-thirds. She has something in mind and isn't talking until we're out of earshot."

Grace collected her shawl and handbag. "That tells me you married a very smart woman."

Dick laughed. "Don't I know it. Ever since that first day, I've stayed in awe. She says that's the correct response to her wisdom."

Father Joe laughed out loud. "This will be fun. Thank you for including a couple of strangers."

Dick glanced around. "In truth, there are many strangers here, but most of them are in residence for research. You all just got swept up in whatever the heck is going on."

"Do you have an idea of what that is? I mean, what is going on?" Grace was genuinely curious.

"Ideas. I have a few ideas, maybe just thoughts. Together we can pool what we know, what we think we know, and maybe a pattern or link will show itself."

The aging priest smiled. "That approach has worked for me for many years. Sometimes the man upstairs needs a little time to put things together."

"My Betsy will tell you it's a woman upstairs, but the taking time thing she'll agree with."

The quartet of senior guests passed the remnants of hubbub as if invisible. "Funny, isn't it. After a certain age, we kind of disappear." Dick was musing out loud.

Grace looked over at him as he reached Betsy's side. "It's very handy to be invisible. I rather enjoy it."

Betsy smiled. "What have I missed?"

Father Joe grinned. "You're up to something, and we want to be part of it."

The offer of aid to the vehicle allowed them to quickly and safely reach the parking lot. When they were in the car, Dick put the key in the ignition and waited.

"Are you going to call him now?" He looked at Betsy.

She smiled knowingly. "Too soon. I thought you might turn on the radio and see if we can hear a score from the game. Such a great way to pass the time. Do we have a dog in the hunt?" Betsy enjoyed sports and wondered if her husband remembered that his Seahawks were playing.

Father Joe chuckled. "The great American pastime is no longer baseball. When did that happen?"

Dick was fiddling with the radio until he found a familiar cadence that said someone was calling a football game for radio listeners. "When TV replaced radio and kids began to play football instead of baseball. That's when." He found a station. "I think they're still playing. Might be halftime. Let's see if we can catch anything helpful."

They listened for a few minutes until they could get a score, then switched it off. Betsy reached for her purse to find her phone. "Do you want me to call?"

"Sure. He hears from me all the time. He might be more inclined to pick up seeing your caller ID." Dick smiled and turned to fill in his passengers. "She's calling our son, Rick."

"Hi, dear. Yes, we're fine. Are you at the house yet? Are you ready for us to join you? I have an idea I think you'll find intriguing. We'll be there in a few minutes. Yes, tell Victory we have her mother and Father Joe with us. Love you." Betsy pressed a button and put the phone back in her purse.

"I got his attention. They're at his house having a drink and starting to make a snack."

"You got my attention too. You devious wench. You've still got it, sweetheart. Let's go have some fun."

Grace smiled. "I think we made a very wise choice to join your adventure."

Dick pulled the small sedan out of the nearly empty parking lot and headed on a familiar route to the house their son shared with their beloved daughter-in-law, Jane. Grateful that the house was so close they could skip holiday traffic. Soon they pulled into the drive, parked next to a strange car, and headed for the door.

Don Grant met them on the walkway, offering a steady hand to negotiate the pavers on the way to the open front door. "I'm very pleased to see you all. I know we need all of your brains to help us sort out what happened."

Betsy squeezed his hand. "I'm more focused on what might happen in the near future."

Dick chuckled. "That's my girl. Not dwelling in the moment but moving on ahead of the train."

Don laughed. "I like it. Let's think ahead. We may be the only ones today." He made sure Grace and Father Joe made it safely into the house before turning to see if anyone else followed. Then he closed the door to join the expanding group. The spry priest quickly advised Rick and Don that their canine family members were safe.

As they moved into the house, laughter and voices rose from the kitchen. Rick looked around the expanded group and suggested. "Maybe it's time for the patio, folks." Still chatting, they all began to head that way. Rick hung back to get drink orders from the newly arrived seniors. Vic and Daniel had picked up bowls of snacks. Don grabbed the stack of napkins and held the door as the parade headed outside.

Once seated on the patio furniture, sipping beverages, Rick turned to his mother. "The floor is yours, Mom. What have you been noodling in that Smith-honed brain of yours?"

"I've been thinking about secrets and how difficult it is to keep them." She swirled and sipped her scotch as the others nodded in agreement.

"Since Nick arrived not so long ago, the list of people who have been let in on his 'situation' has grown. While all of them did need to be told, still, the circle is growing."

Vic spoke. "If I were writing the script for this movie, I would be about to introduce someone who would let the secret slip. There are too many people now who know."

Betsy smiled. "Exactly my thinking. The question is, how do we protect the secret but in such a way that the protection doesn't alert or alarm others and create the problem we want to avoid?"

Vic leaned forward. "Have you ever written a movie script? You have great instincts, Mrs. Stanton."

"Call me Betsy. And no, no movie scripts, but I did meet Dick at a top-secret facility in Tennessee during the War. I watched some smart people, and lots of not-so-smart people, try to keep a lid on something classified."

Vic was intrigued as she noted. "Oak Ridge had the advantage of being off the beaten track, hard to reach, and one might even call it remote. The Institute is none of those. And this secret needs at least one or two." Daniel was leaning forward. Don and Dick were grinning.

Father Joe spoke. "When Grace and I have helped refugees, we value those people and places we can trust to protect our travelers and our secrets."

Heads nodded as Betsy continued. "We have a site that meets those criteria. It's semi-remote, not that easy to get to, and even today it's off the radar, so to speak, and it's run by friends."

Dick raised his eyebrows. "You scamp! I love it. If you're thinking what I think you're thinking."

Betsy smiled. "I am if you're thinking Skyridge Ranch."

Don gasped out a "hah" before saying, "Of course. It's where we took Tommy to keep him safe and out of circulation. That's brilliant."

The expressions on the others said they needed to hear more. Glancing at her husband, Betsy continued. "After the War, we moved here. Then we remembered the youngsters we taught in our spare time in Oak Ridge, Tennessee, who were smart but had limited access to good schooling, especially girls. We came up with the idea of a school to teach science and math to girls. We found a modest Ranch, and with a loan and our GI benefits, we bought Skyridge Ranch about forty miles due east of Pasadena."

Vic was nodding, so Betsy continued. "Our first students were girls from Oak Ridge as well as from the Pueblo near Los Alamos.

We invited our dear friends from Tennessee, Suzanna and George Wheat, to be the first live-in caretakers and hosts for our students since they would be living there. Of course, their children were our first students."

Daniel spoke. "Go on. I think I see where this is going, but I'm curious to learn more."

Dick picked up the story. "Over the years, with George's skill and guidance, the grounds have become more of a campus. It still looks like a Ranch, but the new barn is a high-tech classroom. The main house has a commercial kitchen and dining room to feed up to thirty, and individual casitas house teachers, as well as a quartet of bunkhouses for students of various ages."

Vic tilted her head. "You're right, it sounds perfect. Somewhat isolated, plenty of housing and food as well as technology resources that the researchers can't live or work without."

Daniel asked, "What needs to happen now to put this plan in place?"

Rick raised his palms. "I call Jane. It's her decision, but I think she'll love it. And the current students at the Ranch all love coming to The Institute. Maybe we can just do a swap for a while. It's not like it's a standard curriculum out there. All the teachers and the students can shift residence to The Institute, and the growing membership of the Keep Nick a Secret Club can take up residence at Skyridge."

Vic asked, "Tell me again where this *Brigadoon*-like Ranch is?"

Don chuckled. "I appreciate the reference, but you can see it more than once every one hundred years. That said, it is out in the hills northeast of LA and nicely protected from prying eyes."

Daniel leaned back in his seat. "I like it. A secret place to keep a secret. One helluva secret."

Rick reached for his phone. "I'll call my better half now."

Jane came into sight as the phone in her pocket buzzed. She laughed as she looked around the patio. Her mother-in-law had been about to speak but stopped short both by Jane's arrival and the two fur bundles bounding right behind her. "Did I just hear my name being taken in vain? And, Mom and Dad, you're up to something. You have that look on your faces, I know that look."

At that, the patio erupted in much-needed laughter as the two dogs who were madly moving from one seat to another, nosed hands from laps to be petted and loved.

Don looked at his Sam as she gazed his way. "Now what have you been up to, sweet girl, huh?" At which the stub that was her tail wiggled fiercely. Rick had contained the bulk of Feynman so that his whipping tail wouldn't jeopardize nearby glassware.

Jane reached for the drink Daniel offered, took a long sip, then brought the group up to speed. "These dogs joined our two patients for a while. Mercy believes they sensed something."

Vic cracked, "A disturbance in the Force?"

Chuckles erupted. "Something like that, yes. Tommy and Clary had let them in from the courtyard and followed them as they made a beeline for the infirmary. We let the dogs stay, not the boys. I sent them back to help Gordy in the dining room. When I finally left, Mercy was still sitting between Nick and Theresa. Paul Sanchez was regularly checking their vitals, and Suzanne had delivered a biofeedback rig so that Paul could better monitor what might be going on."

Father Joe added, "You mean what else might be going on."

Jane nodded. Daniel spoke again. "I met Suzanne earlier today. Bright girl, but who's Paul?"

Rick spoke. "Paul Sanchez, MD, neurologist, spending some time at The Institute to work with Suzanne on mind-body research, especially with people who have mobility issues. But the quantum consciousness research of Mercy's should tickle his brain."

Daniel nodded. "Sounds good, as well as reassuring. Who's going to send us updates?"

Jane swallowed a sip. "That would be Paul. Now what have I missed? Mom, spill."

Betsy picked up her thought. "For Jane's benefit, let's reconfirm that we're all here because we care about that young man currently lying in the infirmary at the building we just left."

The eight other people on the patio all nodded their agreement.

She continued. "That he, and we, remain in control of his secret is critical." More heads nodded. "To do that, we need to get all the people who know, or most of them anyway"—she looked at her husband—"somewhere away from prying visitors, cameras, cell phones, and as many incidental risks as we can."

Grace frowned. "Safer than The Institute?"

Dick spoke. "Yes, even safer than The Institute. As many safeguards as there are, it is still a porous place. People come and go all the time."

Betsy continued. "Given the need not only to keep the secret but continue the research into how Nick and Tommy traveled, now that the director of The Institute is among us, I reiterate the recommendation we move the entire team to Skyridge Ranch."

Don grinned. "Absolutely! That's it! That'll work!"

Dick looked at Don. "Now why do *you* think so?"

Don raised his left hand, using his right to tick off the reasons. "One, it's remote. Two, it's secure. Three, it offers top-notch resources for research. Four, they can all live there and not be tempted to be in public. Five, we can keep tabs on them without hovering."

Dick applauded. "Exactly. For the reasons Don so elegantly articulated, we need to pull the team away from the illusion of safety to the reality of a private site until such time as the need for secrecy changes."

Father Joe leaned forward. "And just where is this *Shangri-la?*"

Vic laughed. "I called it *Brigadoon.*"

Rick smiled. "Nothing so rarified. Just about forty miles east of The Institute. Enough acres that prying eyes can't reach, but not so remote that groceries are a problem. And over the years, the property has become self-sufficient as far as energy and water go."

Vic asked, "Who's there now?"

Betsy smiled. "A glorious handful of high school students who would love nothing more than to spend a month or more at The Institute, in residence, to shadow our researchers."

Vic nodded slowly. "Kinda perfect."

Daniel frowned. "Maybe too perfect. What kind of glitches could this plan run into?"

Rick smiled. "I count on Dr. MacLane-Stanton to put the idea through her rigorous process and find the holes."

Jane nodded and grinned. "Thank you, yes, I agree, and I will. The task of keeping Nick a secret feels like it's about to get out of hand. Now who should go and how can I help?"

Don and Vic shared a glance as she spoke. "Well, definitely Charlie and Nicola, and now Fabian. Can Skyridge handle two people in a trance if they haven't come around? Nick and Theresa should be at hand and Mercy."

Rick thought out loud. "They're going to need some more brainpower. D-man just came back. We can read him in. His work on collapsing wave theory will be useful."

Vic smiled. "We met him. Quite a character. What's his story?"

Jane tilted her head. "That's his to tell, but I can assure you that his surfer dude exterior masks a wicked intelligence and one of the brighter minds in quantum theory."

Daniel muttered to himself. "Is there anyone at The Institute who isn't a character and wicked smart?"

Rick heard him. "Not so far. Our research is bleeding edge enough that the safe scientists won't even think about coming."

Dick chuckled. "I don't know if I'd go that far, but Mac and Martha did want a place for ideas that might not be accepted in traditional academic circles."

Don brought them back to the list. "Okay, who else do we need? What about Ben and Michelle? And where are they? Did anybody see them before we left?"

Jane raised her glass. Daniel reached to fill it, and she spoke. "They were with Gordy when I left. Don, have you gotten a text from Ben or, for that matter, Charlie?"

Don pulled out his phone. "Okay, be afraid, nothing from either of them."

Vic laughed. "I heard from Nicola. Charlie, Beta, Mitch, she, and Fabian are all together. I can't speak to Ben and Michelle, though."

Daniel made a suggestion. "Let's list the people who know the secret and then look at who needs to be protected." He pulled out a pen and opened his napkin to give him a writing surface. On the white paper napkin, he started a bullet list.

- Charlie
- Nicola
- Fabian
- D-man?
- Nick
- Theresa
- Mercy
- Ben?
- Michelle?
- Mitch
- Mercy's sister?
- Paul Sanchez
- Tommy?
- Clary?

"Am I missing anyone who knows, other than us here?"

Rick glanced over the napkin list. "Looks about right. Probably ought to add us just so logistics takes us into account. And seeing this list, I think Mom's right that we've got to get the gang away from The Institute now."

Daniel quickly added himself, Rick, Betsy, Dick, Don, Jane, and Vic. Then he whistled at the size of the group.

Jane reached for her phone to text Mitch. "Let me find out what Hands is up to."

Don caught the nickname. "Hands? Why Hands?"

Rick chuckled. "It's from his football days. He could neither catch nor hold on to a football. He was fast, could read plays, but the coach learned not to ever, ever depend on ball-carrying."

Dick smiled. "And that was his and our good fortune. The NFL sniffed around, but our Mitch realized that he had a brighter future off the field than on. But the nickname stuck."

Jane looked up from her phone. "Mitch says he's flying out in the morning with Charlie, Nicola, Fabian, and Beta to Los Alamos.

They want to walk the site and talk with people who know Theresa and maybe were around in the forties."

Betsy urged. "Tell him what we have in mind. He's smart, and if he likes it, he can be a big help making it happen."

Jane's fingers flew on the tiny screen. "Done."

Dick looked around. "Anybody want pumpkin pie? As I recollect, we never got pie because of the hubbub."

Betsy smiled. "That's what you were doing when you were talking with that nice young man who helped us to the car."

"You bet your sweet...brain that's what I was doing. We have two pumpkin and one pecan pie in our trunk." Dick smiled conspiratorially.

Rick was on his feet. "Where are the keys?"

Dick pointed to the kitchen. "On the kitchen table. I figured at some point I could talk someone into fetching them."

Vic rose to follow him. "Let me help. I'll find plates, forks, and do what I can for the cause."

Father Joe stood to join her. "It's a worthy cause at that, *hija*. I am at your disposal."

As the volunteers headed from the patio back into the house, talk turned to the next steps for the big move. Jane eyed Daniel's list. "At first glance, I think the early crew must move—Charlie, Nicola, Fabian, and of course, Nick. Then we should add Mercy because of her connection and her research. Theresa should also remain near Nick, at least until they come out of whatever state they're in, and maybe after. I like adding D-man. His research will be a good addition, plus he has more years of research than the youngsters."

Daniel looked at her. "I agree. This is the core on-site group. Now depending on what the travelers uncover at Los Alamos, we may need Ben and Michelle researching the non-science aspects of the situation."

Jane nodded. "I like that. Yes. And they can always visit as needed, but their research doesn't need to be physically connected to Nick, not as much as the others."

Don weighed in. "What about the doctor, the medical one?"

Jane nodded. "He should be on call and plan regular visits, but we can let him decide if Nick, Theresa, and Mercy are enough of a subject pool for him to shift his lab work."

Vic was thoughtful. "How's security out there? Will Mitch need to set up anything special for this purpose?"

Jane stopped at that thought. "Good point. He'll let us know, but we should include Gordy at some point so that he can set up private communication for the project."

Daniel looked at Jane. "You've mentioned that name a couple of times. What's his story? Gotta be another character."

CHAPTER 6

FRIDAY, NOVEMBER 28, 2008, ALMOST 10:00 A.M., LOS ALAMOS, NEW MEXICO

The small airstrip at Los Alamos had been updated since the War years, but many of the old buildings were visible nearby. Mitch expertly landed the small jet facing the midmorning sun, rolling to a stop near a more modern-looking hangar. Before they left the plane, he wanted to review the plan.

"I just heard from Mom. Things are stable in the infirmary. Paul Sanchez is working with Mercy to monitor both the physical and… whatever else it is that's going on."

Beta smiled. "Sounds ideal. Mercy's in her element when she can bring metaphysics and quantum physics together. If it wasn't for the fact that her subjects are Nick and G-Ma, she'd be giddy."

"Well, while she's holding down that end of the experiment, remind me again what we're doing here at the crack of dawn?" Charlie's stomach was starting to settle from the jet flight.

Nicola took charge. "We're here to learn more about what was in the environment at the time of the experiment. We still haven't found the anomaly that caused the experiment to work on that day and not after."

"Well, I may be doing cyber now, but I'm a trained geologist still. And it's rocks I'll be looking at. "Fabian reminded her. "And, Charlie, it's after dawn a while now." The rest chuckled.

She continued, giving the Irishman a sideways glance. "And now we have the Tommy variable too. But should we keep Tommy a secret for now?"

Mitch jumped on that. "Oh, yeah, Tommy is a *big* secret. *And* because of the chaos yesterday, he hasn't even seen his sister yet, and when he does, it will hit him that she's eighty years old. So when and if we find his contemporaries, they'll be vintage. Let's not cause any heart attacks or create any incidents that we can't control. Let's keep that cat in the bag of secrets. Agreed?"

Beta nodded. "I have a good idea where the old gang will be. Once we leave the hangar, we need to get downtown. There's a place they go every morning."

A vintage silver Ford Bronco was at the hanger waiting for them. Mitch and Beta took the front so she could navigate. Charlie and Fabian jumped in back while Nicola squeezed between them. As they passed the original entrance to The Hill, Mitch pulled up to the white wooden gate. The barbed wire was still visible.

Beta spoke softly, "I think maybe the barbed wire is still here at the old gate just to remind people of the history. You know, people still try to break in even though no work is done over here. Funny that it's such a draw."

Nicola leaned forward. "It's truly haunting. If this is what it was really like, I'm glad I live now. I mean, I know there are still places with barbed wire. It's just that doing research behind it doesn't seem to me to make for a positive, creative environment."

Mitch had his eyes on the road as it narrowed leading into downtown. "Security was more basic then. Guard towers, guns, and barbed wire. Now we have microchips and drones. It can still be creepy."

Beta shook herself out of those thoughts. "Okay, I need to fill you in a little on who I hope we get to meet. I call them the Geezer Gang, but they're really just the oldest guys in and around the Pueblo, and they have no official roles."

"So if they are who we think they are, they'll remember Nick, right?" Charlie was like a dog with a bone.

Nicola, sitting between Charlie and Fabian, leaned forward from the bench seat to speak to Mitch. "We're sure about Tommy and Theresa, yes? Theresa's the girl who was Nick's maid in the living quarters. The one Dick talked about."

Fabian gently pulled her back. "Easy there. We know Nick was here. We know his friend Dick was here. We can work with just that much if that's all we have. Let's just take it easy and be for learning something."

Beta was nodding her head slowly. "I agree with you, though G-Ma tells stories about being a maid at Fuller Lodge. She really liked a guy named Nick and his friend Dick. They were younger and treated her nicely. And then one day, Nick disappeared or stopped showing up. She never saw him again. Well, not until yesterday. And it was the same time her brother Tommy disappeared. She didn't talk about it much, and when she did, she wasn't sad. Well, not tragic sad. I know she missed her brother, but she's always been really calm and peaceful about it."

While Beta was talking, Mitch had found the coffee shop and had pulled into the parking lot. There was a dusting of snow on all the buildings. Mitch warned, "It's not balmy southern California team, bundle up. It looks like Christmas is already here with the snow on the trees."

"Coffee or hot chocolate sounds good. Maybe they have muffins. Do you think they serve breakfast?" Charlie looked at the windows hoping to see some food.

Nicola chuckled. "Charlie, you are always hungry. How do you stay so wiry when I see you eating all the time?"

Beta added, "They have homemade muffins here that are fantastic and a lot more. It's why the old guys come here. That and the bottomless cups of coffee. And they get to be the Geezers, and nobody messes with them."

So they were not surprised to see a table of weathered-looking men having coffee when they walked through the door and into the coffee shop. Nothing happened in the town without their knowledge. Beta recognized one of the older men and walked over to the table. "Uncle Henry, it's good to see you."

A wrinkled face gazed up implacably. "It is good to be seen, hija. To what do we owe the pleasure of your company today?"

"My friends and I are doing some research about what happened here during the War." Beta was serious.

"Which war is that? There have been a few that have touched this place" Henry had a twinkle in his eye.

"Oh, the big one, when it all started here. We're interested in the summer and fall of 1944. Do you remember that time?" she gave as good as she got when her Uncle was concerned.

Charlie tapped Mitch on the shoulder and motioned to the big Irishman. "Dudes. Back over here. Let's get some food and coffee and let Beta do her thing."

The four outsiders settled in a comfortable booth, saving a place for Beta. While they looked around, Charlie studied the menu of southwestern treats and beverages. The windows let in plenty of light, which showed off the polished wood of the booths and tables. The upholstery reflected a southwest motif probably from a local weaver. The smells from the kitchen were not from a greasy spoon, and the visitors raised their noses to sniff.

Nicola grinned. "I'm in heaven. It's more than muffins to tempt me. They have café con leche, tres leches cake, and pan dulce."

She translated for the uninitiated. "All right, you tourists, you're looking at expresso with steamed milk, a rich dessert made with three kinds of milk, and sweet pastry. Does that help?"

"Yeah, it does that. So no tea then?" Fabian was teasing her.

"Not here. If you want hippie stuff, there's probably a place in Santa Fe." Nicola thought tea was pretentious.

Mitch examined the menu. "Well, it all sounds okay, and I like pastry. You choose for me. The muffin might just be an appetizer. I'm with Charlie on food."

"You're kidding, right? You want me to order for *you*? We're in New Mexico, and they speak English here. You order your own food and drinks if you want more."

Fabian smiled. "Let's make it easy then, five of everything." He grabbed their menus and headed for the counter. He loved a local's place. "This puts me in mind of a shop at home. Except the photos there were of football teams, not these desert landscapes and cowboys."

Beta stood near the booth as Fabian ordered food. "You need to come hear them. They've started to talk about the old days."

Then they heard it. A slow rumble of sound from the table of native Geezers. They were laughing!

Nicola had followed Fabian and now returned carrying a tray loaded with silverware and mugs ready for the pot of coffee coming to their table. "Charlie, find out what's so funny."

"Beta, what's up over there?" Charlie called out as he slid from the booth.

"Hush, white man. The Geezers are talking." Beta grinned at him.

"White man, really?" Charlie would play along.

"They get like this. Seeing me has brought back some memories." Beta smiled, thinking of her G-Ma.

"Anything helpful for our mystery?" Charlie wanted to focus.

Mitch perked up. "I just heard someone say, 'It was the summer when everything worked.' Not every*one* but every*thing*. Could that be important?"

Beta motioned for them to join her by the Geezers. "Gentlemen, let me introduce my friends from California and Ireland. This imposing figure is Mr. Mitchell Stans, enjoying his meal is Dr. Charles Grant, then almost Dr. Nicola Acevedo, and at last"—Fabian nodded—"our esteemed Irish colleague, Dr. Nicholas Fabian III."

Henry smiled at her. "Hija, let me return the honor. Here we have Mr. Albert Ortiz, Mr. Oscar Bunelos, Mr. Manuel Ordonez, Mr. Braulio Ontiveros, and I, I am Henry Cisneros, her granduncle. No doctors." He smiled, revealing tobacco-stained teeth.

As the visitors nodded and smiled their greetings to the leathery oldsters, Beta opened her eyes wide. "Braulio? That's your real name? I only ever heard you called Butch." Then she quickly brought them back to the topic at hand. "Uncle Henry, we need to know about what happened here in 1944. That summer, I mean. We know about the bomb, but we know there was more. What do you mean 'the summer when everything worked'? Do you mean people were working because of the war effort?"

Henry shook his head slowly. "No, hija, all of the *machines* worked. The trucks, the pumps, everything with an engine. Nothing broke down like usual. It was really something."

Charlie locked onto this notion. "Why was that different? Were there problems with machines back then?"

Albert smiled. "We had to be the mechanics on call to fix the trucks. Even the Army guys called on us."

Charlie probed. "Do you remember which summer it was?"

"We were going to be seniors in the fall, and it was hot and dry. Must have been June or July. Monsoon was late. There was that giant storm. After that, I don't think it was the same." Henry had drifted back to that summer long ago.

Charlie looked at him. "Must have been some storm if you remember it after all these years."

The other old men nodded. "It was big. Lightning, wind, and hard rain. So much rain. Even some big rocks washed away. We had weeks and weeks of work to clear the ditches and creeks. It washed away some of Miss Wagner's vegetables. She was not pleased."

Fabian picked up the thread. "Big rocks? How big? And they washed away, you say?"

"The roads had gravel on them. Most of that got washed away. A few bigger rocks, nothing we could not lift or pull with a mule." Henry was recalling.

Nicola had grabbed her mug and rejoined them. "Where did the gravel wash away to, gentlemen?"

"Downhill." Men of few words.

"This was the gravel on the plateau you're telling us, where the scientists were working?" Fabian tried to filter the memories.

"Yes. That was it. The general had wanted the roads to have gravel." They all chuckled. "It did not stay. We could have told him. He did not listen." Butch Ontiveros was nodding.

Albert began to laugh. "Remember when the radio started to talk?"

They all started to smile. "We had been without the radio news for more than a year, and all of a sudden, we heard a voice. It was the liberation of Paris. And we could hear it!" Oscar was gleeful. "And it was the British, not the US that we heard!"

Henry remembered. "Yes. It was good to hear about the outside world. We had been isolated for too long."

Charlie spoke. "I heard that the signal was blocked. No news in and nothing going out. It must have been something to hear the voice from England talking about a victory in Paris."

"But after the big storm, the voice was silent." Albert was sad.

Nicola felt an urge to sleuth. "It sounds like the rain changed things. The radio was different. What about the trucks and the pumps?"

Henry sounded sad. "It was back to the way it was before."

"Before what?" Charlie wanted to know.

"Before whatever happened to change things." Henry knew that much.

Charlie jumped on that. "You think the change happened before the rainstorm?"

Manuel looked up. "Yes. It was the time of the Independence Day parade. I remember. I was on one of the floats for the parade. We did not break down." Manuel was sure, and the group nodded in agreement.

Butch added, "But things kept on working, almost until we had to go back to school."

Charlie looked at the group. "When was that? Can you remember?"

Butch thought slowly. "It was September. Early September."

Nicola spoke up. "Hang on. I have that list from the white-board. It might help."

Fabian, Charlie, Mitch, and Beta crowded around Nicola's iPhone. The list said the following:

- White Sands?
- 1944 summer
- Loose material

- Geology
- Activity
- Where did it wash away to?
- Is it still there?
- Are Dick's rocks samples of the stuff?
- Did this make the difference in the experiment?

Albert spoke up. "The summer was very hot and very dry. We all hoped for rain."

Charlie looked up from the list. "Were there any activities on The Hill that were different?"

Henry raised his eyebrows. "There were those men from White Sands. They brought trucks with gravel for the roads. It was dusty for many days."

"How many days, do you remember?" Charlie wondered. "I heard about choking on dust. So it must have been bad, but I don't think Dick said how long the dust lasted."

Albert smiled. "Those guys brought beer. We couldn't get beer around here. They shared at the end of the day."

Charlie raised his eyebrows, making his statement into a question." We heard there was rain, just like you said. Do you remember anything else from before that?"

"Were the guys who brought the gravel still around when the rain came?" Mitch was taking notes.

"No, they were gone. The rain was after they left." Oscar was almost wistful.

Albert reminisced. "I remember that cleaning was a mess for a week while the men worked on the road. We dusted and swept all the time. The sheets on the clotheslines were brown with the dust."

Nicola and Charlie pick up the thread. "After the rain, the dust was gone?"

"Oh, the dust was almost gone after the workmen finished spreading the gravel. Even when the trucks used the roads. It was not so much." Albert was nodding.

Mitch asked, "After the rain was there any attempt to bring more gravel?"

Henry was thoughtful. "There was talk about us taking shovels to the ditches and washes to collect the gravel."

Fabian wondered, "Did that happen then? Did you collect any of the stuff that washed down from the hill at all?"

"I think we took a wheelbarrow once and shoveled some loose rock. But it had gone far." Albert smiled.

Charlie reviewed the whiteboard list. "You had outside workers for days. There were truckloads of gravel and lots and lots of dust that went everywhere. Is that about it?"

Beta looked up. "You said downhill. Do you gentlemen remember which direction the gravel went downhill when the rain washed it away?"

Henry nodded slowly. "It went with the sun."

"Now you said something about the day *he disappeared*. Who disappeared? Tell me more about that day." Beta tried to continue.

The Geezer Gang continued talking, ignoring her question. "Remember when we came home for Christmas that year? So many friends were gone. We could not wait to be eighteen to enlist. School was boring. And the classes in English were the worst." Oscar Bunelos was gazing far away.

His longtime friend Manuel Ordonez smiled. "Yeah, it was just us."

Henry Cisneros nodded. "There was a lot of work for us because of people leaving mostly."

"I remember the lady who helped us with our English. She was young and really pretty." Oscar was smiling.

Mitch wanted to follow their train of thought. "Do you remember her name?"

"We called her Miss Bonita. I don't think I ever knew her name." Oscar blushed at the memory.

Butch Ontiveros spoke up. "I remember the time capsule."

Oscar perked up. "Oh yeah. Miss Bonita was upset about the bombs. She said we would want to remember what happened… someday."

"What happened to the time capsule? Did you ever dig it up?" Charlie smelled a lead on something.

Oscar shook his head slowly. "I don't think so. We buried it by Miss Wagner's at the suspension bridge."

"Buried what?" Beta interjected.

Oscar continued. "I got an empty coffee can from my mom. She was saving it for one of those can drives, but I told her we needed it for the project."

Butch grinned. "Yeah, the can. We buried it under the supports for the suspension bridge at Otowi Crossing. It was hidden there."

Henry straightened up a little. "That is where the work is now. The banks of the creek?"

"Oh man, yeah, they are. I think it is happening soon. They want to build up the banks ahead of the runoff." Butch was concerned.

Fabian jumped on this news. "How soon?"

Butch was remembering more now. "The crew needs a break in the weather. Like today, no wind, no snow. The work will start after the Thanksgiving holiday."

Charlie raised his hand, motioning for the others to come closer. He turned to speak softly to them. "We may have a situation and an opportunity. A time capsule from 1944 was buried under the supports of a suspension bridge a few miles from here."

Nicola spoke first. "Let's go! Who's got a shovel?"

Charlie held up his palm. "There may be a backhoe there now. The banks of the creek are going to be built up ahead of spring runoff."

Beta leaned in. "I know the contractor. Let me call him. He's Butch's grandson."

"And this is exactly why you're here with us today. Thank you." Mitch squeezed her hand as she reached for her phone.

Nicola reached for her phone in response to a buzz. She had a text. "The biofeedback is good on Theresa and Nick. Steady beeps. No spikes."

Mitch added, "And I have confidence in Paul Sanchez. He's the best at what he does."

Beta put the phone down. "We're just in time. John Henry was about to dispatch his crew and get a head start on the job. And he's heard rumors of a time capsule. We all have. Now he's excited to find it. Grab your stuff."

Charlie turned back to the table of leathery seniors. "Gentlemen, you have been a very big help. We are on our way to find that time capsule. How can we find you when we get back?"

Albert looked at his friends. "We will be right here. The food is good, and it is a fine place on a cold day. Perhaps the company is not so…" He didn't finish, and they all laughed.

The visitors shook each of their hands. Fabian nodded. "Smart thinking, sir. It's grateful I am for what you've told us."

The four outsiders followed Beta as they all headed toward their rental. She took her place as navigator as Mitch again took the wheel. "We're about five miles away from the bridge. Let me fill you in on John Henry before you meet him. He went to Skyridge Ranch school like Mercy and I did. He came back to New Mexico State for college and studied anthropology. Right after graduation, his dad got sick, then he took over the family construction company. He's maybe Mitch's age or a little older even. And a good guy." She grinned at Mitch to let him know she was teasing him.

Charlie was building a profile. "Then he knows about The Institute?"

Beta nodded. "Oh yes. As students we would have science field trips there."

Charlie's gaze drifted. "Wow, I can't even imagine how cool that must have been for you."

Fabian picked up on Charlie's earlier thought. "So how much is he knowing, and how much does he need to be knowing from us?"

Beta lifted her shoulders in a half shrug. "Knowing and suspecting are very different. We are all on that continuum. I am now knowing, and John Henry is somewhere in the middle. I will tell him about G-Ma and Mercy. And that attention has again been drawn to the disappearances of 1944. That's enough for now."

Mitch nodded. "I'll follow your lead. I can let him know my role at The Institute. Being head of security may lend to the gravity of the situation. If that's helpful."

Beta smiled. "And John Henry is a man of this culture. He will respect your position and give your words the listening we need. He sees me as a little sister."

Mitch had the wheel in both hands when he turned his head to smile at her. "Then we have a plan." He turned his head slightly to include the others. "You all on board?"

They nodded yes. Beta pointed to the bridge where they saw a backhoe and a man waving to them.

John Henry Ontiveros met them as they turned off the engine. Medium height, athletic build, and straight black hair in a thick braid. Beta hopped out to greet him with a hug. "Hey, JH, how are you? Hair's getting long. Big job here!"

He stood more than a head taller than Beta, so he easily swung her around in the air when he hugged her back, a wide grin splitting his tanned face.

"Little B, what are you up to? I hear good things. Are they true? Are you really at The Institute?"

Beta grinned. "We all are. Let me introduce my friends and colleagues: Dr. Charlie Grant, physics; almost Dr. Nicola Acevedo, also physics; Dr. Nicholas Fabian III, geologist and cybersecurity whiz; and Mitchell Stans, our pilot and head of security at The Institute."

"Whoa. Why the brains and the brawn, Little B? What's going on? What should I know?" John Henry was on alert.

Mitch spoke. "Yesterday was the annual Thanksgiving dinner at The Institute."

John Henry nodded. "Those are great meals and good times. I got to attend a few of them when I was at Skyridge Ranch."

Mitch nodded. "Well, everything was going along like usual, if you can ever really use that to describe the place." Everyone smiled. "But then a new scientist collapsed. He collapsed in the arms of—"

Beta interrupted, "G-Ma! She was greeting him with a hug, and he collapsed. Then on the way to the infirmary G-Ma collapsed. Now they're both there. Mercy is with them."

John Henry reached out to hug her again. "Oh, Little B, I'm so sorry. What can I do, and why are you here and not there?"

It was Nicola's turn to speak up. "We think something that happened here long ago may be a factor in what happened yesterday."

"The Bomb? You think that may still be doing something to our people?"

Charlie jumped in. "Not the Bomb, although I want to hear more about what happened to your people. This is about the other experiment."

John Henry leaned against their SUV. "So it's true about the other experiment!"

Mitch raised his eyebrows. "What did you hear about it?"

John Henry closed his eyes to search his memory. "Some of the girls who worked as maids, your G-Ma, Little B, talked about a small group of scientists who did not work on the Bomb. She called it something else, maybe the Trick. I don't think she knew more than that, and she knew that those men were sent away before the other scientists."

Nicola spoke again. "There *was* another experiment. My greatuncle worked on it. Until recently, all we knew was what the Army told us, that he died a hero. He was a scientist, not a soldier, so there has always been a family mystery."

Mitch saw John Henry trying to connect the pieces. He decided to help. "So we have a scientist who died, maybe, and two people collapsing who may have some knowledge of the Trick. That's why we're here. This is where it started."

John Henry nodded. "And now the rumor of a time capsule may be true."

Beta grinned. "Well, the Geezer Gang says it's true. Oscar even remembers the woman who suggested they do it."

John Henry sputtered. "Not Oscar! Really? You believe him?"

Beta nodded. "If it was just him, not so much, but Henry, Albert, Manuel, and your granddad all said it was true."

"Well, Granddad knows how important this job is here, so if he's willing to cause a delay, then I'm all in. I guess my training in archaeology will finally be useful. So you want to dig here on the banks of Otowi Creek?"

Fabian grinned. "I'm glad to hear that you know how to dig careful like. It would be a disaster for sure to just tear into this area. We risk destroying a box or can of artifacts from the time of World War II."

"Can? Did they tell you what to look for?" John Henry was thinking of the stories he had heard over the years.

"Albert mentioned a coffee can," Mitch shared.

"Any help as to where along here we should start?" John Henry was starting to move away from the group.

Charlie followed. "Oscar said it was under the supports of the bridge. On the west side of the creek."

Beta joined them. "That would have been on the far side of the bridge if you were leaving home or walking with a girl."

Mitch grinned as he matched their gait. "That's where I would go if I wanted to steal a kiss."

Beta blushed. "You plan where to steal kisses?"

"As head of security, I'm a professional at anticipating trouble and nefarious deeds." Mitch was only half joking.

Fabian muttered, "Good to know. Not that I'm about makin' any such plans, mind ye."

Mitch lightly punched his shoulder. "Your reputation is well known and documented, Dr. Fabian. We saw you coming."

"Ach. It's false. The lot of it."

Now Charlie was frowning. "Who else are you watching?"

Mitch smiled. "Your reputation is what *got* you your gig at The Institute. But don't be cocky about it."

Charlie squared his shoulders. "Oh. Okay. It's just that my work hasn't always been well received or respected."

John Henry looked at Charlie with a combination of envy and respect. "At Skyridge, we looked at The Institute scientists with awe. I thought I wanted to be one."

Beta took his hand. "Maybe you still will be. You have time. I think good things are coming for you."

"Is that what your sister says? I hope so. She sees stuff." John Henry had perked up again.

"You'll have to ask her. Come visit us there." Beta smiled.

"Don't tease me about something like that, Little B." John Henry was serious.

Charlie was gazing at the bridge. "Let's find this thing, and then you can come back with us to examine it. The banks still have loads of scrubby growth. I'm hoping we don't have to root around that."

Fabian eyed the banks of the creek as well. "This looks steep and loose-like. How are ye proposing we be going about this?"

Nicola gazed out. "The water is pretty narrow here. Does it ever run higher?"

John Henry shifted into excavation mode. "Yes, it does, but not this time of the year. Okay. We'll start a perimeter five yards on either side of each support and five yards up the bank from the edge of the creek. We don't know how high the creek was running when they buried it."

Fabian offered, "They dug here at Christmas on a visit home. How high does the creek run in December then?"

John Henry was thinking. "It really depends on early snows. I suppose we could google the *Farmer's Almanac* for December 1944. Or you can help me set out a grid, and we can just start carefully."

Nicola looked around. "I'm all for starting. How can we help? Will it be just us, and if so, where are the shovels?"

"My guys are on the clock. We might as well put them to work. Come with me. We'll give them careful instructions, and they can work with us."

It didn't take long. John Henry had his men set up a grid in the likely area. Within an hour, a shovel made a metal-on-metal sound, and everyone stopped to gather around John Henry, Beta, and a worker named Juan. Beta bent down. John Henry joined her. They peered into a narrow trench about eighteen inches deep. "Let me just brush some of this dirt away. I wish I had a real brush and not my fingers."

"Just watch out you don't cut your hands on old rusty metal," Beta warned.

Juan offered his bandana, and John Henry used it to gently wipe away the dirt."

They all gathered around the hole. The ground was soft from recent slushy snow. Revealed near the center was an old, rusty metal can about seven or eight inches tall, wrapped in threads that must have been fabric at one time. As John Henry pulled off his hoodie to use to wrap the can, he spoke. "Guys, this may fall apart. It's from, what, 1944, 1945?" Before any further action, Mitch pulled out his phone and took a few photos to memorialize the find and location. John Henry took the bandana and gently lifted the can into the hoodie. "Okay, let me just wrap it up, and we can go back to work on our original job."

Fabian spoke. "Any chance there's something else here? We've been wanting to get a sample of the gravel that was spread on the roads in July 1944."

John Henry stared at him. "Gravel? Well, maybe there's some in the footers. We'll be careful." He looked over at Juan. "Tell the rest of the guys if they find gravel in any of the footers to bag it up."

Fabian added, "Thanks to ye, man. It's a reach, but all discoveries start as such, yes?"

John Henry nodded. "You're looking at someone who studied artifacts from digs where people had less to go on than what we have here."

Nicola smiled. "When you put it that way, I feel like we just won the lottery."

Mitch eyed the sky. "Let's get this back to your gang of Geezers. John Henry, can you join us? We think you should be with us and your grandfather when we open this."

"I'm honored. Let me hand over the job to Juan. Just give me a minute. I'll be right behind you. Little B, wanna ride with me?" His excitement was contagious.

CHAPTER 7

FRIDAY, NOVEMBER 28, 2008, BACK AT VIC'S HOUSE

While Vic, Daniel, and Don drank their second cups of coffee, her phone rang. Jane's voice was cheerful. "Hope it's not too early for you all. I have an update and a suggestion."

Vic put her on speaker. "Nice to hear your voice. You're speaking to the three of us. We're ready."

"The status of the patients is unchanged. They are still stable, which according to Paul Sanchez is not a bad thing. Mercy reports no change in the flow she feels between them."

Don spoke. "I'm sensing there's more."

"You're so right. I've already been on the phone with our senior quartet—they're early risers—and they suggest, and I agree, that we have another group meeting, but so as not to raise suspicions, we do it at your house, Vic, if that's okay with you."

The trio looked at each other, nodding. Daniel spoke for them. "It's a sound idea. And all of you staying over there had better come in separate vehicles. Let's not raise anyone's curiosity if you and Ben and Michelle all leave The Institute together."

Jane nodded to her phone. "I totally agree. Shall we say eleven o'clock at your place? I'll let the rest of the players know."

Vic switched off speaker with "We'll see you soon then."

Just before eleven o'clock, a silver sedan pulled into the circle drive. Don met the car to help the emeritus members of the group navigate the path to the front door, where Daniel took over. As the last of them crossed the threshold, Ben and Michelle pulled up in a nondescript rental car, followed by Rick and Jane and a guest.

Don and Daniel had helped Vic pull chairs and couches into the spacious room facing the courtyard. The sideboard was loaded with fruit and snacks while savory smells wafted from the kitchen. As the recent arrivals served themselves, Jane began.

"I've brought a newcomer to join us because we have shared history through Los Alamos. He's also a brilliant physicist, and his current work directly aligns with our current investigation."

Rick took over. "We didn't make this decision lightly. When you hear what Dr. Darren Hickson has to say, we think you'll agree with the choice. D-man, take it from here."

D-man gazed at the crowd. "I met a few of you yesterday. Sorry I was so late. For those of you I haven't met, my name is Darren Hickson, Dr. Darren Hickson, also known as D-man or Dr. D-man. I was late because I had just come off a three-month sabbatical studying waves. Why waves? The lab will only take you so far, and sometimes being in nature gets to the breakthroughs that elude us in the lab. It seemed to make sense if I'm studying collapsing wave theory, quantum wave theory, go watch real waves. And now I'm thinking about something I'm calling a quantum tsunami. And that shared history? My dad was at Los Alamos with Dick Stanton here and Mac MacLane. He told me stories and mentioned there were secrets there. Something called the Trick. Then he would clam up. He took some of that stuff to his grave, though my mom finally shared his notebooks with me right before my sabbatical."

Rick smiled and shrugged. "I think you see why he's a good addition. Maybe even the right guy at just the right time."

There were murmurs of agreement all around. Dick chuckled. "Your dad would have loved this."

D-man arched an eyebrow. "The guy I knew? The one who labeled everything and triple-tested every hypothesis?"

"Oh yeah. He was a risk-taker back then. We had to be." Dick reminisced.

Daniel spoke up. "Welcome to our merry band. Have Rick and Jane filled you in on the next move, literally to move the team to Skyridge?"

D-man nodded. "And it's the smart move. Loose lips and all that." D-man leaned in. "I really think my wave stuff is spot-on to help understand how he traveled too." He shook his head slowly and spoke almost to himself. "Just so cool."

Daniel continued. "We've been thinking while we've been waiting for you all. Not everyone needs to take refuge. I can continue my research into the legal issues from my LA office. We suggest Ben and Michelle do additional research in light of Tommy's arrival. That can be done in Arizona, and they can appear to return to their usual routines."

Vic spoke. "This all is making sense to me. At least the planning part. I can do some coordination here. I have the room, and I'm not on the radar. Plus, I can call in a few favors to add another motor home out at Skyridge to add temporary quarters."

"I think I can help by driving Grace and Father Joe home to Indio. Then Sam and I will head home to Vento Junction. Just a normal trip." Don was smiling and looking at the Indio duo. "I'll be back again before Christmas and can bring you both back for the holidays, if you want."

Grace looked at her friend with a smile and a nod. "As long as you give me daily updates, that will be fine."

"I'll call you every day." Jane looked at Grace.

Ben took Michelle's hand. "What Daniel suggests makes a lot of sense. Michelle and I were talking too. About whom to approach and how to inquire to learn more about missing people around that time. Or even unusual arrivals. I want to do a deeper dive into the historical record of that time in whatever geographical range you think we should choose."

Michelle added, "I've been making a list of FOIA requests to the DoD." She looked at blank stares. "Oops, sorry. Freedom of Information Act. And yes, having an Arizona base is a good idea."

Jane's phone buzzed. "It's Mitch from Los Alamos." She set the phone down on the coffee table, putting it on speaker. "Go ahead, Mitch. You're on speaker and the gang's all here."

Mitch's voice was calm, deep, and clear. "This was the right move. Within thirty minutes of landing, we were talking to five of Tommy's friends. Yes, they're still alive and sharp. And they remembered burying a time capsule in 1944. We were able to locate it, and we're on our way back to be with them to open it up, hopefully jogging more memories. We'll be staying at least through Saturday, probably flying back Sunday sometime."

Dick spoke with a shaky voice. "Have they said anything helpful?"

Mitch had a smile in his voice. "Oh yes. They remembered the summer, and I quote, 'when everything worked.' Not every*one*, every*thing*. Then a big rainstorm came, and things went back to the way they had been."

Betsy took her husband's hand as he said, "My, my, my, you *have* done good work."

Mitch spoke hurriedly. "We have Beta to thank for it. Her contacts made this happen. And we're staying at her mom's tonight, all of us. Gotta go."

Jane picked up the phone and took it off speaker. "Be careful. We love you."

"Thanks, Mom." And the connection ended.

Vic rose. "Lunch, anyone?"

Heads nodded, and bodies began to rise from their seats, some faster than others. They moved toward the kitchen, absorbing the plans, the news, and some amazing smells.

CHAPTER 8

ALMOST NOON, FRIDAY, IN THE SUV RETURNING TO THE COFFEE SHOP IN LOS ALAMOS

Mitch watched Beta climb into the mud-caked construction truck before he turned his head and his thoughts back to the road ahead. The precious can wrapped in the bandana and hoodie was in Nicola's hands. She sat safely next to Fabian in the back seat while Charlie eagerly called shotgun.

Beta had plopped into the passenger seat of John Henry's aging truck. "I'm glad you have a step and a handhold. I guess you can date *short* girls now." Beta was teasing him.

"You gotta be kidding me. Date girls—from here? Not tall, not short, just not. Plus, I have no time. I'm busy, and after living somewhere else, I just need more, Little B." John Henry wasn't bitter, just matter-of-fact and maybe a little sad.

"I'm sorry to hear that. You're one of the good guys. You deserve more. Especially after putting your life on hold." She was serious.

"Well, my little brother wasn't ready when Dad died. You know he's graduating from New Mexico State in a few weeks. He's talking about joining the business. It sounds like this *is* what he wants. I hope so." There was a hint of hope in his voice.

The drive felt faster heading back to downtown. They spied the Bronco and pulled in nearby. He turned his head to her. "We're here.

Before we get out, fill me in on the people you're with, especially the big black dude."

Beta grinned. "Well, I've known them all for approximately twenty-four hours. So I'll tell you what I learned flying here from SoCal. They are all wicked smart. Mitch is serious but has a warm heart. He's a big teddy bear, kind of. Nicola is a combination of go-go-go, then stop and think. Charlie is a 'what you see is what you get' guy and always ready to go. Fabian, Nicholas Fabian, is just flat-out funny. Of course, he's Irish, and that helps a lot."

"But you trust them?" This was what John Henry really needed to know.

"More importantly, Dr. Jane trusts them. And Mitch is her son—yes, stop staring—he's adopted. So yeah, I trust them." Beta was nodding, reassuring both herself and her friend.

"Then let's do this thing. I don't know about you, but I'm dying to know what those old coots put in that can all those years ago." He was halfway out of the truck when he stopped to ask, "Want help getting down, Little B?"

"In the interest of my safety, yes, that would be great. I'm a little out of practice." She laughed and so did he. He easily lifted her by the waist, gently setting her down, not missing that Mitch watched from the Bronco nearby.

Mitch looked at what looked like an intimate exchange just a few feet away. He stood leaning on the Bronco and waited for them. He had to know. Better now than to let his heart get broken. As John Henry walked away, he spoke to her. "You guys go back, do you?"

Beta grinned. "John Henry was the big brother we needed and didn't have. He watched out for us. By the time we got to Skyridge, he had left, but he had set the stage for us to be kind of taken care of. Back then, it was a big deal when kids from here got to go away to school. He definitely made it okay for us at a new school. You know it's a boarding school and has its own culture."

Mitch nodded. "I was in a few foster homes before Jane and Rick found me. Being a newbie in an established group can be rough. I'm glad you had him. That's all he is? A big brother?"

Beta looked up at this big bear of a guy and smiled. "And if it was more?"

"Then I'd respect that and know not to think of you, you know, in that way."

She had him in a spot. "And what way would that be?"

Mitch was uncomfortable, not a familiar feeling. "Available is what I meant. If you're seeing someone then, well, then you're not available."

Beta was openly enjoying this. "Available for what, Mitch? What have you got in mind?"

Mitch looked at the coffee shop and began to turn away. "Maybe this was a bad idea."

Beta put her hand on his arm. "It's a good idea, and I'm worth it. Stick with it." And she walked away to join the others. Mitch hung back and let her get ahead.

John Henry had overheard and matched Mitch's steps as they walked to join the others. "You, sir, have just had the Thompson Twins Treatment."

Mitch stopped to stare. "That's a thing?"

"Oh, Beta and Mercy are a handful. Yes, I watched out for them when they were younger and tried to prepare Skyridge. One of them is plenty, but the two of them... Let's just say that all of your security skills may be needed to protect your heart."

"So they're trouble?" Mitch wondered if there was more he needed to know.

"For your heart, definitely. They're identical twins. Identical twin girls. Oops, not girls, women. Think about it." John Henry had raised an eyebrow.

"And they're still that way? They're scientists now. At The Institute." He hoped for a better answer.

"Granted, I haven't seen them for a few years. Just be aware. And she's right. They *are* worth it. Smart, beautiful, funny, and... twins." John Henry nodded knowingly and opened the door to join the action in the now crowded coffee shop.

Mitch muttered to himself as he followed John Henry. "Best defense is a good offense."

In the coffee shop, the Geezers had perked up when the young visitors returned.

Henry was the first to speak. "That was pretty fast. So you found it?"

Nicola had the fragile can still in the hoodie when she set it on the table. "We had great help." Looking at Butch, she said, "Your grandson was the one who found it. He's the reason we were able to be so successful."

For a minute, everyone stared at the rusty can half-wrapped in a red bandana sitting on the now dirty gray hoodie. Then Oscar reached for it. "Careful. It might have some sharp edges after all those years rusting in the ground." John Henry didn't want to tell him what to do, but he also didn't want to call an ambulance.

Oscar picked up a knife and fork and gently pushed the bandana aside, revealing the rusty old can. He gently poked at it. A hole opened. "Good suggestion, young man. I can try to open with this knife and fork."

He continued slowly as the room was transfixed. John Henry offered. "Uncle Oscar, I learned to do things like this in school when we excavated sites. May I try?"

Oscar smiled, handing him the knife and fork while scooting out of the way. John Henry pulled up a chair so he could be level with what he now considered an artifact. "Might need another set of steady hands. Mitch, you want to grab another fork and hold this left side open for me?"

Mitch knelt to John Henry's left and took the fork offered by Butch.

"Okay. While you hold that side, I'm going to try to open this wider and see if it falls apart or if we'll need to pry it open." John Henry carefully used the knife in his left hand to hold the piece of metal beginning to open like a door. With his right, he took the fork and gently pulled toward himself to see if the metal would move or break. It snapped off.

"I'm glad that didn't happen to anyone's fingers. My tetanus shot is recent, but I'd rather not interrupt this reveal with a trip to urgent care," he muttered to himself.

Charlie was on his right side, ready with a bar towel. "Here, let me use this to lift that piece out of your way."

By now, everyone in the coffee shop was paying attention. The owner had brought out more towels and one of the empty rubber basins used for dirty dishes so they could set their findings out of the way.

Someone handed John Henry some tweezers from over his shoulder. "Thank you. Who had this?"

"I did." Mabel Forrester was a regular and knew the boys, as the Geezers were known in town.

"Mabel, I can always count on you. Thank you." John Henry grinned and focused again. "Now that I have a hole, I can see something. Granddad, should I be looking for anything delicate?"

Butch gazed at Henry, who spoke slowly. "There should be a watch, a man's watch. It was a gift from one of those scientists. His name was also Henry. He died soon after we did this."

Manuel snapped his fingers. "I remember something. That man gave us some rocks. He said they might matter someday. What was his name? Dick maybe?"

Nicola perked up. "Dick Stanton? Was it Dick Stanton?"

"Maybe. He was nice. Theresa knew him and that guy, that guy that disappeared." Manuel was remembering.

Charlie spoke softly while keeping his eye on the fragile time capsule. "We've met Dick Stanton. He's ninety years old now, and he will definitely be happy you saved his rocks." Albert was focused on the action on the table as he asked, "Did anyone ever find the one who went missing?"

Nicola looked at him. "He was my great-uncle. And we're still working on what happened that day."

Mitch caught her eye and winked. He approved of her sharing a couple of the dots, but this crowd wasn't ready to connect the whole picture.

Oscar was wistful. "We were all such kids. The world was big, and we wanted to take it on."

Manuel nodded. "This time capsule, we never took it serious. With the war on, school just didn't seem important, you know?"

"So when we met with Miss Bonita to bury it, that was the last time we saw this can. Looks like the wrapping didn't make it." Butch chuckled.

Henry was thinking. "You wanted to know what you will find. A watch, a tin box with Tommy's baseball cards, a rattle, some rocks, a deer hide wrapping a piece of newspaper, and a letter from us. Oh, and a medal. Is that it?"

The elderly men all nodded. Henry spoke softly. "I wonder if that watch is okay. That guy died, remember?"

Charlie was on alert. "Was he wearing the watch when he died? And what did he die of?"

Henry spoke softly. "He worked on the bomb. He gave the watch to me before he died. I'm sure he wore it around the tests. We never heard how he died, but some people said it was some of the bomb stuff that killed him."

"Bomb stuff. Like uranium?" Charlie was stepping back. "Maybe we need a better bar towel to handle the watch?"

Mitch was at John Henry's side and whispered. "Try not to touch anything with your bare hands."

John Henry nodded and whispered back, "I'm with you on that. Any ideas how to handle sixty-four-year-old radioactive stuff?"

"No, but I'll put Charlie on it now." Mitch gave Charlie a high sign and whispered, "Figure out how radioactive this stuff might be and how we protect ourselves."

Charlie turned and walked to the back of the shop and powered up his phone.

Then Albert stiffened. "Geez. Remember that little bag of rocks? The ones we found in that wreck. We put that in there too."

Beta cocked her head at that piece of information. "What wreck Albert? I don't remember talk of a wreck."

"Oh, it was back during the bomb time. A jeep went off the road. Don't know who was driving. Never heard. Nobody told us stuff back then, or now either." He chuckled.

"Keep going, John Henry. We better finish what we started." Beta was encouraging and hoping to redirect eyes back to the rusty time capsule. As the can began to release its contents, it became easier to see what remained.

Using the tweezers, John Henry pulled out the small rattle. Because it was made of bone it had survived in good shape. Next was the small medal and the watch. Carefully setting the items in the rubber bin, he and Mitch turned back to the brittle metal opening.

John Henry looked up. "Who's keeping track? How much more is there to find?"

Butch spoke. "The deer hide with the newspaper, the rocks, the box with Tommy's baseball cards, and our letter. Oh yeah, that little bag of rocks from the wreck. I think that's it."

"Okay. I can see the loose rocks and the metal box. Mitch, I might need you to kind of slide your fork in to nudge the items toward the opening."

Mitch did that. "Okay. I'm trying to give it very little pressure. I don't want anything to turn to powder when I touch it."

"You're doing fine. Keep doing what you're doing. I can almost get the tweezers on the box. There I've got it. Maybe we can use a spoon to lift out the rocks."

A spoon appeared at his elbow. "Thanks. Yes, we've got the metal box, and I can see to lift out the rocks."

Charlie looked at Nicola. "Do those look like the same kind of rocks that were in the box of personal effects Dick Stanton saved?"

"I'm no rockhound, so I have to say maybe. It's worth comparing them." She grinned.

Beta had the rubber bin ready to hold these new items. "What about the bag, the one with the other rocks they got from the wreck."

John Henry arched his back to stretch and leaned again toward the emptying rusty can. "Okay, I can see something else, maybe the letter, maybe something else. I'm just going to use the tweezers to pull gently."

When he eased the letter from the can, the room breathed a sigh of relief. He set it on a paper napkin to go with Beta in the bin.

"So now it's just the deer hide and the bag of rocks, right, Granddad?"

It was Butch who spoke. "Yes, John Henry. The deer hide. It was just a piece. I could not take an entire hide, and we cut just a picture out of the newspaper."

Albert added, "And the small bag of rocks. We thought it must be important. It was stuffed up near the steering wheel, but the steering column was all twisted in the crash. If somebody had pulled the driver out, they might not have seen it."

Mitch was pointing to something that had tilted forward inside the can. "I think that's it. The other items kept it upright. Will the tweezers work, or do you need two forks?"

John Henry glanced at the big man. "Two forks, I think. The deer hide is too thick for the tweezers."

Beta handed them an additional fork. John Henry used them like a European waiter serving filet of fish." Where did you learn that?" Mitch wondered.

"I was a waiter in college at a fine restaurant. A soon as I learned to do this, my tips got better." John Henry was smiling.

Butch chuckled. "Bet that fancy place never thought you would use that skill like this?"

John Henry was concentrating. "No, but I'm glad I learned. Here it comes." And the aged skin flopped stiffly out of the can onto the table. "So that's it? Just the bag of rocks? How big? Then no more treasures in the time capsule?"

Henry looked around at his friends. "That's it, right?"

John Henry poked around with the tweezers and felt something give, just a little. He squeezed the tweezers and pulled slightly. Shreds of fabric began to come. He waited and pushed the tweezers a little deeper to get a better grip. "There. I think I've got the bag."

What John Henry was able to set on the table was once a fabric bag. Near the seam of what must have been the bottom, a handful of small round stones were released.

Butch said, "You might want to give the can a shake to check. We're old, remember? We may have forgotten something."

Mitch used two bar towels to lift the can and rock it gently back and forth. They heard a metal-on-metal sound. "What's that?" several voices said.

Mitch tipped the can with the opening toward the table. A plain gold ring fell out. "That's not ours." Butch was sure. The rest of the friends shook their heads.

Oscar slowly spoke. "I always wondered about our teacher. Maybe she wasn't a miss and wanted to hide her past?"

John Henry used the tweezers to pick up the gold band to see if there was an inscription. "It's really small. Who has good eyes?"

Beta leaned forward. "Tilt it a little my way. I can just make out a date: 7-4-44. *All my love, Gus.* We need to find out what your teacher's last name was."

Oscar spoke. "I bet it's in the letter. We would have called her by name in the letter."

John Henry rolled his shoulders and sat back in his chair. "I don't want to try to open any of the fragile stuff until we have a lab. Sorry, you guys. The mystery will just have to continue for a while longer."

Mitch stood to stretch. "Not much longer. We can take you and the capsule contents back to The Institute, Sunday, if you can get away from the job." The group nodded in agreement.

"I'll pack my bag and be ready to go first thing Sunday morning. What do you want to do for the rest of your time here?"

CHAPTER 9

FRIDAY, NOVEMBER 28, 2008, EARLY EVENING, NEAR LOS ALAMOS, AT THE HOME OF AURELIA THOMPSON

It had been a full afternoon. After the group had finished at the coffee shop, Beta had given them a tour of the town, on foot. They had been able to walk around the grounds of Fuller Lodge, take a tour, and spend time in the Los Alamos Historical Museum. By late afternoon it was time to kick back.

The door of the rambling adobe Ranch house opened as the Bronco pulled into the circle drive. A trim woman with long dark hair streaked with silver stood smiling in the doorway, joined by a madly happy black-and-white border collie. As the weary travelers tumbled out carrying backpacks and briefcases, her arms spread wide in greeting and welcome.

"Hi, Mom." Beta walked into a crushing hug from her mother. "Let me introduce the team."

"Get inside first. The temperature is dropping with the sun. Make sure you bring Rose with you. You know how she can be with an open door."

Mitch was last in. "Thank you very much for your hospitality, Mrs. Thompson."

The group gathered around the oversize beehive fireplace that took up half the facing wall. As they admired the stunning room, thoughts began to spill out.

Fabian scanned the art and the woven rugs filling the room, gazed at the fire, then the group. "Is it a power that I feel here? Or some kind of magic?"

Beta grinned. "You might think so. Definitely magical."

Her mother waved them all to find seats as she took her place in a well-worn wooden rocker next to the fireplace. "There are many places in the world that have power and magic. This place is certainly one. No matter how far I travel, I always come back. New Mexico is called The Land of Enchantment for good reasons."

Nicola mused as she joined Fabian on a cowhide love seat. "I can't speak to magic, but I definitely feel something. I wonder if it had an effect on the Trick? How do you think we could find out?"

Charlie addressed their hostess. "Please excuse our rudeness. I'm Dr. Charlie Grant, and we have Dr. Nicholas Fabian, almost Dr. Nicola Acevedo, and our friend and protector Mitchell Stans. And thank you again for welcoming us."

Nicola added, "I'm so embarrassed. All I can say is that I feel so at home here, so relaxed. I don't feel like a visitor. How can that be?"

Beta's mother smiled. "It pleases me to hear you say that. What you feel is what I hope every person coming to this home will feel, welcome, acceptance, and spiritual peace. And my name is Aurelia, but please call me Lia. And our four-legged Miss Congeniality is Rose. And she approves of all of you."

Beta looked around. "I don't know about the rest of you, I want to clean up, but I also really want to talk about the day."

Her mother smiled. "Let me help you choose. The hall at the end of this room leads to the bedrooms. Beta, you can share your old room with Nicola. And you three gentlemen can decide how to split the remaining two rooms. Each room has a sink and a toilet. The shared tub and shower room is at the end of the hall, and there's a cabinet with fresh towels. We can meet back here in an hour or so to talk and begin making dinner."

Heads nodded and all, but Mitch and Beta picked up their gear and headed down the hall.

Mitch looked at Beta. "How much does your mom know?"

Lia responded, "Know about what?"

Beta tilted her head. "She knows what I knew before dinner yesterday. She's ready for more, and I think she needs to know. It's her mother in the infirmary."

"Go on. I *am* ready, and I want to know if I should be worried about my mother." Lia had shifted in her rocker to lean toward the duo as Rose sat nearby to rest her head on Lia's knee.

Mitch led the way. "At the end of September, three new scientists joined The Institute in Los Angeles, where I'm the head of security and also the son of the director, Dr. Jane Stanton. Her father is Ret. Colonel Mac MacLane, who served at Los Alamos during World War II. He was the military lead of the team of civilian scientists working on what they called the Trick."

Lia was on the edge of the rocker now. "Mother spoke of this Trick and the scientists. But there was more going on, wasn't there?"

Beta nodded and Mitch continued. "The lead scientist was a Japanese American physicist named Nicholas Nishimura. His research was his ticket to the Los Alamos war effort and out of an internment camp. He had done well-respected work on moving atoms across distances. The research team was small, but they put an experiment together, a human experiment. Nick volunteered. That was in September 1944. He disappeared. The Army declared him dead. His friends have quietly continued his research, hoping to learn what happened to him. They got part of their answer in September of this year. Nick showed up in Southern Arizona, sixty-four years after leaving here. And for him, no time had passed."

Beta looked at her mother. "And Tommy came too."

Lia's eye widened. "Tommy? Mother's brother Tommy, who disappeared?"

Beta nodded and Mitch continued. "Yes. There were two travelers, so the mystery is even bigger than we thought when it was just Nick."

"Well, ye gods and little fishes, as my former mother-in-law used to say. Is there more?"

Mitch nodded soberly. "Yes, there is. Yesterday afternoon as Thanksgiving dinner was heading toward pumpkin pie, your mother and Nick met again. When they hugged each other, Nick collapsed.

A few minutes later, as she was walking beside the gurney rolling to the infirmary, your mother collapsed. They are with Mercy and under the care of a trusted longtime friend of mine, Dr. Paul Sanchez."

Lia sat back. "I felt something yesterday. It didn't alarm me, but I felt it. You say Mercy is there. Tell me more," Rose whined, and Lia stroked her head to comfort her.

Beta smiled. "Mercy is in the thick of it. She's sitting between Nick and G-Ma holding their hands, connecting them. Paul Sanchez studies mind-body connection stuff. He says they are both stable, and Mercy says she feels a flow."

Lia smiled to herself. "I bet she does. That helps me. I can direct some energy to her, now that I know."

"Direct energy?" Mitch was curious.

Lia explained, "Our family has different gifts. Mother connects to the spirit world. I am a healer. Mercy takes after my mother. Beta here can grow anything, apparently like her granduncle Tommy."

"The others are going to need to hear this. Are you okay with sharing what you told me?" Mitch looked at the mother and daughter across from him.

They nodded. "We must if we have any hope of learning what's happening." Lia stood. "And now you two should join your friends and get ready for dinner and more talk."

In the Hallway by the Bedrooms in Lia's Home

Nicola gazed through the sliding glass doors toward the fading sunset at the end of the U-shaped courtyard. A flock of chickens poked around the brown grass. As she moved toward the doors to step into the evening air, Fabian stepped to her side.

"Are *you* following me, you big oaf?"

"Not exactly. Is it wrong then, me joining a friend in this curious place?"

"No, just reacting, I guess. You know this trip's been pretty intense." She opened the door, and they stepped into the cooling dusk.

"It's been that. But it's different here."

"You noticed, too?"

"I'm not dense. Why would you think that? I count so little to you then?"

She stammered. "No, no, it's not that. I don't know. So much is happening so fast."

"Sure, I get that. I do, but while we're alone, I need to know something."

"You do?"

"Why do ye call me oaf?" The chickens had noticed them and toddled near to check them out.

She smiled. "It's not obvious? I'm 5'2" and 115 pounds. You're what 6'4" and maybe 200 pounds? From where I stand, you're an oaf."

"Ah, so it's genetics then and not my bearing or any physical clumsiness or such?" He bent to pick up a hen that had taken an interest in his shoes.

"No, you're not clumsy. Don't you remember when we went to that movie, and I made us sit closer to the front? Because I can't see over people who are big like you?"

"Ah, sure, of course I remember. It was our first date. And it's good that you're not seeing me as an oaf. Oafs are not held in high regard, to be sure."

"No?" she was teasing him now.

"Nah. Word is they're pretty dumb actually, easily made fools of." He set the hen in a different direction away from his shoes.

"I would never think that of you. You're dreadfully smart, really kind, and dangerously good-looking."

"Good-looking, you're saying?"

"You know you are. Now you're fishing for compliments."

"Not likely that. Never, not once has that been said to me. Sure, it's always been about bein' smart and large, to be sure, but the looks. No, never."

"That's hard to believe. Look, even the chickens are pecking at you and not me."

"Well, set that aside. The matter at hand is the oaf business."

"And what would you have me call you instead?"

"Well, by my proper name. Nicholas. You could call me that."

"Well, I suppose I could. We have Nick, Nicola, and I guess now, Nicholas." She smiled. "I can do that."

"I like the sound of it from you. And did I hear ye also say I was kind?"

"You heard me say that yes, and gentle too."

"In what ways then? I'm not being coy. Really I don't recall being kind and gentle."

"You're always kind. You think of other people. You watch out for others. Even though you're big, you make room for smaller people. And look at the way you held that annoying chicken. I think I might have just kind of kicked at it."

"So there you have it then. Ma was right all along. And I thought she was just making life harder when she drummed into my head to watch out for others."

"She is a wise woman. Her son is smart, kind, gentle, and wicked handsome."

"He is then?"

"Oh, now you're just begging to hear it."

"I'd rather hear you say my name."

"Nicholas?"

He swept her into a hug lifting her off her feet and planted a kiss full on her lips. When he set her down, she gasped to get her breath.

"That was some kiss."

"You noticed then? Since that first date I been wanting to."

Still speechless, she nodded.

"Well, it's settled then."

"What's settled?"

"You're calling me by my proper name, my kiss was to your liking, and a next date we'll be having soon."

She slowly smiled. "Yes, I guess it's settled."

He reached for her hand, and together, they turned to go back inside to the warmth of the fireplace before they attracted an audience.

CHAPTER 10

IN THE QUANTUM REALM

Her spirits had been vague. He will take a journey. He will return from the journey. *He will be safe.* That message came to her more than sixty years ago.

"Theresa, what happened?"

"We are joined in the spirit world. This does not happen often."

"Are we dead?"

"Oh, no. Our bodies are sleeping."

"How did we get here?"

"I'm not sure how it is that we are here together. I did not leave when you did. It was a few minutes after."

"But you have traveled like this before and with others?"

"I travel this way often. With others, rarely."

"Why me and why now?"

"We are connected. I do not know how. Perhaps your kindness to me when I was timid and young. Your kindness was important to me."

"And why now?"

"What I can tell you about the spirit world is that it has lessons for us. Lessons and clues."

"So you think there is a lesson for me now and here?"

"That is only how it is for me. It is different for everyone."

"But we are here together. Does that mean we both have something to learn?"

"It may be that I was only the guide to bring you here. To make sure you are safe here. My spirits know how to find me. Then they can also find you."

"How soon do they tell us something?"

"There is no schedule. We will be here until we are released."

"Who releases us?"

"I do not think it is a 'who' that releases us back to the physical world."

"This is very confusing."

"It is not scientific. This is an experience of spirit."

"I didn't feel anything like this when I traveled through time. It was fast and I was not aware of anything. I think I'm aware right now."

"It is awareness and also not awareness. My Mercy would say that your consciousness has joined with mine."

"That's not helpful either. I'm sorry to ask so many questions."

"You are curious. Of course, you would ask. I wish I had more answers for you."

"Look. I think I see someone I know. At least someone I remember. Is it someone or something? Do you see him?"

"I feel a presence. I do not see what you see."

"It's coming closer. Do you feel anything bad? Is this what happens here?"

"Sometimes a new spirit will visit. Each visit to the spirit world is a little different."

"I can almost make him out. I think it's a scientist from Los Alamos."

"Are you sure he is coming toward you?"

"It seems that way. His face is clearer. It *is* him"

"I can feel something, but it is not strong. Not strong at all."

"Simon, Simon Constantine?"

"Nicholas. I hope this is you. I have searched for you."

"Are you looking for me here? Are you alive or dead?"

"I died. My spirit, my soul, whatever this is, cannot rest until I find you and give you a message."

"You have a message for *me*? What kind of message? Something from Los Alamos? Something from other dead scientists? What?"

"Find the source."

"That's it. Follow the source? What source? Who gave you the message?"

"No, Nicholas. *Find* the source. I'm free of this place now."

"Simon, don't go. Tell me more." But there was nothing.

"Theresa, he's gone. He was here and now he's gone."

"Did he tell you anything?"

"Yes. He said he had to find me and give me a message. He said to *find the source*."

"Was that all?"

"Yes, and then he said that he could finally rest, and he disappeared."

"Then that must be why we are here."

"He said he was dead. He was still alive when I traveled. Is time different in this place?"

"There is no time in this place."

"How can there be no time?"

"In the spirit world, it is all the same. Yesterday, today, tomorrow."

"How can that be?"

"This may be part of what you are to learn. The spirit world has much to teach us."

A soft voice spoke in the distance. "G-Ma, I can't see you, but I feel your consciousness. Are you here?"

"Yes, Mercy, I am here. And I am with Nick."

"I thought so. I hoped so. I'm holding your hands, and I feel energy running through me."

"Are you here to bring us back?" Nick was both curious and anxious.

"Hi, Nick. I don't know what my job is here. Are you okay? Are you in any distress?"

"I'm fine. I have a lot of questions, but I think I'm okay."

"G-Ma, are you and Nick ready to come back?"

"Not yet. I feel there may be more that we have to learn."

"We're here for you. I'm here to help if you need me. Mom is sending energy."

Mercy opened her eyes to see the top of Paul's head. He was watching gauges bounce around. "What just happened?"

"I connected with them, briefly. They say they are fine and have been contacted by spirits with messages for them."

CHAPTER 11

Saturday Morning, November 29, 2008, Lia Thompson's Home

The smell of strong coffee drew the guests to the brightly painted kitchen. The sun bounced off the copper pots hanging near the stove and streamed into the courtyard. And the chickens were back at work waddling around, poking their beaks into the hard ground. Lia poured and talked. "Those chickens perform a valuable task. Not only do they lay eggs, but none of you saw a scorpion last night, right?"

Eyebrows raised. Heads shook, and Beta chuckled. "The chickens eat them!"

"Whew." Fabian spoke for the group. "Then it's true what they say about them being nasty creatures?"

Lia smiled. "Yes, they can be. So we let the girls have the run of the courtyard at least once a day, and it gives Rose something to do."

"Rose?" Charlie looked around. "Oh, Rose. We met last night, right? I must have been more tired than I thought. I don't usually forget a dog."

"You were, Charlie. But we all were." Beta admonished him. "She's the contented border collie resting in the sun on the porch watching the chickens."

Nicola giggled. "We were all pretty wiped out, although I do recall you petting her head." She glanced over at Nicholas and winked.

Just then, Rose lurched to her feet and began to bark. The front door opened, and John Henry hollered a greeting. "Are you all up? Where is everybody?"

Mitch replied, "Follow the smell of the coffee, bro."

John Henry appeared, insulated travel mug at the ready. "Got a plan for the day?"

Mitch nodded. "See what you think about this. Fabian and Charlie go rock hunting with you. Nicola and Beta nose around for more Geezers and more stories. I'll go back to town and look for more leads on the history and reporting of local events from that time."

Lia nodded in agreement. "Mitch, I think you'll want to check in at the newspaper office, maybe the library, and the high school as well. I'll make a couple of calls on your behalf. The school is closed, but I know the principal. She'll let you in and show you what there is from earlier days. Some of the records came over from the Santa Fe Indian School when this high school opened after the war. Until then, breakfast is coming right up. I've got tamales, chorizo, and scrambled eggs."

The group streamed to pick up plates, napkins, and cutlery hurrying to fill seats at the now-familiar long mesquite dining table.

"Mmmmm. I've missed fresh eggs from our chickens. They really are better." Beta's eyes were closed as she savored the treat.

As Lia surveyed the polished table, she announced, "I'm going to California with you when you fly back tomorrow. She's my mother and I can help."

"You beat me to it. I was going to ask if you wanted to come along. The plane has enough room. And John Henry will be along too." Mitch grinned.

John Henry swallowed and looked at the group. "You weren't kidding. I'm going to The Institute?"

Beta nodded. "You have today to get everything handled here. And you may be gone for a while."

He grinned sheepishly. "I got things in order last night. I was pretty sure you meant it. I really hoped you meant it. And I want to help you on your hunt today. At least until lunchtime."

Mitch was reaching for another helping. "Then let's plan to meet around lunchtime back here. We can share what we learned. And maybe what else we need to check out while we're here."

Heads bobbed, but until all the food was gone, no one moved away from the table. Fabian and Nicola helped clear plates and mugs while Lia went to her study to make calls.

Charlie and Fabian joined John Henry in his truck and left first. Nicola headed to the Bronco. Beta and Mitch lagged behind a few more minutes. Beta hugged her mother as Mitch thanked her again. "You've got my cell number, I know. Call us if you think of anything? We'll be back at lunch."

The Quantum Realm

"I see someone. I think I remember him from The Hill," Nick spoke to Theresa.

"I think I remember you." Nick addressed the figure moving toward him. "But we didn't know each other well, did we."

"We were not encouraged to have friends. But I saw you and your courage."

"Who are you?"

"David Gustafson."

"Why are you here?" Nick was confused by seeing this scientist but wanted to help him if he could.

"Beats me. I was in a jeep. It went off the road down a ravine. Then nothing and now I see you."

"So you don't have anything to tell me?" Nick was frustrated by this experience.

"I don't know. After you disappeared, my team and I kept on working. Say, I saw Reg Hickson here. He told me he died. I must have too. He said he married my wife and raised my son. I didn't know I had a son."

Theresa spoke. "Perhaps you have a message for Nick to take to your son. That is sometimes what happens here."

"I think I was in the jeep for a reason. I found something important. Please tell my wife and my boy that Gus sends his love to them. I'm sorry I didn't get to meet him. I wish…"

Theresa nodded to him. "We will find them and give them your message."

Gus's spirit faded.

Theresa's spirit form grew stronger. "I feel that it is time. Yes. It is time to return. Nick, are you ready?"

"Since I didn't know I was leaving, I trust you about when to return. I still have questions. Will I remember my questions?"

"Yes, you will remember. I have very clear recollections of spirit visits. They may not speak clearly, but I remember clearly."

CHAPTER 12

SATURDAY, NOVEMBER 29, 2008, EARLY AFTERNOON AT THE INSTITUTE INFIRMARY

Mercy felt a change in the flow. "Paul, heads-up. I think they're coming back."

Paul moved closer to the silent figures to watch gauges, as well as their faces for hints. "Why do you say so?"

"I felt an energy surge." Nick's eyes fluttered. He could hear a high-pitched beeping, more than one beeping. Mercy squeezed Nick's hand. "Are you back with us?"

"I can hear beeping. Does that mean I'm back? I feel heavy. Why is that?"

Theresa squeezed Mercy's hand. "I hear beeping as well. Granddaughter, what are you up to?"

Mercy released their hands. The beeping raised in pitch and then dropped. "You are both connected to biofeedback equipment. We wanted to follow your stress levels while you were gone."

"Why does it sound like that?" Ever the scientist, Nick was curious. "And why do I feel heavy?"

Mercy smiled. "We can explain more when you are fully revived. You may be interested to see the waves you created while you were in the spirit world."

Theresa smiled; her eyes still closed. "I think I would like that as well. Will we be able to see these waves soon?"

"I think after you have some water and are able to sit up, then we can talk about taking you to Suzanne's lab." Jane spoke up. "And it's good to have you back."

Behind Jane's back, Paul was shaking his head no, trying to get Mercy's attention. She smiled to let him know she understood.

Nick's head was clearing. "How long were we gone, or out or whatever we were?"

Jane spoke. "You collapsed Thursday afternoon. It's Saturday afternoon now. You've been out for nearly forty-eight hours."

"It seemed like minutes to me." Nick was stunned.

"Welcome to my world." Mercy grinned. "What do you remember?"

"I remember Simon Constantine came up to me. He had a message. He said I needed to find the source."

Theresa opened her eyes. "I was there, but I did not see him. I felt him. Very restless. Then gone."

Mercy was serious. "Who is, or was, Simon Constantine? Is he important?"

Jane sat down and looked at the group. "He was a scientist at the project in Los Alamos. There were concerns that he was a spy. That did not, however, turn out to be the case. What did he say?"

Nick slowly sat up in the narrow bed, "He said I needed to find the source."

"That's all?" Jane was puzzled.

"I asked him for more, but he disappeared. He said he could rest now that he had delivered the message." Nick continued. "There's more. Another scientist. David Gustafson talked to us. He asked us to find his wife and son and tell them Gus loves them. He said he was in a jeep doing something important. That's how he thinks he died. At first he wasn't sure he was dead. But then when he saw Reg. Anyway…"

"Another scientist who was in an accident, doing something important. Interesting. And *find the source*. Even more interesting. While you were out, your team traveled to Los Alamos. They'll want to hear about this." Jane rose from her chair. "Rest as long as you need. I'll send some food and water from the kitchen up to the common area. It's more comfortable there. And you must be hungry. And I'll let the team know you're both awake." Mercy watched as Dr. Paul Sanchez checked Nick and Theresa.

He explained each step to them. "I just want to check your blood pressure. Sometimes when you've been lying down for a number of hours, it's a good idea to take it slow getting on your feet."

Theresa smiled softly. "Young man, I'm in no hurry. Speed has never really served me."

Nick was swinging his right leg. "Doctor, I'm a distance runner, and I'm eager to stand and move a little."

Mercy took his hand. "Let the good doctor take your blood pressure, and you can take a few steps, then we can take a walk if he says it's okay. It's a beautiful day outside. So take a deep breath. This, too, shall pass. Right, G-Ma?"

Theresa chuckled. "You were listening after all."

Paul Sanchez looked up from the blood pressure cuff. "Sounds like you're recovering?"

"She's back all right." Mercy smiled with relief.

Paul smiled. "And you just got yourself a free blood pressure reading for being in the family."

Nick grinned. "Showing off a little? See what happens?"

"Hey, we're scientists. The more data we can collect, the more we might know. This is all good." Mercy rolled up her sleeve.

Paul checked his patients before posing his next question to Nick. "What branch of science are you in?"

Nick smiled. "I'm a physicist."

Mercy twisted her lips before smiling. "Well, I'm a physicist, too, remember, but I don't study the same thing he does."

Paul pumped up the cuff around her arm. "That's right. You said quantum consciousness, right?"

She squared her shoulders, tricky with the cuff tightening. "Yes, quantum consciousness. And yes, it's a thing."

"You read my mind." Paul was smiling.

"See, Mr. Medical Doctor, didn't we cover this already? Yes, it's really a science."

He loosened the cuff and made a quick note. "Sorry. I didn't mean to sound skeptical. I'm new here, and usually I'm the one getting looks. When my colleagues hear that I study the mind-body connection, they usually make noises and wiggle their fingers at me."

Nick snorted. "Then you better be sitting down when I tell you what I study."

Paul moved the cuff to Nick and snugged it while again saying. "Okay, I'll bite. What specifically do you study?"

Nick tilted his head to look at the businesslike man pumping up the cuff before saying. "Up until two and a half months ago, I was working on teleportation, but lately I've added time travel to the mix."

To his credit, Paul kept his eyes on the blood pressure gauge. When he loosened it and made his notation, he stepped back a step to look Nick in the eyes. "Jane told me as much but hearing it from you is somehow even more audacious."

Nick grinned. "You knew? Dr. Jane gave you a heads-up?"

With a practiced motion, Paul slung his stethoscope around his neck, looked at Jane Stanton, and replied, "Yup."

Mercy shook her head. "Well, don't feel too bad about being a skeptic. Until Thursday, when G-Ma talked about people disappearing at Los Alamos, we were never sure what she meant. Meeting Nick cleared up a lot for us."

Nick gazed at her. "I wish I could clear up what happened."

Jane Stanton stood to face the group. "Well, Doctor, how are they?"

"From what I can tell, their reactions to stimuli are normal. Their blood pressures are in normal ranges for their ages. I think my recommendation is just to eat lightly, drink plenty of fluids, and take it easy, especially Mr. Distance Runner. Try walking for a few days instead."

Mercy stood to take Theresa's hand. Nick slid from a sitting position to put weight on his feet, and Jane stepped to his side.

Jane looked at Theresa. "Your things are still in your guest suite. It's next to Mercy and Beta's quarters. Nick, your other musketeers are in Los Alamos following up a lead on your mystery, so you won't be tempted to do too much."

Mercy looked at her. "I can keep an eye on him as well. Anyway, these two have a lot of catching up to do."

Paul gave her a quizzical look. "G-Ma was sixteen the last time he saw her," she filled in.

Jane reached out to shake his hand. "I've said it before, but welcome to The Institute, Dr. Sanchez. Never a dull moment or boring day."

Paul stared at Jane. "So that explains the nondisclosure I had to sign before coming on board. I just figured it had to do with cutting-edge research."

Nick tilted his head at this. "I have to say I think time travel is pretty cutting-edge."

Jane smiled at that. "Here's a new one for you, Nick. Bleeding edge. Takes you a bit beyond."

"Ouch. I'll watch myself." He shared a lopsided grin.

Paul smiled at this. "You do that. I think bleeding for science might be asking a lot this time."

Theresa was feeling strong enough to walk. "All right, youngsters, there will be no bleeding on my watch. Let's find something light to eat and follow this nice doctor's orders."

"If only all my patients listened to what I asked them to do. Thank you, ma'am."

Jane looked at the almost-former patients. "Mercy, have you got this? I'd like to finish up with Dr. Sanchez."

"Sure, Dr. Stanton. I've got this. Now G-Ma, I see a wheelchair. Are you sure you don't want a ride?"

Theresa sniffed. "You insult me, granddaughter. I may not move quickly like you youngsters, but I still walk every day at home."

Nick stepped to her side. "I've got you too. Let's take it easy all the way to the common area."

As the three of them headed to the elevators, Jane pointed to a chair for Paul to sit. She joined him, and when they were out of earshot, she spoke. "Well, what do you think?"

"Clinically?"

"That and any other observations."

"Well, Nick is in remarkable health. Do we know about his parents' health? Does he have siblings against whom I can measure his vitals?"

"Yes, and yes, although his sister is Theresa's age, but she can fill you in on their parents and her own health history. They were all in an internment camp in World War II."

"I'll start a file. And Theresa, well, she reminds me of my abuelas. Feisty and proud. She also seemed to take this 'episode' in stride. None of the tests revealed anything unexpected. I would, however, like to follow her for a while to make sure."

Jane raised a finger. "And Mercedes, what about her?"

"Why would she have been affected?"

"Because she sat between the two of them for almost the entire time. She held their hands and was a physical connection for them while they were, well, while they were wherever they went."

"Then I'll monitor her as well. This really will be a new addition to my studies."

"And you're a master of understatement. Any other observations?" Jane wasn't letting him off the hook quite yet.

"Just that I really like all of them. They're calm, seem to appreciate the unique circumstances of the situation, and are taking it in stride. Or is this a lingering effect of the—what did she call it—trance?"

"From what I've been able to observe, and I've been around Nick almost since he traveled here through time, they are indeed calm and measured about all of it."

Paul starred at Jane. "Then I will follow their lead. There is a certain wow factor as well as *you've got to be kidding me*. But given what you've told me and what I've observed, it's time to get out a fresh notebook and collect my thoughts."

"Nick will like that you take notes. He does too. Always has a small black notebook at hand."

"Then I like him even more. I look forward to getting to know him. And with that, I'm off to grab a bite and kick back. Been a long couple of days."

In the Hallway Outside Nick's Quarters

After they found the food in the commons, filled a plate for Theresa, and made sure she was settled in her suite, Nick and Mercy stood at the door to his rooms, she took the lead. "I want to make sure you're stable, so I'll come in for a while."

Nick raised his eyebrows. "What about your reputation?"

"That's sweet, but it's 2008, and no one will think anything of it." She smiled gently.

Nick just shook his head as they entered the modest apartment space. "Sometimes I think I'm catching up, maybe even fitting in. Then something just catches me being back then."

"I can't even imagine what it's like for you. But there must be some things that haven't changed. Tell me what you've noticed so far."

He grinned shyly. "Well, for one thing, a pretty girl is still a pretty girl. The clothes, though. The clothes are totally different. Then there's baseball. Some of the teams I knew are still around, but there are more teams to keep track of."

Mercy wracked her brain. "Okay, what about food, drink, laughter, tears? Basic human things?"

Nick nodded. "Okay, yes, laughter sounds the same, but humor…different things are funny. I watched Abbott and Costello. Charlie showed me something about a Lampoon, and then somebody called Monty somebody or other."

She shook her head. "Trust Charlie to give you a taste of non-standard, even slapstick humor. And Monty Python is British humor, so all bets are off."

Nick continued. "You mentioned food. Overall, it's much better now, but maybe that's because we had rationing and limited ingredients. I do like the beer now. So many different kinds."

Mercy sat next to him on the narrow bed that doubled as his couch as he thought out loud. "The more I think about it, the more I see that almost nothing *could* be the same. Sixty-four years has changed food, clothing, music, transportation, entertainment, medicine, communication, relationships between men and women. Probably even sex."

Marcy laughed out loud. "Sex! Now how could that have changed?"

Nick blushed. "Well, I'm just guessing. I actually wouldn't know. I have nothing to compare it to."

She looked him in the eyes. "You're twenty-four—no, twenty-five years old and a virgin?"

He straightened up. "Why are you so surprised? Between years of being focused on school, then the camp, and being watched at Los Alamos, there was no time, no opportunity. And besides, there was always the fear of getting a girl pregnant."

"Well, just wow. It didn't occur to me, but when you explain it, I can see why." Mercy was nodding.

"Enough of that subject. What can you tell me about what I just went through?"

Mercy frowned. "Paul and I tracked your temperature, respiration rate and had the biofeedback, essentially a rudimentary EEG following electrical impulses. Nothing pointed to either of you experiencing anything traumatic. And no real physical consequence of the trance state or whatever we want to call it."

Nick focused on her. "Have you ever been in a trance state like that?"

"Not like that and not a shared state. I've been able to meditate and almost reach that state. When I was connecting you and G-ma was the closest I've come to getting all the way to quantum consciousness."

"And what did you feel?" Nick needed to know.

"It felt peaceful for me. I felt your restless energy. And G-ma was like a lighthouse, a beacon of calm light."

"She said there was no time there. How can that be?" Nick was staring into space.

"You know that time is a manmade construct, so no, no time as we know it. Something passes, but not anything we can currently measure." Mercy was hoping this explanation helped.

"But no time? I can't be okay with that. Not if I want to solve the mystery of my traveling. I was in 1944, and the next thing I knew, I was in 2008. Both of those times are real."

"You're right. Time is real for us in this state." Mercy began to ponder Nick's conundrum.

"We're all scientists. We have to study this. Study me. Whatever happened was real!" Nick was agitated.

Mercy was struck by a thought. "Did you think that there was something different about you, and that's why you traveled through time and not just space?"

Nick relaxed and shook his head. "Early on, but not since I found out that Tommy traveled too. In a way, that's a gift. Him being here. That eliminates one line of research and maybe points in a new direction."

Mercy squared her shoulders and straightened her back. "We're not going to solve it today and certainly not when you're depleted."

"Depleted?" Nick squinted at her.

"Your energy, you nerd. You were in a shared trance for almost two days. You didn't really sleep, and now you need to." She rose to leave. "I'll check on you in a few hours. Just try some deep breathing and try not to think about it." She squeezed his hand and headed for the door.

Nick's Notes
Saturday afternoon, November 29, 2008

I can't begin to grasp or even put words around what I have just been through. Since Thanksgiving dinner two days ago. Yes, two days ago, I have not been awake. Alert? Conscious? But I was conscious.

It began when I saw Theresa. She is, of course, sixty-four years older, but I recognized her. Seeing her was not the shock. That came when we embraced. I felt a sharp pain at my temple, and I am told I collapsed. And that's the last thing I remember before waking up this afternoon in a bed in the infirmary.

But that's not entirely true. I remember thinking something and hearing Theresa's voice in my head as if we were speaking. I remember seeing, if that's what it was, Simon Constantine. He had a cryptic message for me. "Find the source." He said it twice, and then he faded away.

At some point, Theresa said there is no time in the state we shared, so I will just think of it as a point during the experience. I saw a man I knew only slightly from the Tech Area, David Gustafson, Gus. He wants me to take a message to his wife and son. I don't know where to begin on that one. And he said he was in a jeep doing something important and then nothing. But I think he realizes he died.

And why did it happen at all? But I'm grateful for Mercy and the doctor, Sanchez, I think. I'm not alone trying to figure out this mystery.

CHAPTER 13

SATURDAY, NOVEMBER 29, 2008, THE COFFEE SHOP, LOS ALAMOS, NEW MEXICO

The lifelong friends had continued to reminisce after the young visitors left with the rusty time capsule. The discovery and the visit stirred up more memories. Now a day later, the reveries were nonstop.

Saturday, December 23, 1944, Near Los Alamos, in the Home of Butch Ontiveros

The friends were looking forward to their eighteenth birthdays in the next few months. It would take Henry another year before he could escape the Santa Fe Indian School. But today was the first day of their three-week break from school, three whole weeks at home. Soon enough, they could enlist. But today, they had something they needed to finish.

Butch led his friends into the small kitchen. "Come on. It's okay. Mom is working at the Lodge today. Albert, you got the can?"

Albert Ortiz held a brown paper bag in his hand and set it awkwardly on the kitchen table. "Yes, I told my mom it was a school thing. Otherwise, this can would have gone to the scrap drive."

Henry Cisneros dug in his pockets. "I found Tommy's baseball cards. He's still gone, so I'm hoping wherever he is he won't mind. You got something to put them in?"

Oscar Bunelos held out his hand. "Maybe this will work. My uncle kept cigarettes in it. The cards should fit." They all looked at the shallow rectangular box.

"Geez, this is kinda nice. You sure you wanna bury it?" Manuel Ordonez had picked it up to look it over.

Oscar nodded. "Mom is angry at my uncle for leaving. She's been throwing out all his stuff."

Butch took it and added it to the pile. "What else do we have?"

Henry pulled out a small rattle made of bone. "Theresa says this rattle will keep the stuff safe. Her spirits will see the rattle or something like that."

Butch nodded. "I trust her. In it goes."

Oscar had a piece of newsprint all folded up. "Here. This is the picture of our baseball team from the newspaper. We're all in it. Tommy too."

The boys nodded that the photo should be added.

Manuel looked around at his friends. "What about this medal for the English language? Miss Bonita was the reason I got it, and this time-in-a-can thing is her idea."

"You don't want it?" Butch took it from his friend. "What about your mom?"

Manuel shook his head. "Mom wants me to speak Spanish. It's okay to send this to the future."

Henry had something else in his pocket. He produced something shiny. "Remember that skinny guy named Henry. He was a scientist. We worked on his car that time? He gave me his watch. Said since we had the same name, I should have his watch. He said it stopped working, but he thought maybe I could fix it. I tried, but no luck. Maybe it will work in the future?"

They all laughed.

Manuel offered one last donation. "These are some rocks Dick, the guy Theresa knows, wants us to leave for the future. Those science men are odd, but we have room, right?"

Heads nodded. Henry had a page of notebook paper. "Miss Bonita said we should practice our English and write a letter to the future to explain what we are leaving for the people who open it."

Oscar looked at him. "Okay, you write it, then."

Dear people of the future,

It is December 1944. Our friend who helped us with learning English said that history is happening now, and we need to save things from now so you can know something about us and our lives. The picture is of our baseball team. We won a lot of games for our school.

The watch was a gift from a man named Henry, who worked on a secret at Los Alamos. He was pretty sick.

The baseball cards belong to my older brother. He disappeared. He played shortstop on the team. We love baseball and hope you still have baseball when you open this. It would be a pretty sad future without baseball.

My sister Theresa wanted her spirit guides to help protect this stuff, so the rattle will help them find it. The medal belongs to Manuel. He got it because he's good at speaking English. It's important at the Santa Fe Indian School that we all speak English.

Whenever you open this time capsule, we hope this war is over. A lot of our friends and family have been hurt.

And the rocks are from a science guy named Dick. He says they might be special. The bag of rocks came from a jeep wreck. Maybe they are special too.

That's all.

Henry Cisneros
Oscar Bunelos
Albert Ortiz

Braulio Ontiveros
Manuel Ordonez

He folded the letter and added it to the contents of the can. Butch had a small piece of deer hide and carefully wrapped the photo. Then with the can filled, they left to meet Miss Bonita at Edith Wagner's Tea Room at the Otowi Suspension Bridge. Their tutor was waiting for them by the front door with a warm smile when they arrived.

"Hi, boys, thank you for meeting me here. Miss Wagner has some milk and chocolate cake for you inside."

As the boys moved inside, eager to reach their treat, Gail Gustafson accepted the coffee can, gently opened it, and slipped something inside. Then she stepped through the doorway to join her young friends. "I have this oiled canvas from the Army that we can use to wrap the time capsule to protect it. Where do you think you're going to bury it?"

The boys glanced at each other and back to her. Butch spoke. "The base of the bridge is a good place. They practice blowing things up a long way from here. Nobody is going to dig here, at least not for a long time." They all hoped that was true. They took the wrapped can, thanked the ladies for the cake, and headed out.

Gail watched them go and slumped a little in her chair. Edith patted her shoulder gently, and then together they gathered the plates to be washed.

CHAPTER 14

SUNDAY, NOVEMBER 30, 2008, AT DUSK, DEPARTING THE INSTITUTE

The small late-model blue SUV rode heavy with Fabian, Charlie, and Nick filling the open seats, leaving D-man to drive. He knew the way to Skyridge from the many visits he and his dad had made over the years. "I want to give you guys an idea of the place you're going to be living in for a while."

"That sounds ominous," Nick muttered.

"Not meant that way. It's just very different from The Institute and totally great. It was your friend Dick and his wife who started the place. They wanted to start a school for girls. I guess Betsy had taught math to some of the local kids at Oak Ridge. She enjoyed it and wanted to do the same thing here. The idea of a boarding school just kind of hit them when they found the original Ranch." D-man enjoyed telling stories.

"So this be not the original Ranch then." Fabian grew skeptical.

"Oh, the original, at least parts of it are still there. They started with about 200 acres, main house, barn, and corral. Over the years, when the surrounding property became available, they were able to grow the Ranch. What you're going to is now 960 acres of pristine California hill country."

Charlie was very curious now. "And how many buildings are there today?"

"Oh, well, the barn became a high-tech classroom. The main house now has offices and a big kitchen. There are a few bunkhouses for students, a house for the head of school, and a couple of guest-houses they call casitas for visiting bigwigs. Yeah, that may be it. Oh, and now there's a vineyard and a vegetable garden. The corral is newer, and there's a barn for the livestock that's also high-tech." D-man was driving and picturing the arrival ahead of them.

Charlie's head was somewhere very different as he poked Nick. "I still can't get over that your Aunt Vic is the actress from the movie that my dad likes so much. And the music. He played that music so much, Ben and I know it by heart."

Fabian grinned. "I guess when she's not your Tia Vic, she really is a famous actress. We never really watched her movies when I was growing up. She sounds down-to-earth-like, not wanting her career to be a big deal."

D-man slipped a CD into the player in his SUV, and familiar chords hit the airwaves. "And just so you know, I'm a fan too. Here is the title track and theme song from *Less Than Nobody*. No groans from the passengers."

Charlie began to sing. D-man joined in, and soon the SUV was rocking to the song from 1977.

Not far behind the singing scientists was another packed SUV with Rick Stanton at the wheel. Jane was checking on the weariness of their passengers. "Theresa how are you feeling and Lia, how about you too. You've both been traveling in the not too recent past." Jane smiled gently at the duo.

"Your son Mitch is very impressive. He's a fine pilot and a caring human being. This speaks well for you and your husband. So I guess my answer is that traveling with Mitch made the trip easy, so I'm feeling a little excitement, that's all. Mom?" Lia nodded to Jane and looked at her mother.

Theresa squeezed her daughter's hand. "I, too, am excited. My travel, such as it was, left me refreshed. And then I slept well last night too."

"Okay then, let me fill you in on what you may find at Skyridge Ranch." Jane looked over her shoulder at the two women seated behind her. "You've probably heard stories about the Ranch since students have been coming here from the Pueblo for years, but some of the bunkhouses have been upgraded. And since the sun sets just after four and we won't arrive until after dark, I want to describe a bit of the layout of the property." Jane was nodding as the passengers smiled in appreciation.

In a late-model sedan that had seen better days, Paul Sanchez glanced at his passengers. "Sorry, my ride isn't fancy. I go to a lot of poor neighborhoods. A clunker like this is left alone."

"I'm glad for the lift and to be making your acquaintance. A doctor are you, then?" Clary McGonigle hadn't been at The Institute long, but he could sense when things around him changed.

"Yes, a doctor. The medical type." Paul smiled at needing to make that distinction.

"So you're along to take care of Theresa and Nick?" John Henry wanted to make sure the woman who was like his own Abuela would be cared for.

"Do you know them?" Paul hoped he was onto something helpful.

"Not Nick, but I grew up in the Pueblo, went to Skyridge, then back to New Mexico State to study anthro," John Henry explained.

"How well do you know Theresa?" Paul followed his diagnostic sixth sense.

"She is like another Abuela. I know all her family." JH nodded.

Clary had been thinking about something. "I'm not too sure where I'll be fitting in on this adventure. You do know it's rocks I'm studying."

John Henry chuckled. "I've run into my share of rocks on dig sites. Never really thought much about them."

"Maybe ye should. Rocks, they be important." Clary was a tad defensive.

Paul smiled as he drove. "I think we're all going to have something to offer. We just need to let things play out a bit. We'll see where we all fit."

"Given you're talking to guys who study really old things, I guess we can handle that." John Henry chuckled.

Clary settled back in his seat to watch the lights of the city fade as the increasing darkness foretold their arrival at the rural edges of Los Angeles.

CHAPTER 15

MONDAY, DECEMBER 1, 2008, JUST BEFORE LUNCH AT SKYRIDGE RANCH, CALIFORNIA

Charlie smiled to himself. The smell of food told him that meals would drive the schedule here in the next phase of the secret. Nicola wandered up to him. "So what did you think when you saw Skyridge this morning?"

"Well, last night, it was getting kind of dark when we got here, and that long gravel drive up seemed to go on and on. Just kinda made me drowsy." She poked him in the ribs.

"Come on. It's been a long couple of days. But the house was all lit up, and it was kind of like being in a western movie set. The deep porch and that triangle hanging there. Does anybody use it to call people to eat?" Charlie teased.

"Of course, you would take note of that. What about the bunk-house, how did you like that?" She kept prodding.

"Well, being in a small house with three other guys reminds me of college. Oh, you want to know 'cause your boyfriend is bunking with me. I get it," Charlie teased her.

"No, I was just curious to hear how you liked the bunkhouse. I'm in one too, with Beta and Mercy. I wonder if we'll have a fourth. Oh, just wipe that look off your face, Charlie Grant." She pushed at his arm. "I think the bunkhouses are really nice. I never had anything this nice when I was in the dorms. Really. Two shared bedrooms with bathrooms and a sitting area where we can study or just sit and talk."

"I am impressed with the barn classroom. It looks like a bunch of smart boards on the walls, just like at The Institute. And it's cool that it turns into a dining room." Charlie looked around.

"I heard that the Ranch is huge, like a square mile. I hope we get to walk around pretty soon. I'm curious." Nicola craned her neck to look around the room. As the newly arrived greeted colleagues and friends who had been on-site since early evening the day before, Mitch struggled to get the group's attention.

He had phoned Rosemary Edwards early Sunday evening. As interim head of school, she was key to the safe house concept being a success. As Rick Stanton's sister it was nothing less than a sign from Theresa's spirits that this was the right move at the right time. Her curiosity had been raised by her parents, and she was direct with Mitch on the phone. "I know my parents all too well, and now my brother and his lovely wife are involved. What's up, Mitchell?"

"Are you sitting down?" He wasn't kidding.

"I am now!" Rosemary Stanton Edwards set down her coffee mug.

"We've been keeping a major secret at The Institute, and it's time to move to a safer place and Skyridge is it."

"Safer than The Institute?" She was confused.

"Uh-huh. And this is coming from Betsy, your mother."

"Okay, then. What the hell is that secret?"

"Time travel." He just let that one sit with her for a minute.

"This is about Dad's time at Los Alamos, isn't it? Holy shit, they found him? The guy who disappeared came back. When I started to write science fiction, Dad told me a bit about his time there, but it was so vague."

Mitch was smiling. "Well, you're about to get two of them. The one who knew about the experiment and the other was an accidental or incidental traveler. I'll send you an encrypted file with the profiles of everyone who will be on-site, as well as the ones who will be back and forth. And there will be a couple of non-science types. Theresa Cisneros and her daughter Lia Thompson, an archaeologist named

John Henry, and a Dr. Paul Sanchez… That's another part of the story. You'll just have to wait until I get there tomorrow."

"That's all? When Rick and Jane suggested I take the interim job after the divorce, did they know about this?" Rosemary was suspicious.

"I gotta go. You'll have to take that up with them." The line went dead.

And now they were all here in the barn-like classroom and dining hall.

"I'm guessing everyone is hungry, so I'll be brief. We're here because this secret"—Mitch looked at Tommy and Nick—"is in danger of getting away from us. The knowledge in this room could put Nick's safety and freedom in jeopardy, not to mention Tommy's here." His gaze shifted to the youngest member of the team.

Heads nodded as they glanced at the pair of time travelers.

"While you all are here putting your fine brains to work on the question of what happened in 1944, the rest of the team will either be at The Institute or their own safe spaces. The full team will assemble here on weekends in person or via digital means so we can share what we have learned and move forward."

Murmurs of agreement and appreciation echoed in the barn dining hall and classroom.

Mitch continued. "Who in particular will be off-site? I'll be at The Institute, as will Beta, Dr. Jane, and Paul Sanchez. Victory and Daniel Acevedo will be working their own lines of research and resources. Ben and Michelle will be in Arizona soon and will be pursuing in-depth history and missing persons from that time and the area around Los Alamos. Grace, Father Joe, and Don Grant are already back in Indio and Arizona. These decisions reflect concern for everyone's safety and the need to keep as low a profile as possible." Mitch was assessing the impact of his sober message.

He continued. "And last, we come to communication. Thank you for turning over your cell phones. There will be two points for communication in and out of Skyridge, Rosemary as head of school, and Dr. Nicholas Fabian as on-site head of cybersecurity. If you have a need to contact anyone, you are to go through them, please. Once we get past this first week, we will review the situation and consider changes. Any questions or comments?"

Nicola raised her hand. "Thanks, Mitch. It all makes sense. I just wanted to pass along something my Tia Vic said as I was saying goodbye. She said that hiding in plain sight is a proven strategy. And my dad agreed with her. Then she said we could call her if we wanted to know more."

Rosemary perked up at this tidbit. "I think I'll take her up on that sooner rather than later. Mitch is her contact info in the system?"

As he nodded, he scanned the room. "If that's it then, let's eat. We have Thanksgiving leftovers and more."

As John Henry gravitated toward the food line, Mitch tapped him on the shoulder. "I just wanted to say thank you for running interference for us with security at the old site so the guys could go rock hunting. I think we avoided or at least postponed the alert system at the site."

John Henry smiled. "Formal security is a lot easier to get around. But there's not a whole lot that can be done to stop the Geezers. That said, they gossip and tell the old stories all the time, so it may be a while before the pieces all come together for anyone."

"Just the same I appreciate what you could pull off with a phone call." Mitch wanted John Henry to know he had earned his respect.

As Mitch turned his attention to the food line, John Henry spoke softly. "She's special. Be sure you mean it."

Mitch glanced at him. "I do. And I'll watch over her. We'll see you when we come back here Friday."

Nick and Mercy grabbed two chairs at a table for four. D-man waved to them and dropped into a chair. Charlie quickly followed. "Have you found a running route yet?" Charlie was looking at. Nick.

Mercy jumped in. "He's been told to take it easy for a few days."

"I'm thinking of walking the fence line this afternoon just to stretch my legs." Nick was examining his full plate.

"I know the grounds. Why don't I walk with you?" D-man offered to Nick.

"I'd welcome that, yes. After lunch?" Nick smiled tentatively at the shaggy-haired scientist.

Mercy was about to speak, and Charlie leaned toward her." It'll be good for them, and they won't be far."

John Henry had sat with Rosemary, Mitch, and Lia. "When do we open the time capsule again?"

Rosemary asked, "Do you have everything you need?"

He nodded. "Thanks to Mitch, we're all set, gloves, tweezers, video camera, not to mention the equipment to analyze the rocks. We need someone to shoot the video. Any suggestions?"

Rosemary grinned. "Who's the youngest person here. They are the most likely to have those skills."

"Good plan." This was Lia. "But my money is on the young Irishman and not my Uncle Tommy."

Heads nodded. She continued. "Should we let everyone here know so they can be here?"

Mitch nodded. "That will keep everyone on the same page, so to speak."

"So around one o'clock?" John Henry was in planning mode.

They all nodded. "Maybe one thirty to give people a chance to walk off the turkey tryptophan. And in the meantime, you can ask that young man to help you with the video camera." Rosemary suggested.

Mitch rose to let the room know. "If you want to be here when John Henry opens the time capsule, then be back here by one thirty. If you have questions about the property, Ro and I will be here to answer them. The vineyard is a good place to stretch your legs. There are horses in the corral, but riding should be for later. If you forgot something you need in your bunkhouses, I'm making a list. Please stay on the property. You know why."

Nicola raised her eyebrow at her Irishman, who grinned back.

"Are you for exploring then?"

"Oh, I could be persuaded."

"In private then lass, do you not agree." They moved away from the group to explore on their own.

CHAPTER 16

Monday, December 1, 2008, Immediately after Lunch, Skyridge Ranch, California

Nick and D-man headed for the door as the barn cleared out. D-man pointed away from the buildings, and the two strangers headed toward a split-rail fence.

"So what's your story?" Nick scanned the acres ahead of them.

"Not as interesting as yours." D-man smiled.

"Well, your name, for starters. D—"

The older man interrupted him. "D-man." He chuckled. "Something my dad started. Not sure why. He was a beatnik. They came before hippies."

"Came before what and beat what?"

"Oh, yeah. They were after you too. Beatniks were in the 1950s and hippies came in the 1960s."

"Your dad gave you this name." Nick was getting him back on track.

"Yeah, Dad liked to surf, and the other surfers weren't into formality. So I became the D-man or just D-man, and it stuck."

Nick nodded. "I guess that makes sense, but I don't know much about surfing, at all."

"Aren't you from California?"

"Yes, but even in the 1930s surfing was happening in Long Beach, and we lived in Pasadena." Nick kept up his walking pace.

"It definitely has quite a history in California. For some people, it's more than a sport or a lifestyle, it's a profession." D-man was keeping up with the younger man.

"Just more that I don't know. You'll find that the more we talk, the less I'll know." Nick shrugged.

"Hardly, dude."

"Okay, I'll grant you I know physics. But then again, clearly not enough."

"Let's get back to your story." D-man wanted to know a lot more about this enigmatic visitor.

"I'll grant that my arrival is interesting. Maybe more than interesting. More mystery than anything. But how did you come to be part of the inner circle here?"

It was D-man's turn to shrug. "Oh, that. My folks were at Los Alamos with Dick and Mac. When the War ended, they all headed back to SoCal. Dad taught with Dick, and Mac started The Institute. So I grew up hangin' with Rick and Jane."

"That doesn't explain why they think you should be here."

"Oh, you mean my work. I've been studying collapsing wave theory."

"You're going to have to say more than that." Nick challenged his walking companion as they reached a junction in the fence.

"Let's turn here. We can walk for about fifteen more minutes and be back in time for the time capsule. You do want to be there, right?"

"I do, but I still want to know more about your work."

"Single-minded. Good to know. How much do you know about Erwin Schrödinger?"

"Of course, the cat, his thought experiments, and Heisenberg's uncertainty principle as well." Nick had his head down, studying the ground.

"Good, because what came after that is a lot more interesting. At least to me. Do you remember hearing about a guy named David Bohm at Los Alamos?" D-man had slowed his pace as he warmed to his subject.

Nick stopped to look at D-man. "Yeah, he worked on the Gadget with Oppie."

"Well, a lot of stuff happened after Los Alamos, but Bohm's idea was that there's just a single wave function governing the universe. He thought that quantum particles travel with and are guided by waves. And that everything depends on everything else, so nothing really collapses, it only seems like it does locally."

Nick looked him dead-on. "You've got my attention, and I can see why you're here. We definitely need to spend some serious time with my research and yours. Have you met Charlie Grant and Nicola Acevedo? They've been working on this too."

"Dude, I'm ready. In the meantime, you gotta breathe in this air and just be here in the moment."

"Not sounding like a scientist now."

"I sound like a guy who lost his wife and whose daughters are worried about him and whose son has been riding his ass to give life a chance again."

"I'm sorry. I didn't know." Nick was taken aback.

"How could you? She died three years ago. That's when I came back to The Institute full-time. I needed to get out of my head, and Jane literally came and got me. She and Rick put me in the van and brought me to the quarters I'm still in."

"They're an amazing couple."

"They are that. And Ro is Rick's sister, Rosemary that is. We all grew up together."

"What's her story?"

They had started walking again but at a leisurely pace. "Not sure. It's cool that's she here, though. She was married for a while, and I heard now that she's not. You'll have a chance to ask her. I'm sure she's going to want to talk to you. She's a writer, and she's known for science fiction. You are just too, too tantalizing for her to resist."

"Like H. G. Wells kind of stuff?"

"Hers is more hard science-based, as you might guess with her family influence."

"Are there other kinds?"

"Oh man, you have no idea how many. There's fantasy, historical, new age."

"How do you know so much about it?"

"Ah yes, that. My daughter Darcy is a teacher. One of her courses is called Great American Science Fiction of the Twentieth Century, la-tee-da."

"I think I should take her course." Nick was serious.

"I'll get you her syllabus, and you can download the books." D-Man was eying the barn just a few steps away.

"Download?"

"Man, I forgot. I'll show you later. We're back and it's showtime."

CHAPTER 17

MONDAY AFTERNOON, DECEMBER 1, 2008, BARN CLASSROOM, SKYRIDGE RANCH, CALIFORNIA

Jane looked around the room. It was full but not packed, and the screen on the wall showed eight more tuning in to see what the time capsule from 1944 had to share. Clary was a natural with the video camera, so typical of an eighteen-year-old. Mitch nodded and John Henry moved to the center of the rectangular table facing the audience and near the front of the large room. "Lia, are you ready to assist?" She smiled at the implication this was a medical procedure. "Ready." He motioned to her to signal the room that they were starting. "Do you prefer latex or cotton?" He offered two pairs of gloves.

"Why don't you wear the cotton, and I'll take the latex, and we can divvy up the items depending on which gloves will be best to handle the item." Lia reached for the latex gloves.

"Good plan." John Henry looked around as he began pulling on the clean cotton gloves. "Hey, everyone, it might be easier to watch on the screen as we start to pull the items from the can."

Theresa, Tommy, Mercy, and Nick sat near the table and to the left of Lia. Charlie, Nicola, Fabian, and D-man stood to the right of John Henry. Jane, Paul, Mitch, Beta, and Rosemary edged toward the back of the room and gazed at the screen. Paul leaned in toward Jane. "I want to keep an eye on Theresa and Nick during this process.

We still don't know what triggered their shared trance. I'm glad you asked me to come with you today."

John Henry pulled the shreds of the decayed canvas wrapper from the fragile can. The opening gaped from their first attempt a few days ago. The items they had extracted were in a circle around them. Photos from Mitch's phone were also up on the screen so everyone could see the order in which the items had been removed. "Okay, I'm going to pull lightly on the deerskin now." The long tweezers grabbed the brownish hide and eased it open.

"Lia, will you use the other tweezers and hold the skin lightly as I try to unfold it. It's pretty stiff." John Henry gently grasped his tweezers and gripped the corner of the hide. As the hide creaked open, a yellowed piece of paper appeared, and the room gasped.

Beta spoke softly. "Henry said that there was a newspaper photo and a letter. Maybe that's one of those."

John Henry proceeded slowly to release the paper from the hide. As soon as he did, a black-and-white photo of two people tumbled forward. The image was still clear. Clary zoomed in. Three voices spoke at once.

"That's my mom!" D-man announced.

"That's the man who came to me in my visit." This was Nick.

"That's Miss Bonita!" Tommy was surprised to hear his voice out loud. He thought he had kept that information to himself. His sister reached for his hand.

John Henry muttered, "Maybe this is part of the mystery of the wedding ring."

He kept going. Using tongs now, he reached into the depths of the can to scoop out the loose rattling rocks. Lia held a small dish for him. One at a time, he pulled the rough stones from the base of the can. Only one remained. This one was smooth and almost round. Tommy was staring at the table now filled with the contents assembled by his friends years ago.

Gently John Henry lifted the can to tilt it from one side to the other to listen for any other treasures or clues. "Clary, do you want to zoom in and get some images of the inside of the can?" John Henry moved to the side to let the teenager lean in to have access.

Charlie spoke into the silence. "John Henry, why don't you try opening the small metal box to see what survived?"

Nicola suggested, "I'd like to see if the letter is intact."

Rosemary suggested, "Maybe the letter will give us clues before we go ahead with any of the items."

Lia looked at John Henry. They nodded." Makes sense. We'll start with the letter. Let's see if it will reveal more contents."

Lia took tweezers as did John Henry, and they carefully maneuvered the paper. One flap lifted and was laid flat. While Lia held it flat with her tweezers, John Henry lifted the other flap to lay it flat. They saw another piece of something that must have been folded with the letter. It looked like newsprint. Together Lia and John Henry worked their tweezers to unfold the item. When it was flat, they heard someone suck in a breath.

Then a youthful voice spoke. "That's our baseball team. That's me, and Henry and Albert and Butch and Manuel. There's Oscar on the end." Tommy was grinning.

Clary leaned the camera over John Henry's shoulder to project the photo and the contents of the letter onto the screen.

Tommy began to speak. "I recognize Henry's writing."

Theresa spoke softly. "So do I. He always had nice handwriting. Probably the Indian School." She began to read aloud her brother's letter from sixty-four years ago.

Dear people of the future,

It is December 1944. Our friend who helped us with learning English said that history is happening now, and we need to save things from now so you can know something about us and our lives. The picture is our baseball team. We won a lot of games for our school.

The watch was a gift from a man named Henry, who worked on a secret at Los Alamos. He was pretty sick.

The baseball cards belong to my older brother. He disappeared. He played shortstop on the team. We love baseball and hope you still have baseball when you open this. It would be a pretty sad future without baseball.

My sister Theresa wanted her spirit guides to help protect this stuff, so the rattle will help them find it. The medal belongs to Manuel. He got it because he's good at speaking English. It's important at the Santa Fe Indian School that we all speak English.

Whenever you open this time capsule, we hope this war is over. A lot of our friends and family have been hurt.

And the rocks are from a science guy named Dick. He says they might be special. The bag of rocks came from a jeep wreck. Maybe they are special too.

That's all.

Henry Cisneros
Oscar Bunelos
Albert Ortiz
Braulio Ontiveros
Manuel Ordonez

"Yeah, that sounds like them. And they took my baseball cards. I wonder which ones." Tommy was oblivious to the impact of the letter on the others in the room.

John Henry leaned back to stretch his back and shoulders. Lia did the same. "I think now we can start to assign people to assess the items. Geologists, you want the bag and dish with these rocks?"

Charlie spoke up. "I'd like to take a look at the watch and see if there's an obvious reason why it wasn't working."

Dick spoke from the screen. He and Rick were watching together at the house. "I'd like to see the comparison of the rocks you have in front of you and the ones in the box of Nick's personal effects. You have those, right? They look the same to me. I hope I included one of the smooth round ones. They always bothered me."

Theresa said softly, "I'd like to examine the rattle. It has been in the family, and I had hoped it would find its way back."

Rosemary jumped in. "I think it would be valuable to open the box with the baseball cards. What do you say, Tommy?"

"Sure. But they're just kid stuff. Why would you care?" Tommy was reaching for the tin.

John Henry put his hand gently on the teenager's. "Baseball cards can be valuable. Especially older ones. Let's be careful. It could be real money in this box."

"Real money? Like ten bucks?" Tommy was grinning.

"More like thousands depending on which player, what condition, things like that." Paul Sanchez volunteered this info.

Tommy stepped back. "You gotta be kidding me. Baseball cards are valuable?"

"They can be. Let's see what your friends decided to send to the future." John Henry grasped the metal rectangle and attempted to open it. He ran into resistance. "Tommy, do you know how to open this?"

He stepped closer to take a look at it. "I think so. It looks like something Oscar's uncle had. I think there's a little lip here." He pointed to the left corner. "And you give it a slight twist."

The box popped open to reveal a pristine image of Ted Williams. Next up was Hank Greenberg, then Joe DiMaggio. Lefty Gomez was next. Finally, they saw Morris "Mo" Berg.

"Are they worth anything?" Tommy was curious.

"We can make some calls and get an idea of what we have here. The Ted Williams rookie card may be special. Maybe all of them." Jane was thinking out loud. "Rick will love to do this, won't you, dear." She looked at the screen. Her husband was nodding and wearing a big smile.

As the room began to collectively breathe again, they heard voices from the screen. They had forgotten about the audience. Daniel spoke first. "Let's be careful about the inquiries regarding the baseball cards. We will want to think about some way to protect the finds and prove provenance."

Jane nodded. "Of course. The Institute should be able to be the third party making the inquiries."

Daniel nodded. "That sounds safe."

Dick spoke next. "What about the photo of Gail and Gus and that wedding ring. I remember them. He died around the time I was sent to Oak Ridge. It was an accident in a jeep."

Nicola spoke softly, but D-man heard her. "Gus looks a lot like D-man."

The man of the hour leaned down to her ear. "I was thinking the same thing. It's time to give my mom a call anyway. Mom always said I took after her side of the family. But I didn't look like any of them either."

Theresa and Nick moved closer to Tommy. "This has all been very strange for you, I think." Theresa looked at her very young-looking older brother.

Nick put his hands on Tommy's shoulders so he could look him in the eye. "The situation you and I are in is unique, perhaps in history. We have moved across space and time. It's a lot to take in, even for me, and I was in charge of the experiment. I can't imagine what it's been like for you."

"At first, I was just happy to not be crazy. Especially after the juvey jail place. But the longer I'm around all of you, it kind of gets better and worse at the same time. Does that make sense?"

Nick nodded. "It does because it's the same for me. I saw my best friend, and he's old now. My parents are dead, and my little sister is eighty years old."

Tommy nodded. "Uh-huh. My little sister here looks like my abuela. Not that you aren't still beautiful." He took Theresa's hand and squeezed it. "But you know, you're a lot older. I guess everyone is, unless they're dead."

"I think what I'm saying is that you can talk to me." Nick was speaking gently now. "About the experience, probably about anything. Nobody else can really understand what it's like to be in 1944 and then 2008 all in the same day."

"When you put it like that, it's even weirder." Tommy sat back down. "What happens now? How do I live my life?"

Theresa held her brother's hand. "What were you going to do before you traveled?"

"I was going to join the Army and fight in the war."

"If there hadn't been the war, what were you interested in doing?" Theresa smiled at her youthful brother's short-term thinking.

Tommy gazed into space. "I've always been good at growing things. I guess in the back of my mind I thought I would be a farmer or rancher."

"You and Beta have much in common. I think it would be good for the two of you to talk. Would you like that?" Theresa raised a hand to catch Beta's attention.

Beta joined the trio. "You called, kind of?"

"My brother has a gift for plants and growing things. Do you think you and he might have a conversation about your work?" Theresa spoke in a tone that told Beta it was not a request; it was a gentle command.

"Of course, G-ma. Tommy, let me show you some of the cool gardens and the vineyard here on the grounds."

As they walked away, Nick looked at Theresa, now older but still wise. "I'll make sure he has someone to talk to. I was honest about how challenging it is just to be here. I need to think about my research, and I'm also trying to speak a new language. Not to mention all of the scientific advances. It's a lot."

"I'm happy he has you, and this school, and so many of your new friends. He will be fine. It all just takes time." Theresa was nodding to herself as much as to Nick.

"Ah yes, time. The thing that we have here, and we don't in your spirit world. That one still confounds me, but Mercy is helping me understand." Nick was smiling.

Nick's Notes
Monday, December 1, 2008, Skyridge Ranch, California

Watching Tommy Cisneros trying to both figure out what happened and adjust to this new world allows me to observe from a new point of view. I need to talk with Mercy about this. Just the fact that another human being was transported is both exciting and alarming. Now we must wonder if there are others.

And now we have the time capsule. The rocks in it may help; I hope they do. And the mystery of Gail and Dave Gustafson keeps growing. Maybe Ben and Michelle can look into that. Tommy was surprised to hear that baseball cards are valuable, but not as surprised as I was. What a strange world this is. What may be next?

I'm grateful to be in a bunkhouse with Charlie, D-man, and Fabian. I can speak easily with them as scientists and as men of this time. There is that word again. Does everything come back to time?

CHAPTER 18

TUESDAY, DECEMBER 2, 2008, EARLY MORNING AT SKYRIDGE RANCH, CALIFORNIA

"I thought I might find you here." D-man greeted Nick then sipped his mug of steaming coffee.

"Why would you think I'd be here?" Nick was stretching on the wide front porch as he prepared to take a long run.

"Because Charlie just said so. He, on the other hand, is having a full breakfast and has no intention of doing anything strenuous from the look on his face." D-man chuckled.

Nick nodded. "Yes. He and Nicola used to drive me from The Institute to a park where I could run in the early mornings. They would wait for me. I felt like they didn't trust me alone, but then again, I do not have a driver's license or a car and needed a ride."

"Yeah, paperwork must be problematic for you right now. What are they doing about that?" D-man leaned against the fence.

"Grace has identification for me in the name of Nicholas Brown. The story is that I was raised by survivalists and did not attend school until I went to Skyridge. Father Joe has friends in a mission near the Four Corners of Arizona, and they helped create my story."

"And that story includes a driver's license?" D-man was curious.

"Yes, it does, but I have not had the opportunity to drive a modern car, and the traffic is not something I'm ready for right away." Nick was starting to jog in place.

"Sounds reasonable. I won't keep you. I suggest you stick to the fence line. If you want to follow the perimeter of the property, it's about two miles to circle back for breakfast. If we don't see you by what? Seven thirty? We send out the dogs?"

"If I'm not back by then, you can send them out, but I'll be back." Nick grinned and headed off at a trot.

He had just reached the edge of the buildings and was looking up to the rolling hills when he had company. "You're a runner?"

Tommy grinned. "I play baseball, and none of us had cars, so we ran everywhere. Does that make me a runner?"

"Maybe. I used to swim. I only started to run at the Camp because there was no pool, and I needed to stay moving." Nick had not slowed his pace.

"Was that pretty rough?"

"Yes and no. The living was hard, and the food was bad, but I was with my family. Now that they are gone, well, my parents anyway, the camp doesn't seem so bad." Nick had a faraway gaze.

"Life in the Pueblo was simple and maybe hard. The school we went to was pretty awful. We played sports to keep from going crazy." Tommy was easily keeping up.

"What school was that?"

"Santa Fe Indian School. We stayed there during the week and came home on the weekend. They wanted to make us white."

"Whoa, that sounds bad. Wanted to make you white?"

"No speaking Spanish and stuff like that. Me and my friends, we were all waiting to be old enough to join the Army and get out of there."

"I would have enlisted, but the whole Japanese thing. People thinking I'm Japanese. But I'm not, really. My parents were born in Pasadena. I'm full-on American, but try telling that to Roosevelt." Nick clenched his jaw.

"Me too—American, I mean. But my family has always spoken Spanish. That doesn't make us less American."

"Things are better in this time. Nicola says that speaking Spanish is a good thing now. There are jobs for people who are bilingual."

"Maybe that will help me when I look for work."

"School first. Let's get you graduated from high school."

"Okay, okay. You sound like my sister. But she's probably right. I guess in this time you need more school to get good work."

"Definitely. Not to mention you have been rescued by a bunch of people who really believe in the value of school." Nick chuckled.

They were out of sight of the school buildings now. "I got something I need to tell you." Tommy spoke in a low tentative tone.

Nick slowed just a step. "Okay. Should we stop or do we keep running?"

"We can run. It's about the rocks. The ones in the time capsule. There was one that was different."

"I noticed that. It was almost round, very black and shiny. Not like the others."

"Yeah. I had one of those rocks. It was bigger. The guys and me we found it when we were tracking rabbits. The gravel trucks dropped a lot of stuff when they took the curves on that road."

"How much bigger was your rock?"

"Almost the size of a baseball. That's why I had it. I wrapped string around it, and we used it to practice catching and throwing."

"What happened to it?" Nick was looking ahead but listening intently.

"I had it in my pocket that day. We had been throwing it around. I stopped to have a smoke, and the guys went on. That's why I was outside the building. Your building."

"And…"

"They took it from me with my clothes at that reform school place. Well, I guess it was also kind of a hospital. I don't really know what it was. I slept a lot. They kept giving me pills."

"And when you left, did you ask about it?" Nick had started to slow as buildings came into sight.

"Nah. I was pretty groggy. I hadn't even thought about it till I saw the rocks from the time capsule. Do you think it's important?" Tommy was both concerned and excited.

"I don't know, but we're going to find out who has that rock and get it back. I'm glad you told me." Nick was sincere.

"How you gonna do that? Get it back, I mean." Tommy matched Nick's pace.

"The same people who rescued you are gonna rescue that rock. Don, Ben, and Michelle. I think they will track it down as soon as we let them know."

"Then let's get a move on, old man. I'm hungry and we have a rock to find." Tommy raced Nick to the main house and breakfast. Nick laughed at being called an old man and raced Tommy to breakfast.

Nick's Notes
December 2, 2008

I need—no, I want to talk to Mercy. After spending time with Tommy and being at this place, I feel different. The visit to what she calls her quantum realm has made me think about the role I have always played, both as a scientist and in my entire life. Not that there has even been much difference for me.

I am and always have been an observer. It is the way Father taught me to see and to be in the world. But now it's different. I am no longer that way. Something happened to me, and not just the time travel. When I decided to be a test subject, I left my old role behind. I just hadn't thought about it in those terms.

And then recently, I slipped back into it. Just observing. It's safe. But I don't think I want to be safe anymore. I don't even know if I really can. I look at Grace and the courage it took to survive the Camp, to marry, to have a career. Grace has lived her life fully.

Tommy is thinking about how to get a job. He's not watching. He's living. And he's just seventeen.

That's what I want, to start living my life. I'm not sure how. Maybe asking Mercy to help me is the first step.

CHAPTER 19

WEDNESDAY, DECEMBER 3, 2008, IN THE WAREHOUSE DISTRICT OF LOS ANGELES, CALIFORNIA

Gordy Chambers counted himself a very lucky man. Great wife, beautiful, healthy children, a successful business, and lifelong friends. Friends like Mitchell Stans—or Hands, as he would forever be known to a special small circle.

Concern for his friend moved him to send an urgent, encrypted, and coded text: "Taco time. Today. 30 minutes."

Mitch's phone alerted. "Something's up." He was in the director's office at The Institute.

Jane Stanton looked up at her oversize son. "Your face says trouble. Speak to me."

"Foot just sent me a text. It's our code to meet in ninety minutes at this week's designated safe zone. I think you might want to come. My gut says it has to do with *the secret*." Mitch was moving toward the door.

"How soon do we leave? Do we need your dad?" Jane was reaching for her phone.

"A mother and son out for a picnic is good cover. Let's limit the fuss. Will you call the kitchen and ask them to fix something? The site is thirty to forty-five minutes away depending on traffic." Mitch was thinking and planning out loud.

Jane dialed the kitchen. "Hey there. I'm heading out for a picnic. Will you fix a basket for two, and one of them is a big eater. Yes, I'll be there in fifteen minutes. Thank you."

An hour and a half later, Jane, Mitch, and Gordy sat at a picnic table in an almost-empty park. As Jane and Mitch spread out the food, Gordy began to casually speak softly. "It just never gets easier. Knowing even the watcher is being watched. Tell me again why I'm in this business?"

Jane smiled and handed him half a sandwich. "Because you are brilliant and committed to the safety of your family, your friends, and even your country."

Mitch had his sandwich almost to his mouth. "They watch even you?"

Gordy just nodded and took a bottle of water from the basket.

"Who is this mystery 'they,' young man?" Jane smiled disarmingly at the two friends who had spent so many hours studying and planning in her family room.

"And that is why we're here. This time 'they' is a little out of the ordinary. Ever since you filled me in on our visiting scientist, I've added some filters and alerts to what I watch, not for you personally, but for The Institute. I do watch out for you all, but that's not what prompted the text."

"Come on, Foot. Out with it." Mitch had an apple in his hand and was about to take a drink from his water bottle.

"DARPA sent messages to a group of researchers, and the words in that message included Los Alamos, experiment, 1944, and Nishimura." Gordy took another bite of his sandwich.

"Holy shit!" Mitch put down the apple and barely kept himself from choking on his water.

Jane calmly reached for the other half of her sandwich. "What's the timing on these messages, or was it just one message?"

"The first one was Sunday." Gordy picked up a corn chip. "Then each day since. That's three consecutive days. Today they called a meeting."

Mitch focused on his friend. "Do you have a location, names, more than just this?"

Jane spoke softly. "Breathe, Mitchell. Let Gordy give us the full brief."

Mitch leaned back. "Sorry, Foot. This has become very personal, and I kind of…well, Mom's right. I need to take a step back so I can do what I'm good at, and so can you."

"Thank you both. The meeting is in Northern Virginia. The recipients of the messages are almost all on the East Coast. The invitees are all scientists, no military addresses, and they have been invited as a group, which means something. Not sure exactly what, but letting them all know about each other may mean it's not top secret."

"East Coast scientists. That's interesting. We have many colleagues on the East Coast. Any names you can share that might show on The Institute's list of hosted researchers?" Jane was folding up the wrapper from her sandwich.

"I knew you'd ask. I already cross-correlated names and institutions. There's only one name." Gordy paused.

"Well, out with it." Mitch was frowning.

"It doesn't make sense, though. He's not an East Coast guy." Gordy frowned as well.

Jane tilted her head. "It's okay. We'll figure this out together."

"Okay. It's Dr. Darren Hickson. Why do they care about D-man, and why is he connected to any of them?"

"Damn. I don't like what just flashed into my brain. He was gone for three months. He was supposed to have stayed in touch, and he didn't. And now he's in the heart of what's going on in a supposed safe place." Mitch's jaw was tight.

Jane nodded. "Agreed. It looks suspicious, but it could also be innocent. D-man shared his newest research with Rick, and it's cutting-edge, even for him. Rick thinks he's onto something with his theory of a quantum tsunami causing unexplained events."

Gordy and Mitch exchanged a look. Gordy asked, "What kind of unexplained events?"

"Oh, just the usual Area 51 UFO stuff, but that stuff gets a lot of attention." Jane was calm.

Gordy shook his head slightly and reached for a cookie. "I think it's more than that. MIT and Johns Hopkins aren't usually on the list when those topics are in chatter."

Mitch nodded. "Okay, what else you got?"

"None of the people invited are under sixty years old. Everybody has some tie to what happened at Los Alamos in the 1940s. But there are also people *not* on the list that are interesting." Gordy was clearly puzzled by his own discovery.

Jane spoke. "Like who?"

"Well, your father-in-law for one. He's one of the last survivors of that time, and he worked on the Trick." Gordy was matter-of-fact.

"There were only a handful of people who knew about the Trick, much less were close to it. Who other than Dick are you aware of?" Jane wondered. "It sounds like it's time for a visit with him."

"And there's one more thing." Gordy's head was down.

Jane put her hand on his shoulder. "It's Robert, isn't it?" He nodded.

Mitch set his jaw as he and Gordy began to put the trash from the picnic in the basket. Mitch turned to his trusted friend to ask, "How much time do we have?"

Gordy stared at the nearby tree. "Let's plan dinner tonight. Will that work?"

The group split apart, and as Jane and Mitch headed to the van, she pulled out her phone. "I'll tell your dad we're going to need one of his kitchen miracles. Who else should we call?"

"If Daniel and Victory are available, I think it may be time to assemble our A team. You agree?"

"My thoughts exactly." Mitch opened her door, put the lunch basket behind her, and headed around the front of the van.

As he climbed in the driver's side, he muttered, "Maybe this is a good thing."

"Then why do you and Gordy look like you've been given bad news?"

"We don't like surprises, and I feel uneasy when Uncle Robert starts sniffing around." Mitch powered up the van.

"Then it's definitely time for the A team." Jane smiled and hit new numbers on her speed dial.

CHAPTER 20

DECEMBER 3, 2008, EARLY EVENING AT THE HOME OF RICK AND JANE STANTON, LOS ANGELES, CALIFORNIA

Feynman joyfully barked greetings as his humans arrived. Mitch spent several minutes focused on his furry sibling, just the most recent in a series of creatively named canines. "Hey, let me know what I can do to help." This was directed toward the kitchen, where clanging sounds were increasing.

Rick's voice traveled from the kitchen. "You're doing it. Keep him busy. I've got a lot going on in the kitchen, and a hungry four-legged assistant is not the helper I'm looking for."

"And just what kind of help might you be looking for?" Gordy peeked his head into the familiar kitchen.

"Now you I can use. Get an apron and help me get the fish ready for the grill." Rick grinned in greeting.

Jane welcomed Vic and Daniel in the driveway as she helped her in-laws negotiate the walk to the door. "It's fish tacos, and I hope you brought an appetite. Rick went a little crazy at the market."

Mitch looked away from Feynman to greet the newest guests. "You know the big guy here. He's a lotta happy, so watch your balance."

Daniel sat near the big dog and bigger man and gave them his undivided attention. "Not that I need an excuse to visit you all, but your mother left me a very mysterious message. Any idea what's up?"

Mitch nodded. "I do and we actually have a new mystery. And you and your sister may be critical in our next steps."

"Food and a mystery. You're talking my language." Vic sat down to join them, and Feynman redirected his tongue and tail to the vivacious woman now at his eye level.

Jane glanced at her living room, relieved to see her in-laws had seated themselves near the bar. "Mom and Dad, do you want to be served, or would you like to pour? Rick's making fish tacos, so there's a pitcher of margarita's as well as chilled Coronas, but there's always the other stuff." She knew their fondness for single malt scotch.

Vic tore herself away from her newest hairy friend to rise and help. "I'll be happy to tend this bar if you tell me what you want."

"You are a dear to do that. I'll have scotch neat, and my beloved will have..." Dick looked at Betsy.

"Oh, heck, I'll have a margarita. For God's sake, it's fish tacos. What are you thinking having scotch, you old coot?" Betsy was grinning at her husband of too many years to count.

"I didn't say I was *only* going to have scotch. I'll get to the rest. I just want to take the edge off." Dick was teasing her.

Vic loved to hear their banter. Being around a couple like Dick and Betsy, who had endured for so many years, raised her hopes that her own life would soon hold such loving banter.

Daniel looked at Mitch. "I'm getting a beer. What would you like, and does Feynman drink?"

Mitch grinned. "He's been known to slurp beer when it spills, but we don't want to contribute to the delinquency of a minor even of the canine variety."

Voices from the kitchen said, "Beer, please, and hurry. We're working hard." Gordy wasn't shy in this house, and Rick was having a blast.

Soon enough, Rick and Gordy emerged from the kitchen to take a break. All eyes turned to the cooks, and Rick raised his bottle to Gordy. "The man of the hour. The floor is yours."

Gordy took a sip. "I see a couple of new faces, though I know who you are. Mitch has been kind enough to fill me in. Turnabout is fair play. I'm Gordy Chambers. I've known this family since I played football with the Big Guy. Both he and I had our eyes on futures off the field. You see where his has led. I stayed in IT and began to specialize in communication, specifically encrypted comms. I started working for college friends helping their start-up tech businesses. That caught the attention of the DOD…and others. For the past eight years, I've run my own company with the kind of clients that I can never tell you about."

Eyebrows raised around the room. "That has, in turn, allowed me to watch over my extended family." Gordy continued and glanced to the Stantons. "The Institute is an off-the-books client. I watch the comms for every reason you can think of and a few more. A lot of research starts and ends under its roof. Research that corporate spies and state actors would love to get hold of."

Vic muttered, "Okay then, I think I need to talk to you when I need story ideas."

"It's you all's not-so-little secret that brings me here tonight," Gordy continued.

"Damn, I was afraid of that." Daniel drained his beer.

"Let me tell you what I told Mitch and his mom at lunch today. Sunday, the day his team was returning from Los Alamos, a message was flagged that had key words I was watching, Los Alamos, 1944, experiment, and Nishimura. That was Sunday. There was another message on Monday. Then another on Tuesday. Today there was an invitation to a meeting. Oh, and this is coming from DARPA."

Vic looked puzzled. Daniel explained, "Defense Advanced Research Projects Administration."

"How do you know…never mind." Vic focused on Gordy.

"The invitees are all on the East Coast, save one. I compared the list of invited scientists against scientists who have been at The Institute…since it began. And only one name popped up." Gordy paused. "Dr. Darren Hickson."

Jane looked around the room. "And there's one more concern. My brother Robert is the one who initiated the messages and the invitations."

"I think I'm going to be ill." Rick blanched.

"There must be an explanation." Betsy spoke calmly. Dick took her hand and nodded numbly.

Jane spoke. "That's what we believe and what we hope. But you are here because it's time to talk about Vic's suggestion, about hiding in plain sight. While we investigate Darren's connection and Robert's involvement, we must also initiate a distraction and perhaps some camouflage."

Vic set her drink down. "It sounds like Robert has baggage. Anything you care to share? And what's his rank while you're sharing."

"My brother, the not-quite-retired full bird colonel, can be a complete full-on jerk. He and my dad haven't spoken in more than two decades. Robert wanted The Institute to become part of DARPA. Dad refused."

"Whoa. So how bad is it that he showed up?" Vic wrinkled her forehead.

Rick spoke. "We don't know, but he's a family sore spot for sure."

"Then the plan to start hiding in plain sight is even more important. I liked the idea when we thought the secret was contained to the people we know, and now it's critical." Vic leaned forward.

Mitch stood up, causing Feynman to wag his tail. "Not yet, big guy. There's something else. Mom, this came in this afternoon. Ro called me from Skyridge. Nick and Tommy have been running together in the mornings, and Tommy opened up to him. Tommy recognized one of the rocks in the time capsule. He recognized it because he and his friends had found a bigger one like it and had been using it for baseball practice. Yeah, space rock or whatever it is as a baseball, but the point is he had it in his pocket when he traveled. And they took it from him at that place in Arizona. And no, they didn't give it back to him when Don, Ben, and Michelle rescued him."

Daniel leaned back. "Let me summarize. The smartest part of the military is sniffing around, led by an estranged family member. An insider, who may be compromised, is at the heart of the biggest secret in history, and a juvenile facility in a small town in Arizona has what may be an alien artifact. Have I got this right?"

Mitch nodded. "I couldn't have said it better."

"In that case, we need to eat before we try to stress our brains on just alcohol." Betsy was ever practical.

"Yes, ma'am," Gordy, Rick, and Mitch said in unison.

"Let's move this dinner to the patio. Rick, is the grill ready?" Jane was in motion.

"Grill and grillers are ready. Time to get the rest of the food out there." Rick and Gordy moved to the kitchen. Vic, Daniel, and Mitch headed to gather the rest of the dinner items. Jane hung back to help Dick and Betsy.

"You do give the most interesting parties, dear." Betsy smiled.

"Oh, stop it. You know this is hard on her," her husband gently chided her.

"Well, I'm partly serious. This is the most fun I've had since Oak Ridge and then starting Skyridge. I feel really alive with all of these things going on," Betsy admitted.

"I admit that it has put a bounce in my step that's been missing for a while," Dick muttered.

As Jane helped them both get to their feet. Betsy added, "I have to say that on a very selfish level, I am enjoying the new people, the camaraderie, and even the intensity of this whole thing."

Dick added, "If only our friends weren't at risk."

Jane and Betsy nodded and followed the group to the patio.

After the first round of grilled fish tacos, Vic decided it was time to share her ideas. "Can everyone eat, listen, and focus? Yes, then let me tell you what I've been thinking since the safe house at Skyridge became a reality. The best lies are mostly true and then have just enough falsehood to accomplish their purpose. In our case, the falsehood will be writing and filming a movie about time travel. This conveniently explains research queries into history at Los Alamos. It explains a gathering of talented and diverse people in a quasi-remote location. And I have a thought to explain Tommy as well."

"We're all ears." Rick was on his second taco, and his helpers were going for thirds.

"He was at a facility, right, kind of a clinic?" Heads nodded. "And then he was removed to go to a place that specialized in his *problem*, yes?" Vic was building her story line. "And the nature of his *problem* was unclear, yes?"

Jane said, "We thought the less said, the better at that time. And from what Don said, the facility was glad to hand him off. Frankly, they thought he was crazy and more than they could handle."

"Sheesh." Mitch paused in reaching for another beer.

Vic was gleeful. "This is great. I have an idea of how we can use Tommy's *condition* to establish the premise for the movie. The story the movie tells is about people who have 'social temporal displacement disorder.' You can look it up, but it isn't in any textbook. I checked."

Rick set his beer down. "Social temporal displacement disorder. If I follow where you're headed with this, social is about interacting with people or maybe history? The temporal has to do with time, displacement means the person thinks they are in a different time or place, and disorder because…well, of course, it's a disorder to everyone else. Do I have it right?"

Daniel nodded. "You're spot-on. It sounds medical. The explanation is rational. It gives Don, Ben, and Michelle a great ruse with which to return to the facility now that we know they took something from Tommy. And more importantly, it's just a great concept for a sci-fi movie. She even has a title."

Heads swiveled as Vic shrugged. "Temporarily temporal."

Laughter exploded, and Feynman started to bark.

"I guess that's an acceptable working title from your reactions." Vic smiled broadly.

Gordy was pensive. "I think it's even better than that. In addition to listening in to monitor Robert, I can also plant messages. I do it very rarely. I'm able to mask myself and insert a mention of this disorder into the message thread."

Mitch tilted his head. "Is that smart? Do we want to add another element at this point, or do we want to save it?"

Daniel was nodding and began to speak. "I see what you mean. Wait until we really need to throw them off. However, if we throw them off now, will that buy us more time and allow us to fully deploy our camouflage? More discussion is called for. Sister mine, it's time for you to call in your squeeze."

Vic blushed. "Happy to do my part."

Mitch smiled. "That would be great if you would. I was going to call him about the rock thing and just haven't had a chance." Heads nodded in understanding.

Jane gazed at the remnants of dinner and the now relaxed group on her patio. "Next steps, team?"

"I think we need Ro. She's the science fiction writer. She's already on-site, and her name will add some legitimacy to the genre of the film." Rick was nodding.

"I think I see what needs to happen." Mitch was squaring his shoulders. "Vic calls Don, and he and his bunch chase the rock. She will also put together a one-page treatment of the movie. Don can use it to get the rock back. The treatment also goes to Rosemary to get her thinking. The movie plan is explained by yours truly to the Skyridge bunch when I go out Friday. Gordy plants the social temporal displacement disorder in a message on this DARPA thread. But who—and, Dad, I'm looking at you for this one—makes a call on Dr. Darren Hickson before Friday to find out why he's getting this invitation from Uncle Robert?"

"If you're planning to unveil the ruse on Friday afternoon, then Feynman and I are taking a drive tomorrow. Taking Mr. Happy with me always disarms people, and it says that this is a casual visit. Don't want to set off alarm bells to warn D-man." Rick was petting his cohort in the plan.

"Next question. How many of us want to be, plan to be, at Skyridge for Friday dinner? Beta, Paul and I will be there. Anyone want a ride?" Mitch was starting to gather plates.

"Your mom and I will definitely be there." Rick was moving toward the grill.

"Maybe Saturday. I like the drive during the sunlight." Dick was looking at Betsy, who nodded her agreement.

Gordy looked around. "I think I'll stay in the shadows for now. Are you all on the MRC?"

"Oops. Egg on my techno face, Gordy. I haven't added our newbies to the network." Jane was embarrassed.

"Murk?" Daniel asked.

"Actually MRC, short for Mobile Relational Communication. It sounds like *murk*. It's a private encrypted comms tool. We use it at The Institute. It has enough range that it's useful within about 150 miles," Gordy explained. "A perk of working for brilliant friends. One of them created the tool. I created the encryption. A tech marriage of sorts."

"When do we get ours?" Daniel was eager. "This solves a lot of issues that I was just beginning to list in my lawyer brain."

"Tomorrow. I'll make it a priority first thing. Mitch knows how to reach you?" Gordy glanced.

"I'll make it happen. You get 'em to me, and I'll take them to Vic and Daniel." Mitch had his hands full of bottles now.

"I don't know about the rest of you at the grill, but with the exception of the D-man uncertainty, I'm feeling a lot better." Rick was standing and stretching. Feynman barked his approval, and everyone laughed.

When the last of the visitors had said good night and Rick, Jane, and Feynman headed to bed, he smiled at his wife. "I need to thank Mitch again for suggesting Feynman could be a therapy dog. I know the trainer questioned his wisdom but look at him now." The big dog wagged his tale but didn't take his eyes off Jane.

Her canine shadow had not escaped his notice. "All right, all right. Yes, I have something on my mind. And you already know what it is." They said together. "Robert."

Jane climbed into bed, reached for a book and smiled when the furry therapist laid his head on her ribs. She pulled his head close and kissed his nose. "It's okay, big guy. I'm okay now." He seemed satisfied and moved to the end of the bed to drop to the floor and curl into sleep.

"*Are* you okay? Your little brother doesn't usually add calm to situations. Especially anything having to do with The Institute." Rick pushed his reading glasses lower to watch his wife.

"I just don't know how long he can carry this grudge. Dad turned down the offer to merge with DARPA decades ago. And for very good reasons." Jane shook her head.

"We know that. But Robert has never accepted that science cannot thrive in a hierarchy. They figured it out at Los Alamos, and your dad paid attention." Rick closed his book. "Not to mention the damned agency couldn't decide whether it would actually be called Defense or just work on defense projects. It went back and forth how many times? Just crazy."

"So what do we do about Robert?" Jane turned to look at her confidant and partner in the biggest secret of their lives.

"Nothing. And doesn't that just grate against our urge to act." Rick scowled.

"It does and I have to agree. If he's involved, I don't want him to suspect that we know anything. I don't want to alert him to the possibility that anything is going on. Ahhhhhh. I knew when he moved from military intelligence to DARPA that someday we would have this conversation. I just hoped not too much would be at stake when we did. Maybe just a nuclear energy breakthrough or cloaking technology." She chuckled.

"And that's why Dr. Furry Feynman and I are visiting Skyridge tomorrow morning. Our fine four-legged therapist will know if D-man is holding something in. I won't need to drag it out of him." Rick smiled a conspiratorial smile.

"It will break Ro's heart if Darren is making some kind of mistake. I know she still has feelings for him." Jane gazed into space.

"She does? After all these years. They were kids. Well, she was. He was in college. Then he met Serenity. I know she was heartbroken, but that's been years." Rick was sometimes a little obtuse.

"When Edmund left her, for another man, she held it together. In fact, it was a relief to have it out in the open and be free of a marriage that wasn't. It's been long enough now that it's time, and Darren has just landed in her lap, or at least her neighborhood." Jane was concerned.

"You've been talking with my sister." Rick was not entirely surprised.

"Of course, I've been talking with your sister. We were friends before you and I got married. Her friendship is one of my longest and most treasured. So yes, I've been talking with your sister. And it was *such* a relief to be able to read her in on the Nick secret." Jane was warming to the conversation.

"I wish you could come with me, but that might be too much tomorrow. And we'll both be there Friday. I'm hoping there is a rational reason D is part of DARPA's interest in 'the situation.' I'll let you know as soon as I can. Given the communication quarantine, I won't be able to call until we're on the way home. How would you feel if I left Feynman there? We can bring him home after Friday dinner." Rick was thinking out loud.

Jane turned to kiss her husband good night. "That's all good. I'll miss you both and will be waiting to hear from you. I'm sure Mitch will keep me busy until then." She chuckled slightly at her understatement, then turned out her light.

Earlier that Same Evening at Skyridge Ranch

Nick caught Mercy's eye after dinner. "Want to go for a walk?"

She grabbed his hand, and they headed toward his now-familiar route. "We're walking and not running, right?" she teased him.

"I'll run if you will."

"Not after that meal. Exercise, yes. Running, no. I have to watch out that I'll grow out of the clothes I brought with me." She chuckled.

"I wanted to talk with you about something. I could use your help."

"Of course. What's on your mind? Or is that a loaded question?" She smiled.

"Maybe my mind is loaded. Ever since I woke up I've been aware of something."

"Something from the visit?"

"After it. More of a realization. All my life, I've been an observer. I learned from my father. He taught science. Maybe it's been a safe place to be, observing. But after experiencing what you call the quantum realm, I don't think I can be just an observer anymore. More important, I don't want to just observe." Nick was looking at the ground and squeezing her hand.

"Okay. You want to do more than observe. What are you thinking?" Mercy wanted to probe, but gently.

"I look at my sister. Even in the Camp, she made friends, she fell in love, she found a career. She didn't play it safe." Nick lifted their hands together as if to shake them at his past.

"Yes, she did choose. She has led a wonderful life, and it's far from over. I'm not following, though."

"She didn't just watch. She did things. She made friends. Fell in love. And I don't know how to do that." Nick dropped her hand.

Mercy stopped walking. Nick turned to look at her. "I don't know where to start. I didn't before even when I knew the rules. Now I'm here, and everything's different. How do I start, Mercy?" he was almost pleading.

Mercy pulled him by his hand, walking slowly.

"Let's look at what you admire about Grace. She made friends even at the Camp. You have made friends here. Charlie, Fabian, Nicola, even crazy D-man. Not to mention me and my sister. We're your friends now. Maybe at first, we looked at you differently, but that didn't last. You're one of us." Mercy was earnest. "And you're a fine scientist. I hope it's still the career you want. The world really needs your mind working on your discoveries."

"I want more than friends and a career." Nick blushed.

"Oh, you mean falling in love?" She was aware that the conversation was shifting.

"At least having a date. Nicola and Charlie were starting to write a…a…some kind of ad to get a date. That's when Fabian told her he thought she was smart and beautiful. Then they went to a movie together. But I can't do one of those to find someone. What am I going to say? Single Japanese-looking guy, twenty-five, acts older. Knows a lot about World War II."

Mercy burst out laughing. "Okay, That's just flat-out funny. Not to you, but when I think about some of the personal ads I've read, that one, well, I would email you." She squeezed his hand.

"You're not being serious and I am." Nick was hurt.

"Actually, I am serious. I like you. And I'm interested. Maybe the timing sucks. I mean, we're here and can't really go on a date, but we're walking. We're alone. It's a beautiful night. I bet that was good enough for Grace and her husband-to-be when she was in the Camp." Mercy gazed at Nick.

"So you think we can be like Grace and Hector. Grab the moments we can, to be alone?" Nick sounded hopeful.

"Why wouldn't we? This isn't a practice life, Nick. You, more than any of us, know that. If this is what we've got, then let's take advantage of it. No one's watching us out here. Maybe it's not a movie theater, but we're alone." She leaned toward him.

He leaned in and lightly kissed her. She stepped into his arms and deepened the kiss. He pulled back a little. "I don't know what I'm doing."

"You're doing fine." Mercy pulled him back to her. "And just think. No need for a car, no parking, no dinner, no movie. Just us under the stars. It doesn't get any better than this." Mercy was smiling.

Nick clasped her hands in his. "Okay then. We're dating? You and I?"

"I sure hope so. I'd hate to think you were practicing on me so you could ask someone else to go on a moonlight walk." Mercy was teasing him.

"No, just you. Ever since I met you at Thanksgiving dinner, I've wanted to kiss you. I just didn't know…"

"Yeah, there was the whole collapse and quantum thing that got in the way." She grinned slyly.

"Yes, there was that. I'll try not to collapse again when I'm thinking about kissing you." Nick smiled back.

"If I have that kind of effect on you, maybe we should find a place to sit down?" She was still smiling.

"I hope we're safe from collapsing. And it was your grandmother who brought it on. Say, you don't think it runs in the family, do you? The making me collapse thing?" Nick was joking.

"It's not happening now. But we could try another kiss and see if we can push the limits." She looked at him.

"In the interest of science." Nick reached for her.
"Science, yeah, right," Mercy mumbled into his lips.

Nick's Notes
December 3, 2008

When I decided to ask Mercy to help me to stop just observing and start living my life, I wasn't sure what she'd say, what would happen, or what it might mean. I hoped she would say yes, but I had no idea I would start feeling so much, so many different things all at once. I was excited. I was afraid. But it felt right. And then we kissed. Then so much more feeling. Not as afraid, but still. I don't know what I'm doing. That's not comfortable for me. I guess I had no idea how much I had been holding in. How much effort it was to hold it in. I feel lighter now. How can that even be?

And it wasn't just one kiss, so it wasn't an accident. I think she meant to kiss me. I'll have to ask her tomorrow. Maybe she knows what happens next. I sure don't. But I want to know, and I'm looking forward to tomorrow in a way that I haven't before. Is this romance? And what if romance is faster in this time since everything else seems to happen so quickly. But feelings can't be instant, even in the future, I hope. I want to get to know her better. I hope she thinks that's okay.

CHAPTER 21

AUGUST 30, 2008,
ON THE OREGON COAST

Dr. Darren Hickson sat on a bench to watch the waves ease against the beach. It was a calm day, mostly gray with a few breaks for weak sun. Seagulls called to each other, and the smell of seaweed was blowing out to sea, but the saltwater perfume was strong. He pulled the battered envelope from his backpack. He'd been carrying it around for almost three years. He couldn't put off reading it any longer.

Dear Darren,

Being your dad has been an honor and the privilege of my life. Because of you, my life has been full beyond what I could have wanted or expected. Know always that your mother and I love you with all of our hearts.

Know also that she *is* your birth mother, and, as you have long suspected, I am not your birth father. He was my best friend and your mother's first love. His name was David Gustafson. He died before your mother knew she was pregnant. It was a jeep accident. I thought it was suspicious, but there was no one willing to listen to me. This was late October of 1944.

We were all at Los Alamos, but without a husband, she had to leave. She was only allowed to be there because of him. Days after she left, the project I was working on, the Trick, ended; actually, it was called off. The scientists working on it wanted to keep going, me included, but we were not allowed. A couple of weeks later, I was ordered to Hanford, Washington.

It was a confusing time, and communications were difficult and slow. Your mom had told me she would take the train to Sacramento to visit an aunt. Before I got to Hanford, I sent her a ticket and a ring to come join me there. She did. You were born almost seven months later.

Your mom wanted to tell you about us and your dad when you were old enough. Then we got so comfortable. We became a great family together.

It's just that part of it is a lie. I'm gay. Your mom helped protect my career by marrying me. Things were different then, and I was the friend she needed, then and always, as we have come to realize.

I do love her. She is my closest friend. We have been discreet with our private lives. After you married and moved away, it didn't seem necessary to tell you. But the lie has always been there lurking.

The other secret is about Los Alamos. In a way, those years never ended for me. I continued, along with Dick Stanton, to quietly pursue research into the science behind the Trick. Mac MacLane kept both of us in the loop on the work that continued at The Institute. None of us could forget the courage of our friend Nick Nishimura. He's the man who went missing, causing the

project to end. We have never found him or figured out what happened that day.

These are my two secrets. Maybe you will
understand why I didn't tell you. I hope so. Please
do not blame your mother.

I love you, son, and am so very proud of
you. The man you have grown into is a credit to
your mom and Dave would be happy to know
you. I miss him every day.

Please forgive me.

Your Dad,
Reg

The letter rocked him. He was glad he had not had a chance
to read it while Serenity was still alive. She would have spent her
precious energy on comforting him when she needed all of it to fight
her cancer.

The sabbatical now became a convenient cover to do some
investigating without the scrutiny of well-meaning friends.

He still had someone he knew in a key place. And now he had
names and a few rough dates. The mystery of his birth father was
calling him as strongly as the waves. He would respond to both.

He folded the letter and carefully returned it to his pack. The
rhythm of the waves lulled him as his thoughts roiled. He wanted to
call Rick, but it was too soon. He needed to know more before he
called him and made the request to meet with the senior Stanton.

CHAPTER 22

THURSDAY, DECEMBER 4, 2008, EARLY MORNING AT THE LA, HOME OF VICTORY ACEVEDO

She dialed the number she knew by heart and heard the familiar ring. "Hey there, good morning." Her voice did not hide her excitement.

It was early in Arizona, but Don Grant was awake. "Good morning yourself. To what do I owe this special wake-up call?"

"I wish it was only to tell you that I'm thinking about you, but you know I'm thinking about you every day. You know that, don't you?" She was only half teasing.

"I do and it warms me in all the right places." He had a smile in his voice.

"I'm glad that's settled. But we have a wrinkle. Tommy told Nick that he had a rock in his pocket when he traveled." Vic continued.

"I've heard of a rocket in my pocket, but that's not what you mean." Don was only half teasing.

"No, Tommy said the guys found this roundish smooth black rock when they were rabbit hunting. He wrapped it in string, and they used it for baseball practice. He had it in his pocket. But it wasn't with his things when he got to Skyridge," she explained.

"When we were able to get him out of there, he was pretty loopy. I'm not sure what they gave him. The clothes he had on looked vintage, but I didn't think to ask about personal effects when they released him to us." Don was serious. "Why do we care about a rock?"

"Tommy said it looks like the big brother to the rocks in the time capsule. There were other smaller rocks like his big one, but it's the bigger one that we want to track down." Vic sounded businesslike. "If you have any trouble with them Daniel's at the ready to come down like a hammer, especially given all the drugs they put in his system."

"So Tommy had this rock on him...when he traveled...I think I get the urgency now. I'll head over there right away. I'll give the director a call and let him know. He owes me. And speaking of owing, well, kind of. I have something for your mom if you think she'd like it." Don set his mug down as he reached to pet a furry roommate.

"Something for Mamacita. How sweet. What?"

"Well, it's more of a who. Grace seemed to enjoy having Sam stay with her. And some friends of mine are moving into a retirement place, and they can't keep..."

She didn't let him continue. "A dog, is it a dog? You found a dog for Mom?" She was excited.

"Not just any dog. It's Sam's littermate. Her name is Amy June, and she's a total sweetheart. They left her with me yesterday, and I was thinking of giving you a call today to run the idea by you."

"That's perfect, so perfect. How soon can you bring her to Mom?" Vic was eager.

There was no hesitation. "I was thinking of tomorrow, and then maybe I could see you over the weekend."

"And we can go to Skyridge and see everyone. I have my motorhome there so we can have privacy." Vic had almost forgotten why she called. "And maybe you'll have the rock."

"We don't know yet if it's dangerous. It may need special handling." Don was in science mode.

"Great thoughts and I have no insights. But if Tommy and the guys handled it wrapped in string, then you should be safe putting it in a box and bringing it with you." Vic was hoping she was right.

"I'll call you when I know something but count on me being at your place by late afternoon tomorrow." Don was happy, and his voice showed it.

Vic continued. "Will you bring sweet Sam?"

"If that's okay with you. She loves Skyridge." Don was still smiling. "And she's good company on the long drive. Plus having her in the car will help Amy June stay calm. She's missing her home right now. It will be good to get her settled at Grace's. I have her bed, dishes, food, and all her vet files."

"I'll be looking forward to hearing what you find out about the missing rock. This is all great stuff for the movie. Too bad it's real." Vic's voice had lost some energy. "I have something else on my mind, if you have another minute."

"For you as many minutes as you want."

"I've been giving it a lot of thought, and maybe I'm crazy or bold, or worse, but would you consider spending more time here in California? With me?"

"For the record, I do not think you are crazy, I like a woman who speaks her mind, and I would very, very much like to spend more time in California, with you." Don was blushing.

"Then let's talk about how we can make that happen when you're here this weekend. Deal?"

"I'll call you as soon as I have an update. I miss you already." And Don clicked off.

He then dialed his longtime friend who ran the facility that had housed Tommy. "Hey, John, It's Don Grant. Remember the young man with the undiagnosed issue? Yeah, him. Well, it turns out he had a personal item with him when he arrived that wasn't returned to him. Can you help me out and find it for me?"

The voice on the other end was silent. "What kind of personal item?"

"This may sound odd, but it's a smooth black rock with some twine around it. About the size of a baseball. The boy is Native American, and it's a family item."

"I have no idea, Don. That young man was very ill. I wouldn't believe anything he tells you. I have to go now." And the phone line went dead.

A Couple of Hours Later.
Near Skyridge Ranch, California

Rick called his sister from the car. "Ro, I'm on my way to the Ranch. Feynman and I need to see D-man. Is he tied up with anything?"

"I'm looking out the window, and it looks like he's catching some rays and expounding to a couple of the youngsters. Do you want me to let him know you're on the way?"

"No, this needs to be casual. At least it needs to start that way. Mitch clued you in?"

"He did. And I'm as baffled as you are. And I'm looking forward to meeting with Victory. She'll be here later today. *Temporarily Temporal.* I love it. This will be fun to write. I have loads of ideas." His sister had a smile in her voice.

"I have no idea what to expect when he and I talk. But this can't wait." Rick was not looking forward to the conversation.

"It's Darren. There has got to be a reason, maybe a squirrelly one, but a reason. He's just not a nefarious kind of guy." Ro continued to watch the group enjoying the sun.

"That's what I want to think. We'll find out soon enough. I'm about thirty minutes out." Rick clicked off to focus on the road.

When he was about five minutes away, there were few cars on the narrow rural road. He lowered the windows for his passenger. Feynman immediately lolled his head out the window tongue first. Rick spoke softly to the therapy dog. "Okay, buddy. We're going to see your friends. I want you to check out your old friend D-man. He's been having a rough time since his wife died. You may sense sadness. I hope you don't feel more than that. Just be yourself. And we're here."

The *whap, whap* of his tail against the rear bench seat told Rick that the therapy was about to begin. He pulled up to the main house,

and Feynman was almost out the window with excitement. Ro came out to greet her brother and the four-legged wiggle storm about to descend. "Hi, big bro. How was the drive?" She gave her slobbering friend a hug. "He's over with Charlie, Nick, Nicola, and Fabian. Not sure where Tommy is. Probably with Lia and Theresa in the garden. How can I help?"

"Not sure yet. I'm going to let our therapy friend here find the people who need him. I just hope that's not the D-man." Rick and Feynman turned and headed toward the cluster of scientists basking in the midmorning sun.

The familiar faces turned his way as Feynman announced their arrival, nosing each one and greeting them as old friends. After licking Darren, he turned to nose Nick and then sat by his side. Rick breathed a sigh of relief. "D-man, got a few minutes for a walk?"

His old friend grinned slyly. "Wondered when you were going to get around to it. Sure. The youngsters have plenty to ponder. Let's head out to the usual place." He stood easily, and the two friends pointed themselves toward the vineyard and the bench at the far end of the dormant vines and their destination.

"How is George's bench? Does it need a new coat of paint?" Rick hadn't been out to the old bench in a few years.

"That was the first thing I checked when I got here Sunday night. It looks like someone has been taking good care of it. They'd better. George's ghost would raise holy hell if it wasn't cared for. That bench was his favorite place on the entire property. I remember in his final days, finding him snoozing out there in the sun. Suzanna would just smile and shoo us away to let him sleep."

The two men arrived at a low, wide wooden bench at the top of a rise. From this vantage point, the entire property spread out in rolling waves of green growth, both cultivated and wild. They took familiar places to take the measure of the place and perhaps each other. Darren began. "You're wondering why I got an invitation to a meeting from DARPA. Right?"

Rick nodded as he tilted his head. "Thanks for not wasting any time. Yeah, I'm wondering."

"We have to thank Robert for that." D-man shrugged.

"Man, that was not the answer I was hoping to hear." Rick was grim.

"Hear me out." He pulled the battered envelope from his pocket and handed it to Rick. "This is why I reached out to Robert."

After Rick read the letter, he refolded it, slipped it back into the wrinkled envelope, and handed it carefully to his friend. "That's a lot to take in. When did you get this?"

"Oh, I got this at the reading of the will, Dad's will."

"That's been, what, three almost four years ago?" Rick was confused. "Did you read it then?"

"Smart guy. No, I did not. We had just gotten Serenity's diagnosis. I figured Dad was gone and anything in the letter could wait. I didn't want her to use precious energy on anything but herself. So I didn't read it until I got to Oregon three months ago."

"Let me understand this. For three months, the people who are your friends and surrogate family have been in the dark, worried about you, and you reached out to Robert MacLane. More specifically, Colonel Robert MacLane. The thorn in his dad's ass for the past twenty-five years or more. That Robert MacLane? That's who you decided to call?" Rick was a little pissed.

"Did you read the part about Dave Gustafson's supposed accident? You think you could have helped with that?" D-man was getting testy now too.

Rick's jaw clenched. "My dad was mentioned. You didn't think it might be, oh, let's say, nice, to let him know?"

"Of course, I thought about it, but I had nothing to go on. I figured I'd see what Robert could find out, and then I'd call your dad. This kind of thing could be hard on a ninety-year-old heart. I didn't want to risk that for no reason." D-man was sincere.

"Okay. I get that. But you could have called me. My heart is just fine." Rick wasn't going to let him off the hook.

"The truth is I didn't do anything for the first eight weeks. I read the letter. I watched waves. I did yoga. I walked on the beach. I missed Serenity. I didn't call Mom either. I just didn't even know where to start." D-man gazed off to the horizon.

Rick softened. "Okay. When did you finally call good old Robert?"

"Right before I headed back. The day before Thanksgiving, I think. It's kind of blurry. I wasn't using a calendar. That's why Thanksgiving kind of took me by surprise. I had planned to be back earlier."

"Let me understand this. A week ago, you called Robert. And in just one week, and a holiday week at that, he's assembled a list of scientists who he thinks have something valuable to add to a case from sixty-four years ago. Is that what I'm hearing?" Rick had never trusted Jane's younger brother.

"Sounds kinda slick, doesn't it? Do you think I ought to go? I'm totally into what we're doing here now."

"I think since you started it, or at least this chapter of whatever *it* is, you have to go. But let's you and Ro and Jane and my dad all talk before you leave. We'll all be here tomorrow night. Have you responded to the invitation yet?"

"No, and they sent me a follow-up, wanting to know if I need a ticket or how they can help me."

Feynman came into view and picked up his pace when he saw Rick. "Here, big guy, over here," Rick called.

They both rose to greet the happy four-legged therapist. When he arrived, his tail was wagging his delirious joy at being outside and with his friends. Not a worry in sight.

"When is the meeting scheduled?" Rick patted the huge head.

"Next Wednesday in some small town in Northern Virginia." I have to fly out Tuesday if I'm going to be there in time."

"I think you have to respond and say yes." Rick was pensive as the trio began to amble back to the main house.

When Ro saw them walking toward the main house, she came out to greet them. "Can you stay for lunch, Rick?"

"Nah, but if you don't mind, I'll leave the furry one with you. Jane and I will be coming back tomorrow for dinner and the weekend, and he loves it here. If you'll have him, I think he'd love it." Rick was absently patting the giant dog's head.

D-man spoke first. "He can stay with me and the guys in the bunkhouse. I love the big dude."

Rick and his sister laughed. "I guess it's settled. I'll see you both and the rest of the gang tomorrow in time for happy hour. Do you need me to bring anything?" Rick was checking for his car keys.

"I'm going to be the DJ for the evening. I was wondering if you have some stuff that Nick and Tommy might appreciate. I plan to introduce them to the music of the '50s and '60s, but it might be nice to start with the '40s. Might even get some folks out dancing." D-man was smiling.

"Are you spinning discs or using something else?" Rick started to think.

Ro smiled. "We've got it all, turntable, CD player. I think we may even have an eight-track player!"

"I'm sure I've got something then. See you around five, okay?"

Ro stepped alongside her childhood friend to join him, waving goodbye to her brother. "Join me for lunch?"

"How could I refuse. What's on the menu?" D-man grinned at her.

"A veggie frittata and a long-overdue confession." Ro climbed the two steps to the wide shaded front porch of the main house.

"The one sounds tasty, and the other sounds confusing. Care to explain?" He held the door open for her.

"Let's start the conversation in my office. The kitchen is kind of Union Station nowadays." They walked down the corridor lined with colorful paintings and sketches by local artists. When they reached her office, she sat in one of the two chairs in front of the large desk so he could sit at her side.

She began. "I owe you an explanation or certainly a confession." D-man raised his eyebrows. "Just go with me on this. Maybe you know that I had a mad crush on you when we were all growing up. Our parents all hung out, and we just seemed to be one extended family. By the time I figured out and was brave enough to tell you that I had feelings for you, it was too late. It was the end of my freshman year at Smith. I had dated a few guys back east, and it helped me realize that what I felt for you was special. But you had met Serenity, and I could see it in your eyes. She was the one. I decided to keep my feelings to myself."

"Ah, Ro, I'm sorry." He began.

"Not yet, there's more. I went back to Smith, and near the end of my senior year, I met Ed. He seemed great—smart, talented, athletic. The things I liked about you. Great family. It felt right. And he looked a bit like you too. We took a fast track and after we both graduated, we got married that fall."

"I remember. We were there. Back in Connecticut or Vermont?"

She nodded. "And we did okay for a few years. Ed got a job teaching at a small college. I taught writing and had time for my own projects as well. I thought we were settling and in, and maybe it was time to start a family. But that's not what happened."

Darren took her hand, concerned at the turn the conversation had taken. "What happened. Did one of you get sick?"

"Nothing like that. In fact, you could say we both got healthy. Ed admitted to me that he had thought when we met that he was bisexual, but now he knew he wasn't. What prompted the realization? He fell in love with one of his students. Too cliché, right? A young man from London." She smiled ruefully.

"But this must have been, how long ago?" Darren was confused.

"Yes, this was a long time ago. But we had the house, our jobs, my writing. It was…comfortable. We made the decision to just live as friends. Remember this was long before a gay man could live in the open with a partner."

"Yeah, you're right. And you agreed to this arrangement?" D-man was concerned for his lifelong friend.

"I did. My life was full. My writing was successful, and Ed was okay when I found the occasional special friend. And so it went for a long time. Too long. We finally realized that by staying together, in whatever kind of relationship that it was, we were denying ourselves the opportunity to find real love. Then Ed found someone, found real love, and they wanted to get married. Which they did as soon as it was legal."

"So that's when you got divorced and moved back to California. I wondered what had happened, but Dad died, and then Serenity got sick. It's just been a lot to take in the last few years. I'm sorry I didn't call you." D-man was shaking his head.

"It wasn't expected. I came back, restarted my life in California, put some pieces back together, and quietly became a single woman. Though I haven't tried much dating. It's so awkward." Ro grinned.

"In what way? Lots of people are divorced."

"Most women's husbands didn't leave them for another man… after decades." She cocked her head to look at him.

"When you put it that way." He chuckled softly.

"That's the story and my confession. I care about you. I'm emotionally unencumbered. And I wonder if you have feelings for me." She laid it out.

"I gotta say, Ro, your timing is awkward and great at the same time. I came back from Oregon with my heart lighter than it's been. And yes, I have feelings for you. Always have, but you're right, I met Serenity, and that was it for many years. And now I've gone and stepped in it by calling Robert." D-man stopped when she gasped.

"Robert the nemesis of all that is open and loving? Robert the skeptic? Robert the asshole? Jane's brother Robert?" She was in shock.

"The same. I needed to ask someone with government connections for something, and he's the only one I know. I just explained it all to your brother."

"Okay then, explain it to me. This I just gotta hear." Ro was suspicious.

He explained about the letter, his birth father, the mysterious death, and when he took a breath, she stopped him. "Okay. You're right. I'd have called the ass myself if I had read what you did and had a sixty-four-year-old mystery plopped in my lap. Then again, we all *do* have a sixty-four-year-old mystery here. Jeez, is it in the water?" Now she was genuinely smiling.

"Now we've both confessed." He took her hand. "What's next?"

She stood and held out her hand. "Lunch? I promised you a frittata."

He stood slowly and embraced her, then lightly kissed her. "Frittata it is then."

CHAPTER 23

THURSDAY, DECEMBER 4, 2008, AFTER LUNCH AT SKYRIDGE RANCH

Nick had asked Charlie, Nicola, and Fabian to join him after lunch.

"Okay, we're here, under a tree. What's up?" Charlie was still finishing his sandwich.

"I'm not sure who we want to share this with. That's why we're out of earshot," Nick explained.

"Sharing what, now?" Fabian sat down and leaned back against the sprawling eucalyptus.

Nicola dropped down next to him. "Is it a secret? Should we even have secrets here?"

"It's about the rock that Tommy told me about. He started opening up to me when we were running." Nick clarified.

"Rocks. Gah! We're *still* talkin' about rocks?" Fabian chuckled, and Nicola lightly punched his shoulder.

"Actually, yes. This was a bigger rock. The size of a baseball. And Tommy says it looked like some of smaller round shiny ones in the time capsule."

"And this is of interest why?" Charlie brushed crumbs off his short.

"Two reasons: first, this baseball-size rock was in his pocket when he traveled, and second, they didn't give it back to him when he left the juvenile place that was keeping him." Nick sat across from the couple leaning against the tree.

Charlie stood behind Nick. "Holy shit! You think it means something, don't you, that he had a hunk of this on him at the moment—"

Nick interrupted, "Uh-huh."

Nicola joined in. "And why the hell did he not get all of his private property back?"

Nick held his hand up to calm her. "I told Ro, who called Mitch on Tuesday. He told the gang on the outside, and your dad, Charlie, is making a call to find out where it is."

"It's just twistier every day." Fabian was nodding almost to himself.

Nick continued. "I wanted you all to know. I was thinking maybe today we should bring Tommy into the lab to help with the rock analysis. We can ask him some more questions. After all, he's handled one or more of them."

Nicola nodded. "He seems fine. The doctors gave him a clean bill of health. So yeah, let's bring him in. He's cool, right Nick?"

Nick looked at Charlie, who translated. "He won't freak out, get panicked or stressed."

"Oh, no. He's okay. In fact, he's adjusting really well." Nick smiled.

Fabian hauled himself up, offered a hand to Nicola, and asked Nick. "So who then does not know about this maybe powerful rock?"

"D-man. Ro told me that he had reached out to a guy on the outside before he got here, and now they're watching him." Nick spoke softly.

"Yikes," Charlie blurted. "Well, who keeps him busy while the rock work starts?"

"He has some interesting ideas about wave theory, Charlie. I was hoping you could learn more while you keep him away until we know more." Nick looked up at his friend.

"I can do that. Oh yeah, I can do that!" And he headed off to find his assignment.

Nicola held out her hand to help Nick get up. "Then let's find Tommy and get to it. The sooner we know something the better."

Late Afternoon in the Ridgeview
Bunkhouse at Skyridge Ranch

"Does this bunkhouse make anyone else feel like they're back at summer camp?" Charlie looked at the other three guys who shared the bunkhouse.

Fabian scowled. "Summer camp? In Ireland? You're daft. Either workin' or in school we were. Summer camp. Americans."

"Now, now. Let's be understanding of our cultural differences. I myself went to surf camps. So it's not quite the same. Mine were a lot wetter." D-man grinned.

"My most recent camp experience was not a good one, and the quarters were much different," Nick spoke softly.

"Gah, of course it was. Sorry, Nick. I think of you as one of us now. Truly. And a right good mate to have." Fabian was chagrined.

"Actually, that's great to hear. I don't want to wear it on my sleeve. Sorry I said anything." Nick shrugged.

"Don't be sorry, please. We want to know you as a person, not just a scientist working on a compelling problem." D-man was serious.

"Then as a person," Charlie grinned. "What's going on with you and Mercy? I've seen the two of you go off for long walks, holding hands."

Nick blushed. "She's helping me with something."

His bunkmates all burst out laughing. "Oh, is she now?" Fabian chuckled.

"Not so fast, you Irish devil. What are *you* up to with our Nicola?" Charlie turned the tables on his other friend.

"Speaking as the voice of experience in the room," D-man started, and the room again burst out in laughter. "What? Why are you laughing at me?"

"I saw you disappear with Ro. Now fess up. What are you two up to?" Charlie was relentless.

"We go way back. Kinda picking up where we might have begun a long time ago. And it's kinda great." D-man smiled happily.

"Kinda great is the way it is for sure. So different from the girls at home. So, so very smart, and funny, and independent, and beautiful." Fabian looked besotted.

"Goners, both of you. That leaves you, my serious friend. How goes it with the mysterious Mercy?" Charlie circled back to Nick.

Nick began. "I'll let you in on what I asked her to help me with, and maybe you all can help too. I realized after the—"

Charlie interrupted, "When you went quantum?"

"Yes, that's a good way to say it." Nick continued. "When I went quantum, that I couldn't observe that experience. I just had to feel it. I had to live it. And in that moment, I realized that all I have ever done is observe. Now I want to live my life, not just observe it." Nick had his hands spread palms up, offering up his declaration.

"Well said, young man. And spoken with more wisdom than young men usually achieve." D-man was nodding.

Fabian was nodding as well. "That nails it. It's easy as scientists to fall into observing the world around us. My family keeps my attention on the world, but temptation is at hand always to step back into my head and away. I know what you're saying."

"Okay then, I'm just bummed. I'm the odd man out. No love life. But then again, I am living a great life here. No complaints. And there's always hope, right?" Charlie looked around the bunkhouse.

And everyone laughed again and started to throw pillows at Charlie.

CHAPTER 24

FRIDAY MORNING, DECEMBER 5, 2008, IN THE CAR DRIVING FROM ARIZONA TO CALIFORNIA

"I'm glad you kids decided to ride along with me. It's a long, lonely ride, even though the destination is calling me." Don smiled to his passengers.

"Are you talking to Sam and Amy or to us, Dad?" Ben teased.

"Maybe all of you, but I'm especially grateful for two-way conversation. And given the new rock wrinkle, I wanted time with you both." Don's eyes were on the road, but he was recalling an unsatisfactory call he had made in search of help to find Tommy's missing rock.

"A rock wrinkle. We'll have to remember that for the movie." Michelle tried to take a light tone about the latest twist in the corkscrew tale of their time-traveling friends.

"Tell me again what happened." Ben wanted to keep their conversation focused a little longer.

"I hung up the phone with Vic and immediately called the director. We go back to my teaching days. I thought it was going to be a friendly call. But it didn't go that way. It started with a little catching up. Then I mentioned Tommy and the facility. As soon as that came up, his tone shifted and became abrupt and official. I made sure he knew I wasn't making any accusations, just looking for a personal item that belonged to the young man I had picked up." Don replayed the call as he spoke.

Ben prodded. "And then what?" He was next to his dad in the passenger seat of the rented SUV.

"I decided to make another call. I played innocent and called another friend on staff there and asked for the rock."

Michelle was in the back seat with two very happy four-legged travelers. "And how did that go?"

"It doesn't seem possible that there was enough time for the director to have called in the thirty seconds it took me to find the number, but that's the sense I got." Don was shaking his head. "Maybe I don't know our little town as well as I think I do."

Michelle had both hands full scratching two dogs but was not too busy to follow a train of thought. "Is the rock dangerous? Do you think there could have been some kind of incident at the place? It sounds like they were prepared for a call."

Don shook his head slowly. "Vic didn't say anything about any danger. And apparently neither did Tommy. But that doesn't mean that something hasn't changed. There's just a lot more we don't know."

Ben continued. "Do you think we tell Daniel right away? You said he was willing to kind of be the hammer."

"I think we have to. I'd hate to delay and have an opportunity slip away. Besides, he has resources that we don't and might be able to find out if something else is going on." Don saw a pull-out on the interstate so they could all stretch their legs, and the dogs could have some water.

As they watched the dogs sniff the scrub brush, Michelle asked a happier question. "Does Grace know about Amy June?"

Don grinned. "No, but Father Joe does, and he'll be there when we arrive. He agrees with all of us that Grace will love our little Amy, and it's the right time for her to have some company."

Ben continued this line of thinking. "And we're leaving Sam to help her get acquainted, or does Sam come to Skyridge?"

"The good Father and I talked about it and decided that it could confuse Amy to have Sam there and that this is a good time for Grace and Amy to get to know each other. I think he's right, but I wanted to offer just in case."

Michelle nodded. "I agree with him. Poor little girl. Her parents moved out, she came to stay with you and Sam, and now she's moving again. The sooner she can feel safe in a new home with her bed and dishes and food, the faster she'll settle down."

They all piled back in the SUV. Ben looked back at her and continued the train of thought. "I wish it was as simple for Nick and Tommy. I wonder how they're getting along?"

"Vic gets reports from Nicola. It seems like everyone is settling in. Nick and Darren Hickson seemed to be making friends, and Nick and Mercy have been taking long walks in the evening, alone." Don was smiling.

Ben hooted. "Way to go, Nick. Mercy is a total catch for him, and with all of the history they have with her family, I guess maybe it was bound to happen."

"You won't guess this one, though. Mitch and Beta are keeping company." Don was nodding.

Michelle joined in. "You're right. I did not see that one coming, but I'm happy for both of them. Any idea what the plans are for tonight at Skyridge?"

"Music and food for sure." Don began. "Maybe some canoodling."

Ben nearly spit out the sip of water he had just taken. "Canoodling? What, are we in 1920?"

The dogs whined. "Better give me their squeeze bottle-water dish. They can smell your water and want a drink, either that or they think they want to canoodle!" Michelle was laughing.

"Vic assures me there are plenty of beds, bunkhouses, and motor homes, so everyone who wants it will have privacy." Don was still smiling.

"Okay then. I suppose that's all we need to know for now. I'm looking forward to sharing what we've found and run up against with the team." Ben was gazing at the horizon.

Michelle nodded. "Who knew missing-persons files would be such a touchy subject, especially files from 1944."

Before too much longer, the turnoff for Indio was in sight and they slowed. As soon as they hit surface streets the windows were rolled down so the dogs could get a whiff of the new place. Ben had called Grace thirty minutes earlier so that she was at the door when they pulled into the driveway.

As the Arizona travelers spilled out of the SUV, Grace's eyes grew wide when two dogs whirled up to greet her. "I know Sam, but who is this sweet baby?"

"Her name is Amy June, and she's looking for a new home. We wondered if you'd like her?" Don passed her the leash.

All Grace could do was nod and quickly sit in one of the front porch chairs as Amy nosed her hand. "Oh, my friend. This is a wonderful gift. Since your Sam has been gone, the house has been a little emptier than usual."

Father Joe sat in the chair next to her, and Amy switched her nose to his hand. "You're right, Don. She is a fine addition to this home."

Grace looked at the conspirator. "You knew? And didn't say anything?"

He nodded and smiled. Then they both laughed. Amy looked from one to the other in a full-body wiggle. At this, Sam barked. There was more laughter, more petting and the group moved into the tidy house. Ben and Michelle carried the bed, dishes, and food so that Amy June would feel at home in her new house.

Several Hours Later at Skyridge Ranch

By the time Don, Ben, Michelle, and Samantha Jane pulled up to the main house, they were greeted by an eager crowd. Sam found Feynman, and they headed out for a romp to stretch their legs.

Vic and Daniel had just arrived and were greeting Rick, Jane, and Ro. Vic eyed Don and headed his way. "How long has it been?"

"One very long week." He gave her a hug and a quick kiss.

Ro smiled at them and motioned to Lia to join the new arrivals. "Lia, you've met the young people. Now meet the parents and a very proud aunt or, better, tia."

"And a brother and his girlfriend too." Ben jumped in. "I'm Charlie's brother, and this is my girlfriend, Michelle. And that is my dad, and Charlie's, Don Grant. He's currently attached at the hip to—"

Vic broke in. "I'm Vic, proud tia to Nicola Acevedo, and this is my brother Daniel, her father. And perhaps of greater import, we are Grace's kids, and Grace is Nick's sister."

Ro and Lia smiled, nodded, and tilted their heads as they absorbed all of the connections that had just been tossed out. Vic continued with a grin. "Got all that?"

Everyone laughed. Lia arched her eyebrows." Nick has quite the web of friends and family. As a healer, it fills my heart to feel your love and pride in him and the rest of them as well. But especially for him, he's had a rough path for one so young."

Daniel looked at Lia. "We know about your mother and her spirits. I'm curious, what kind of healer are you?"

Lia smiled at the barely disguised skepticism in the tone of his question. "I am both a native healer and a registered nurse. I run a small clinic from my home between the Pueblo and Los Alamos."

"Interesting. So many people with so many talents. I'll have to thank my daughter for finding you all." Daniel's face said that he knew he had been busted and bettered by this new woman.

Lia opened her arms. "Speaking of daughters…" She embraced Beta and Mercy.

Daniel blurted. "Twins! Oh, you brave woman."

Everyone laughed, especially the girls. Mitch and Paul walked up and caught the end of the laughter. Beta peeled away from her mother to pull Mitch into the mix, and he tugged Paul along. "Some of you met Dr. Paul Sanchez at Thanksgiving, last week. Yes, just last week. He was the MD on-site when Nick and Theresa collapsed—"

He was interrupted by Lia. "Thank you so much for the care you gave my mother. She looks wonderful."

Paul nodded and muttered, "I think I need to sit down, and someone needs to fill me in. I think I missed a step."

"Stick with me," Daniel offered. "I think I can help." They all laughed at the thought.

Ro looked around. "And where are the Four Musketeers?"

As the four residents of Ridgeview bunkhouse came into sight, Feynman and Sam returned and began to bark wildly. D-man broke away from his bunkmates. Jane and Rick climbed out of their SUV, laughing at the dogs and the wild welcome. From the other direction, Samantha Jane was barking and herding Nicola and Tommy to join the gathering. Rick was pulling a box from the back of his SUV when his friend D-man appeared at his elbow. "Did you bring the music I asked for?"

"And then some. Ro assured me the turntable works. Is the dance floor ready?" Rick was grinning.

"Oh, yeah. I haven't told anyone but you what I have in mind. Say, do you and Jane know how to dance to the old stuff?"

"Are you kidding? All of our folks made us go to cotillion dance lessons when we were at the most awkward possible age, thirteen. Just old enough to be thinking about the opposite sex and too young to know what to do about it. It was awful. We had to learn the fox-trot, the waltz, even a little jitterbug."

"Well, that's good. I don't want to have an empty dance floor when Benny Goodman makes sound waves." D-man was chuckling over his plot.

Ro was standing on the porch about to ring the dinner bell when she looked around to take in the crowd of connected friends and family. She marveled and wanted her notebook to start writing the story that was buzzing in her head, but first, dinner. She rang the weathered iron triangle.

Nick's Notes
December 5, 2008

Darren surprised me. Well, me and Tommy. His consideration for us is touching. He asked Rick to bring some records from our era so Tommy and I wouldn't be left out tonight when it was time to dance. I had forgotten what fun it was to hear music and dance with a partner. It was before graduation, the last time I danced. Before the war started and everything changed. And now it looks like that time really is gone. Tommy is adjusting quickly, as far as I can tell.

Dancing to our music and then listening as the music of the 1950s and then 1960s was played, it was overwhelming. The music and the different beats and rhythms kept washing over me. Darren says it's one of the feelings that made him think about wave theory. I can see that, or feel it, I guess.

Smart and thoughtful and a little strange describes Darren, but that's most of us here. And it's what they say at The Institute, too, that we're all a little strange. Are all scientists strange? Or maybe just physicists? I'll ask Mercy what she thinks.

Mercy fills my thoughts now, but in a good way. I like to talk with her. She's smart and understands my work. And she can dance. She said that her mom made sure she and her sister could dance to lots of music. I'm glad for that. I had fun. I can't remember the last time I had fun. That needs to change.

CHAPTER 25

SATURDAY MORNING, DECEMBER 6, 2008, BARN CLASSROOM AT SKYRIDGE RANCH

The chatter lowered to a murmur as Mitch moved to the front of the room with Dr. Jane. She led off. "I hope you all enjoyed the amazing breakfast this morning. Food is fuel, as I see you all agree, and we're going to need that fuel for the next couple of hours."

Mitch glanced at her and went ahead. "Last Monday, we suggested splitting into three teams to focus our efforts. We have a new one to add. The mysteries team. And no, to respond to what you're all asking, isn't it *all* a mystery? We have a new one, folks." He nodded to D-man, who rose.

"My story has recently taken an interesting twist, and it turns out to be part of this whole web of lives, science, and secrets. In a letter my dad left for me in his will, I learned that he was not my birth father. Mom has now confirmed this. My birth father was another scientist at Los Alamos. Nick encountered him when he went quantum, yes that's what we're calling it."

Charlie muttered, "I said it first. Going quantum is my phrase."

Nicola nudged him. "We know, Charlie, hush."

"His name was David Gustafson. And he died in a jeep accident under mysterious circumstances."

Nick spoke up. "He also said he was in the jeep because he was doing something important, but he didn't remember what."

Vic raised her hand. "Do you think this might be related to the spy recordings we got from the box of Nick's effects?"

Jane nodded. "It's entirely possible. Rick's mom and dad are inviting D-man's mom to lunch on Monday. If Gail is open to the idea, they'll play one of the recordings for her to see if she recognizes anyone."

"Miss Piggy thought the woman's accent was East Coast, from one of the Seven Sisters colleges, probably," Charlie added.

"Thanks for following up, Charlie. I was hoping Piggy was okay. I guess she is?" Vic smiled, thinking of her former vocal coach. "Sorry, everyone, Miss Piggy is a vocal coach and dialect specialist. I call on her when I have parts that call for accents."

Charlie added, "And she's a sci-fi fan. I know her from chat rooms. I did her daughter a favor. Stop looking at me like that. It was a science project."

The room erupted in laughter. Mitch attempted to circle the conversation wagons back to the topic. "This is one of the mysteries the new team will be working on. There is also the mystery of Tommy's missing rock. For those of you who may not be aware, our youngest time traveler had a fist-sized rock in his pocket when he was transported. He and his friends had picked it up down the hill from the farthest plateau near where the scientists were doing their work. They used it like a baseball to practice catching. When Tommy was in residence, shall we say, at the juvenile facility in Arizona, the rock, along with his clothes, was taken from him. When he was rescued by Don, Ben, and Michelle, he got his clothes back, but not the rock. Don has called the director of the facility and is being stonewalled, pun intended. Hence mystery number two."

It was Rick's turn. "And to add to the mix, we now have a threat. Not just the threat of the secret getting out, as in why we're all here. This is a new threat. Some of you know that Mac and Martha had a son named Robert. Yes, my brother-in-law. Robert pursued a career in the military and has been estranged from the family for a couple of decades, ever since Mac refused the offer of a merger with DARPA, the Defense Advanced Research Projects Administration." A hush settled over the room. "Mac had learned from the scientists at Los

Alamos that research doesn't thrive in a military structure. Something that Robert still won't accept."

"Why does this Robert know anything that's a threat?" Fabian was baffled.

"Ah, that's partly my fault." D-man hung his head. "When I read about my birth father's mysterious death, I called the only military dude I knew, Robert. We all grew up together. I was hoping he'd have access to old records and might shed some light on it."

Mitch added, "And that was right at the time that our group went to Los Alamos to look up the Geezers, ask questions, and poke around looking for information about 1944."

Vic and Ro looked at each other and started to laugh. "This is just so perfect, though. We couldn't have written a better setup for a script. And here we are pretending to be writing a movie script." Ro was choking on her laughter.

Jane smiled at her sister-in-law. "She's not wrong. Even though the timing seems inconvenient, the smokescreen of the movie really is just about perfect."

Mitch continued. "Glad you think so. We need to make sure that the old adage 'where there's smoke, there's fire' doesn't snare us. Because we have a few potential traps ahead of us that we hope to avoid. The first is the matter of the meeting in DC that Robert has set up. D-man is invited along with a handful of other scientists of note. The movie may not be enough to throw him off."

D-man stood again. "I think I can head him off, though. The jeep accident and a scientist with some kind of important message. Spies on the ground in a top-secret site. That's plenty to pucker up an neurotic military guy like Robert. The movie will just be a bit of fluff to be dismissed if you ask me."

Don tilted his head and looked at Vic. "He may be right. At least it should buy some time to get further into the movie and the science research here without worrying about visitors. We're going to need both time and help to find that darn rock."

Fabian raised his hand. "It's a rock report we're ready for then?"

Mitch grinned. "Yes, thank you. A rock report it is. The floor is yours."

Fabian clicked a remote, and the periodic table of elements appeared on a screen behind Jane and Mitch. "You recognize this then, the periodic table of elements as we currently know it."

Clary stood with a dish of rocks in his hands. "Sure, and this dish of rocks I'm holding here has something in it that is not to be found on that table up there."

"Whoa. All of the rocks are new?" Charlie was surprised.

"Nah, Charlie. Only just the round black ones. Like the one that was not about being returned in Arizona." Fabian nodded sagely.

"Is it related to anything you're familiar with?" Dick Stanton had arrived quietly, and heads swiveled to greet him.

"Not at all. It be dense, but light. It has properties that seem like we, like I, should recognize. Confound it all, they be not like anything I know. Not like anything I have ever had my own hands on. I know magnetic rocks. They be dense and these, they be not. Sharp implements and drills are of no usefulness on these, and still, they will not register hard on the scale. These round black fellows be new. That's the truth of it." Clary shrugged.

John Henry frowned. "I think I've heard of some sites, abandoned tribal sites, near White Sands. Really old places. I wonder…"

Charlie grinned lopsidedly. "Doesn't that count as another mystery, maybe two? Is someone keeping a list?"

"Agreed. It goes right after time travel." Nick laughed, and the room cracked up.

D-man spoke up. "Which brings us to the science team. Of which the mystery rocks are certainly a part. Our merry band has been looking into my recent work on waves and collapsing wave functions. We're hoping Dr. Paul over here has some EEG waves to share with us. We thought perhaps the waves of Nick and Theresa's quantum trip might be interesting to compare with particle waves."

Paul spoke up. "I brought the file, and we can put it up whenever you're ready."

Rick was ever the physics prof. "And what interests you in the waves?"

D-man played off at his lifelong friend. "Glad you asked my good man. I had this notion when I was sitting on the Oregon

Coast watching the ocean waves lap gently at the shore. Waves are not always regular. They are driven by tides, unless another source is introduced to drive the waves. Like what you ask? Like tectonic plates shifting. Large waves become larger waves—a tsunami."

Charlie couldn't keep in his excitement. "A quantum tsunami! Wow. Yes. And Nick's experiment is the tectonic shift."

Rick and his dad locked eyes. "Maybe that's it. But maybe there's more. Do the rocks matter or not?" Rick stared at his dad.

Dick spoke almost to himself. "This is so much more than we had ever considered, but as soon as you started to talk about it, this has got to be the key or at least one of the keys."

Vic spoke up. "It's rare in my experience that talk of a movie being made is not the most exciting topic in the room. But hands down, you all have just put our little movie on the back burner. And that's okay. This science stuff is cool. And will, of course, be helpful going forward."

Ro was nodding in agreement. "Oh yeah. I love this. When we're looking at social temporal displacement disorder, any kind of external cause will help add twists to the story."

Vic continued. "D-man, Ro was saying that we could really use the help of your daughter Darcy. Any chance she might be available to join us?"

"The thought had crossed my mind, but I wanted to be sensitive to both nepotism and increasing our circle. If you think she can help I'll call her today. Oops, Ro, you have the phone, you can call." D-man grinned.

Mitch looked at his mom. Jane filled him and the rest in. "Darcy Hickson teaches a course on American science fiction at a community college in Oregon. There's usually a waiting list to take her course."

Mitch looked around the room. "I think we have done a major info dump on each other. Let's say we break until lunch and come back to share any new ideas, requests, and movie suggestions to watch tonight. See you back here at 1:00 p.m."

Mitch motioned to Nick to join him in a quiet corner of the noisy room. When he was close enough to hear Mitch said, "I wanted you to hear it from me. I'm interested in Beta, and I've let her know."

Nick raised his eyebrows. "Interested? Oh, interested. That's great, but why are you telling me?"

Mitch leaned his head and lifted his chin in the direction of the other side of the room. "Because they're sisters and not just sisters, they're twins. Identical twins. See them right now?"

Nick looked at saw the two sisters, heads together laughing. "Oh."

"Yeah. And that's not all. John Henry gave me some inside information." Mitch found JH in the crowd and raised his hand to bring him in on the conversation. When John Henry reached the corner, Mitch asked, "JH, would you tell Nick what you told me about the twins?"

This question evoked a wide grin on the newcomer's face. "You mean about the Thompson Twins Treatment?"

Mitch nodded. Nick looked concerned. "What do you mean?"

"Oh, just when they weren't being watched at Skyridge during their teen years, they played tricks on guys at home. They were kinda known for it."

"What kind of tricks?" Nick didn't like the sound of that.

"Back then, they wore their hair the same way and dressed alike. Get the drift?"

Mitch turned to look at Nick. "You're new to dating in this time. I'm not sure if women were tricky back then, but these two were known to go on each other's dates."

"But not now, right? They're not teenagers."

"They're still identical twin sisters," JH reminded them.

Mitch noticed something happening across the room. "Guys, Lia is talking to them. She looks stern. Maybe this is good for our team."

"I can find out after lunch. I've known Lia all my life, and as they say, I got no dog in this hunt. Not that either of the girls is a dog. But you get my meaning." JH was enjoying this.

Nick was somber. "Yes, John Henry, if you would do that, I would feel better. I do like Mercy, and I am not interested in being toyed with."

Mitch nodded. "Me either. I want to believe that they've out-grown those tricks. I hope they can take us seriously. I'm not joking about my feelings about Beta."

"I feel the same about Mercy. It's all new for me, and I'm anxious enough as it is," Nick added.

John Henry patted them both on the shoulders. "I think you're safe. They are fine young women and have grown up considerably since those years. Let's get some food. All this talk of women has made me hungry."

Nick laughed. "Now you sound like Charlie. Everything makes him hungry."

They continued laughing as they moved toward the buffet table.

Across the room, Lia was finishing a chat with her daughters. "Are we agreed that your old shenanigans with boys are over? Nick and Mitch are not the kind of men you trifle with. I would be heartily disappointed in you both. And you know that JH will tell me if you try anything."

The twins looked at each other, then their mom and back at each other. Then they blushed. "It seemed like fun back then." Mercy shrugged.

Beta grimaced. "I guess it was meaner than we thought. I'm sorry. Does everyone think we're jerks?"

"Or worse," Mercy added.

"I think most people who know you have written off your teen-age tricks as just that. However, all that goodwill and benefit of the doubt will evaporate if you try anything, and I mean anything. So if I hear that Mercy has cut her hair…" Lia almost wagged a finger.

"I really like Mitch. I wouldn't want to screw things up."

"And I really like Nick. And he's way too special to play any kind of joke on."

"Okay then. Mitch will be flying me back home Sunday afternoon. I don't want to worry about either of you." Lia stood from where she was sitting. "I think I'll see if I can be useful and help Ro."

As the room shifted to lunch mode, Dick Stanton caught his son's eye. "Rick, how can I help? It sounds like you have some interesting lines of research to follow."

"Agreed. It's almost too much. We need to look at the wave hypothesis and then at whether a literal new element caused the change in the power or the effect of the machine that you all built." Rick was nodding.

"Not for the first time have I thought of the scene in the film *Raiders of the Lost Ark* at the end when we see the crate being stored in the huge warehouse. Never to be found again. Is that what happened to our machine?" Dick frowned.

"Damn, Dad, you're right. And it's another thing for Robert to look for. Maybe. Or would that tip him off?"

"Too bad about young Robert. And with his dad getting worse. I wish there was a way they could patch things up. But I don't know if Mac could recognize him now." Dick was saddened at the thought of his friend with Alzheimer's nearing the end of his journey.

"I'll talk with my good wife. Maybe she can come up with a way to get Robert's help and mend a fence or two." Rick gave his dad a soft pat on the shoulder.

"I heard that. What kind of mending are you thinking I can do? It doesn't involve needle and thread, does it?"

"Not unless you think something sharp and pointed could be used on your younger brother to bring him around. Dad and I were thinking that maybe Robert could find where the machine went that dad and the team built. We were laughing about it being stored with the Lost Ark of the Covenant." Rick smiled.

"Well, you've given me an idea for movie night as well as a new thought that we can back-burner until Robert shows his true colors." Jane was skeptical where her brother was concerned.

CHAPTER 26

SATURDAY, DECEMBER 6, 2008, THE SCIENCE TEAM MEETING AT SKYRIDGE RANCH

Charlie, Nick, and Nicola followed D-man as he headed for their now-favorite spot. Fabian followed a few strides behind.

"Does this tree have a name?" Charlie looked up the branches that provided welcome shade.

"Let's call him Oppie. Maybe it will help us have a break-through," Nicola said.

"Is it an American thing then, to name everything. Can a tree be not just a tree?" The Irishman settled his bulk against the base of the focus of their attention.

D-man looked at the younger scientists. "Naming the tree could be a code for us. Let's talk with Oppie about that. And we all head here. I kinda like that."

Nick nodded. "If it helps us figure things out, I'm for it."

The older man smiled. "You know we're all still relative unknowns to each other. Indulge me for a few minutes. Tell me how you came to be following this line of research. I'll go first. It sounds kinda lame, but it's the family business, and now, as it turns out, it's in my DNA. And I find it compelling."

Nicola went next. "Like you, I guess it's a family thing, although I didn't know it until recently. I was always good at science in school, and my grandparents encouraged me." She looked at Nick. "Yes, your sister. So when I got to Rick's classes, it just clicked. Particle Physics is just an unending source of mysteries. I was hooked."

"Mysteries is the way I think of rocks." Fabian spoke. "Each one holds a story. They each are bits of the universe, you know. They're unique and will not give way to casual study. I like that. The serious nature of rocks. Yeah. Then along came cyber and a new mystery to be teasing my brain and calling me to travel a new path."

"*Star Trek* did it for me. When I first heard 'space, the final frontier.' Oh yeah. I was in love. And then, when Scotty stood at the transporter and beamed people around, I wanted to do that. Physics is the closest I can get to *Star Trek*." Charlie was grinning at himself.

"What about you, Nick? We never asked you." Nicola looked at her friend.

"I share this in common with D-man. It was my father who first drew me into the study of physics. He taught science, and at home, he would talk about what his classes were studying. When he talked about Einstein and general relativity, I was a goner, not unlike Charlie."

"That's as good a transition as I've had in a long time." D-man looked around the group. "I've been thinking about good old Albert. You know he predicted gravitational waves. Ripples moving at the speed of light across space-time."

"Is that what sent you to Oregon then?" Fabian asked.

"Pretty much. That and I needed to get past a lot of sadness. I knew my wife would have kicked my butt to see me moping around. Then Jane did it instead. But yeah, the action of waves is where it's at for me."

"Did the Oregon Coast help with your sadness?" Nick was quiet.

"It did. I couldn't escape my own thoughts. Between that letter from my dad and the waves, my brain did some churning," D-man admitted.

"Was that when you came up with the quantum tsunami idea?" Charlie asked.

"It was a combination of things. Looking at the waves, thinking about gravity. Wondering what else could make or change waves. Remembering Hubble saying that the universe isn't static. Stuff like that."

"Not static like electricity?" Fabian teased.

"Even though we can't ignore the presence of that electrical storm the afternoon of my experiment. It hadn't started, but the air was heavy with the threat of the storm," Nick remembered.

Nicola mused, "Remember Wheeler's famous statement: 'Matter tells space how to curve, space tells matter how to move.' Does that add to our thinking? Maybe in light of the air being moist and heavy that afternoon. Nick, you used electricity to power your chamber. Had your other experiments been done with similar conditions?"

"Mostly things were really dry and dusty. Really dusty from all the gravel being brought in for the roads. Funny you would quote Wheeler. He was in Chicago when I was at Los Alamos. He stuck with research?" Nick smiled.

"Yeah, he did. But about all that dust, that means lots of particles, huge particles. And maybe some of the crazy rocks, huh, Nicholas?" Nicola looked at her beau.

"I canna say, but I can speculate. Given the properties we revealed, it has to be possible they played a part."

"How had you managed the directionality of the previous experiments, Nick?" Charlie followed their thinking.

"Pretty simply. We shifted the angle of the chamber. Usually toward the northeast, away from the rest of the buildings, just in case."

"And what direction was the storm coming from?" D-man was perking up.

"That day, the skies were swirling. First one direction, then another. Like it couldn't make up its mind." Nick remembered.

Nicola was making notes. "I bet we can get weather reports from that time. It can't hurt to look into it."

Heads nodded. "Are there particle wave images or projections that might help us?" Nick was thoughtful.

"Way ahead of you. They've been requested. Good thing weather reports don't seem to raise any flags if you know what I mean." D-man smiled.

"The soup has become a stew, hasn't it? From just a couple of bits, we have more ingredients." Fabian was nodding.

"Not sure if we're making progress or if this is just a necessary step before we can weed out the distractions from the core of what made the difference that day." Nick looked around.

Charlie added, "And then there's Tommy. How did he get transported with you? And were there others…"

"Does it make sense to proceed until we know about others?" Nicola was wondering.

"Our research involves a lot of thinking and a lot of math. None of it is without value. I think we have to get to a whiteboard and start creating some equations." Nick rose.

Charlie joined him. "And get a snack on the way. Where are we going to find a whiteboard?"

Fabian stood. "Each bunkhouse has one, and a couple are empty. Let's find us one and start working."

D-man brought up the rear. "I'll stop at the main house and get markers. See you in ten. When you choose a bunkhouse, prop the door of the bunkhouse open, so I'll know where you are."

"And remember everyone. Our tree is now called Oppie." Nicola chuckled and headed off.

Nick matched his speed to join the Irishman in their walk. "If you don't mind, I'd like to ask you a question."

"Go ahead." Fabian was curious.

"You and Clary, you're both Irish, but you don't sound the same, and I was never around anyone who was Irish until I met you both, so I'm just curious." Nick was a little shy about asking the big man.

"Ah, that. Well, there's a good reason we don't sound quite the same. Clary, he's just recently off the boat. And me, well, I've been in the states for nearly five years. I sound more like a Yank every day, at least that's what my Ma says when I chat her up." Fabian was chuckling at the recollection of his last call.

"Off the boat? Did you come by boat when you came to the states?" Nick was even more curious now.

"Ach, sorry about that. Turn of phrase. Off the boat implies that you're new in the country and unfamiliar with American ways and language," he explained.

"I think I'm a little bit off the boat myself. The new slang and technical terms leave me shaking my head a lot. Charlie started a list for me on his phone. On his phone. I would never have said that a few months ago." Nick was smiling.

"Is it helpful, then, to know that about Clary and me?" Fabian wanted to make sure his new friend was at ease.

"It is. Thank you. I appreciate you telling me, and I guess I feel a little less like a stranger knowing about you and Clary."

"Happy to be of service. And we're here. I think this bunkhouse is empty, and we can use it." Fabian reached for the handle on the door, and they went in to get to the task at hand.

On the Porch of the Main House

Paul Sanchez grabbed a chair to join Theresa, Lia, and Mercy. He began. "I've been curious ever since I met you all, when did your gifts, powers, skills, however you choose to call them, begin to show up?"

The women smiled at each other. Theresa spoke. "I think of my visits as a gift. I have not had occasion to call on my spirits, so I do not think it is a power that I have or control."

Lia joined in. "I, on the other hand, do call on my gifts as a healer to supplement my training as an RN."

"And I am actively cultivating the ability to call on my quantum consciousness." Mercy shrugged. "No help, are we?"

"Not necessarily. Just because you, Theresa, have not reached out, or you, Mercy, want to use your gift differently doesn't mean you're not a help." Paul leaned forward.

Lia arched her eyebrows. "Do you think they could do what I do?"

"That depends on how you do what you do, not to sound coy." Paul continued his thoughts.

"I've watched you, Mom. You close your eyes, hold out your hands, and then you begin to treat your patients. What are you thinking then?" Mercy followed Paul's thinking.

"I'm doing what Mamacita taught me to do. I center myself to open the flow. Of what I can't articulate. But it comes to me." Lia spoke softly.

Mercy's mouth had opened, and no sound came out. Paul looked at her. "I'm guessing this is the first time you've heard this?"

"It's certainly the first time I've heard it in the context of how to access the family gifts. I guess I never asked. I was so focused on trying to make quantum consciousness legitimate science," Mercy admitted.

Paul grinned. "Then we're making progress. In my mind-body work, I begin with this step, asking people how. Helping them see their access pattern and process. Often it's unconscious. Something someone has done instinctively all their lives. Sometimes it was taught by a family member. Like a rite of passage to learn how to do or cause something."

Theresa looked at the group. "Is it time to include Tommy and Beta in this discussion? Remember, he, too, has gifts."

"I'll go find him. This is exciting. I'll be right back." Mercy tore off to find her teenage granduncle.

"Theresa, what do you remember of your brother's gift?" Paul probed.

"I remember him talking in the garden behind the house. He had his hands out. Not like he was pushing or pulling them. More that he was having a conversation with them and using his hands to gesture." The older woman smiled at the memory.

"I talk with the plants in my garden too. Nothing happens, but when I chat with the chickens, they seem to lay better and are more energetic. I've never thought about the idea that I might have influenced them too. I've always focused on people. Oh my God, I have to help Rose." Lia was alarmed.

Theresa looked at Paul. "Rose is her middle-aged border collie. She has some arthritis, bless her heart. Don't fret, hija, Rose gets your love which is healing."

"I can't believe I never thought about it. I was just so focused on helping people. And, of course, my formal training was all human-oriented." Lia was shaking her head slowly.

Mercy, Beta, and Tommy arrived out of breath. "What's so important? Is something wrong? Are you going to fall down again?" Tommy reached his sister's side.

"No, nothing so serious. We have been talking about our family gifts. And we want to include you in the conversation." Theresa took her brother's hand.

"Oh, that. It's just plants. Nothing like healing or talking to spirits." Tommy sat on the steps near the group.

Paul moved to sit next to the teenager. "Plants are living things too. And if you have a connection, then let's talk about it and maybe find out more about it."

Lia added, "Just now, talking about what I do, we realized that I also influence animals. I had just never thought about how I treat the farm animals or even our pet dog. Now my eyes are open."

"What do you remember of your time in the garden at home?" Theresa asked her brother.

"Mostly I just talked with them, the plants. Like they were friends. I liked to see them get tall, especially the corn. I would tease them when the tassels grow out. I always liked the peppers too. And the fruit trees. I always talked to them. The blossoms were beautiful, and then the tiny fruit would show up. I guess I didn't have a purpose. I just liked them all." Tommy shrugged.

"Do you think I can go back with you to New Mexico? I'd love to see you all in your surroundings." Paul spoke to them all.

"I can't speak for everyone, but I plan on staying here as long as Nick is here. I want to be on hand if he needs me," Mercy said.

"I agree, hija. I will go home for a time, but I may return very soon depending on Mitch and his corporate jet." Lia grinned. "Maybe I can bring Rose here. Do you think she would like it here?"

Theresa added, "I, too, choose to stay here a while longer. Tommy, it may be too dangerous for you to go back and see your friends just yet."

"I hadn't even thought about that. Sorry I asked." Paul blushed.

"No, I want you to come back with me. Beta will join us when AirMitch flies again, and you can tour the area. It will give you a chance to see us in action." Lia laughed.

"For now," Mercy looked at Tommy, "you can spend some time in the garden and the vineyards here. Let's take pictures today, and then next week compare them. I'll ask to borrow Ro's phone unless there's an old-fashioned film or Polaroid camera around."

"It sounds like a plan, or at least some steps on the path to learning. How do you all feel about this?" Paul asked.

Heads nodded in agreement. All rose except for Theresa, who stayed to enjoy the warmth of the sun on her creaky bones.

Inside Casita Bonita

"What are we going to do about your younger brother?" Rick looked at his wife.

"I'm waiting for inspiration. Nothing I've tried in the past ever worked. I can't figure out what drives him. What makes him so angry and suspicious." Jane shook her head.

"I don't remember him this way when he was a kid. I thought he was like us. What changed?" Rick gazed into space.

"Only Robert can answer that. Maybe D-man can have a real conversation with him. The mysterious death of his birth father is real, compelling, and something that he could actually use help with."

"Enough mystery-mongering. Let's go find the others and see what our collective brains are noodling." Rick grabbed her hand and headed toward the door.

Nick's Notes
Saturday, December 6, 2008

Having everyone here almost feels like it did at Los Alamos. Except there are single girls here. So it's better. Mercy and I find time for a walk every day. We talk a lot. And there's kissing too. She says I'm pretty good at it. I have to take her word on that. I talked with her about taking things slower. She said okay, but then she kissed me. Maybe slow means something different nowadays.

The conversations about science are good, thought-provoking. D-man has some fresh ideas on how my particles may have moved.

The collapsing wave theory has promise. It may help to explain how Tommy was swept along. I'm concerned that there may have been others, other waves and even other people. I'm glad Ben and Michelle are taking on a missing person search.

The movie tonight was in black and white. Lots of people groaned. Tommy and I are still used to them. I guess the others are spoiled by having everything in color. The name of the film is *The Day the Earth Stood Still*. The theme was timely, being afraid of what you don't know or something unfamiliar. I can appreciate that one. It reinforces why we're out here. To think that all these years after that film, people are still fighting wars and killing each other. We were so naive when we thought we were fighting the war to end all wars, no that was World War I. Maybe there will always be war. That's sad.

Nick's Notes
Sunday, December 7, 2008

It's Sunday, December 7, and still fresh for me, this date. Such an awful day to remember. I find that I do not think as much about the War anymore. Maybe it's because it's peacetime. Don was the first one to recognize that not only the date but the day of the week is significant, at least to me. I'm glad he did. I was unsure how to bring it up. Once he did, there was an interesting discussion about remembering certain days that are meaningful. And why we do so even when they are sad. Many spoke of September 11, 2001, and what happened. I have only seen the video. Hard to believe.

Part of me is glad that the "day that will live in infamy" is still remembered. Tommy and I both were a little quiet today. Everyone understood. We heard about how the day is remembered even today. Flags are planted by headstones in graveyards. War veterans are honored. Every year there are fewer of them alive.

Mercy spent some extra time with me. I assured her I was fine, but she made sure I didn't spend too much time alone.

CHAPTER 27

MONDAY, DECEMBER 8, 2008, LUNCHTIME AT THE HOME OF RICK AND JANE STANTON, LOS ANGELES, CALIFORNIA

Jane pulled into the driveway and noticed several empty cars. As she opened the front door, a whoof met her and a wet tongue. "Hello, Mr. Happy. Where is everyone?" Feynman trotted off toward the patio, wagging his tail like a directional flag.

The sound of voices met her, then familiar faces looked up to greet her. "Hey, sweetheart, glad you could tear yourself away. You remember Gail Hickson, yes?" Betsy wore the mantle of hostess easily.

"I do. It's good to see you, Mrs. Hickson. It's been too long. We're thrilled to have Darren among us again." Jane found a seat while Rick handed her a glass of iced tea.

The newest guest smiled. "Gail, please. We're friends here, old friends, or is that fact obvious?"

Vic was smiling at this new acquaintance sitting next to her. "I enjoy listening to stories about the War. My mom's were so different, and it helps fill in a lot of gaps that the history books don't cover."

"And I can't imagine how it must have been for your mother to have been treated so badly by the government. Those internment camps were a permanent stain on our character, not that anyone remembers today." Gail shook her head.

Rick looked around. "I think we're all here, and the show can begin."

"I am curious about this invitation. A show, you say?" Gail leaned back in her chair.

Vic stood. "A couple of months ago, my mother unearthed a box of her brother's personal effects. They were returned after he was declared dead in 1944. At the time, her parents just put the box with other things to be stored, and life kept going. My niece, Rick's advisee, is studying my uncle's work. Mom remembered the box. When she took off the lid, she saw an oversize manila envelope from the War Department. In it, there was a shallow square box holding a reel of tape." Vic took a breath. "Gail, he was at Los Alamos around the time that your first husband was there."

Jane continued. "With Victory's connections in the movie community, she had engineers who have the right equipment to carefully convert the old reel-to-reel tapes to CDs for us to listen. The first time we heard them, Dick and Betsy were with us. There were two men and one woman speaking. Dick thought he recognized one of the men's voices. Vic's dialect coach has weighed in on the woman's voice. Says she probably went to one of the Seven Sisters colleges in the east. We're wondering if you would be willing to have a listen and see if any of them sound familiar."

"Gosh, yes. It's been a long time, so don't get your hopes up." Gail smiled crookedly.

Vic pressed play. The voices began. As soon as she heard the woman's voice, Gail went rigid. Vic halted the recording. "Are you all right?"

"Oh my God. I haven't heard that voice since the night Dave died. Her name is Marilyn. Marilyn Bledsoe. She was on the road the night Dave had the accident. I never could figure out why she had been outside the gates." Gail spoke rapidly.

"Was she a scientist?" Vic wondered.

Now Dick spoke. "Damn. That's who that is. I never did spend much time around her or her worthless husband."

"What did she do there?" Rick prompted his dad.

"Like so many wives during those years, she wasn't allowed to work. I know it's hard to understand now. Anyway, she had too much time on her hands. Was always hanging around sticking her nose into things. But as a civilian, there wasn't much Mac could do to stop her. I think he tried." Dick was recalling.

Vic asked, "Do you think she arrived as a spy, or did it happen because she had time on her hands?"

Dick scoffed. "Given the quality of work her husband did, I think she arrived as a spy and he was her cover. He certainly didn't add anything to the team he worked with. I heard grumbling about him. In fact, I think they were gone even before I got transferred to Oak Ridge."

Rick spoke. "I wonder if there are records of where they went?"

"Finally, something Robert could actually help with," Jane spurted out.

"I take it your younger brother hasn't changed?" Gail smiled.

"Sadly no. He's as much of an ornery jerk as ever. But maybe he's in a position to help us with something, I hope." Jane sighed.

"But why do you even want to know? It's a lot of years ago. And she's probably dead." Gail was puzzled.

"Darren shared Reg's letter with us. We know about his birth father. And we also know that there were suspicions about the cause of the accident." Dick looked at his longtime friend.

"Oh…that. Reg has been gone for almost four years now. I was glad to hear that Darren finally read the letter. I even understand why he put it off. Serenity's death hit him harder than Reg's death, but the two of them. One after the other, it was a lot for him." Gail nodded.

"And there's more." Vic continued. "My uncle's work was the cause of speculation back then and maybe even now. It would be safer for everyone involved if we could solve at least one of the mysteries surrounding deaths and disappearances at Los Alamos."

"When you put it that way then, of course. Pursue the name. And I wonder, but it's silly to even think about." Gail looked at her lap.

"Trust me, nothing is silly around here." Betsy smiled. "Have you remembered something?"

"I'm embarrassed, but yes. It was almost Christmas of 1944. I had been tutoring some local boys, helping with their English. I suggested that they create a time capsule. When they did and we all met, I slid my wedding ring and a photo into the coffee can. I was just at my wit's end. I was being sent away, and when I wore my ring, I remembered Dave, and people would ask about my husband. It was an awful time. Anyway, I put them in their time capsule. Do you know if it was ever found?"

Vic smiled. "Yes, it has been unearthed, just recently, in fact. The items in it are proving helpful and a bit mysterious, but you have just solved one of the mysteries. I can make sure the ring and the photo are returned to you very soon."

"Oh, thank you. Now the ring holds good memories. I think I'd like to have it again. And as far as the other mysteries, please, see what you can learn. I do hope you can keep Reg out of it. He worked so hard to protect his reputation. Of course, once he married Archie in Massachusetts, it was all in the open. Even Wikipedia updated his page." Gail shrugged.

Betsy reached for her hand. "I can't believe I forgot. We were there! Good heavens, I'm losing my touch."

"Nonsense. You have a full life here. And the days march on. I was just happy for him and for Archie. They had to be discreet for so long. By the time they finally did get married, Reg was retired and the university couldn't do anything about it." Gail dusted her hands together as if to rid herself of the prejudice against her former husband.

Jane spoke softly. "What about you. All those years. Did you find someone?"

"Oh yes. I did. And now he's gone as well. As they say, old age ain't for sissies." Gail smiled.

"I, for one, admire the heck out of you. You've led a full life. Your son is brilliant." Vic smiled. "And now you may very well help to solve a sixty-four-year-old mystery."

Gail's face wrinkled. "Now that we're talking about Los Alamos, something has always bothered me. After Dave was killed in the wreck, I never heard about anybody investigating the accident.

I don't know if the wrecked jeep was ever pulled from that ravine where it landed. I was in shock, pregnant, and then almost shoved out the door. I may not have had the presence of mind to follow up even if I had been able to stay. Do you think it's possible that spy had something to do with the accident?"

"I say this is another mystery to add to the list. And this time, yes, it really is something Robert could help us with. He would have better access than we do on the civilian side of things." Rick sounded eager.

Dick chuckled. "Doesn't that beat all? I sure hope Robert puts the bit between his teeth and doesn't let go until he finds the truth."

Betsy patted him on the forearm and announced. "And on that note, let's eat."

"All this talk has made me a tad peckish." Gail grinned.

The group hooted at that. "Peckish? Did you learn that from Archie?" Dick wanted to know.

"As a matter of fact, I did. That term always endeared him to me. When I say it now, I think of him and Reg. Good memories." Gail smiled.

Santa Fe, New Mexico, Airport, Just after Lunch

Mitch taxied the corporate jet near the reserved hangar. John Henry helped get the stairs released so the travelers could emerge into the crisp air of the sunny high desert.

Beta helped her mom gather their bags while Ben and Michelle did the same. Daniel clicked his phone to life. "Hey, bud, I just landed. Yeah, made great time. No, I've got a ride. Are you still up for a midafternoon conversation about a mystery? Great. I'll see you at two thirty at your office. Thanks." Daniel clicked End.

"I'm starting my part. What's taking the rest of you so long?" They all laughed at his comment.

Ben looked at Michelle. "Did you say you have a friend here we can stay with?"

"I did and we are. I texted her last night, and she's ready to take us in, wine and dine us, and probably ask a few questions. You can handle it. She's a former college roommate." Michelle hoisted her backpack on her shoulder. "We talked about this. She can know how I met you and why we're here, the missing persons stuff."

"I can handle that. I'm just a dusty history teacher from a small-town community college. Yeah, I've got that part. But is there something she may know that I should be listening for?" Ben was waiting for her to move toward the doorway.

"That's an interesting question. I don't know. Perhaps your history brain can find a thread to pull as we catch up with her." Michelle was pensive.

Mitch gathered Lia and Beta apart from the others then surveyed the passengers. "Daniel, how are you getting to your friend's office?"

Daniel looked back at the man-in-charge. "You, I hope."

"Okay. I can do that. We have the same silver Bronco as last time. Plenty of room. Ben, you and Michelle?" Mitch looked at them expectantly.

"Renting a nondescript little two-door something or other. We'll be fine. And we'll be driving it all the way back to Vento Junction. We'll be out of your hair in no time." Ben grinned.

"John Henry? How about you?"

"I see my brother right over there in the vintage pickup."

Mitch cautioned, "Just stay in touch. I'll be wheels up in a couple of hours, and back in SoCal by dinner. Beta, you're with me, or do you want to check in at your mom's now?"

"Thanks, yes. I want to pick up a few things as long as we're here."

Lia surveyed the group. "Well then, let's get a move on. I have a dog to greet, emails to answer, and plans to make."

"Depending on what I find, I very well may stay here for the next few days. I'll let you know by Thursday." Daniel was calculating his next steps.

"Say, just out of curiosity, what's the name of your friend here?" Lia looked over her shoulder at Daniel.

"Duke Dumont, a friend from law school days. He still has his practice here, at least that's what he says in his emails." Daniel smiled at the memory of law school days.

"You may be interested to know that Duke handled the mediation for my divorce." Lia sounded smug.

"And how did he do?" Daniel wasn't letting her just drop that bomb and not follow up.

"It was the easiest divorce he ever had, or so he told me. There were no arguments, no acrimony, just two people ready to move in different directions." Lia shrugged.

"Well, it certainly seems to be a small world." Daniel hoisted his well-traveled leather bag in the back of the Bronco.

"I didn't think Daniel Acevedo ever went for understatement." Lia grinned.

Mitch cleared his throat. "Okay. Everyone knows the drill. Low key. Low profile. Anyone asks, we're doing research for a movie." The former football player smiled slyly.

They all nodded, thinking about next steps.

CHAPTER 28

OCTOBER 29, 1944,
AT SUNSET, OUTSIDE THE BUILDING
HOUSING THE TRICK ON THE HILL

"Tell me why you're commandeering a jeep and heading into Santa Fe. It sounds mysterious." Dick Stanton eyed his friend.

"I wish I could fully explain it. These rocks are just too strange, and I can't explain them. I need to get them to a friend there to examine them. I think they may be important. I need to do this." Dave Gustafson pleaded with his buddy.

"Does anyone else know you're doing this little errand?" Dick asked as they began to walk toward the edge of the camp.

"I let Mac know I needed to take a sample to Santa Fe. He asked a few questions and then gave me a pass." Dave was looking toward the motor pool.

"Want some company? I got nothing going on tonight," Dick offered.

"I think it's best if it's just me. We don't want to raise any suspicions. You know how the rest of them get." Dave glanced around.

"Fair point. How long do you think you'll be gone?" Dick looked at his friend.

"You mean when should you call out the search party?" Dave smiled ruefully. "I suppose by midnight."

"Show me the sample you're taking." Dick wanted a look at what was so important.

Dave held out a small cloth drawstring bag and pulled it open. "You mean those little round black ones? That's what you're all hot over?" Dick arched his eyebrows.

"Yeah, the little round black ones. I can't figure out what they are. And when these are near anything mechanical, things change. Motors work, watches don't. Go figure. There's something about them that's different and maybe really important." Dave neared the jeep with his name on it.

"I think you're more than a little crazy, but then again, we all are out here. Anyway, my transfer is coming any day. Mac said to be ready." Dick stood by the jeep.

"Mine too. Probably Hanford. How about you?"

"Maybe Oak Ridge. I've never seen Tennessee. Of course, I'd never seen New Mexico either." Dick smiled.

"And we still haven't. All we've seen is this place," Dave groused. "I dragged Gail all this way to live in heat, dust, bad food, and secrets. So many secrets."

"Yeah, there's that. Be careful tonight, okay." Dick patted him on the shoulder.

"I will. I told Gail I'd be back before midnight. She'll worry. Maybe you can check on her," Dave asked.

"I can do that." Dick waved as Dave fired up the jeep and headed for the gates.

CHAPTER 29

TUESDAY, DECEMBER 9, 2008, EARLY EVENING AT A LOCAL WATERING HOLE IN WASHINGTON, DC

"Tell me again why we're meeting here." Colonel Robert MacLane was grumpy.

Darren Hickson smiled. "Because I'm staying with friends nearby and I've just traveled across three time zones to be at your meeting." Darren looked around at the Tried & True Tavern. "Why, you don't like dark polished wood, worn chairs, and no loud sports blaring at you?"

"Friends. Humph. Science friends, surfing friends, hippy friends. I guess your people don't stay in hotels like regular people." Robert was looking around the bar at the crowd.

"Not that it's any of your business, they both teach at local institutions of higher learning and like this neighborhood. And so do I. And so do a variety of people as you have been observing. Stop frowning, Robert. People are looking at you." Darren was enjoying this.

"I'll frown if I goddam want to. Now start talking."

Darren leaned back in his chair and looked around. "I like a place with character. Look at that bar. It glows from all the elbows that have leaned on it over the years. Every chair could tell a story. And look at the tiers of bottles against the mirror behind the bartender. Every kind of spirit you could ask for. They wouldn't have the bottles if they didn't have patrons that asked for them. This is a great place, Robert. Give it some time. It might even rub off on you." He chuckled.

"I won't be here that long, trust me, dammit. Now what couldn't wait for tomorrow's meeting."

"You'll recall that my dad died going on four years ago?"

Robert nodded.

"He left me a letter. A letter that I chose not to read until recently."

Robert's eyebrows raised.

"Come on. You'll also recall that my wife had cancer and died. I had a lot going on. The girls and I were grieving. Doug climbed into his shell just like his father. It's taken some time, dammit. But time does pass, even when you're feeling things like grief, loneliness...I could go on." Darren wasn't going to let him off the hook if he was going to act like a jerk.

"Please don't. Just get to the point, why don't you." Robert was still grumpy.

Darren leaned back in his chair and took a slow sip of his scotch. "Glenlivet 12-year never disappoints. Your sister sent me on a sabbatical for a few months. The Oregon Coast was a soothing place for my soul. And I finally read the letter."

"And you found God," Robert said like the cynic he was.

"Nope. I found a mystery. Turns out Reg Hickson was not my birth father."

Robert leaned in. "I never thought he was. Always thought he played for the other team, if you know what I mean."

"I do and he did. He was also a great dad. He loved my mother, obviously not in a married kind of way, but I grew up with parents who laughed, talked, liked each other, and loved me. But that's not the mystery."

The uniformed man stiffly tilted his head as if to pose a query and muttered, "I'll bite. What's the damn mystery then?"

"My birth father was a man named David Gustafson. Your father knew him because he was a scientist at Los Alamos during the war years. But David Gustafson didn't leave like the rest of the men we know. He died in a jeep accident carrying a message away from the camp on an evening in late October 1944." Darren took another sip.

"I sense there's more. Keep going."

"There were spies on-site. I have a recording of several conversations. One of the spies talks about sabotage." Darren took another sip.

"Now how would you get a hold of a recording of spies from Los Alamos?" Robert scoffed.

"Turns out Dick Stanton returned a box of personal effects to the family of one of the scientists who died there. Like my letter, the box went unopened for a long time, a very long time. When it was finally opened, it was by the grandniece of the dead hero. She's studying under your brother-in-law Rick Stanton."

"Okay, there are still a few gaps here. Keep going."

"This young woman's aunt has connections who were able to transfer the contents of the reel-to-reel tape to a CD. When Dick heard the voices, he said they were familiar. When my mom heard it, she recognized the woman on the tape and had a name." Darren set his glass down.

"And I should care why?" Robert could be such an ass.

"Because I'm hoping you would rather solve a real mystery than go down whatever rabbit hole you dragged me and my colleagues here to talk about." Darren waited.

"What makes you think I'm going down a rabbit hole?"

"Because you've been wanting to make your dad wrong for the last thirty years. And based on the names on the email list, you think you have something to do that with."

"Look. People are sniffing around Los Alamos and asking questions about what happened back then. Not the bomb, the other stuff." Robert was always suspicious, but this was new.

"You mean the Trick. All of our dads chased after that for years. What makes you think there's anything real there now?"

"I just have a feeling. These are not the usual people. There's no reason for people to go asking locals about that time more than sixty years ago." Robert wasn't going to let it go.

Darren was going to draw this out a little longer. "Just what kind of people, and how do you know all this anyway?"

"Reporters, security people, locals are talking to visitors." Robert was losing steam.

"I'm going to disappoint you, buddy. Whatever you think, hope, or suspect is going on just isn't. A movie is being developed. I know this because my daughter Darcy is a consultant on it. A science fiction movie. That's why people are visiting and asking questions. Now I've offered you a real mystery. One with a couple of good leads and at least one real bad guy or gal. Which one are you going to go after?" Darren rested his case and crossed his arms.

Robert's jaw was tight. "A movie. A goddamn movie. You're sure about this?"

"My daughter Darcy is so excited about it. She's taken a semester off teaching so she can help with the script. Yes. I'm sure."

"Well, what am I going to tell the people coming tomorrow morning?"

"Not my problem."

"I'll just tell them I had something come up and apologize." Robert was calculating his loss of face.

"Sure. They'll buy that." Darren felt a little smug.

"Where's the letter and the CD? If you want me to solve your mystery, I'm going to need those." Robert had shifted gears.

"I have a copy of the letter and the CD right here. But before I hand these over, I need to know that you're going to be serious about this. You know there were spies at Los Alamos, and I'm giving you something that no one has heard, maybe ever. Not to mention entrusting you with my dad's confession of his sexual orientation. This can't get out, Robert. It just can't. A lot of people would be hurt." Darren wanted Robert, a man he had grown up with, to see beyond whatever resentments, frustrations, and disappointments he had. It was asking a lot.

"You really don't think much of me, do you?"

"Give me a reason to think better of you. Have you been out to see your mom lately?" Darren was softening his approach.

"I call her once in a while."

"I saw them when I was on the coast. She's as lovely as ever. Your dad is weaker and mostly, well, not your dad anymore. He still recognizes your mom, but he didn't know me. It's hard, I know, to watch someone go like that." Darren really did feel for Robert.

Robert squared his shoulders. "What are you going to do now?"

"I'm going to hand you an envelope with information I hope will help you learn who murdered Dave Gustafson. I'm going to have dinner with my friends. And I'm going to catch a plane tomorrow back to sunny California. That's what I'm going to do." Darren smiled.

Darren rose to leave. "Oh, and, Robert, don't have the meeting. The scientists you've invited are doing real work. Let them keep thinking you're as serious as they are." Darren handed Robert an envelope and walked out of the bar.

He walked for a few minutes and turned a corner into a long-established residential neighborhood. The homes were well-kept. Most of them painted white with contrasting shutters or awnings. When he walked up the sidewalk toward one of the modest two-story colonials, the door opened, and Ro smiled at him.

"How did it go?" She wanted to know.

He motioned to get inside and close the door. "I wore the wire. Didn't you hear?"

"I did, but you were there. You could see his body language. Do you think he bought it?"

"Gordy will tell the tale. I hope he did." He leaned down, gave her a quick kiss, and headed for the kitchen. "I still can't believe you got this place in the divorce. I'm also glad you haven't sold it."

Early Evening, Lia's House, Outside Los Alamos, New Mexico

John Henry had knocked on Lia's door out of breath. "Got a minute or ten?"

Lia was walking from the dining room to greet him with Daniel Acevedo trailing behind her. "Sounds like you've got something to tell us."

"I'm glad you're both here. I need level heads to help unravel what the Geezers remembered to tell me today." John Henry headed for one of the cowhide love seats.

"Well, go ahead, son, spill." Daniel smiled.

"It's about that small bag of stones they remembered. The ones they pulled from the jeep wreck."

"That was definitely interesting, yes, continue." Lia nodded.

"I saw them, the Geezers, just now. I stopped in to grab a cup of coffee and there they were. When I stopped to say hi, Albert tapped me on the arm. 'I remembered somethin' else,' he said almost so just I could hear. He said he had taken the stones to his Uncle Benny to see if he knew what they were. You may not remember, but Benny Ortiz was a well-known jeweler back then. Anyway, Albert says that Benny couldn't do anything with them damn black rocks. Couldn't cut 'em, polish 'em, nothin' as Albert reported." John Henry looked for their reactions.

"Okay. We don't know what they are, but neither does a jeweler who's spent his life working with the rocks and stones from this area. He tried the methods available to him to try to work the stones, and he couldn't. I say that's pretty interesting." Daniel was nodding and smiling.

Lia reached over to grab John Henry's hand. "Thank you. We wouldn't have learned even this much more about the black rocks if you hadn't had the patience to listen to one of those sometimes-annoying old men."

"I'm glad you think it's important too. I just can't help but think that the more we learn, the closer we'll get to what they are and maybe what they mean." John Henry was nodding.

Daniel spoke. "If you don't have dinner plans, would you like to join us?"

Lia nodded in agreement.

"If I'm not intruding, that would be great." John Henry smiled almost shyly, recognizing that the two older people in the room might have had plans.

"Please stay. We can call Skyridge, and you can give your report, and we can all catch up." Daniel was nodding and smiling.

"Okay then. Dinner it is. How can I help?" John Henry stood and looked toward the dining room.

"Wash up, and I'll have you set the table while Daniel finishes at the stove." Lia grinned.

Nick's Notes
Tuesday, December 9, 2008

I can't stop thinking about Darren. D-man, as he likes to be called. He's back in Washington, DC, meeting with Jane's brother, Mac and Martha's son. Just listening to them talk about him makes me shake my head. How could two of the best people I know have a son that is so different and difficult. Ro went with him. She left Fabian in charge. He does have the most experience in security.

We should hear something tomorrow. Until then, Charlie and Nicola and I are looking further into collapsing particle waves. I think that's what they called them. There were just so many variables at the exact moment of the experiment. Variables I had not even thought of, considered, or for that matter, known about. Dick says he and others have tried to tie them all together over the years. No luck.

I don't know if I should feel urgency about figuring this out or not. Maybe if the missing persons search reveals something, my urgency will rise. Right now, I'm okay with just trying to understand how to live in this time and maybe who I am in this time.

CHAPTER 30

WEDNESDAY, DECEMBER 10, 2008, HOME OF VICTORY ACEVEDO, LOS ANGELES, CALIFORNIA

Victory welcomed Jane and the newest member of the movie team to her house, "Hi, you must be Darcy. Your father has told us a lot about you." Vic led them into the spacious living room. "I'm Vic. Welcome."

"Gah, I hope not. Dad gets a little carried away." Darcy Hickson shook hands with the lovely woman speaking to her.

Jane laughed. "All fathers get to do that about their kids. It's a rule. At least I think it's a rule. We boast about Mitchell and, of course, the dogs." Jane joined the newcomer on the couch.

"Darcy, can I get you anything. Something to drink? Are you hungry?" Vic was hostessing with enjoyment.

"I'm good. Stopped at The Institute to pick up some stuff before coming here. Man, I can't believe how much things have changed in the last few years. What a place. But why aren't we developing a movie from there? What is up?" Darcy leaned forward.

"You said she was sharp." Vic looked at Jane.

"More than sharp. Darcy, we stopped at The Institute because that's where the nondisclosure documents are. You recall signing them now, right?" Jane looked at the young woman.

"Well, yeah. It's The Institute. Everything that happens there requires an NDA. Something different about this one?"

"You could say that." Jane's eyebrows had risen.

Vic spoke. "Do you want to fill her in, or do I have the honor?"

"This is your territory. Have at it." Jane grinned.

"Did your grandfather ever talk about his time at Los Alamos during the war?" Vic decided to start from the edges of the story and move in.

"He told us about meeting Grandma Gail. About how awful the food was. How much he hated the desert. Go figure, from a surfer," Darcy spoke eagerly.

"Nothing about why he was at Los Alamos, his work there?" Jane had to butt in.

"Nope. And I guess we never asked. Why?"

Vic continued. "Your grandfather, Jane's dad, and her husband's dad were all working on a project together. And it was not the bomb." Vic waited for that tidbit to sink in. She continued. "They all left the project and started over when the War ended. But not everyone who worked on the project was so lucky. Your dad's birth father died in an accident. That information only recently came to light. And my uncle, the lead scientist on the project, was declared dead but was in truth missing as a result of the experiment."

"What experiment?" Darcy was hooked.

"Teleportation." Vic smiled.

"Get out!" Darcy almost shouted.

Jane continued. "It's true. That experiment and the resulting loss of a scientist was what drove my dad to visit Stanford after the war. He found my mom, and they started The Institute together. He and Rick's dad quietly continued the research all these years to learn what happened to their colleague."

"Have they found out? Is that why I'm here?" Darcy was almost on her feet.

Vic grinned at her. "Yes and no. There's more."

"No way!" Darcy was hooked.

"You have *no* idea yet, smart girl." Jane smiled at Vic. "See why she's a good addition?"

Vic was nodding. "Yes, they found out what happened to their colleague. And yes, that's very much why you're here. And more compellingly, they still don't know why what happened, happened."

"Okay. I give. Keep talking." Darcy pushed on her hostess.

"They found their colleague," Jane said.

"Dead? It's been, what, more than sixty years?" Darcy furrowed her forehead.

"Far from it. He's alive and well and twenty-five years old." Vic let that sink in.

"Nooooo. You're telling me this person time traveled. You're telling me that my grandfather and your father"—Darcy looked at Jane"—were part of a time travel experiment?"

"Don't cringe. Yes and no." Vic waited to see how Darcy would react. "Yes, they were part of the experiment. And no, time travel wasn't part of the plan. Just teleportation. Time travel turns out to be an unexpected bonus."

"Why do I get the feeling there's even more." Darcy leaned back in her chair.

"Oh, there's more. My evil younger brother has inserted himself on the scene." Jane grimaced.

"Oh man, Dad's talks about Robert sometimes. I know he doesn't trust him. Maybe doesn't even like him. He never talked about why." Darcy shared.

"Robert is military all the way. Black-and-white, no gray areas. In his world you are either friend or foe. We are pretty much all in the foe column at this point." Jane shook her head.

Vic summarized, "We have a time traveler, two actually." At this, Darcy just raised her hands to hold her head in disbelief. Vic continued. "A mystery death. A collection of brilliant minds in a bucolic setting. And the need for a credible ruse to protect them. Oh, and a handful of rocks of an unknown origin and nature."

Jane put out her hands with their palms open. "Now do you have an idea why you're here?"

"Oh man. I get to be part of writing a movie script to deflect interest away from the real thing. Brilliant. What's my next step?

Unless you think this is writing itself, which I think it may be." Darcy was reaching for her laptop.

"Not so fast on the technology there. We are going old school on this for now. The walls have ears, and they tell us that our technology may be vulnerable. Notebooks, pens, and pencils are the order of the day. And not here." Jane was in here element.

"Okay, then, where and when?" Darcy put her laptop down.

"Skyridge and we'll be heading out this afternoon to be there for dinner and movie night." Vic crossed her arms to signal the reveal was over.

"Why not now?" Darcy was ready.

"We have some errands to do, some food to prepare. A dog to collect from the groomer. A husband to snag. Don't worry, they'll all be there waiting for us." Jane finished.

"All? How many are there?" Darcy was getting concerned.

"There's a bunch," Vic started. "Charlie Grant, Nicholas Fabian, Clary McGonigal, Tommy Cisneros, Mercy Thompson, who has a twin sister who's in New Mexico right now, her grandmother, Nick Nishimura, and your dad and Ro will be back by tonight too."

"And there will be more on hand for the weekend. We have quite a few who spend the week working on complementary research, and then we all compare notes on Saturdays. It's a lot of fun. Your Dad DJs on Friday night." Then Jane added, "You caught that Nick and Tommy are the travelers, right?"

"OMG, of course. So I get to meet them!" Then Darcy stopped and stared. "Wait a minute. You're older, of course, but you're Victory! You starred in *Less Than Nobody*. Mom and Dad watched that movie loads of times and the soundtrack. Well, those songs were part of my childhood. They played them so much. He and mom would sing along and sometimes dance. Oh my God, you're her. You're victory!" Darcy just shook her head in disbelief.

"Does Dad know? Of course, he does. Oh my God!"

Jane had a wide grin directed at her new friend. "Does this ever get old?"

Vic smiled back. "Never."

CHAPTER 31

WEDNESDAY, DECEMBER 10, 2008, NEARLY DUSK AT SKYRIDGE RANCH

Cars began to pull up to the main house shortly after four. The sun was barely bright, and the air temperature was feeling Decemberish for southern California as D-man and Ro climbed out of her SUV. "Have you thought of getting a Ranch dog for this place?" D-man was looking around for a welcome.

"I'm interim, remember? But if I get the job, and I would very much like the job, then I think a Ranch dog is a grand idea. A little unconditional love is always welcome." She smiled at him.

They hadn't gotten to the front door when the next car arrived. Vic, Darcy, Rick, Jane, and Feynman surged out.

"Hey, I was just saying how great it would be to have a Ranch dog, and here you are." D-man came back to greet the furry wiggle storm. "Not you, big guy. You got a great home. Another big guy or gal needing a home. Somebody for you to play with." More tail wagging.

Jane glanced around. "Before the crowd realizes we're here I want to fill you in on the latest. Let's get inside."

When the door closed behind them, all faces turned to pay attention to Jane as she continued, "Mitch heard from Gordy. It sounds like Robert is not being honest with Darren. The meeting went on today as planned, even though Darren did not attend."

"Yeah. I heard from a couple of the scientists wondering where I was. I told them I had a last-minute conflict. Maybe we can look at them individually and find one or two we can tell about the movie." D-man set down his backpack.

"I'd like Mitch to be part of that strategy and probably Gordy as well. But I agree that poking a few holes in Robert's balloon is promising." Jane smiled.

Rick shook his head. "Damn, that man is stubborn."

Vic and Darcy looked at each other. "No, it's great. Every movie needs a villain. This is playing into our hands. Just wait till we actually make the movie, and we list him in the credits!" Darcy was gleeful.

Her father grabbed her and gave her a big hug. "Now who taught you to think devious thoughts like that. Not moi, certainly." Everyone laughed.

There was a knock at the door, and a voice called out. "Is it at home you are?" Fabian had a smile in his voice. "And are you decent, or shall I barge in?"

Jane answered, "Come in and be admonished of your lecherous thoughts." She teased back.

"Ack, I'd hoped to find you lot inflagrante delicto, or some such contortion, but all of you are dressed? So am I late then or early?" Fabian held his head in mock horror.

D-man shook his head. "I'm gone for two days, count 'em two, and already you've gone to the dark side."

"Sure then, it's *Star Wars* you've chosen for movie night. With all this talk of a dark side." Fabian was not backing off.

Ro intervened. "Nicholas, we are showing *Contact* tonight starring Jodie Foster as a scientist who has an extraordinary experience."

Rick clapped his hands together. "I *love* that film. That's a great choice." Feynman was excited by the clapping.

"Perhaps it's time for Mr. Happy Wags to greet all of his friends. Fabian, will you do the honors?" Rick handed him the leash.

Handing a ring of keys to Ro, the large Irishman sighed. "Here are the keys to this Ranch kingdom. Very glad I be you're back and not to wonder. This place it be a great concern to have on my shoulders. I thank you for believin' me up to the task. I must hand it to you Ro and an admirer I certainly be now even more than before. And I'll be taking this wee beastie in trade for the keys." He headed off with a grin.

When the door closed behind them, Jane continued. "Anything else to share before the hordes realize we're here?"

Ro asked, "When will Mitch be here again for a strategy session. Can Gordy come as well?"

"If we can wait until Saturday morning, things will feel more natural, if that's even a possibility. All bets are off, though, if our Darth Robert does something stupid." Jane shared a twisted smile.

"I can set that up. Now let's get the gang together for movie night and see who's sitting with who. Or is it *whom*? I'm a writer and I should know." Ro was happy.

Vic took Darcy by the hand. "Like we warned you, there are a bunch of folks to meet and you may need a lineup, but I'll do the best I can." They headed out the door. "I'll take you to Skyview bunkhouse. That's where Nicola, Beta, and Mercy are staying. Beta and Lia, her mother, are in New Mexico, so two bunks are open, right?" Ro nodded yes, and the two women sped out to join the gathering residents who by now were greeting Feynman.

Vic and Darcy had not reached their vehicle yet to get their bags when the siege began. Mercy started. "You must be Darcy. You're staying in our bunkhouse, right? Let me get that for you. It's right over there." She pointed up the hill and to the right of the main house.

Nicola added, "Lia's bunk is the top on the right. I hope that works for you. If not, we can figure another arrangement."

Vic pointed to the two women who had spoken. "The one with your bag is Mercy, and the other is Nicola. They can fill you in on who they are in life and why they're here."

Charlie appeared. "Looks like you got it handled. Vic, do you need help getting your stuff to the motor home? Is Dad coming?" Charlie was curious.

The actress turned screenwriter shook her head. "Not till Friday night. I hope he brings Ben and Michelle too. I haven't heard anything new on the hunt for the missing rock. That makes it sound like some kind of jewelry caper. Yikes. What have I gotten myself into?"

A latecomer spoke up. "I think it's way too late to ask that question, Vic." Nick chuckled at his niece.

As she assessed the young people milling around, she decided introductions should continue. "Darcy, here we have Charlie Grant and Nick Nishimura. Again, they will fill you in on who they are and what brings them here."

"You were right. I do need a list of players. A cheat sheet would be great." Darcy was only half kidding as she looked from new face to new face.

"It'll get easier. Oh, but Friday or Saturday my twin sister arrives. Her hair is different. You can tell us apart easily." Mercy was walking away from the group toward the bunkhouse.

Darcy spoke to herself under her breath. "Oh yeah. This will be big-time fun."

Nick's Notes
December 10, 2008

Things are changing. I think for the better. Today I met a member of Darren Hickson's family, his daughter Darcy. She is energetic and outspoken. She reminds me of Charlie. Her invitation to join the movie team comes because she teaches a college course on American Science Fiction. I cannot conceive of that as a college-level course. But then again, sixty-four years have passed, and more since I was in college. Things have changed. Fabian would tease me for that understatement.

I sound so old. Sometimes I feel it. And still, the energy of this place is infectious. I like it so much.

Tonight, the movie was *Contact*. I am told it is based on a book by a noted astrophysicist. He died, but his research, thinking, and of course, this novel and this movie live on. The main character, Ellie, has an experience and then is given cause to doubt herself. But she believes herself and her experience in the face of facts that challenge her. I feel like Ellie. I am more fortunate, though. No one here doubts my experience. I do not take my good fortune for granted. I need to talk with Tommy about this.

CHAPTER 32

THURSDAY, DECEMBER 11, 2008, BREAKFAST TABLE AT SKYRIDGE RANCH

"Charlie, I just don't know where you put all the food you consume." Nick was teasing, but only partly.

"Hey, I have a metabolism that should be its own dissertation topic," Charlie joked.

Darcy joined them as Nick and Mercy appeared at the end of the long table. "Are people functional at this time of day? It's not prime time for me." Darcy had a death grip on her coffee mug.

Mercy laughed. "There's no schedule. The Ranch is a creative space. The goal is to nurture solutions to tough problems. To open our minds to thoughts that might be pushed aside in the *outside world*, so to speak."

Nicola and Fabian appeared in time to lead the Greek chorus. "Ooooo, the *outside world*."

"Okay, so that's how it's going to be. I can play as long as the coffee keeps coming." Darcy pushed her empty mug to the edge of the table as Charlie appeared with a freshly brewed pot to fill her up. "Anyone else, as long as I'm here?" All the mugs were pushed his way.

Ro had joined the group. "Nick, I'm curious about your thoughts after watching the movie last night. Do you think Ellie had any guilt about being the one person to get to experience what she did?"

"That's an interesting question. I was impressed by her belief in her own experience in the face of the story that she was told. I hadn't thought about her being the one who got to live and experience the trip in the machine." Nick held his mug with both hands and got quiet.

"I think they should have told her the truth. It was deceitful and cruel not to." Nicola set the mug down.

Fabian leaned toward her. "Now then, if the world learned that the machine sent her to a realm where a being could present as her dead father and share secrets of the universe, you think this is a good thing. But no, that is not the case at all. A wee bit of global panic it would be. Then every, yes, every major religion would be in an uproar, to be followed on by a new space race to build more machines to send more scientists into the brave new beyond. Was there really another choice? I think not."

"You make an excellent point, Dr. Fabian. And a sad one as well. To think that the public, American and worldwide, would panic at the thought that a realm exists beyond what we can see or conceive of." Ro was standing at the buffet table, looking at the spread.

Charlie joined her. "Well, was that what it was like, Nick? When you went quantum?"

"Nothing so sandy and sunny. More foggy really. Figures appearing out of a mist and only developing features as they grew closer. And they didn't stick around for entire conversations. Much more cryptic." Nick frowned.

Darcy was nearly finished with her second mug. "I'm thinking more clearly now. Thank you for the coffee. It's really good. Back to the thinking about what the public would do if faced with dramatic information that challenges everything they know and believe. Consider the history of religious prophets carrying 'the word.' It didn't go well, not for Jesus, or any of the Christian martyrs, hence the designation, martyr. The Jews are still waiting for the return. No religion has achieved what they strive for. Therefore, I share Dr. Fabian's assessment that keeping the secret was the prudent course."

"I hear you telling me that Tommy and I had better work on blending in." Nick smiled.

Clary and Tommy joined them. "What's that then about me chum here? Should our ears be burning?" Clary reached for coffee.

"Just that the world isn't ready to believe that two guys from 1944 arrived in 2008. That's all." Nicola smiled at him.

"You're only figuring that out now? And I thought you were the smart ones." Tommy huffed.

"Glad to hear you agree. We are pretty much a walking, talking afront to common beliefs about the way that life works," Nick mused.

Darcy leaned back in her chair. "I gotta say, though, a whole lotta books and short stories have been written about 'what if time travel was real.' You could put a lot of fiction writers out of business if you go public."

The room erupted in laughter.

Darcy grinned. "I hadn't considered the economic impact of truth on the science fiction market. Excellent point if anyone ever asks about why I didn't share my story with—"

Ro broke in, "The *New York Times.*"

Charlie added, "The *National Enquirer.*"

The room kept laughing.

D-man appeared at Ro's elbow. "Your phone, madam. It rings for you."

"It's Mitch. I'll take it outside." Ro rose to answer the call.

Once she was out of earshot, she pressed the answer button. "Sorry about that. We were talking at the breakfast table about the benefits of keeping secrets. Pretty interesting actually."

Mitch replied, "Good thing because we're going to need to keep a tight lid on things for a while. Just heard from Gordy. Robert is making plans."

"Damn. Robert really is the villain here. I had hoped he wouldn't be." Ro clenched her jaw.

"Gordy can monitor all of the conversations going forward. Might not be a bad idea for D-man to reach out to one or two of his colleagues and probe a little." Mitch's tone was measured.

"I'll suggest it. I'm sure he'll agree. And he'll be disappointed. We had such hopes that Robert could let go of his grudge." Ro lowered her head.

"I'll let Mom and Dad know. You'll take care of sharing the word there?" Mitch got ready to sign off.

"I will. And I look forward to seeing you tomorrow. The gang here is ready for more music and dancing. I think we'll all be ready to relax together and talk about what's next." Ro heard the click after he agreed.

Ro entered the breakfast area, and every face turned to her. "Not only did Robert go ahead with the meeting, now he's making some sort of plan."

D-man slammed his hands on the table, shaking several mugs. "Dammit all to hell. I gave Robert a great option, real mysteries, a reasonable way forward. I wore my heart on my sleeve. Dammit."

Darcy spoke softly. "Dad, it was Dorothy Parker who said, 'You can lead a horticulture, but you can't make her think,' remember?"

D-man's face split in a wide grin. "I remember that was one of your mother's favorite quotes. All too apropos of Robert." The room relaxed.

"If we're goin' to be in the secrets business, we're gonna hafta eat hearty." Fabian reached for another muffin.

"I couldn't agree more." Charlie reached for the last muffin.

An Hour Later at The Institute

Rick was on the phone with Jane and Mitch. "I can't say I'm surprised. Robert always has been supremely sure he's right about anything he decides."

"It's just that this is terrible. And it's even worse. I got a call from Mom. Dad is getting worse. Hospice is on hand, and they check him several times each day." Mitch reached for his mother's hand to squeeze it gently.

"We knew it was coming. Dementia has affected his balance, and now it's his ability to swallow. The hospice nurse said this is what happens. It's to be expected. So I'm alarmed, relieved, and comforted. How can that be?" Jane gazed into space.

"How can I help? What can I do?" Rick was hurting for his wife.

Mitch spoke swiftly. "I'll prepare a flight plan for Oregon so we can be ready whenever you want to go."

"Thank you, honey. I appreciate that, and it's a good idea. Rick, let's take Feynman to Skyridge tomorrow, and he can stay there for a while in case we need to leave in a hurry." Jane shifted into planning mode.

"Will do. I'll get our bags out so we can pack and be ready to go when we get the call." Rick was eager to have something to do.

"Good. We have a short list. But let's plan to let off some steam tomorrow night. Could be a while before we can be lighthearted again." Jane hung up the phone.

CHAPTER 33

FRIDAY, DECEMBER 12, 2008, SOMEWHERE IN SOUTH LA'S WAREHOUSE DISTRICT

Gordy picked up his MRC and tapped in. "Update. Not great. Basketball for breakfast?"

Mitch felt the small device buzz with an incoming message. "Damn" was all he said when he lit the screen to read the message. Then he walked directly to the director's office.

"Uh-oh. You have that look," Jane said to her oversize son.

"The 'I'm in trouble' look? The 'I need to spend money' look? Or the 'Uncle Robert has again proven to be an ass' look?" Mitch tried to make light of the situation.

"Damn," Jane Stanton groused.

"Not quite the word I was thinking. We heard what D-man said to him, and he won't give it up. The man is not well, Mom." Mitch slumped into a chair near the desk.

Jane nodded. "You get no argument from me. I think we send word to Vic to leak the story. Let's see if a little egg on his face will slow him a little. I presume you got this word from Gordy. Anything specific?"

"We can get more in about forty-five minutes if you want to come with me." Mitch tried to roll the tension out of his shoulders. Tension that had Robert's name etched in his muscles.

"I'm free. Is it lunch this time? What can I bring?" She reached for the phone on her desk.

"Midmorning, I'd say muffins and coffee will be about right. Pick you up in fifteen minutes at the back gate." And he was out the door.

Traffic had been light, and Mitch had made good time to reach their destination. He pulled the SUV up to a small park across from an elementary school. Many small students were outside for lunch, and the noise of their play lifted all of their spirits. "Mom's got the muffins and a thermos of coffee. What have you got?" Mitch glanced at his friend as he lifted the basket to the small concrete table under a sprawling eucalyptus tree.

Gordy reached for a muffin and handed Mitch his travel mug for a refill. "I suppose we could be grateful that Robert is predictable. He didn't accept a rational explanation like a normal human being. He didn't call off the meeting like a serious professional strategist. Instead, he's rambling like a man who is leaning heavily toward fixation on a wildly improbable thought. And he's not being subtle at all. The group receiving his messages has doubled."

Jane took a sip from her mug. "Is anyone taking him seriously?"

Gordy shook his head. "That's the thing. The scientific community wants nothing to do with this. No one is replying to him. I've followed their responses to D-man after he sent them his story. The scientists want to help D-man and can't figure out what Robert's deal is."

Mitch finished his second muffin. "His deal is that he's coming unglued. It's taken a long time, but Uncle Robert has lost his grip."

"Fortunately, following Darren and Ro's return, Vic prepared something special for the press about the movie and is ready to leak it whenever we give her the signal. I just MRC'd her and told her to pull the trigger." Jane smiled.

Gordy chuckled. "I never thought when I created the MRC that a handheld low-frequency comm device would become a verb. What have I done to the English language?" He held his hand to his forehead in mock dismay.

Mitch lightly slapped his friend on the shoulder. "Gotta head out. Thanks, as always, for the heads-up. I'll MRC you when Vic has let loose the leak."

"Thanks, Gordy. Hi to the family." Jane gathered the vestiges of the snack and put them in the basket before the group parted ways.

Distributed at 11:45 a.m., Pacific Standard Time

Dateline: Hollywood
Confidential Preproduction Alert

Powerful Women Productions is working on something small that could be big. Legendary actress, activist, and savvy business-woman Victory Acevedo is teaming up with sci-fi novelist Rosemary Edwards, and up-and-coming genre literature and film professor Darcy Hickson on a project that promises...well, we don't know what it promises. All this reporter knows is that with these three top talents involved, this is a sure winner. Smart investors better start calling before this opportunity is gone.

CHAPTER 34

SATURDAY, DECEMBER 13, 2008, FOLLOWING BREAKFAST, SKYRIDGE RANCH

D-man decided to clear the air with his team. "Well, the news about my trip back to DC was a bummer. I had really hoped that Robert would follow up on the real mysteries, my birth father's death, and the spies. But I guess John Henry, Ben, and Michelle will have to do the heavy lifting on them."

"There is nothing my brother and his squeeze like better than a mystery, maybe two, especially real ones like what was handed to you. Man, it's just hard to believe that Robert wouldn't want to solve a mystery that his dad let go." Charlie was shaking his head.

"Sounds like this Robert character has trouble in him." Fabian plopped onto a chair. "To what do we credit his untimely fixation on Los Alamos?"

Nicola pushed his shoulder." You know this. Robert is Mac's son. Sometimes a successful father is a tough act for a son to follow."

D-man added his two cents. "It's always been like that between Mac and Robert. From what I could see, Mac didn't start it. This is all on Robert. Then when Mac turned down the merger with DARPA, Robert just lost it."

"And he never found it again?" Charlie asked.

"Hell, he never even looked for it again. His identity is now Robert *I-hate-my-father-Mac* MacLane." D-man shook his head in disgust. "Such a waste. And what it's done to the family." D-man continued.

Nick was silent, then looked up. "Having had years with my father taken from me, even by my own hand, I can't imagine not wanting to talk to my father and spend time with him."

Charlie nodded. "I'm with you, Nick. I can't imagine not having the relationship that I do with my dad. I sure wouldn't be the person I am now."

"And just what kind of person might that be, Dr. Grant?" Darcy sat down next to him.

"Well-rounded, friendly, thoughtful, rational…" The laughter stopped Charlie from continuing.

Nick looked around. "I do have something serious I want to ask you all. When Ben and Michelle spoke about searching for missing persons, it felt like the air was knocked out of me. I just hadn't considered that other people could have gone traveling. As soon as I learned about Tommy, I should have considered it, but I just didn't. Now I can't stop thinking about it. Wondering if somebody or more than one somebody might have had their lives uprooted by my experiment."

Mercy had joined the team to listen to their discussion. She reached for Nick's hand. "If you're feeling guilty, know this—guilt never changed anything. Until we know something, you can set that worthless emotion aside."

"Hear, hear," several voices cheered.

She continued. "I'm serious. We don't know anything more than Nick and Tommy were transported on that day. Until Ben and Michelle learn something, the best thing we can do is keep trying to figure out how you two teleported."

Charlie nodded. "Agreed. And I have been doing some pondering on the whole question about why Nick and Tommy were affected and no one else in the building, that is to our knowledge. But we would have heard if somebody in the room was affected, right Nick?"

"Dick would have said something. I'm positive. So, Charlie, do you have a hypothesis?" Nick poked his friend.

"Not so much a hypothesis as a 'what about' or 'what if.' What if the crazy rocks made the difference?" Charlie looked around.

Nick nodded. "I've had a similar thought. Especially since I remembered that we brought in a couple of buckets of gravel to spread under the metal base of the chamber so that we wouldn't have metal touching the wooden floor of the building."

"Nick. This is big!" Nicola exclaimed.

"She's not wrong there, dude." D-man nodded.

Nick lifted his shoulders with his palms open. "But what does it mean? We don't know. Until we know what the rocks are, it's just coincidence."

"Sorry I'm late. I was helping in the garden. It's so big and has so much stuff in it. Oh, and I heard what you were saying about the rocks. When the guys and I found them, we did notice some things." Tommy plunked down next to Nicola.

Fabian asked, "And what was there to notice then?"

"Our watches, if we had them, didn't keep time." Tommy was gazing into the distance thinking about those days.

"Okay, that's important." Nick smiled. "Anything else?"

"Any time any of the guys was called to the motor pool to work on one of the jeeps, they made sure to have a couple of the rocks with them. Kind of a good luck charm, *because all summer everything worked*—anything with an engine."

Nicola spoke up. "The Geezers remembered that everything worked, but they didn't say anything about the rocks."

"Maybe I'm the only one that thought so. The guys always thought the engines worked because they were so good at it." Tommy grinned.

Fabian nodded. "That I can see. And more than sixty years have gone by now. Are you thinking they don't recall carryin' rocks in their pockets to make engines work?"

Nick wanted to go back to something. "Proximity. Tommy, you had a kind of big rock in your pocket. My chamber sat on top of a bunch of them. That's proximity. The guys had a few rocks with them when watches didn't run, and engines did. Don't you see what this could mean?"

Darcy nodded. "Yes. Unless someone was near the rocks, they would not have been affected by the experiment."

"And maybe there's even more going on." D-man continued. "I've been trying to figure out how Nick and Tommy's particles rode the quantum tsunami and stayed intact. The rocks might solve that puzzle too."

"Man, we need to find that rock." Charlie shook his head, thinking about his dad in Arizona.

After Lunch at The Institute, Preparing to Share a Video Feed

"I hope you're all well-fed. We have a lot of updates today." Mitch spoke to his distributed audience. Ben, Michelle, and Don were in Ben's office at the college. Mitch, Beta, and Paul were in the small conference room at The Institute. Betsy and Dick were at Rick and Jane's house. Lia and John Henry were in her clinic office. Vic and Daniel were in his downtown LA office. Gordy was in an "undisclosed" location.

"I know the missing rock team has an update. Don, you want to start us out?" Mitch invited Don to turn on his video camera.

"I got a strange call from the local middle school science teacher this week," Don began. "We met when she student taught under me. She was trying to grade a local geology project brought in by one of her students. Thing is, the student included a shiny round black rock and called it something she knew was wrong. But she didn't know what it might be. Hence the call to me."

"And what did you tell her, Dad?" Ben asked off-camera.

"First, I asked if I knew the student in question. Small town. It's a logical question. When I heard the last name, I knew it was our rock. The mom works at the juvenile facility." Don continued.

Michelle urged the reluctant speaker. "Tell them what you told her, Don."

Don grinned. "I told her how relieved I was to hear that the rock had been found. I shared with her that it had gone missing after having been in possession of a young man with a serious mystery illness. The rock was needed to rule out contamination." They all laughed out loud.

"She could *not* get rid of it fast enough!" Ben was enjoying this.

"Would you like to see it?" Don held it up to the screen. "If you can wait, we'll be out to join you this coming Friday and will bring it along. Maybe a lead-lined box?" the laughter continued.

"Thank you for solving one mystery. And speaking of mysteries. How is the missing persons team doing?" Mitch was moving things along.

Michelle began the report. "I've reached out to the local sheriff and municipal police in the Los Alamos and Santa Fe area. I also reached out to the tribal police, just in case. I filed a FOIA request for the military records for September 1944 in New Mexico. I didn't want to tip *anyone* off. So far, no one has gotten back to me, but I'll send email reminders Monday."

Ben reached for his notebook. "I took a slightly different angle. I went to look at microfiche records of the newspapers locally and as far as Tucson to see if any Jane or John Does showed up around the time Nick and Tommy did. Then I did the same search, but online, for areas as far as Salina, Utah, Cheyenne, Wyoming, Yuma, Colorado, Midland, Texas, and Juarez, Mexico. These form a loose circle around Los Alamos as a center point with Vento Junction being the farthest point traveled. I'm about halfway through and no sightings so far."

Don noted, "This time of year, a lot of people start taking time off. It could be a while before we hear anything."

Mitch replied, "Noted. Thank you all for your reports, your efforts, and your creative thinking."

Rick spoke up. "Dad remembered something you may want to hear."

Dick's face appeared. "I recalled talking with Dave Gustafson the night of his accident. He had a bag of the rocks with him and was taking them to a friend in Santa Fe to be examined. So those rocks could have fallen out of the jeep went it went off the road."

"I can check with the Geezers." John Henry spoke up. "I'm sure they know which curve to check out. I wish we had the sheriff's report to tell us how far off the road the jeep went."

"The Historical Society may have something for you. I recall the docent saying something about copies of local incidents," Mitch added. "Thank you, John Henry and Dr. Stanton."

Vic's voice was next. "You don't need to see me, just know that the leak has done its work. My phone has been ringing, and my poor assistant can't keep up with the messages on the machine. I've had half a dozen emails from producers who say they have money and want to take a meeting."

Ro and Darcy chimed in. "We're writing like mad and actually have a pretty great little script shaping up. And it all starts with a time capsule in Southern Arizona. Should make Robert squirm a little."

"Speaking of Squirming Robert." D-man was chuckling. "I've got a few friends on his list of scientists, and they have begun referring to him as Colonel Kurtz from *Apocalypse Now*. He has no credibility with them. None whatsoever. Not sure what he'll gin up, but the science angle is not going his way."

"So your colleagues think he's lost it?" Rick pushed.

Jane tapped his shoulder. "Don't sound so gleeful."

Charlie spoke next. "Getting back to the science angle, we've been looking into why Nick and Tommy moved, and the rest of the scientists in the building didn't. The quantum tsunami notion explains part of it. But then how did Nick and Tommy's particles know to stay in some coherent state and arrive in Vento Junction. Our best speculation is the mystery rock or rocks have something to do with it."

Dick's voice came in from a few feet from the microphone. "Dave Gustafson thought they were important. Important enough that he was killed. Maybe that's why. Without an insider, we may not ever learn if any investigation was done."

"Anything else for the good of the order, as they say?" Mitch looked at the various screens showing on his smart screen. "Okay then, tell us what movie you're going to watch tonight."

Nicola piped up, "*Miracle on 34th Street*. After all, 'tis the season."

"Oh, before I forget, and I can't believe I almost did," Rick broke in. "I've got a line on a private collector of baseball cards. He wants to remain anonymous and is interested in buying all of them as a lot. I'll be meeting him sometime this coming week. Vic, maybe Daniel could tag along?" Rick finished.

"I'm sure he'd get a charge out of it. I'll text him as soon as we click off." Vic chuckled, and the screens went dark.

Nick's Notes
Saturday night, December 13, 2008

We watched a black-and-white movie tonight. I can't believe how quickly I've come to expect color. This film is from 1947, so things looked familiar. It's a simple story but with complex messages. I liked the redemption theme most of all. The mother who had closed her heart because she had been disappointed and learned that she could love again. But using the post office as proof of Santa Claus was a stroke of genius.

Mercy says she has a soft heart and always cries at movies like this. She says be prepared. She'll be sniffling all through the coming holiday movie nights. Maybe she didn't notice that the movie got to me a little too.

The meeting this morning was unlike anything I have ever been a part of. Instead of everyone being here at Skyridge, cameras made people appear on the screen in the barn classroom. Just amazing.

And the mystery rock has been found. I think Clary is eager to put it through testing to confirm what it is or is not. We're lucky to have him.

I'm still a little, or maybe more than a little, concerned about Colonel Robert MacLane. The team has nibbled away at the grounds for his suspicions, but he is proving not to be rational in his attachment to them. It's so hard to believe that Mac and Martha's son would be so mean.

CHAPTER 35

Sunday, December 14, 2008,
After Lunch at Skyridge Ranch

Charlie caught up to Nick and Mercy as they left the lunch tables. "Hey, I've been thinking about things Nick doesn't know."

"My first thought is why, followed quickly by 'what did you come up with'?" Mercy stopped to quiz their friend.

Nick wondered, "Can you be more specific? Science? Sex? Cooking? History?"

"I would never venture to wonder about your sex life. Just so you know that *is* off-limits. No, I've been thinking about the life skills we take for granted today. Using a microwave, a cellphone, sending email, *driving a car*." Charlie emphasized the last one.

Mercy was nodding. "I get it. We've been focusing on the mystery at hand and wasting an opportunity to teach basic skills. I love it. I don't say this often, Charlie, but you're right."

"I haven't driven a car in several years. Not since right after I graduated. Father let me drive a couple of times when Mother needed something from town and he was teaching. Our car was very different." Nick was very serious.

"Lighten up, dude. My old beater is here. I can teach you on it. No matter what happens to it, it's okay. It's mostly indestructible." Charlie warmed to the topic.

Mercy reached for Nick's hand. "This is really a great idea. You may need to know how to drive. We don't know how soon. So this is perfect. It's Sunday afternoon. Nothing's planned. Let's do it."

"I'll just let Ro know what we're doing so she won't think we're making a break for it," Charlie said over his shoulder as he walked to the main house.

When Charlie got to the main house, Ro was deep in conversation with D-man, Darcy, and Tommy. "I just wanted you to know that we're going to teach Nick to drive this afternoon. Didn't want you to think we were planning an escape." Charlie chuckled.

"Can I learn, too?" Tommy asked him. "I used to drive the Ranch truck, but that was really different. I want to learn to drive a modern car."

Glances were exchanged. D-man grinned. "Let's join you. Driving is a skill that everyone needs. Let's make this happen." He led the way while reaching for his MRC to spread the word about the upcoming entertainment.

When the group reached Nick and Mercy, it felt almost festive. "Thanks for being here, I think," Nick said to the group.

"I think you're going first. Then I get a chance," Tommy spoke to Nick.

"Makes good sense for both of us. Mercy was convincing me that every red-blooded American can drive a car. I find that a stretch, but given the uncertainties that surround us, I now consider driving a survival skill." Nick was walking with Charlie toward the older sedan.

Charlie handed the keys to Nick, who climbed in the driver's side. "How do I move the seat? Where's the gearshift? I don't feel a clutch pedal."

"In reverse order. There is no clutch. It's an automatic transmission. You change gears to drive, to park, and to go in reverse. That's all. And reach under the seat in front of you and there's a lever. Ah, you found it." Charlie was buckling his seatbelt. "Remember to buckle up. It's the law."

Ro was at Nick's window. He rolled it down after finding the button. "There's a single-lane gravel road that circles the perimeter of the entire Ranch. Why don't you try that for your maiden voyage?"

"I use that as one of my running routes. I actually know it a little bit." Nick looked at her.

"I wouldn't go over ten miles an hour. Five is better on your first trip." Ro looked at Charlie.

"Agreed. Granny at the wheel it is." Charlie grinned.

Nick turned the key.

"Give it a little gas and get the feel of the pedal," Charlie spoke evenly.

"I see you took care to point the car forward so I wouldn't have to back up. Thank you." Nick glanced to his right.

"Next step, check your rearview mirror to see if anything is coming behind you. Unlikely here, but a good habit. Then check the side mirrors. Now use this and put it in drive. Yes, like that." He watched as Nick moved the shifter in the center console from P to D. "Now give it a little gas."

The car leaped forward, and Nick slammed on the brake. "I didn't expect that," Nick said.

"That's why we're practicing. Now try it again a little lighter and see how it goes." Charlie was calm.

This time the car moved gradually, and Nick breathed a sigh of relief. "Let's just take it easy this first lap. You don't need to go any faster than this until you're comfortable with it." Charlie's voice was soothing.

"Okay. I like that plan. Slow and steady. Here I go." Nick was rigid behind the wheel.

"Dude, this is a rite of passage. I can understand why it didn't happen when you were a teenager, but now every teenager in America wants to get their license as soon as they turn sixteen." Charlie was recalling his driver's test.

"I wonder how soon I will need to drive?" Nick was relaxing a little as they moved further away from the Ranch buildings.

"That's hard to say, but there may come a time when there won't be anyone else to help you, so this is a good thing to know how to do. Maybe I should teach you how to hotwire a car." Charlie was not entirely kidding.

"Hotwire? Like stealing?" Nick was a little alarmed.

"Probably not a good idea. I think you'll have access to vehicles legally. At least I hope so. The Robert thing is unsettling." Charlie continued.

"One thing at a time. Let me be proficient at driving a car using a key before we go on any tangents." Nick smiled.

As the group came in view, Nick waved and they continued on lap number two. "Okay, do you want to pick up your speed a little?" Charlie asked.

"Ten miles an hour?" Nick wondered.

"Yeah. Go for ten miles an hour. And then when we finish this lap, let's find a place to practice reverse." Charlie was planning ahead.

Nicola pulled on Fabian's arm to get him away from the moving vehicle. "You make a big target and we don't know how well Nick is managing the car quite yet."

"Good. You're still sweet on me, so I'll be steppin' back since you care to protect me."

"Yes, I want to protect you, and I would also hate to see Nick's face if he happened to bump you as he was trying to navigate this gravel road. You do not want to be the cause of him feeling badly, now do you?"

"Ach, that was not occurring to me. It's a kind heart you be having. I'll not be bruising it with my carelessness."

She squeezed his hand and pulled him back and away from the glances they were attracting.

"I'd be for driving on the wrong side of the road if I had the chance," Clary muttered to Tommy as they watched the progress of Nick's lesson.

"What do you mean the wrong side of the road?" Tommy was baffled by his friend's statement.

"You really do be sheltered then. Where I come from, we drive on the left, and the car comin' at you is on your right," Clary explained with a touch of condescension.

"Oh, I get it. You *do* drive on the wrong side of the road." Tommy was starting to understand.

"No, we do not. The correct side of the road is the left." Clary decided to stand his ground.

"Maybe if you're in Ireland, but we're in America now, and the left is the very wrong side of the road, bud." Tommy was grinning.

"I'll give you that then, but when we're in my home country, you'll be driving on the right side of the road, I mean the left." Clary started to laugh at himself as they both chuckled.

Forty-five minutes and more than a few laps later, it was time for Tommy to take the wheel. Charlie turned his task over to D-man, saying, "You're a dad and he's a teenager. This one's for you."

Tommy and D-man eyed each other and grinned. "Okay, we'll take it from here." D-man opened the passenger door. "No heart attacks, young man. I have plans for tonight."

Tommy's departure was a little smoother. "I can't believe how smooth these engines run. They sure got a lotta power." Tommy was smiling at the horizon.

"They do, but today is not the day for power. Don't worry. I'll get you out on the road this week in my SUV. They did get a driver's license for you, didn't they?"

"I think it's in my wallet. I'll have to check. Good point. Since I haven't been driving, I just didn't think about it." Tommy blushed.

"Did you have a license in New Mexico before this happened?" D-man suddenly wondered about the range of skills of the young driver.

"Not exactly. It cost money, and nobody ever seemed to care. It's not like we had a family car or anything." Tommy was focused on the single gravel lane and his slow progress around the Ranch.

"Let's be clear, young man. You don't lie to me, and I won't lie to you. Agreed?" D-man shifted his body to stare at the teenager.

"Yes, sir. No lies. I didn't have a license. We all figured we were enlisting soon and who knew if we'd be alive after the War to need one." Tommy relaxed his shoulders as the truth spilled out.

"Thank you. Now I'll confess to you that I drove a few times before I got my license. Caught holy hell from my dad. The time that made me stop was when he took me to the emergency room at the hospital on a Saturday night. It's the worst night for teenagers getting in wrecks. What I saw that night I never want to see again." D-man was grim.

"What was the worst thing you saw?" Tommy was driving slowly, making the first turn.

"It was the families in the waiting room. Most were crying. Some were shrieking when they learned their kid died." D-man shook his head. "I never wanted to do that to my parents. I can still hear those parents. Don't do that to us. We're kind of your parents now. Okay?"

"Okay. When you put it that way, it's different. It's not so much fun."

"It can still be fun. Right time, right place, right vehicle. This time and place are for learning. Even though this is an older model car, it still has more power than what you drove in 1944. Let's make sure you learn about it." D-man pointed ahead of them to the next stretch of road. "Now, give it a little gas here on the straightaway… That's it…Good. On the next lap, we can try reverse."

Tommy blanched. "I never did reverse."

"Well, you're going to today, and it will be fine." D-man smiled at the young man who had now dropped his attitude.

CHAPTER 36

MONDAY, DECEMBER 15, 2008, THE INSTITUTE, LOS ANGELES, CALIFORNIA

Beta hurried to catch up to Mitch. "Hey, Big Guy, I need to talk to you."

"Something serious?" His concern showed on his face.

"I hope not, but can we go somewhere kind of private?" Beta was looking around the hallway.

"Mom's office is right here. She's out this morning so we can use it." He opened the door marked "Director."

As soon as the door closed. "Thanks. It's about Suzanne." She began as she sat. Then she froze. Her eyes scanned the wall behind the desk. Countless framed photos, certificates, and diplomas filled almost every square inch. "I guess I never knew your Mom was so…"

"Accomplished. Yeah. She's pretty amazing. She's done a lot with her life, knows a lot of people, and she's still got a lot ahead too." Mitch sat on the edge of the desk nearby. "Now what about Suzanne?"

Beta shook her head to refocus her thoughts. "She asked me when D-man was coming back. And she kind of acted like they have, like there's something between them, if you know what I mean." Beta was uncomfortable.

"Whoa. I never even considered that she might, well, that D-man could have been interpreted as…as flirting. Am I under-

225

standing that's what you think is going on?" Mitch decided to drop down to sit in the companion chair next to her.

"I'm new here, and maybe she thinks I'm safe to talk to. I never really saw them interact together. What did you see? I don't know how old she is, but he's older, right?" Beta tried to figure out the situation.

"Old enough to be her father. Suzanne has been at The Institute for about three years now. Dr. D-man lost his wife about the time she arrived. She's never seen him as a married man, a happily married man." Mitch was thinking out loud.

"Has he always been at The Institute?"

"No. He used to be at UCLA. Mom thought he needed the emotional and collegial support here when Serenity was dying. She wasn't wrong. I can't imagine what he might have been like left alone. I mean, he has his kids, but they were hurting, too," Mitch explained.

"So we have a vulnerable, charming, clueless widower teasing a vulnerable engineer/scientist with an edgy exterior. Am I painting the right picture?" Beta was following the clues.

"And they share a sense of humor. Ye gods. All this was happening on our watch. How bad is it?" Now Mitch was concerned.

"I really don't know, but somebody needs to talk with her and let her know." Beta stopped.

"Let her know what? That the guy she thinks likes her is falling for an age-appropriate woman out at Skyridge? And just who might be able to deliver that message?" Mitch was the one who was uncomfortable now.

A knock on the door roused them from the dilemma. "Dr. Stanton is out. Can I help you?" Mitch responded.

The door opened to reveal Dr. Paul Sanchez. "Well, what have we here. A tryst in your mother's office? Mitch, you devil." Paul grinned at his friend.

Beta got up and closed the door. "It's not like that."

"It could have been. And it's okay by me." Paul was enjoying this.

"If there's any trysting, it won't be in my mother's office. Yech." Mitch was grossed out at the thought. They all laughed.

"Okay then, why are you two in here, alone?" Paul continued.

"You first," Beta bantered back.

"I have an opportunity to work with some mobility-challenged teens at a place in South LA. I wanted to make sure Dr. Jane was okay with me giving them some of my time," Paul admitted.

"That sounds amazing. I can't imagine Dr. Jane would object," Beta blurted.

"Tell me more about the teenagers. What's your interest in them? Mind-body stuff?" Mitch was thinking.

"That, and each of them has lost something, and they could use an outsider to bring some perspective to their situations." Paul was earnest.

"Do you think Suzanne could help?" Beta raised her eyebrows and glanced at Mitch, who nodded his assent.

"Hadn't considered it, but she'd be great. Former skateboarder, now engineer and scientist. Yeah. That could be a big hit." Paul was grinning.

"Then you may be the solution or part of the solution to the problem that prompted us to have our private conversation in this office," Mitch announced.

"Something about Suzanne?" Paul worried.

"She thinks there's something romantic between her and D-man Hickson," Beta stated.

Mitch continued. "And as you may have noted, the good Dr. Hickson is besotted with my Aunt Rosemary at Skyridge."

"Yeah, about that, how did that happen so fast?" Beta was curious.

"They all grew up together. When Ro was a teenager, she had a crush on him. He was a few years older. Their ships did not have favorable winds. D-man's blew him to Serenity. Now they both are single and have another chance," Mitch explained.

Paul refocused them. "Where do I fit in?"

Beta drew it out for him. "You've seen them at Skyridge. You can mention something about it when you have your conversation with Suzanne about joining you in the work at the clinic."

"Like how? I know you think D-man has a thing for you, but he doesn't, so why don't you help me instead?" Paul recoiled.

"Nah. More like you saw how well she worked with him, and you thought she would be an asset to you in this work," Mitch suggested.

"Okay, kinda smooth. And how is it that I get to be the one to break her heart?" Paul was still not sure.

Beta was nodding. "She'll bring it up. Trust me, you'll have an opportunity, and it will be natural. You won't have to push it."

"Okay. I'm not really sure, but now that I think about it, Suzanne would be great. Where is she this morning?" Paul stood ready to open the door.

"Start at the dining hall, then her lab. Catch you later. Oh, and I'll tell Mom about the clinic opportunity." Mitch rose and patted him on the shoulder.

When the door closed, Beta rose. Mitch said, "Not so fast. We are alone here."

"Why, whatever are you thinking, sir?" Beta grinned.

"Just a down payment on some time with you later, I hope." He kissed her lightly.

A Few Minutes Later by The Institute's Lobby Elevators

"Suzanne, just the woman I want to see." Paul winced inwardly at the stale greeting.

"What up, Doc? Got anything juicy to share?" The woman of the hour grinned devilishly.

"I'll tell you as we head up to your lab. That is where you're headed, right?"

"Score, Doc. I'm headed in to tweak an experiment." The elevator doors opened, and they entered together.

As the doors glided closed, they both began to speak.

"So how are you liking—"

"How long have you been here—"

Then they laughed.

"You first, Doc. You're new." She smiled in a friendly way.

"Okay. I just wondered how long you've been here. I know some people come for as little as a week, and some, it seems, are, well, lifers, I guess." Paul grew uncomfortable.

"I've been here a little over three years. So not a lifer, but I know what you mean. And long enough that I know some stuff." She chuckled.

"I bet you do." He raised an eyebrow. "Now you."

The doors opened, and they began to move toward her lab.

She looked his way. "I was just wondering how it's going for you. I mean, there's been a lot going on, more than usual. It's a lot to take in on a normal day."

"I think since I've known Mitch for so long, it was a little easier to roll with the events of the past weeks. But it is very different from what I'm used to."

"That's right. I forgot that Mitch said you guys go back. That really could help. So what else is up? You were looking for me." She opened her lab door, and they entered a clean but cluttered space.

"My work here isn't the only thing I do. I keep my hand in at a clinic near south LA where some kids who are new to mobility challenges go for rehab and therapy. I thought it might be fun for you and helpful for them if you'd come with me."

"Woah. Now that I did not expect. I didn't know what to expect, but I kinda thought it would be white coat stuff. Do you wear a white coat when you go there?" She was shaking her head.

"I do not. I wear jeans and a shirt. Some of the kids are Spanish-speaking. Some are from really bad neighborhoods and got shot in the wrong place. Most of them were either gang members or were nearby when the shooting started." He decided to lay it out straight.

"And it's safe?" she needed to be a little careful.

"We're there in the daytime, and the families have made it clear that the clinic is neutral territory. I think it's as safe as it's gonna get around there." He had to be honest with her.

"Then I'm in. I wish somebody had been around to talk to me after my accident. Oh, the docs and the therapists were great. But it makes a difference when someone is in the chair talking to you." She was nodding almost to herself.

"Thank you. I know it will mean a lot to them. My next visit is tomorrow. Is that okay with your schedule?" Paul was wondering how he was going to weave in the D-man info.

"Yah. That's good. What time?"

"I usually get there around ten, and I bring doughnuts." Paul grinned.

"Now I'm really in. Can I pick them out?" She nearly spun in her chair.

"The kitchen here makes them for us." Paul hoped she wasn't disappointed.

"Even better. Total yummmm." She started to hum and move toward a counter with some gear.

"There was one other thing." Paul began, clearly uncomfortable.

"I wondered who the messenger would be." She looked at him with a half smile.

"Messenger?" Paul was confused.

"Uh-huh. Messenger. To give me the news that would break my heart. That D-man is, well, not gonna ever be my squeeze." She was enjoying this immensely.

"You know already?" Paul was still uncomfortable.

"He left me a note. He's such a softie." She turned back to her gear.

"So you've known all along?" he needed to figure something out about his new colleague.

"I suspected. Come on. He's old enough to be my dad. That alone is creepy. He's so much fun, though. I couldn't help teasing with him." She looked over her shoulder.

"You've made this easy on me. Thank you. I thought I was going to be the one to break your heart, and I didn't want to do that." Paul was relieved and chagrinned.

"That doesn't mean that we can't have some fun with this. We can figure out a way to milk this situation when we're in the van tomorrow." She gave an evil leer.

"I may like that. It was my friend Mitch who put this task on me. I think I can have some fun at his expense." Now he was seeing the possibilities.

"Oooo. The big guy. Yes, indeed we can have some fun."

Laughing together, he waved goodbye and headed out with a weight off his shoulders and a lighter step.

CHAPTER 37

Monday, December 15, 2008, Early Afternoon, Vento Junction, Arizona

"Thanks for coming, Dad. We have something we want to run by you." Ben Grant welcomed his father to his small apartment near the community college.

"Always happy to see you both, and I have something I wanted to discuss with you as well." Don sat on the love seat as Samantha Jane jumped up to join him.

"Do you want to go first?" Michelle Mathews was in the kitchenette, preparing iced tea for three.

"You may want to sit down for this." Don grinned as Michelle delivered a tray with their cold drinks.

"Dad, what have you got up your sleeve? Another time traveler?" Ben was only half joking.

"Nothing so earth-shaking. Just, well would you like to move into the house anytime soon?" Don took a sip of the tea.

"Are you okay?" Michelle raised an ever-present concern when she thought about parents.

"Oh, it's nothing to worry about. I didn't think about your dad having been sick. I'm fine. In fact, I'm more than fine. I'm in love." Don grinned.

"Well, that's not news. In fact, it's pretty obvious," Ben kidded his dad.

"And it's also pretty serious. When I head over this week, I'm not coming back, well, not to live here anyway. Vic and I started to talk about this a while ago. The driving back and forth is getting old. No cracks from either of you." Ben and Michelle tried to stifle their chuckles. "She and I, well, we want to spend more time with each other. Especially while we're healthy and active. This movie project is a handy excuse to try this out. I'll be taking a trailer full of things that will make me feel at home, but I'm not ready to sell the house." Don raised his shoulder in a half shrug. "What do you think?"

"What about Sam?" Michelle was petting the happy pup.

"She'll be coming with me. Vic loves her almost as much as I do." Dan gave Sam a squeeze. "Doesn't she, sweet girl?"

"It's pretty soon, isn't it? What's it been, three months?" Ben was being protective.

"Son, when you have loved and lost and find love again, you don't sit around and wonder when it will look right to outsiders. Vic and I have both talked and talked about that very fact. It's fast, and it also feels right. What is second-guessing going to get me? I'm not selling the house, remember? I'm just letting you guys have it for the foreseeable future." He nodded to communicate it was a done deal.

"Well, okay then, how can we help you?' Michelle asked.

"Tell me you'll move into the house," Don said simply.

"If it's okay with Ben, I'm in. I've been staying with my mom for the last month. My lease was up, and I wasn't sure about my next step. Sounds like it's right in front of me." She smiled. "I have a cat, is that okay?"

"Well, son, are you okay with it, the house, the girl, *and* the cat?"

"Never lived with a cat before. I'm willing if you are. My lease is up at the end of the month. I'm glad you brought this up when you did. The landlord just sent out a notice wondering if I wanted to renew." Ben sat back in his worn chair and addressed Michelle. "And I've been wanting to bring up the topic of moving in together. Then this lease thing came up, and that brings uncertainty. But now that I have a place, would you and Miss Kitty join me?"

Michelle hugged her dusty history teacher-cowboy.

"Good. Now what did you both bring us here for?" Don took a long sip of the tea.

"It's about the missing persons search," Michelle began. "We're thinking we're asking the wrong question, or questions."

"Interesting. Continue." Don nodded.

Ben picked up the thread. "I began to think about Nick and Tommy. They were indeed missing, but they also disappeared. And that's a different kind of alert and a different kind of search." Ben was nodding to reinforce his thinking.

"And I started to search old headlines for disappearances. Mysterious disappearances. I'm starting to get some hits!" Michelle was excited.

"Okay. That's interesting and exciting. Other than newspapers, where are you searching?" Don leaned forward.

"I'm going to go back to historical records, and instead of missing persons, I'm going to query for unexplained disappearances," Ben offered.

"I'm going to do the same for the sheriff's reports. Not sure what they will reveal. Missing and disappeared might be euphemisms in some cases, but in the headlines, I found they were different." Michelle was earnest.

"Where were these headlines?" Don was curious.

"Nothing north or east of Los Alamos. Which alone is curious. But when we now think about what our science team was talking about, it makes sense," Ben said.

"I'm guessing you have more?" Don was laughing, which made Sam wiggle her butt.

"There are a lot of newspapers in New Mexico today, but it was a pretty small state in the 1940s. I'm focusing on Albuquerque, Santa Fe, Artesia, and a few others." Michelle continued. "Once I finish with those, I'll look at Silver City, Las Cruces, and maybe Gallup and Farmington."

"Okay, but where did the stories come from that grabbed your interest?" Don prodded.

"Los Alamos. Right under our noses." Ben laughed. "And there were also a few animal disappearances, but I'm not really thinking those were part of the experiment."

"And who or what disappeared?" Don kept on.

Michelle's eyes got round. "A young GI. Supposedly disappeared, or went AWOL, on perimeter patrol. On September 8, 1944." Silence.

"Oh my God. Nick's worst fears. Someone else may have traveled." Don was stricken.

"We're not finished corroborating the disappearance yet. We're checking railroad and bus records, as well as marriage licenses and any other kind of records that might be connected with a GI leaving the camp," Ben added.

"Anything I can do to help?" Don felt helpless.

"Well, if Robert wasn't such a toad, he could help. Hey, Dad, do you have any contacts left in the VA or any of your service connections?" Ben raised his shoulders to emphasize the possibility.

"Let me think on it. I have one buddy who's a military history buff. This might be the kind of thing he would sink his teeth and keyboard into." Don was nodding.

Michelle had a thought. "Let's ask Father Joe if he has connections in the churches around Los Alamos whose records would reveal weddings that day or soon after."

"And the court as well. I'm guessing that marriage records are more readily available." Ben hoped.

"We're going to have an interesting report to share this Saturday. Are you both coming over?" Don rose, and Sam jumped down.

Michelle nodded. "With you moving, maybe we should rent a truck or something and help you move."

"I'd like to say we don't need it, but I do have some things I want to take. If you two could drive the truck, I'll pay for the rental of a vehicle for your return." Don smiled.

"Depending on how much we get done, I was thinking we might come out and stay through New Year's Day." Ben was hopeful. "School is out. It's kind of perfect."

"In that case, there's gonna be a whole lotta movin' goin' on. Let's get to it." Don clapped his hands, Sam barked, and they laughed.

Nick's Notes
Monday, December 15, 2008

We got good news about Tommy's rock. Don has it in his possession now. I look forward to hearing how it is that he got it back. Clary, our geology prodigy, is looking forward to having a larger specimen to study. I sure hope that Charlie's speculation is right and that our proximity to the rocks made the difference in the success of the experiment. I would feel terribly guilty if my experiment caused anyone else to lose their life. Well, not exactly lose their life, but certainly everything they knew and everyone they knew and loved. I never thought about me being alone as fortunate, but in light of what happened, maybe it was better that I didn't have a girlfriend.

Mercy says that guilt never changed anything and all it does is use psychic energy. She may be right. About guilt never changing anything. I'm still learning about psychic energy. And not too sure about it.

Tommy has continued to join me on my morning runs. He was a baseball player, and he has great stamina. I like him as a running partner. And it's been a good chance for us to get to know each other. Only having a sister, I rather like the feel of being an older brother. I think he will soon outpace my knowledge about life. If he asks me about sex, I'll have to recommend Charlie. Or maybe D-man. Mercy says I am doing fine in the kissing department. I do wonder what comes next nowadays. I imagine she'll tell me if I ask. But that means I need to be ready to hear the answer.

CHAPTER 38

Wednesday, December 17, 2008, Barn Classroom, Skyridge Ranch

Ro and Darcy looked up at the large screen filled with the attractive face of Victory Acevedo. "I like your idea. The time capsule triggers something for our protagonist. It shifts his brain into 1944, even though he was born in 1990." Victory was excited that they might have the hook for the story.

Darcy continued. "Having the diagnosis of social temporal displacement disorder was a great source of both mystery and conflict. Now this trigger incident helps explain its origin."

"Why would this particular time capsule provide a trigger? Something in it? Something about our protagonist?" Ro pondered.

"Don't know yet. Don't need to know yet. Right now, we can create a series of mishaps and incidents as our poor hero, for lack of a better name, bumbles along. Now we get to introduce a cast of characters. People who help him, hide him, like him." Vic was nodding as her ideas spilled out.

Tommy came in to join them. "Sorry, I'm late. I was in the vineyard. The vines can sure use some pruning. I think I got here just in time."

"For us or the vines?" Darcy joked.

"Maybe both. What have you guys been cooking up? Do I get to meet any beautiful girls yet?" Tommy grinned.

"Not a bad idea." Vic smiled. "How many did you have in mind?"

Tommy blushed. "Maybe one, at least one. Or two. I'm a young guy. I want to play the field."

"You're on the run in the movie. I think you're going to meet a series of young lovelies who take a fancy to you." Ro punched him lightly on the shoulder.

Darcy grinned wickedly. "Lots of kissing."

"Yeah, but it's gonna be some actor, not me, right?" Tommy was glum at the thought.

"Okay, yes. But you can dream, can't you?" Vic smiled.

"Maybe I can audition the actresses?" Tommy hoped.

"Let's not get ahead of ourselves. Back to our hero. Tommy, what was it like when you first arrived?" Darcy had her notebook open and her pen poised.

"It was strange. I felt like my head was buzzing. I looked around, and I didn't recognize where I was or any of the people. The clothes were strange, and then I saw the cars and trucks. I nearly passed out." He was remembering.

"Then what?" Darcy prompted.

"I saw some guys playing baseball. That looked like something I knew. I asked if they needed a player." Tommy was gazing in the distance.

"What happened when you asked that?" Vic hadn't heard Tommy tell his story.

"Things started out fine. I was playing shortstop. My usual position. When our side sat down, somebody asked me where I was from. I told them Los Alamos. It's easier than saying the Pueblo, you know." He continued. "They said, 'Where the bomb was made?' and I asked, 'You know about that? It's supposed to be a secret.' And then they all laughed."

"They said that everybody knew about it. That the bomb ended the war when they dropped it on Japan."

Rosemary took his hand and asked gently. "How did you handle that information?"

"I told them I didn't believe them. That's when somebody called somebody. The next thing I know, I'm in the back of something, not a car, not a truck."

"A van?" Darcy asked.

"Yeah. I've seen a van now, and yes, it was a van. They took me to a hospital. A doctor poked at me and asked me questions, lots of them. Then they took me to that place. When I got there, they kept asking questions. I told them the truth. Next thing I knew, I was sleepy. And pretty much until Don, Ben, and Michelle broke me out, I slept." Tommy rested his elbows on his knees.

"I'm so sorry that happened to you. Do you remember anything about the other people being kept there?" Darcy tried to be gentle with her questions.

"When we had meals, nobody sat with me at first. After a while, they figured out I wasn't dangerous. I didn't talk much. I listened. Most of the guys there broke laws. Stealing, even shootings."

"It's hard to believe anyone thought it was okay to put someone who sounded crazy—sorry, Tommy—with criminals. We've got to put this in the script. Maybe people will get angry enough to do something about it." Vic was fierce.

Ro had a thought. "Tommy, did anybody take you into an office and ask you questions, kind of quietly?"

"It's fuzzy, but yeah. A younger guy. Longer hair. Tried to act like a buddy. I wasn't buying it. He kept asking me about where I came from. Learned my lesson on that. I just played tired. Couldn't think. That kind of stuff." Tommy frowned.

"Did they ever give you anything to 'unfuzzy' you?" Vic was still pretty angry about the way Tommy had been treated.

"Only right before I got pulled out. Even then, things were still pretty foggy when Don, Ben, and Michelle took me out of there." Tommy was nodding almost to himself.

Darcy had one more question. "How long did it take for things to clear up for you once you were out of the place?"

Tommy paused. "It was still a couple of days. And really, it wasn't until I got here and could put my hands in the earth again. I really missed my garden. They let us outside in what they called a yard, but I figured putting my hands into the ground would look crazy. Didn't need that."

Ro's eyes had gotten big. "Putting your hands into the earth clears your mind?"

"Yeah. Always has. Even as a little kid. Mom put me in the garden to play. And I get things to grow. Mom says...said, it was my gift." Tommy was matter-of-fact.

Vic shifted her tone of voice into soft mode. "Your sister sees spirits, your niece is a healer, your grandniece connects to the quantum realm, you connect with the earth and growing things. Is that why Beta is studying sustainable agriculture. Did she get your gift?"

Darcy was nodding to herself. "You know the Druids referred to elementals—air, earth, that kind of thing. Tommy, you might communicate with the elemental of the earth. Wow."

"What's a Druid?" Tommy was confused.

"It's an ancient religion. Not much practiced now. Very much based in nature and rituals," Darcy explained.

"Kinda sounds like tribal stuff," Tommy replied.

Ro added, "Studies of people around the world reveal more similarities than differences. I think we just found one. Not sure what to do with it, but let's share it Saturday."

Nick's Notes
Wednesday, December 17, 2008

D-man said we needed something totally different for movie night. He thinks a heavy dose of Christmas is coming. Maybe he's right, but the movie tonight was unlike anything I've ever seen. I don't know if I have words to describe it. *Woodstock* is a real place, and the concert that the movie shows really happened. I can't believe it lasted for three days. And all that rain and mud. The people looked like tribes from National Geographic, except more clothes. Some of the music was compelling. I'm still not accustomed to listening to rock and roll. Folk is more tuneful, but there wasn't so much of that.

I talked with Tommy this afternoon. He was excited about the meeting he had with Darcy, Ro, and Vic. Said something about

Druids and that he told them about his gift. I think that's good. Tommy needs to trust more than just me. We're all in this. I need to ask him what he thought of the movie.

Mercy rolled her eyes when D-man said we'd be watching *Woodstock*. She agrees that it captured an important event in the 1960s and that it's very special for people who were young then. She doesn't think it translates well to others. I agree with her.

CHAPTER 39

Thursday, December 18, 2008, After Breakfast at Skyridge Ranch

Clary McGonigle was on a mission to track down the only other teenager at the Ranch. He spied him just leaving breakfast. "Hey, Tommy."

Tommy Cisneros turned around with a grin. He liked the energetic Irish kid. "Hey, Clary, what's up?"

"Let's us be gone away then." Clary looked around at the breakfast hubbub.

"Sure. Where to?" Tommy was curious about what had Clary eager to leave the crowd. "Wanta take a run?" Tommy glanced at his lanky new friend.

"Sure. I was a footballer. You call it soccer here. No sense to that. It's with your feet that the game is played, dontcha know. Soccer, as you call it, is played with the feet and not the hands. It's football. You, Yanks, you have no sense then." They took off at a trot.

It didn't take long to reach a grassy hill where Clary indicated they could stop. He still glanced around before starting. "Yesterday I could hear ye talkin' about the movie. When that Darcy talked about Druids, my ears perked up. Do ya remember that part?"

"Yeah. That was pretty interesting. My people believe all kinds of stories about mother earth and how people came to be here. And then there's my family and our gifts. At home nobody thinks it's strange. Here, though, I'm not so sure."

"Sure, even at home, not everyone is being tolerant, about gifts, I mean. My family is known to be, shall we say...unusual." Clary hesitated.

"Go on. Does someone in your family have a gift?"

"My da. It's about water. He can find it. Calls it dowsing. But I hear that happens here as well. But..." He stopped.

"Are you trying to tell me that you have a gift?" Tommy raised his eyebrows.

"I do that. With rocks. When that Darcy, she was talkin' about elementals, well, I am told that I talk with such like." Clary blushed.

"That's pretty great. Darcy thinks I connect with an earth elemental. What do you connect to?" Tommy was grinning.

"I have no name for them. I hear and feel them. Like you said you feel the earth when you put your hands in it." Clary hoped he was making sense. "What is it feeling for you when you do it, put your hands in the earth?"

"When I start moving soil with my fingers, I feel tingles. Sometimes I feel warmth. Sometimes both. It's like the plants and the earth want to get my attention," Tommy admitted.

"And how is it the earth lets you know such things?"

"Sometimes the feelings are stronger in one direction or another. Sometimes when I push my hand in deeper, the feelings get stronger. Sometimes weaker. It's kinda all different. But when it's planting season, I get lots of great feelings. The earth really likes having growing things in it." Tommy was smiling at the memory. "How about the rocks. What do you feel?"

"I'm feeling many things, and sure, it depends on the rocks. That's why I'm choosin' geology. It's fond of all of 'em I am, but that rock you be having, I wanta feel it. Even the small ones give me a feelin' I never had on me ever." Clary was looking into Tommy's eyes.

"Did they scare you?" Tommy was concerned.

"Not so much that. But never, in all the years of the holding and touching of rocks, felt I what I did from those small round stones. They're not being of this earth, Tommy. That's all I can say."

Clary plopped down to sit on the ground. As he joined him, Tommy asked, "Do you hear anything? Can you talk to rocks? I only ask because I talk to plants. They seem to like it. They grow better." Tommy was nodding his head.

"Maybe like a whooshing sound in my head. Not so much words. And it's a kind of pull it is that I feel," Clary admitted.

"What kinda pull? Like a direction?" Tommy was even more curious now.

"Like the rock, it be wanting me closer. But that, well, how do you be closer to a rock? And the pull I felt when walking near mines I was. Only one time did I venture into the opening. Closing in around me they were. I escaped sure, and I'm not for going into any mines again." Clary shuddered.

"Okay, that's scary. I can't imagine feeling like rocks want to close in around me. The earth doesn't feel that way to me." Tommy was nodding and thinking. "Are your family Druids?"

"Ah, it's a bit of curious that. My people, they were Druids long ago. My great-great-gran, I think. But nowadays the public thinks Druids are to be the same as witches then. It's not good."

"No, I guess not. I can see why you wouldn't go around telling people either. You never know how they could act," Tommy agreed.

"Mostly I'm wanting you to know that I'm being like you. I have a gift." Clary was looking around, kind of shy now that he had spoken.

"Thanks, thanks for telling me. Good to know. It sounds like Don has my rock, and it'll be here Friday. I'll stand next to you when you hold it. Just in case you need my gift to help." Tommy stood and held out his hand to help Clary to his feet.

"Thanks. It's better I'll be feeling then." Clary smiled shyly.

"Want to go back or have a bit more of a run?" Tommy shrugged.

"Yes, go on, then. The running be feeling good on my legs, sure." Clary smiled, and they both headed off.

The Institute, Dr. Jane Stanton's Office

Her cell phone rang. It was her husband's ring. "Hi there. Are you calling about dinner?" she wondered.

"Good question, but no." Rick laughed. "Got a taste for something in particular?"

"Just kind of enjoying a respite from the intensity of the Ranch. Let's just have something light." She smiled. "But that's not why you called."

"It's much more fun than dinner, although we might want to invite Vic and Daniel to join us." He was being mysterious.

"And why might that be?" His wife was intrigued.

"Because we're going to need some advice on handling a great deal of money." Rick had a grin in his voice.

"That lottery ticket you bought?" Jane was teasing.

"Nah. Better. The baseball cards from the time capsule. I put out some feelers, and I found a buyer. He wants to buy all of them as a lot."

"Who is it? How do you know they're legitimate? When did this happen?" Jane peppered him with questions.

"No more info until dinner. Are you okay if I invite Vic and Daniel?" Rick was excited.

"Go ahead. Maybe you should MRC them. Seems secrecy is the order of the day," Jane cautioned.

"I'll include you in the group. See you by six. Will that work for your schedule?" he asked.

"I'll make it work. This sounds both fun and important. And isn't that just the best description of the past three months!" Jane rang off, shaking her head.

Office of Ben Grant, Vento Junction Community College

The MRC sitting on his desk alerted. The text told him to reach out to Michelle. They had burner phones for this purpose. "Hey, what's wrong?" He was concerned.

"Nothing yet," Michelle replied. "But I had a thought."

"Care to share?" Ben smiled through the phone line.

"It's just that Robert MacLane seems like he needs a bigger push to get him off his current trail and on to a different one."

"You're right about that. His dogged insistence on nosing into the Trick is unsettling." Ben was nodding.

"And we really would rather have him following up on Dave Gustafson's mysterious accident, yes?" Michelle was building her case. He could feel it.

"That would be better all around, yes." Ben waited for her to get to her idea.

"Well, what if Sedona Searsy put a story in my former employer's rag of an online paper about a mysterious death in 1944 at Los Alamos during the time of the Manhattan Project?" She waited for his reaction.

"I think that would ruffle some feathers. Especially if you mentioned a certain colonel who had information and chose not to act on it." Ben was liking this.

"This weekend, I'd like to bring it up at the check-in meeting. In person." She was hopeful.

"We're driving Dad's stuff over because of his move, so I think we should plan to stay through the weekend. Maybe through Christmas unless you have plans." Ben hoped she would say yes.

"I'll let Mom know. I think it'll be fine. She's got plans with friends for Christmas, anyway. And the cat seems to like her more than me now. Now that I think about it, maybe you won't be living with a cat after all. I think I have a green light to pack enough things for a longer visit and head west." Excitement was in her voice.

CHAPTER 40

FRIDAY, DECEMBER 19, 2008, LATE AFTERNOON, SKYRIDGE RANCH

It had only taken about an hour to unload Don's "worldly goods," as he called them, into Vic's spacious home. They picked up the non-descript rental car for Ben and Michelle, and the three-car caravan headed out to unwind at Skyridge. Don and Vic led the way in her SUV, Ben and Michelle next and Daniel in his red BMW convertible sports car bringing up the rear.

Energy filled the small rental car as Michelle burst out, "I'm so excited to get there and see everybody and share our ideas. I know we can do a call, but it's just not the same as in person."

"I'm with you on the human interaction. Technology is great, but humans are subtle creatures. Nothing beats the classroom, the dining room table, the front porch. I'm eager to get there too. Is it just me or are things moving along really fast? I wonder if Nick's life will ever slow down." Ben pondered as he guided the car away from the Friday traffic headed toward the coast.

The miles dissolved in the rearview mirror, and then they were under the iron archway that announced Skyridge Ranch. It was another few minutes on the slow single-lane drive before they reached the main house. The Arizonans drew near the growing crowd and eased in to park.

When Daniel pulled up his convertible a few minutes later, Mitch walked over to see if he could help. "Hey, slowpoke. We've been here for an hour. What's slowing you down?"

"Well, I decided to obey the speed limit and not raise suspicion. You know a car like this is a cop magnet, and we don't need to draw that kind of attention right now," Daniel teased.

The sun was setting, and clusters of friends, colleagues, and hand-holding couples headed for the barn to help lay out dinner for the crowd. Ro and Mitch both felt the vibration of their phones. They shared a look. As they were the only people allowed to have phones on the property, it felt ominous that they both would receive a call at the same time.

Ro answered while Mitch listened. "Oh, Rosemary dear. It's a blessing to hear your voice." It was Martha O'Hara MacLane.

"It's wonderful to hear you as well. Jane and Rick are here nearby. Do you need them?" Ro wondered what might have prompted this call.

"That might be best, dear, if you would." Martha waited.

Mitch signaled to his parents to hurry over. "It's Gram. She wants to talk to you."

Jane accepted the phone. "Mom. We're here. Is there something wrong?"

"It's your father. The hospice nurse says his time is near. I thought you'd want to know." Martha spoke softly.

"Oh, Mom. Are you all right?" Jane asked in a rush.

"Oh, darlin', this has been coming for such a long time. I'm all right. Sad surely, but it's his time."

"Mitch can fly us up in the morning. Will there still be time?" Jane wondered.

"I canna say. But it should be fine. The guest room will be ready for ye." Martha's voice still carried the warmth of her Irish roots.

Mitch looked at Rick. "I can have you there by ten if you're ready to go by seven forty-five."

"Mom, we'll be there around ten tomorrow morning. Is there anything you need before we get there?" Jane was concerned about her aging mother.

"You and Rick are all the balm I'll need. And Mitchell, too, of course." The proud grandmother spoke from her hurting heart.

"We love you. We'll be there soon." Jane hung up the phone, and Rick took her in his arms. The crowd had gone silent. Mitch spoke clearly. "It's Mac. They think his time is coming soon."

There were gasps and hugs. Nick spoke first. "We need to call Dick and Betsy."

D-man added, "I need to tell Mom."

Ro handed her phone to D-man to make his call. Rick took the phone from Jane to call his parents. "What do I tell them?"

Mitch advised, "Tell them what we know and what we're doing tomorrow. If they want to be around friends, they can come here to wait for news."

Don suggested, "They may be shaken. We should offer to come pick them up and bring them here."

Rick nodded numbly.

Vic looked at Ro. "Until then, we all need to eat, and the food is getting cold. Let's share each other's company and support."

Ro pointed to D-man. "Time to use your DJ skills and play something appropriate."

Vic looked at Daniel. "Wanna help me handle the bar? I'm guessing it will be busy tonight."

Soon the crowd fell into the now-familiar Friday evening routine. The sound of conversation filled the space. Nick took Mercy's hand. "I guess I didn't think about Mac dying. Even when I saw him and he seemed so fragile. Why didn't I consider it?"

Mercy squeezed his hand. "It was better that you didn't. From what you've told me about that experience, you needed all your wits about you to be in the moment to get useful memories from him. If you had been looking at him as someone who was about to die, well, you might not have been as effective."

"Thank you for that. You make a good point. I wouldn't have known what to say. And now that's he's dying, I know I don't know what to say." Nick wore a haunted expression. "He's the first person I know who's…"

"Dying? That's right. You skipped over all those years of people passing away. Oh, Nick. How can I help you?" Mercy's realization startled her.

Ben and Michelle were speaking in low tones between themselves. "Do you think Robert will come?" Michelle asked Ben.

"A normal son would come. What we've heard about Robert is not that. Let's ask D-man." Ben moved to the DJ area as D-man keyed up the Nitty Gritty Dirt Band performing "*Will the Circle Be Unbroken.*"

As voices began to sing along with the familiar song, Ben leaned in to speak. "What are the chances Robert will be coming to Oregon?"

D-man looked up at the ceiling and then turned to Ben. "He loves his mother deeply. He may well be moved to come to her side. Rick and Jane should be prepared for that."

Michelle had joined them and added her thoughts about logistics. "How soon would he be able to get to Oregon?"

"That depends on where he is. We need to ask Gordy about Robert's whereabouts." D-man raised this possibility.

"I hadn't even considered that he wouldn't be on the East Coast. Do you know for certain he's on the move?" Ben was worried.

"The last I heard wasn't specific. We need to ask and soon." D-man turned to his duties again and keyed up "*I'll Fly Away*" by Alison Krauss and Gillian Welch in a new version of a song from the 1940s.

With the room singing along, D-man moved over to talk to Mitch. "Ben and Michelle brought up the question of the hour. Will Colonel Robert MacLane be flying to his mother's side? Has Gordy heard anything helpful?"

"Shit. I bet he'll do just that. I'll MRC Gordy right now." Mitch set his jaw and turned away.

D-man moved back to guide the mood in the room through music. Soon people were moving to the sounds of "*My Back Pages,*" Dylan's lyrical insights set to a singable tune.

The mood was serious but not somber as plates emptied and refilled. Daniel and Vic were relieved of bar duty by Beta and Fabian.

Tommy and Clary had both grabbed beers before anyone noticed and headed for the far end of the room. "I remember him. Mac that they're talking about." Tommy looked at his friend.

"Who is he then?" Clary was new to the web of connection in the room.

"In 1944 at Los Alamos, he was one of the military guys in charge." Tommy nursed the bottle of beer.

"So he's old, you're telling me?" Clary was trying to follow.

"It's hard to think of him being old. I think of him as he was just a few months ago. I'm not good with ages, but he sure wasn't old." Tommy was gazing into the distance.

"But that was long years ago, yes?" Clary was trying to get an image.

"I guess so. Sixty-four years. They're all old now. Look at my little sister. She's eighty!" Tommy was still amazed at the reality of what the years meant to his family.

"But Mac, he's being the one who started The Institute." Clary was starting to connect the dots.

"I guess."

"My God. It's Mac and Martha we're talkin' about. That's the Mac who's being about dying?" Clary had connected the final dot.

"I can't say. I didn't get to go to The Institute. I've only heard about it, but I think that's right." Tommy was a little worried about his friend.

"It be Fabian I need to be seeing." Clary moved away to find his fellow Irishman. Tommy looked around for someone to sit with. He spied Vic. She waved him over to join them.

"Lotta hubbub tonight." Don made space for the teenager at their table. "Is that a beer I see in your hand?"

"Yes, sir. I didn't think one could hurt." Tommy blushed.

"As long as it is just one." Don smiled the knowing smile of the father of sons.

Vic joined in. "It's a tough night. We all arrived in high spirits, and this news is so very sad. I know Mac has been ill for a long time. Even though it's not a surprise, it's sad all the same."

251

"Some of the older guys from school. The ones who enlisted right after Pearl Harbor. Some of them died. But we only heard about it. There were never any bodies to bury. There were some ceremonies. They were sad and long. They always seem to be so long. Why is that?" Tommy looked at his older friends at the table.

His sister reached for his young hand to take it in her wrinkled one. "It is a hard lesson you learn when someone near to you meets their death. This man, Mac, is a good man and has helped many of the people in the Pueblo. It is indeed sad that he is moving on, but do not fear for him. I know his spirit is strong."

Tommy looked at Theresa, her face familiar, even with the passage of sixty-four years. "You would know about spirits. Thank you. I feel a little better."

Daniel had joined them. "Don't ask me. I don't like funerals. I don't like to go to funerals. Or celebrations of life, as some people like to call them. Doesn't matter what you try to call them. What they are, are funerals." Daniel was not a fan.

Beta came over to see how things were going. "I'm thinking of calling Mom. She's a healer, and we're all going to need some healing."

"Now that is an excellent idea." Daniel smiled, remembering Lia Thompson, and lifted his glass in a toast.

"Do you think Mitch could fly her and John Henry back here before Christmas?" Beta started to smile at the thought.

"Well, my buddy Duke in Santa Fe has a small plane. I bet he'd do it. He still owes me a favor or two or three." Daniel was planning.

"I'll go ask Mitch now. I know he's hurting, but I need to know." Beta hurried off.

Don stood up to stretch. "I think I'm going to make some musical suggestions to our DJ. Maybe lighten the mood." Vic smiled and nodded her head in agreement.

CHAPTER 41

SATURDAY, DECEMBER 20, 2008, MIDMORNING ON THE OREGON COAST APPROACHING THE MACLANE'S CABIN

"I wish my stomach felt as calm as the flight was. No reflection on you. You're a talented pilot, son." Rick patted Mitch on the shoulder.

"There are plenty of reasons not to be calm. Gram is facing the last day or days of the man she loves. Mom is losing her father. Uncle Robert may show up with who knows what kind of attack. Yeah, calm is not a description of what's behind that door up there." Mitch was steering the rental car into the narrow driveway.

"Damn and double damn," Jane muttered.

The door had opened to reveal one grim-faced Colonel Robert MacLane.

"There's nothing for it but to face the situation, honey. I'll be at your side. Mitch, you get to back us up." Rick wasn't kidding about that last part.

By the time they got to the doorway, Martha had joined Robert to welcome them. Tears began to flow as mother and daughter hugged. Mitch and Rick stepped back, almost into Robert. "They're going to need a moment," Rick said to whoever cared to listen.

Mitch asked Robert, "Who's with Gramps?"

"Nurse." Robert spared no words.

253

"How is he?" Rick wanted more information.

"Nonresponsive." Again, Robert displayed his verbal skills.

Martha and Jane had recovered enough to join the three men still on the front porch, relieving Robert of the need to respond to questions. "Your father has had trouble swallowing for a day or so. The hospice nurses said that's a sign of the end nearing. Yesterday his eyes were open until almost noon. When they closed for a nap, they didn't reopen. I squeeze his hand, but he no longer squeezes back." Martha was drained sharing that news.

Jane pulled her mother inside to the small couch so they could sit together. "I'd like to see him, if that's all right."

"Of course, dear. They say he can hear you when you talk. I hope so. I keep telling him I love him, and it's okay to go when he's ready." Martha's smile was tired.

After Jane walked down the hall, Robert muttered, "I don't believe he can hear anything. And even if he could, what would it matter. That old man is dying, at last."

"Robert!" His mother was aghast. "How could you say that?"

"He never listened when he could. Why would he listen to me now?" His anger seethed.

"Where does this anger come from?" Martha was concerned about her son.

Rick and Mitch made themselves scarce by heading down the hall to join Jane.

"Dad never listened to me. I got tired of trying to talk sense into him." Robert crossed his arms in front of his chest.

"What was he supposed to hear?" Martha wanted her son to reveal the root of this uncomfortable anger.

"The Institute should have merged with DARPA. That's what he wouldn't hear." Robert spat out the words.

"You know very well why he said no to that. He learned at Los Alamos that innovation does not thrive within a government structure." Martha was confused.

"That's bullshit, and you know it. Plenty of innovation has come from structure." Robert began to pace.

"Mind your language, young man. Your father and I made the decision together to keep The Institute private and independent. So if that's the source of this anger, you can direct it to me as well." Martha's spirit was showing.

"I don't believe that. You always did what Dad wanted." Robert wasn't giving up.

Martha ignored the insult. "You know, behind most anger is fear. What are you so afraid of, Robert?" Martha's tone was soft but firm.

The steam ratcheted higher. "I'm not afraid of anything. You don't see it, do you? You chose her." His voice was still tight.

"Chose who?"

"My sainted, science-brained, overachieving sister, that's who." Robert's years of frustration showed. "Of course you don't see it, can't see it. Won't see it." His voice rose.

Jane interrupted, "Because there's nothing to see, that's why."

Martha shook her head slowly from side to side. "Oh, Robert, no. There's nothing like that at all."

"I repeat, bullshit, mother dear. I don't believe you." Robert stood and walked out to the front porch.

Rick had heard the exchange and returned to sit next to his mother-in-law and friend. "I'm so sorry, Martha. For Robert and for your loss." He put his arm around the older woman who only moments before had been fierce and now felt frail.

"If I've learned anything in my many years on this earth, ye canna save people from themselves. Robert is making choices. He wouldn't admit it, but he is." Martha was saddened by her own words.

"He is that. The fact that he is so stubborn concerns me because of his rank. Is anyone watching over him back at the Pentagon?" Rick stared after the man who had disappeared from sight.

"That they are. Before Mac went so far away, he would get an occasional call from a friend. They are indeed keeping an eye on Robert. And there are concerns." Martha was sad and relieved to divulge what she knew.

"Well, that's something then." Rick found the news prickly comfort.

Early Afternoon, Skyridge Ranch

D-man gathered the remaining visitors and residents together in the barn conference room. "We might as well be useful while we wait for news. Let's do our team reporting if you all agree." Heads nodded.

Vic started. "The movie team made progress this week. We think we have the cause for the social temporal displacement disorder. We had been trying to figure out what could trigger something so strange. Then it came to us. A time capsule. Whether he found one and opened it or just heard about it, a time capsule provides the connecting point in time. It just seemed to fit."

The room erupted into applause. "Brilliant!" Fabian declared.

"I like it." Nick was nodding yes.

"Makes as much sense as anything ever does in a movie." D-man grinned.

Daniel spoke next. "I may be telling tales out of school, but Rick spoke with me about the potential sale of the baseball cards from our very real time capsule. He put out feelers in collector's circles and has an offer to buy the lot from a private collector who chooses to remain anonymous. Rick wanted suggestions for an attorney who could set up a trust and a foundation. It's a whole lotta money."

"That's great news." Don smiled at Daniel.

"What does that mean exactly?" Tommy asked.

Daniel explained. "The details need to be worked out, but there will be enough money that some of it can help your friends who are now getting older. The rest will be in a trust protected for you and from private investigators so that you have enough time to figure out your life without having to worry about how to make a buck."

Charlie patted him on the back, and Nick nodded his pleasure at the news. "Okay, I guess that's good. I like to work, but I wasn't sure what I'd do in these times." Tommy half smiled.

Ben spoke up. "Michelle and I have been giving the Robert problem a lot of thought." Heads nodded around the room. "We'll check with Gordy to make sure, but from what we can gather, Colonel Robert MacLane hasn't shown any interest in the real mysteries at Los Alamos. And they are, how did Dave Gustafson die and why, what happened to Marilyn Bledsoe the spy, and what the hell happened to the machine or chamber or whatever you want to call it, that Nick, Dick, and the others built."

"Thank you. I was wondering if anyone else cared about the real mysteries." D-man was pleased.

Michelle picked up the thread. "Many of you know that I used to write for a national online tabloid, and it was less than reputable. It remains drawn to outrageous conspiracy theories, and the editor loves a juicy story involving the government." Grins appeared on faces around the room.

"What if Sedona Searsy, yours truly, were to write an article about this cluster of mysteries and then let it leak that one very important colonel was aware of said unsolved murders and spy threats and did *nothing*." Michelle sat back.

This time people stood and clapped and hooted.

"You go girl!" Ro shouted.

"Give 'em hell." This was Vic.

Ben looked at Daniel. "Any downside from where you're sitting, Counselor?"

"No, as a matter of fact I like it a lot. Why? Because it's the truth. I enjoy standing beside truth tellers. I'll do that any day." Daniel was nodding at Ben and Michelle.

Tommy glanced at Clary, who nodded in the affirmative. "We have something to tell you." Tommy got shy.

Clary stood up to join him. "So it's talking about gifts we are. Tommy has it for the earth and rocks then be mine. As if you weren't already knowing it."

Mercy joined them. "For you uninitiated into the realm of people with unusual gifts, you recall that my grandmother communicates with spirits, and my work in the quantum realm builds on our shared gift. My mother is a healer, my sister can make plants, well anything, grow; and Tommy shares that gift of connecting with the earth, and now Clary. His family, too, has gifts. Clary here can feel rocks. And he hears them, not in words, but as if an elemental from the Druidic tradition is communicating with him."

Darcy was excited, turning to Vic and Ro. "Can we use this in the movie? Oh, please let's use this in the movie."

Don looked at the young men. "Well done, well done. And thank you for the courage to share something so personal."

Ro felt a buzz in her pocket. "Hang on, everybody. Might be Mitch. "Ro was stone-faced as she heard." He's there and in rare form."

"Tell me what we should do." Ro shook her head to the listening crowd.

"As soon as we know what his plans are, I'll let you know if you need to initiate a return to The Institute. So far Mac is still with us, and so is Robert." Mitch spoke softly. "Later, gotta go."

Ro shared the news. Vic spoke. "Do we really think he'll come back here for the burial?"

D-man was grim. "He's just enough of a son of a bitch to do it. It makes no sense, but Robert has stopped making sense."

Ro turned to Michelle. "How fast can Sedona get that story to the online rag?"

"I wrote it on the drive here. It's ready now." Michelle grinned.

Daniel held up his hands. "Let's think about timing. In order to throw Robert off the track and keep him from Skyridge, how much time do we need and how long will it take for the story to percolate?"

"I can make sure it also gets to national news outlets. It should be a matter of hours if it's a slow news day." Michelle was sure of herself in this familiar territory. "So far, the most interesting headline I saw was that the FBI agent who was Deep Throat for those two *Washington Post* reporters died."

"I think there's irony here. Give me a minute. "Don looked rueful.

"One more call. Let's ask Gordy if he's picked up anything." Ben suggested.

Ro was ahead of him. Her MRC in hand, she texted the tech whiz. Her phone rang a few seconds later. "Hey, Foot. Things are getting serious. Mac is about to die. Rick, Jane, and Mitch are up there. So is Robert. We have a story from Michelle that she can drop to both legit and questionable news outlets that might distract Robert from this trail. Have you heard anything that would cause us to hold off?"

"No, in fact, it's a great time. The scientists are laughing at him, and there is rumbling in other circles that he's losing it. Let's push him." Gordy clicked off.

"All systems go. Michelle, do you need to head back to town to plant the story?" Ro was in head-of-school mode.

"That would be best. Vic, may I go back to your place, or should I go back to The Institute?" Michelle hesitated.

"Let's go to my office. If anyone tracks a true story to its origins and finds out it came from my office, I'll be ready for them." Daniel's smile had a sinister glint.

Vic hugged her brother. "You have your scary-lawyer face on. Be off with you. We'll see you in a few hours. Travel safely."

Nick's Notes
Saturday, December 20, 2008

Sad, but not unexpected, news today. Mac is near death. The idea of hospice care is new to me, but it makes a great deal of sense. According to their nurse, Mac is very near the end. How amazing to think that such knowledge exists now.

The next concern is over his son Robert. What will he do? Will he be a problem for us? What kind of trouble could he make? Mercy is right when she tells me not to worry. So much is out of my hands, our hands. As a precaution, we are all prepared for a quick departure, and all of my notes are secure. I suppose knowing that something is pending is better than being surprised.

Thinking of being prepared, I have enjoyed learning to drive, again. Learning with an automatic transmission is both easy and way too relaxing. I could imagine my attention drifting. And just the thought of talking on one of the tiny telephones that Charlie, and everyone else, has is unthinkable.

The movie tonight, *White Christmas*, was heartwarming. I remember Bing Crosby and Rosemary Clooney but from radio and not movies. That makes sense because this movie was made after the

War. But the nostalgia for the bonds between friends made me tear up. Interesting that a movie from so long ago is considered a classic and required viewing every year. Mercy said that it's not Christmas until she watches this movie.

Maybe that is why I am so comfortable around her. She appreciates aspects of my life from before. It may be years until that life feels like history. Right now, it's still just my life.

CHAPTER 42

SUNDAY, DECEMBER 21, 2008, JUST AFTER BREAKFAST AT SKYRIDGE RANCH

MRCs were buzzing with alerts, and short messages as residents and visitors hurried to prepare for the unknown.

"Michelle, have you heard anything yet about Sedona's story?" Ro stopped her as she headed for the barn classroom.

"Gordy said he would watch. I expect that once I can check my phone, there will be an avalanche of texts from my old bosses." Michelle both dreaded and looked forward to the familiar hyperbole and innuendo to come.

"Thank you for being willing to step back into that world. Ben said that you were relieved to leave it behind. Only Robert could make me even think to ask you to consider this." Ro grimaced.

"Sometimes it's where you have to play when you're dealing with scumbags." Michelle's smile twisted.

"I hope it's worth it. For you and for our cause." Ro began to walk away.

"Me too. I hope this isn't one of the 'careful what you ask for' situations. D-man better be ready." Michelle pulled her backpack up over her shoulder.

Vic, Don, and Daniel cradled coffee mugs and watched the action from the front porch of the main house. "She's sharp. We're lucky to have her on our team." Daniel nodded toward Michelle.

Don nodded. "Couldn't agree more. I was so relieved when Ben was finally able to pull the truth out of her and realize that she is a normal person. And one with ethics and values. There are fewer and fewer like her out there today. I worry for Charlie."

Vic patted him on the forearm. "Don't you give Charlie another thought. Remember how he was getting along with Elaine on Thanksgiving? And now Darcy? Honey, your son is a babe magnet. Not that he knows it."

Don nearly choked on his coffee, Daniel did. They both sputtered. "Babe magnet? Charlie?"

"Of course, you don't see it. He's good-looking, funny, totally without airs, and so very smart. How can any girl resist?" Vic smiled.

"When you put it that way. I guess he could be." Don smiled.

"Then I guess I can count myself lucky that my daughter fell for the large Irishman?" Daniel teased.

"To be sure, Nicholas Fabian the Third has met his match. Nicola wouldn't be happy with someone who didn't challenge her." Vic smiled at the thought of her niece with the dark-haired, blue-eyed charmer.

Ro slumped down next to them. "I really hope we don't have to see all of you disappear just because Robert is an ass."

Vic reached out to touch her forearm. "I think the movie team needs to stay right here. If we all leave, it may look suspicious. And having to spend the holidays on location, if that's what this is, is perfectly normal for a film crew. We're all nomads. I think just the at-risk among us should make themselves scarce."

Daniel nodded. "My brilliant and savvy sister makes a good point. Let's keep a full complement here."

Don nodded. "Who should prepare to head back, and back to where?"

Ro paused. "Only as far as The Institute, maybe. Robert wouldn't dare, at least I hope he wouldn't dare, intrude there. Ben, Michelle, Nick, Mercy, Mitch, Beta, Tommy, and Clary. Theresa and Paul too. Anyone else?"

The others nodded in agreement. Ro stood. "Then let's gather in the barn and let everyone know our thinking." She moved to ring the large iron triangle used to call people to meals.

Heads swiveled, and bodies began to move toward the familiar converted barn. Ro moved to the head of the room.

"Thank you all for responding so quickly. We want to share our concerns, and we appreciate your grasp of the serious nature of this threat. Once we have an idea whether or not Robert is planning to come to the funeral, we'll let you know and then put our plan into action. If he's coming, the movie team will stay in place to reinforce the credibility of the story. The rest of you will hightail it back to The Institute. No, not to your homes, not yet. This will be a short incursion, if it happens at all, and Christmas is Thursday, and we want you all here to celebrate."

Heads bobbed and smiles were shared.

Ro felt the familiar buzz of her MRC. The message was brief. Her eyes filled. "Mac is gone."

More eyes filled and hugs were shared.

Charlie stood. "How soon do you think we'll know?"

D-man leaned back in his chair and announced. "Don't know, but until I do, I want to raise a glass to one of the finest men I ever knew."

Voices calling out "Hear, hear" filled the barn.

Vic called out, "Who's bartending?"

Her brother stood. "I will if I can have some help bringing out the booze."

Half a dozen helpers leaped to help. Soon there were drinks, toasts, and stories began to circulate from those who knew them to tell.

Nick stood and raised his glass. "Mac never got in our way. He fought for the project. He was a good man. I want to carry on my work in his memory. To Mac."

"To Mac," echoed in the space.

"And Martha." This was Ro.

"To Martha," the voices filled the air.

Nick's Notes
Sunday, December 21, 2008

We got the call. Mac died today. I can't imagine what Martha is feeling. So many years married to him. My memories of her from school are still so fresh. She was passionate about teaching. I saw that in her still when I went to Oregon to see them.

And Mac. He was a good man. What Dick has told me about what happened after the experiment tells me I wasn't forgotten. Mac didn't need to keep looking, but he did. He kept believing. I think that was even more important. The Institute is the legacy he leaves behind.

Mercy warned me that Mac's death could bring up a lot of feelings for me. I am sad. More than just Mac dying. She says it's normal. That doesn't help me. I feel helpless. It's not a time to feel helpless when we may have trouble coming.

I used to resent studying Shakespeare when it took me away from science, but now I'm remembering a line from Hamlet. He was talking about his father. "I shall not look on his like again." I wish Mac's son felt that way.

CHAPTER 43

MONDAY, DECEMBER 22, 2008, HOME OF LIA THOMPSON IN NORTHERN NEW MEXICO

Lia answered the special phone she had been given by Mitchell Stans. "This is Lia."

"Good morning." It was Mitch, and she smiled. He continued. "I wish I had good news for you. Mac, my gramps, died yesterday, and his son, my Uncle Robert, is about to arrive in Los Alamos looking to stir up the past and maybe a lot of trouble."

"I'm sitting down now. Walk me through this again, please." Lia was still learning who was who.

"Sure. And I'm sorry this is so abrupt. We just got the news about Gramps yesterday. He was diagnosed with Alzheimer's almost nine years ago, but when he neared the end, the deterioration accelerated." Mitch filled in some background.

"It can happen that way. I've seen it with some of the seniors around here. All you can do is make them comfortable and relieve any fears." Lia nodded to the phone as if it could see her.

"My Uncle Robert is a career military man and was estranged from my grandfather. Just recently, he showed up on our radar at The Institute again."

"Oh, that's right, Darren Hickson reached out to him about his birth father." Lia recalled the confession.

"Even though Robert has been told about the movie and the real mysteries, he has decided to chase conspiracy theories."

"Let me guess? Teleportation and time travel? Because it's a threat to national security." Lia could speculate about the implied yet nonexistent threat.

"Exactly. We've tried to throw him off by explaining the movie development. But he's still pursuing the conspiracy. Our sources reported to me this morning that he's headed to Los Alamos. I wanted you and John Henry to be ready. And to get to the Geezers and ask them to keep their mouths closed about the time capsule." Mitch had gotten to the point.

"I can see your concern. I'll call JH, and we'll head over to the coffee shop as soon as I hang up. Any idea of Robert's ETA?" Lia was looking for her phone and her purse.

"He'll be flying in from Oregon. At least that's where he was yesterday. I haven't checked commercial flights." Mitch was not feeling better about this.

"Don't worry, Mitch. We can handle whatever Robert decides to throw at us. Remember, we've had military types around here for more than sixty-five years. We know how to share non-fact facts." Lia smiled.

"Be careful. We don't want any consequences to be directed your way." Mitch was now a little worried about what might happen.

"And after this Robert comes, what then? Are John Henry and I coming there for Christmas? And if so, I'd like to bring Rose. It's hard on her when I'm gone." Lia was shifting the conversation to a happier topic.

"We hope he won't be there long. I can fly up to get you all on Christmas Eve morning. Will that work?" Mitch was smiling now.

"That will be perfect. I can get friends to take care of the house and the rest of the critters. How do you want me to let you know what I find here?" Lia thought she knew but needed confirmation.

"Continue to use this phone until we're…well, maybe for a long time. It's the only secure method we have." Mitch was grim.

"That confirms what I thought. Over and out or whatever you say in this situation." Lia chuckled.

There was a smile in Mitch's voice when he replied, "Over and out, Lia."

Her next call was to John Henry Ontiveros. "Morning, JH, what've you got on your schedule?" Lia was cagey.

"Nothing that can't be adjusted if you need something." Lia and her girls were family.

"I do. Why don't you meet me for coffee downtown in ten minutes." Lia was heading for her door.

"I can be there in five. I'll be sitting with Abuelo and gang." John Henry was already in his truck and made a quick course adjustment.

"I'll see you there." Lia clicked off and smiled.

When she arrived at the coffee shop, the Geezer Gang was in good form. She could hear laughter. She sat down and greeted them all. "Buenos dias and good morning, mis amigos. I have a favor to ask," she began.

Heads turned to look at her with curiosity. "For you, hija, anything." Butch Ontiveros smiled.

"Remember when the young people came to visit, and you found the time capsule?" Heads nodded, and they smiled. "I need to you to forget that if a military man comes and asks you questions. He is not a friend."

John Henry put his mug down. "Better give me a little more than that."

"Okay. The man and woman who started The Institute have a son who doesn't like or respect them. He is headed here and may want to stir up trouble." Lia tried to keep it simple.

"What is this military man called?" Henry wanted to know.

"Colonel Robert MacLane." Lia spat out the name.

"Holy shit, Lia. Robert's coming?" JH asked. "I thought he was made up. I guess not."

She nodded. "He's investigating the old stories about the experiment. So let's not say anything that could hurt our friends. He knows that a team of people is writing a movie script, and it involves Los Alamos in 1944. That's why those people were here."

The old men all nodded. "We can just play like we forgot everything. Maybe we're not playing." Henry smiled.

"It's okay to talk about the movie. But not the time capsule. Okay? Now I have to talk to a few more people. Thank you." Lia hugged each one and headed for the door. John Henry followed.

They spoke in the parking lot out of earshot. "And if you want to share Christmas at Skyridge, Mitch is coming Christmas Eve morning to give us a ride. I'm bringing Rose." Lia smiled.

"Man, I would love that. Let me make sure little brother is all set. But hell yes, I'm coming. For how long?" JH was grinning.

"I think I can be there until a few days after New Year's. Does that work for you?" Lia was thinking and planning ahead.

"I think that works. We really have nothing big going on between Christmas and New Year's. It gives the guys on the crew a chance to spend time with their families." JH was nodding.

"I'll let Mitch know. Now who else do we need to talk to about this threat?" Lia looked around.

"The newspaper because Mitch was asking about old issues. The historical museum, same thing. Face it, a large black dude is memorable around here." JH was recounting and retracing their steps. "And the security guard. My buddy. He gave us a chance to go look for rocks. He loves to mess with the visiting military types."

"Can you think of anyone else?" Lia was wracking her brain. "Your brother? Do you need to fill him in just in case? Oh, the high school! I almost forgot."

"Not a bad plan, plus he'll have abuelo duty when I'm gone." JH was nodding in agreement.

"Mitch didn't know exactly when Colonel Threat was arriving, but it should be today. I'll check back with you as soon as I've had my conversations with the newspaper, the high school, and the museum. I hope the movie story works. At least it gives them something to say that sounds credible. And I guess now they really are working on a movie. Vic has investors!" Lia moved toward her truck.

"Go figure." JH walked back to the café. "I'll give the gals in the café a heads-up too."

Lia slapped her forehead in mock dismay. "Of course. Good thing you remembered."

Midafternoon, Los Alamos Airport

The helicopter stirred up dust and gravel when it circled and landed near the main military hangar. The man who got out didn't speak to the pilot but headed for the open door of the gray metal building.

"Welcome, Colonel. We got word this morning that you were coming. Didn't get much info on this visit. How can we help you?" The young man greeting him was accustomed to visits from military brass, but usually, he knew the purpose of the visit.

"All I need is a car and a driver who knows the area." Robert was terse.

"Then we can help. I have an SUV and a driver ready. Just let me—"

Robert interrupted, "Just point me in the direction."

The young officer pointed to the door Robert had just come through. "On your right, sir."

Robert charged out of the building toward the startled man in fatigues leaning against the SUV. He jerked to attention. Robert barked, "Get in and drive. I'm looking for information on some people who were here the day after Thanksgiving. I'll start downtown."

The driver headed toward the heart of the town. There were only a handful of places to visit, and he knew a parking lot where he could stop and let this cranky visitor get out. "This is a central place, sir. Do you want me to come along?"

"No, just wait here. I won't be long." Robert slammed the door and headed for the coffee shop.

With each stop, he heard the same thing. Movie people had been here. One of them a big black man. Very nice and polite. The museum, the newspaper, the high school, all the same basic story. Nice people, working on a movie.

"Shit," Robert muttered to himself. "They know more than they're telling. I just know it."

Back in the SUV, he told the driver. "Head out to the Pueblo. Maybe someone out there knows something."

"I'm not familiar with that area, sir." The driver only knew the general direction. "I've only been here a month. Do you want me to radio for another driver who knows more?"

"No. Just get me out there. You can do that much, can't you?" Robert was in no mood.

"Yes, sir." He put in the GPS information, and a map appeared on a small screen.

Before long, they pulled up to a small building with a sign out front that said "Pueblo Council." Inside a middle-aged woman sat at a welcome desk.

"May I help you?" she said this with a gentle smile, aware that the man in uniform standing in front of her was agitated.

"There were outsiders visiting the area after Thanksgiving. I need to know what they were looking for and what they may have found." Robert was out of patience, not that he had much to begin with.

"Ah, the young people. Yes, they came here, but they just talked with a few of the old people here. People who like to tell stories." She nodded.

"What kind of stories?"

"The old days."

"What old days?"

"When they were strong and brave." She was still smiling and nodding.

"I don't think you understand. I want to know about 1944." Robert was increasingly frustrated.

"Yes, the old days."

"Where are these people?"

"They mostly go to the coffee shop in town." She was still smiling and nodding.

"I talked with them. Are there others?" Robert was turning red.

"Most of them are dead now. Their spirits visit." She nodded again.

"Then what do the spirits say." Robert was more than skeptical.

"They said an angry man would come looking for something. They said he would not find what he was looking for here." She smiled at him.

"Oh, for God's sake." He turned and walked out the door. The woman kept smiling as she watched him get into the SUV and drive off. Then she picked up her cell phone and dialed a number. "You were right, John Henry. He was here. And he was angry, like you said. I do not think he will return." She hung up the phone and chuckled.

Robert was seething. "Take me back to the airport. This was a waste of time."

Gordy Chambers's Office, Somewhere in Los Angeles

"Mitch? Robert blew in and blew out of Los Alamos. Not sure what he may have learned, but he was on the ground for less than two hours." Gordy was on a secure line but was keeping his messages brief.

"Thanks, Foot. I'll reach out to my other sources and let you know what I find out." Mitch hung up and turned to share the news. On a screen were his parents and grandmother. "Robert spent less than two hours on the ground in Los Alamos. I need to call John Henry and find out what he knows."

"When will you be back here?" his mother wanted to make plans.

"I should land right at dusk. Is there anything I can bring you?" Mitch was preparing his flight plan.

"Just you. We'll be ready with dinner when you arrive. And then we're returning tomorrow, yes?" This was his father.

"Yes. We can leave whenever you're ready in the morning. I have the ground crew ready here to receive Gramps's remains when we land and take everyone out to Skyridge." Mitch had laid the plans long before he needed to put them into action.

"Then we'll see you in the morning. We love you." His grandmother's voice quavered.

CHAPTER 44

TUESDAY, DECEMBER 23, 2008, SKYRIDGE RANCH

With the news of Mac's death, the rhythm at the Ranch changed. Clary had not yet had a chance to track down the man he needed to see.

"Mr. Grant, might I be talking with you?" Clary had finally found Don Grant.

"Sure, son, what's on your mind?" Don smiled at the wiry teenager.

"It be the rock then, the one you were for bringing back with you." Clary was eager.

"Of course. I'm sorry I didn't think of this sooner. I hear you have a sense about these things." Don smiled.

"I do that. Where does it be now, if it isn't a bother for you." Clary was focused.

"It's in the main house. Shall we go take a look?" Don turned around to head toward the sprawling Ranch house.

"Please, let's do. I'm having been with the smaller ones, and an idea is about to be growing, but clearer it might be when the bigger one is in my fingers." Clary wanted to explain the importance of this.

As they walked, Don took on his familiar teacher role. "Tell me what you think and why you think it."

"Strange it is for sure and not being at all scientific." Clary was leery of sharing what he had felt when he handled the small round, black stones.

"I think we've moved beyond the limits of science; don't you agree?" Don smiled at the young man.

"That we have, sir. That we have." Clary was relieved. "When holding the wee stones I was, they were feeling, they were feeling like babies. Now most of the rocks I handle, sure they be truly old. Being on this earth a long time they are. These ones, they are not being like that at all."

Don and Clary had reached the porch. "Now that's an interesting observation and well said. Let's go find the big rock and see what it feels like." Don opened the door, looking forward to hearing what this prodigy would say next.

Ro and Vic looked up when Don and Clary walked into the kitchen. "What an interesting pair. What brings you here now? Fresh coffee? Muffins are still in the oven. You're about ten minutes early, but you're welcome to wait." Vic smiled at them both expecting to hear a reply having to do with food.

"We're here to handle a rock. Ro, will you open the safe for us?" Don raised his eyebrows and tilted his head toward Clary, signifying who was in the lead.

"Happy to oblige. Let's go. Vic, will you watch the oven?" Ro smiled at her fellow writer.

In her office, Ro lifted a painting from the wall revealing a metal plate about ten inches square with a digital numeric pad on it. A few quick presses and the door released. "I presume it's the round black rock you're interested in?"

"That be the one." Clary had his hands extended.

Don nodded, and Ro handed the wrapped bundle to Clary. He gently moved the padding aside to reveal the smooth black surface. He set the padding on her desk and held the rock in one hand, then the other, then he cradled it in both hands. His eyes were closed and his breathing even. More than even. He was taking deep breaths, almost like he was breathing in the rock as well as holding it. Suddenly he sat down.

"Gah! It be like I said to you. Babies, they're being for sure in this world. It's all new for them. It's not knowing where they are then, and nothing be familiar or known to them. Mighty confused they be." Clary was marveling at the rock in his hand. "Miss Ro, would ye turn on the lamp here? I'm for trying something out." Clary looked at Ro's halogen desk lamp.

When she turned it on Clary's eyes grew big. "Ach. I thought so. It's liking the light. That be sorely odd for a rock. Makes me wonder if it be light had something to do with how they be here." Clary stroked the rock as if to soothe it.

"Should I turn the light off, now?" Ro was both curious and concerned.

Clary nodded yes. "It be more confused when the light is being on. Huh. Out to the sunshine, let's be going." Clary moved, and the two adults followed with rapt attention to what this youngster was revealing through his gift.

When they stood on the porch, Clary opened his hands to let the rock feel the sun. "Sure, and I'm for having almost the same feeling, but I'm thinking it be knowing the difference, then, from manmade and natural. Curious, I'm thinking."

"That, young man, is an understatement." Don smiled broadly. "I think we need the scientists to hear what you've told us. They may have some theories."

Ro took out her MRC and sent out a quick text to gather. "Why don't you head to the barn. Everyone should be there soon. I'll help Vic with the muffins and join you as soon as we can."

When they were all in the barn, Don asked Clary to tell the small group what he had just shared. Charlie, Nick, Fabian, Nicola, and D-man looked at each other. After the teen finished talking, Charlie spoke first. "If these rocks are attracted to light, maybe Nick's experiment triggered something in them. You used light, right?"

Nick nodded. "We did, and we had a lot of power. It could have been a very strong attraction."

Nicola was thinking differently. "But why. If these are baby rocks, as you say, Clary. What do babies want?" The men at the table looked at her blankly. "They want their mother, dummies."

Fabian scoffed. "So the baby rocks are wanting their rock mommy. You're daft."

Nick smiled. "Maybe, maybe not. Remember what Simon Constantine said in the quantum realm: 'Find the source.' Maybe the rocks are trying to find the source too."

"If we think of Mommy as the source, then where does that leave us?" Charlie was thinking out loud.

D-man's eyes grew round. "The rocks wanted a ride. They perceived Nick's light source as a way home."

"Why do I hear ET?" Don grinned.

"They didn't want to phone home; they wanted a ride home. Little did they know that they were the ride." Nick was nodding to himself. "I think they rode the light, but they also directed it."

"Whoa. Now that's a theory." Charlie leaned back in his chair.

D-man had scrunched his face hard, and when he looked up, he said one word. "Waves. They rode the waves. They didn't know where they might go, but they felt the particles, they felt the movement." Heads nodded. He continued. "And if my theory about the quantum tsunami is even partially right, these visitors either caused the Tsunami or played a part in it."

"Maybe not so daft after all," Fabian admitted. "The particle waves, of course, sure we know about. But how might the waves be influenced? That's a question, isn't it?"

Charlie picked up the thought. "If the waves didn't collapse. If they expanded. Then maybe, just maybe, we get Nick and Tommy here in 2008."

Ro arrived in time to hear that last bit of the conversation. "Hold all of these thoughts. I just heard from Mitch. We have an ETA of 3:00 p.m., folks. When Rick, Jane, Martha, and Mitch arrive, we need to be ready to either hold the interment ceremony or at least gather to grieve. I don't know what they have in mind. He asked me to let Beta and Paul know to come out as soon as they can. I've called Dick and Betsy. They'll bring Gail too."

Nicola stood up. "What can we do, how can we help?"

Vic had just arrived with the muffins. "First, everybody take a muffin and some coffee. Then we'll figure out who does what."

The group nodded, passed around the basket, and brought pots of coffee to the now filling tables in the barn.

Dusk at Skyridge Ranch

The procession of friends and family wound its way through the vineyard up to the top of a ridge overlooking the familiar valley. "Mac always loved this view," Martha breathed out.

A green burial had been permitted. The grave was only a few feet deep because the body was wrapped in a mushroom shroud to promote rapid decomposition and Mac's return to this place he loved. Once he was carefully interred and covered with moist soil, Martha faced the group. "Mac thanks you, and I thank you for your love. Now he wouldn't want sadness. There is joy in this next adventure for him. I'll miss him. I'll mourn him, but I canna be sad. Not for knowing him and certainly not for loving him. A finer man..." She couldn't continue.

"And a finer friend. He stood for something. I'm proud to have known him and called him my friend." Dick's voice was unsteady. Betsy and Theresa stood on either side of him, a united front of war-era witnesses mourning the passing of one of theirs.

"I imagine George will be happy for some company out here by his bench." Rick smiled at the thought.

Martha smiled widely. "Now there's a fine thought. It's one I'll hold onto in the coming days. You'll find me sitting on this bench. And I'll be talking to them, so don't worry when ye hear me."

Jane hugged her mother. "I love that image."

Rick stepped next to Jane, and she pulled her mother into a three-way hug before they walked slowly toward back toward dinner in the barn.

Don gripped Vic's hand, and they didn't speak for a long time. As if to himself, Don softly said, "I didn't know what to expect and how I might feel."

"I was worried, mostly for you. I didn't know how much emotion might come up." Vic turned to take both of his hands.

"That makes two of us." He squeezed her hands. "I'm okay. The feelings washed over me. It felt somehow soft, almost not even sad."

"That's unexpected, yes? Maybe it's the Skyridge effect." Vic looked at his face and realized he was smiling.

"Yes. I'm okay with that and with us." They started the winding walk to the barn and dinner.

Nicola was walking alone, and Fabian caught up with her. "I'm okay, you don't need to worry about me." She smiled as she looked up at him.

"It's not so much a worry over you, then it's care I'm feeling. And there was more than a bit of emotion just then. "He stopped to check and see what he could read on her face.

"That's sweet and kind. I did feel a lot, and then it slipped away. I can recall it and not be sad. Pretty amazing, actually." She shook her head slightly.

"Well, you must know that it's you that's being amazing. No surprise here. "He took her hand as they followed the others slowly toward the gathering group and a big dinner.

The group on the ridge thinned as people began to wander back to the barn for dinner. Nick and Mercy were the last to leave. "I think I just want to sit here for a little while, if you don't mind," Nick said.

Mercy squeezed his hand. "May I stay with you?"

"I hoped you would." Nick smiled and squeezed back.

"I feel him. At least I think I do." Marcy had her eyes closed.

"How does he feel?" Nick was always curious about Mercy's gift.

"At peace, but not quite. He's going to be around for a while, I think. Sometimes that happens." She turned to look at Nick.

"If you say so." He smiled back.

Nick's Notes
Tuesday, December 23, 2008

Mac was buried here at Skyridge today. They called it a green burial. He didn't have a casket. Someone they know made a shroud of mushrooms. By wrapping his body in that shroud decomp would be quicker. What a thought and what a concept. My parents never talked about such a thing.

I wonder what Grace wants. Maybe Vic knows. No, she would have told Father Joe.

Mercy said that lots of people have been choosing cremation rather than a traditional burial. It's kind of a grim topic, but with Mac dying, the discussion turned to how people wanted their deaths to be handled.

I suppose talking about it is better than leaving your loved ones wondering. I like becoming part of the earth again rather than being burned up. Even though I know I wouldn't feel anything, it's just a gentler thought. Yes, I think a green burial. I'll tell Mercy that's what I want too.

CHAPTER 45

WEDNESDAY, DECEMBER 24, 2008, SKYRIDGE RANCH

Shortly after lunch, Mitch drove up with Lia, John Henry, and a very excited Rose. Feynman and Samantha Jane rushed the car to greet the new member of their furry tribe. Lia laughed. "This will be so good for her. She spends too much time with people and chickens. These two will give her a good run."

The crowd on hand swarmed to welcome the newest arrivals. Voices rose, and words like rocks, waves, breakthrough, green burial, and more were on the air. Lia looked for her girls. "Mercy? Beta?"

John Henry hung back with Mitch as two identical faces parted the crowd to hug their mother. "There's so much to tell you." Mercy said first. "Where's G-ma?" Beta noticed her grandmother was not among the crowd.

"She was with Paul the last I saw," Beta recalled.

"Is she all right?" Lia said with concern.

"Oh yes, they just really enjoy talking about the mind-body stuff that Paul's into." Mercy smiled.

"You had me worried for a minute," Lia softly chided them.

"She likes to spend time with him, and she and Dick and Betsy are thick as thieves. And now they have Martha as well." Beta had noticed.

"Can you blame them? Sometimes it's nice to have people around who know the same history, recognize a reference to early radio or movies," Lia explained.

Vic appeared at their sides. "Let's get your mom to her casita. You don't want to miss dinner and movie night."

"What's the movie tonight?" Lia was smiling.

"We thought we'd try a modern classic. Yikes, can you even say those two words together? *Love Actually* is the feature tonight." Vic chuckled.

"Oh, I love that one." Darcy had joined them. "And you can too say modern classic. I should know, I teach them." They all laughed.

Nick's Notes
Wednesday, December 24, 2008

I can't get over how many people we have here. Ro says that every bed is full. And it's hard to believe it's already Christmas Eve. It seems like Thanksgiving was yesterday.

We needed the respite of a festive meal. And families are together, even mine. I have Vic, Nicola, and Daniel. It still stuns me that I have so much family in this time and that they are each amazing. I have a lot to be thankful for. We called Grace. She's spending the holiday with Father Joe and Amy June. She loves her new dog.

Yesterday we may have made a breakthrough. Young Clary has an amazing gift with rocks. He told Tommy about it because Tommy has a gift too. If Clary is right, then the smooth black rocks are the anomaly we were looking for. But we don't know exactly how they had the effect they did. This is not scientific at all, and still, I believe what they tell me. Interesting.

Mercy suggested I take a break from questions for a night and try a state of gratitude. Better than quantum, I suppose. I'll have to tease her about that.

The movie tonight was called *Love Actually*. I didn't quite understand the title, but the intertwining stories were skillfully told. I enjoyed it. So many people. All connected. It felt a lot like Skyridge. I hope we can all be just as happy.

Nick's Notes
Thursday, December 25, 2008

It was a quiet day. Instead of gifts, there has been no time to go shopping, we shared memories and Christmas traditions. I learned more than I expected to. Mercy and Beta and Lia talked of lining driveways with luminarias. Theresa recalled making Christmas tamales. That made my mouth water.

Don, Ben, and Charlie remembered Ruth and how she would make dozens of decorated cookies. Paul and John Henry sang a few carols in Spanish. They sounded great.

Rick and Jane talked about their first Christmas after Mitch arrived. It sounded so special. D-man and Darcy remembered Serenity. Her tradition was an open house for neighbors and refugees. I guess we are those refugees this year.

Fabian and Clary told of Irish holidays and the stories of fairies and selkies. Vic, Daniel, and Nicola laughed about reading "A Christmas Carol" with extra dramatic effects. I can only imagine.

It all sounds so beautiful and intimate. Mercy kept watch on me. She whispered that I was sticking to my plan to live rather than observe. Especially when I was asked about the Christmases I remember. The last couple weren't so good. I tried to put myself back with Mother, Father, and Grace. I just don't seem to see much of anything when I recall memories. I think the holidays were modest. That may also reflect the scarcity of food and goods. I think that's it.

Mercy says people protect themselves from feeling pain, emotional pain, by denying facts. That sounds impossible to me. How can a fact be denied? She said that withdrawing from people is another way to try to be protected from being hurt. She said that sometimes people do it without being aware that they are doing it. I'm pretty sure I do that. There has been so much pain since Pearl Harbor. It's easier to focus on today and new people. But today, hearing my friends talk about their sadness was hard. I think I have been good at protecting myself from pain.

Sometimes I think about what I left behind, the people mostly. I have mixed feelings. I know I don't want to go back. Every day I'm more at ease with the new inventions, new styles, new everything. And still, watching a classic movie, what they all call my movies, can send me back in time through my memories. It can be overwhelming, that sense that I belong in the movie, maybe not here. Mercy says it's normal. I wonder if it will ever end.

Overall, this may be my best Christmas ever. It all feels new and heartfelt. I look forward to next year. I haven't been able to say that in a long time.

CHAPTER 46

FRIDAY, DECEMBER 26, 2008, SKYRIDGE RANCH

Lia offered to lead a ceremony to remember and celebrate Mac and all the friends and family lost by those gathered at the Ranch. The group assembled along the ridge near the new gravesite.

The practiced healer spoke in a husky voice. "We begin by burning some sage and listening to the rhythm of the drum. Let the sage smoke and the rhythm seep into you as you close your eyes and breathe deeply."

Beta and Mercy had bundled dried sage into sticks and lighted them. Then they walked slowly around the group softly waving the smoke while Lia kept a soft beat on the small goatskin drum. After the smoke settled, Lia began." If you are moved to do so, please share memories and let us all celebrate them with you." The soft beat continued.

D-man was sitting next to Darcy. He began. "Serenity was a shining spark who made me a better man. I will always miss her. The spirit world is brighter for her being part of it."

Darcy continued. "Mom taught me so many lessons just by being her. She was kind, generous, there might be more words, but I think you get the idea. I will work to live my life the way she would."

Don spoke of Ruth. Nicola of her mother. Daniel stood silently next to her, overdue tears sliding from his closed eyes. Hearts poured out memories of loss and love. No one was untouched in the small group.

Finally, Nick spoke. "My losses do not feel as sharp as all of yours. The people who are gone for me left, and I didn't even know it. The life I might have led escaped my grasp without my even having tried to hold on to it. I choose not to wonder what might have been. I am grateful to be here with all of you."

The drumming faded and stopped. In the silence, Nick heard soft weeping. Lia spoke gently. "Thank you all. Stay here as long as you choose."

Ro added, "A light lunch will be ready in about an hour. It's a grazing buffet, no designated time to start or stop."

Last to leave were Rick, Jane, and Martha. "Mom, are you doing okay?" Jane was concerned because her mother had been silent.

"Ach, I'm fine. This was a beautiful thing here. Lia has a gift. She didn't say it, but her healing energy filled this place. It was peaceful just to be here and be near my Mac."

Jane arched her eyebrows. "How did you know about her gift?"

"I didn't. I felt it. And what a gift it is." Martha smiled.

Rick smiled crookedly. "So much for my scientific knowledge."

"Ach, you know plenty. And it's quite all right not to know everything in this world." Martha semi-scolded him. Then they all laughed. As they turned to walk back to the barn, Martha remembered something and called out to Nick. "Nick, Nick, I've something to tell you," she called out.

Nick and Mercy stopped and walked back to where the trio were standing. Nick took her hand, and she began. "When Mac could still speak, one afternoon right out of the clear blue, he grabbed my hand. "Marty," he said," Marty, it worked. He came back. It worked after all.' And then he slipped away again. I thought you should know that your visit gave him some peace. He was happy, Nick."

Nick gulped to swallow the lump that had suddenly grown in his throat. "Thank you, Martha. I'm happy to know that the visit made a difference." He squeezed her hand and stood still to watch the trio walk away.

"I wonder if teleportation can work without time travel," Nick spoke almost to himself as Mercy next to him smiled.

Late Afternoon at George's Bench

"I'm glad you agreed to come back here. I think we both are a little unfinished." Mercy spread out a blanket near the bench.

"What do you mean?" Nick sat down beside her.

"You're doing better at expressing your feelings. And I think you have more to say. That's all." Mercy smiled.

"I'm not sure I understand what there is to gain by going over some of these things. But I do want to make sure that I'm not moving too fast." Nick gave her an utterly serious look.

"Okay, now I'm a little confused, too fast? What do you think is moving too fast?"

"You and I, kissing, that kind of moving too fast."

"Sometimes I forget that you're not from this time. You've become just one of the guys, part of the group and all of the action. So just know that we are not moving too fast for me. In fact, we could move faster, but you might not be comfortable with that." Mercy smiled.

"Faster than kissing? You'll have to guide me. I told you that all this is new to me. And my only frame of reference is old-fashioned, to say the least." Nick blushed.

"How about you set the pace." Mercy squeezed his hand. "You said yourself that you observed most of your life. This is a chance to think about what the events and people you observed made you feel."

"Okay. Let me just stretch out on the blanket and let my mind wander." Nick stretched out next to her. Suddenly he grabbed her hand. "My head is hurting."

In a blink and a breath, he was out, like the last time. "Ahhh, Nick, I think..." Mercy didn't finish.

"Mercy, are you here?"

"Yes, I'm here."

"And here is?"

"I think you know, but I'll confirm it for you. We're in the quantum realm."

"It's only my second time."

"And my first with you."

"Why are we here now?"

"What were you thinking right before?"

"About Mac. Wishing I could talk to him again."

"It may be too soon. Some spirits need some time before they appear."

"But Theresa said there is no time here. This is really confusing."

"Think of it this way. The newly arrived spirits need to sort out what happened to them and what may be holding them back."

"Back from what?"

"From what's next for them."

"Still confusing. But I'm seeing something, maybe someone. Do you see anything?'

"Kind of. Describe what you see."

"A figure, maybe a man, moving toward me."

"I see that too."

"It's different than last time."

"What's different?"

"Me maybe. This time I'm looking for a visitor or maybe two."

"That makes sense. This is more familiar."

"I think it's Mac."

"But younger, yes?"

"Yes. Like the man I met during the War."

"The figure is close to us now?" Marcy wasn't sure.

The figure speaks. "Nick, is that you?"

"Yes, Colonel, it's me."

The figure continued. "Who is that with you? Theresa?"

"This is her granddaughter."

Mac's spirit continued. "But I saw you, and you looked like you did then."

Mercy spoke. "Time is different here, Colonel."

"Must be," Mac's spirit said.

"Are you okay, Colonel?" Nick was looking for the reason for this visit.

"I don't know. This is all strange. But before I died, I guess I died, I saw some people. People I knew were already, well, dead. I think I have something I have to do."

Mercy nodded to him. "That is often why spirits, or consciousness, is active here."

"Was something on your mind at the end, Colonel." Nick focused himself.

"Yes, I think so. Yes. You must continue your work."

Nick felt a shudder. "What work is that, Colonel?"

"And tell my son that I love him. I always loved him."

"But, Colonel, what work do you mean?" Nick needed more.

The spirit faded from their sight.

"I felt pain and then relief from him." Mercy reached for Nick.

"Yes. I felt that too. Strange to have feelings here without my body."

"We can talk more about that later." Mercy's voice faded.

Nick opened his eyes. He raised his wrist, but it was under a sheet.

And they weren't on the hill.

"Welcome back." Paul Sanchez took his wrist in a familiar firm grip.

"Where's Mercy?" Nick was concerned." And where are we?"

"I'm right here." Mercy had a smile in her voice.

"Did you come back first?" Nick wondered.

"No, I think it was when you came back."

Paul looked at the two of them. "We carried you to the main house. And you opened your eyes at almost exactly the same moment."

Early Evening Gathered in the Barn Classroom

"What do you think it means?" Charlie looked around at the group.

"Continue the work," Daniel repeated the message Nick had shared.

"Is it as simple as it sounds?" Ro wondered.

Martha spoke almost to herself. "He was not a man of mystery. My Mac said what he meant. His thoughts were clear."

"How do you think he knows what we're working on?" Nick muttered.

"Really, after all this, you think the spirits aren't aware?" Mercy laughed.

"If they are so aware, it would be nice to have some help then." Fabian chuckled.

"If you take him, or whatever you met, at his word, then you must be on to something." Daniel was nodding.

Rick picked up the theme. "That also means that Robert is more of a threat than he might have been."

Mitch and Ro both reached for their pockets at the same time. Mitch spoke first after reading the terse message on his MRC. "Robert is getting ready for something big."

Ro continued. "Gordy thinks we should prepare to have only a few people here and soon."

"That sucks. I hoped we could all be together for New Year's Eve. "Charlie grumbled.

Darcy, Vic, Daniel, and Ro said all at once. "New Year's Eve!"

Ro said, "Something big."

Darcy grinned. "Doesn't get much bigger than New Year's Eve."

Vic punched her arm lightly. "And how great is this for the movie. Do we dare have a camera ready?"

Daniel was firm. "We absolutely cannot appear to be prepared. And if for some reason he begins to search the premises, not that I'll let him, but if we have to have everything cleared out and looking like that's the way it's been."

"We have four days. If indeed New Year's Eve is it." Don looked around.

Martha smiled. "Who's on first?" That broke the tension, and everyone laughed.

Charlie added, "No one expects…"

Several voices chimed in, "The Spanish Inquisition."

The shared laughter broke the tension.

Nick's Notes
December 26, 2008

Mercy and I went quantum together. It was somewhat familiar but still so strange. Her presence is comforting, there and here. I'm pleased that it was Mercy with me this time. And we met Mac. He had a short message. These darn spirits still don't seem to want to explain much. "Continue your work." That's what he said. Oh, and "Tell my son that I love him.' I don't see me being the one who delivers that message.

We got word that Robert is planning something big. The biggest idea we had was New Year's Eve. Now we are all preparing. I'm getting ready to leave with Mercy, Clary, and Tommy. Nicola has alerted Grace. Just in case, she is telling us only what we need to know. In case of what, I hesitate to consider.

We are so close to figuring out what happened. I feel, not a word I usually use, but I feel that the answer is at hand. Mercy will be pleased to know that I feel this. I had almost relaxed.

CHAPTER 47

SUNDAY, DECEMBER 28, 2008, SKYRIDGE RANCH

A small group sat on couches around a table in the living room of the main house. Mitch spoke first. "I don't like the idea of leaving, but I understand why."

"I'll feel better with you at The Institute just in case Colonel Jerk-of-the-Year decides to go there first," Rick muttered.

Jane nodded. "And we need to have Theresa, Beta, Paul, Lia, and John Henry all away from here."

"I know, I know. I just don't like that we have to do this because of *him*." Mitch's jaw was set. "But The Institute van will do for the purpose."

Ro looked around the table. "I think our plan is sound. The people remaining here all have a tie to the movie. Martha has just arrived and will be staying in residence, so she has a reason and a right to be here. You guys as well." Looking at Rick and Jane. I feel like we have a secret weapon with Daniel here. Betcha Robert won't be expecting that!"

"Speaking of me, do you have a role in mind for me?" Daniel appeared in the doorway.

His sister appeared at his elbow. "Why our lawyer for the movie, of course."

"And I'm Nicola's father." Daniel smiled.

"Does that mean being a dad is enough of a reason? Then Charlie is my ticket to stay?" Don joined the group.

"And that explains the motor home. That means I only need someone to drive one of them back to LA." Vic was nodding and ticking items off her fingers.

"Ooo, that's also a good way to spirit a bunch of people off-site without a lot of vehicles going anywhere." Jane smiled.

Don thought out loud. "Do you want Ben to drive the other one back to your place? He can ferry Nick, Mercy, Tommy, and Clary. Michelle can drive the rented sedan behind them."

Jane smiled. "I think that gets the people who need to be protected out of the way of our impending trouble. All that's left is for us to clean up and identify anything that should be taken off-site before Wednesday."

"How soon does this all begin?" Rick wondered.

"The cleanup could use all hands. Let's look at departures starting tomorrow afternoon." Ro looked around for approval. Heads nodded.

"Who's going to tell them?" Mitch asked.

"You are." Jane smiled.

Mitch used his MRC to text all the visitors on the Ranch property. They all streamed to the barn classroom immediately.

After everyone was seated, Mitch moved to the head of the room. "Thank you all for coming so quickly. The warning of Robert's imminent arrival is confirmed. It is critical that we prepare for him and protect all of you. We have a plan to share with you."

Don stood next to Mitch. "What we have in mind is a two-stage exodus. The motorhome is a convenient way to get several of you off-site without being noticed if there is anyone watching the roads. Since Vic and Daniel are staying here, Ben, you will drive Vic's extra motorhome with Nick, Mercy, Clary, and Tommy in it. Michelle, you will follow in your rental car so it can be returned as we planned.

Mitch picked up the lead. "I'll drive The Institute van. In that beast, I will be ferrying Lia, Theresa, Beta, Paul, and John Henry. You all will stay at The Institute until it's safe for me to fly back to New Mexico with three of you."

Don picked up the thread. "Ben and Michelle, from Vic's house, you'll be driving one of The Institute's passenger vans all the way to Indio, with passengers. When you get there, Grace and Father Joe will have a car for the two of you to drive back to Vento Junction. The van stays in Indio, and Nicola and Charlie can come to pick it up when things settle."

Daniel took over. "Nick, Mercy, Tommy, and Clary, you can take a breath at Grace's house and rest for a night. Then she and Father Joe have a plan for your next step. Beyond that, she's not saying, and we understand why. Just know that her refugee network is coming to your aid." He explained.

Ro continued. "Everyone else remains here to 'work on the movie.' That's the story and the game plan. Any questions?"

Charlie raised his hand. "What about the dogs?"

Mitch smiled. "They all come to The Institute. To get them off the Ranch and keep them together, Ben will bring them to Vic's in the motorhome. I'll get them all in the van a little later and bring them to The Institute, where they can hang out with us."

Heads nodded, and murmurs turned to grumbles. "When do we get to come back?" Clary wanted to know.

Nick took this one. "We really don't know. The situation with Robert offers no certainty and we must go into hiding."

Mercy added, "It won't be for long. Between the story planted about Dave Gustafson's death and the movie turning into something real, Robert will not be credible."

D-man suddenly jerked up. "What about my mom and Dick and Betsy?"

Jane smiled. "They will also enjoy the relaxation and protection of the guest quarters at The Institute."

He sat back visibly relieved.

"Then what is there for us to be doing?" Fabian wondered.

"That's an easy one." Ro grinned. "Everyone staying, make it look like you've been the only ones in your quarters. Anyone leaving, pack up everything, clean thoroughly, and be prepared to head out tomorrow evening."

D-man added, "And for all of us here right now, we party tonight until we can all gather together again."

Nick's Notes
Monday Morning, December 29, 2008

I have a better feeling this time than when the family headed for the Camp in 1942. Even though it's not the US government making me move. Mercy reminds me that it's only one man and that the man is not the president this time. Small comfort.

The boys are excited. I made sure Clary has the rocks in a safe package and on his person so he can alert us if he feels something from them.

It feels right to be traveling with Mercy. There's that word again. But there is not another better word to describe this anticipation. I'm at ease with her. I think she trusts me.

Nick's Notes
Tuesday, December 30, 2008

With the exception of dinner last night, though it seems longer ago, everyone has been in motion since Sunday when we heard about the plan. The dogs loved it. They thought we were all playing. Traveling in the motorhome today was pretty amazing. It combines the best of luxury train travel with the privacy of a personal bus. I can see why Vic has one. Really it's a house on wheels, a house you can take with you.

We reached Vic's at dusk and quickly transferred to the van Mitch brought. It is safer to travel at night. We benefit from the early sunsets this time of year. It gets dark soon after four. Ben and Michelle took turns driving. Maybe because of the dark, the six-hour trip went quickly. Grace and Father Joe were up and waiting for us. Amy June, her new dog was so, so happy to see all of us. We were so tired we spread out to couches, beds, and even the floor right after we got there. Mercy says stress can make you tired. There was plenty of that to go around.

Ben and Michelle will go home to Arizona in the morning. The adventure begins for Mercy, Tommy, Clary, and me tomorrow night.

CHAPTER 48

WEDNESDAY, DECEMBER 31, 2008, MIDMORNING NEW YEAR'S EVE AT SKYRIDGE RANCH

Ro felt her MRC buzz. "It's him."

Rick, Jane, and Martha all clustered to look at the small device. "All safe." Mitch had texted them the words they needed to hear. The last of the travelers as on the next stage of their journey.

"It's out to the barn to keep decorating."

Ro looked to the door and pushed her friends out. Martha lingered. "I'll be resting here, if you don't mind."

"Martha, just rest and relax. The excitement is all yet to come." Ro smiled.

Dusk, and the Party Was Underway in the Barn Classroom

Ro felt the familiar buzz. The text was one word: "incoming." She alerted the group.

Thuka, thuka, thuka, thuka, thuka, thuka, thuka. The sound grew louder and louder. D-man kept the music playing, but the group stopped dancing. The doors to the barn were open to let the evening air in. Black helmeted men streamed into the room, winding like a smooth black snake around the perimeter. One man stepped forward.

"Where is he?" Colonel Robert MacLane shouted.

"There's no need to shout, son." Martha spoke.

"*Shut that damn music off!*" Robert shouted.

Jane had moved next to her mother, not that this fierce mother hen needed backup. Martha tried again to get her son's attention. "Robert, what's this about then?"

"You know damn well what this is about."

"If she did, she wouldn't have asked, asshole. So why don't you tell her?" Rick stood next to Jane.

Several of the helmeted soldiers turned their heads to look at each other.

"There is a dangerous fugitive being sheltered here," Robert insisted.

"Dangerous fugitive? There is no fugitive, dangerous or otherwise, here." Ro stood up.

"Sit down, Ro. I wouldn't expect you to tell me the truth." Robert began to move toward them. Helmets around the room began to look back and forth.

Martha tried again. "Robert, can you be more specific about what you're doing here?"

"*You're protecting him! You're as bad as Dad was!*" Robert was yelling.

One of the helmeted soldiers muttered, "Dad? Is this his mother?"

"Robert, please be specific. You've said fugitive. What else can you tell me about what you're looking for?" Jane calmly continued.

Sarcasm dripped. "Oh, sister dear, as if you didn't know. You have the man that our father looked for all his life."

Another helmet muttered, "Sister?"

"Robert, your father looked for a man who *the Army* declared dead and a hero in 1944. His family has the medals to prove it," Rick stated.

Robert's voice was shrill. "But he's not dead. You have him here. I know it. I know it. He's alive, and you're protecting a national security risk."

Daniel stood and moved forward. "Do you have any grounds to accuse these people?"

"I don't need grounds. I'm the goddamned US government, and *I'll accuse whoever I want!*" Robert was red-faced.

A radio crackled. One of the helmeted men spoke. "Colonel, the general wants to talk to you."

Robert didn't pay attention. "You have him. He came back. He's here. He's not dead. Give him to me."

"Oh, Robert, no," Martha moaned.

"Dammit, my father was part of an experiment in World War II."

Martha spoke. "Yes, he was. It was teleportation, dear. And the experiment ended tragically. The lead scientist perished. He was one of my students."

The black-helmeted soldiers continued to look around.

Robert nearly screeched. "No, he didn't, he's *here.*"

Jane said calmly, "Robert, if indeed there was a time traveler, what you want is the technology, not the traveler. And if this happened under Dad's watch, then the military already has the technology."

"*No, we don't!*" Robert was sweating and red-faced.

D-Man lost his patience. "Robert, what about the murder? What about my dad? I called you to help find out what the Army covered up in 1944."

"Robert waved his hand in dismissal. "Forget that. It's not important."

"A real murder. An unsolved murder. An Army cover-up? Not important?" D-man's voice had risen.

Robert turned to look at the pony-tailed scientist to shout." Not when you're hiding a national security risk here."

The radio crackled again. "Colonel, the general demands to talk to you, sir."

"*Not now,*" Robert shouted.

The helmeted soldier held the radio up near Robert so he and the rest of the room could hear. "Colonel MacLane! *Stand down! Stand down immediately!*"

Robert screamed. "*No! I will not! He's here! They have him here, I know it!*"

The general's voice bellowed, "*Colonel MacLane! If you do not stand down, you will be relieved of command! Do you understand?*"

"*I will not stand down! I will not stand down! I will not stand down!*" Robert was screaming.

The voice on the radio barked. "Captain Hayden. Relieve Colonel MacLane of his weapon, secure him, stand down, and retreat. You will report to me as soon as you return to base. Do you understand?"

"Yes, sir." Captain Hayden moved to take Robert's sidearm. Robert lunged, but there were men to stop him.

Robert was still screaming as the soldiers restrained him and carried him to the helicopter. Captain Hayden turned to the stunned gathering. "I regret what happened here tonight. And if you really are Colonel MacLane's mother and sister…" He paused, at a loss. "I am so very sorry." He turned and left the room.

After the *thuka, thuka, thuka* sound had faded, and the sound of crickets had again filled the silence, Daniel spoke. "This isn't over."

Approaching Midnight at The Institute

Mitch's MRC alerted, "Robert secured and removed by his own men. All clear for now." He shared the message with his group of Skyridge refugees.

"All clear for now doesn't sound reassuring." John Henry was skeptical.

Beta nodded. "I'm not in any hurry to leave this panic room based on that message."

Lia chuckled. "Good for you, daughter. I'm with you. This is comfortable. We have food, water, even champagne. I say we stay until morning at least."

Theresa nodded. "My girls are wise and smart. We stay put, young Mitchell, if that is all right with you."

"I know when to throw up my hands. Ladies, consider us in for the night. Now who wants to play a little gin rummy?" Mitch looked at John Henry, and they all laughed in relief.

Approaching Midnight, Indio, Grace's Living Room

Nick and Mercy felt the MRCs in their pockets alert them to a message. They had been waiting for news ever since Ben and Michelle had dropped them in Indio and continued on to Arizona. Nick turned to his fellow travelers. "Robert came. He was taken away by soldiers. Daniel says, stay alert."

Mercy shook her head. "That must have been quite the scene."

Tommy and Clary looked at each other. "Awesome, it would be for certain." Clary was becoming an American teenager.

Grace and Father Joe gently chided him. "You can say that because you are here and did not have to feel the terror of the Army coming to take you from your home."

Tommy nodded. "I remember the soldiers. So many of them. They didn't like us either. But I still wanted to enlist. I'll be eighteen in a couple of months. If I was still back there, I would enlist. I guess it's better I'm here. Maybe I would have died. A lot of guys did."

Mercy nodded. "I think we all need to be grateful for where we are tonight and the people around us."

"This is a New Year's Eve to remember for sure." Nick smiled.

Nearly Midnight at the Now Home of Ben Grant and Michelle Matthews in Vento Junction, Arizona

Ben's MRC alerted. "Dad says Robert went full Colonel Kurtz and his own men hauled him away."

"Not exactly the way I played it out in my head as we were driving across the desert, but I'll take it. I wonder how long they can keep him?" Michelle's reporter brain was in gear.

"I imagine a psych evaluation will be requested. If he keeps saying what we think he said, I don't see a rosy future for him." Ben looked grim.

"I wonder if I should goose the Dave Gustafson story a little?" she wondered.

"I think that's a question for Daniel. We can reach out to him tomorrow. I think we may just lay low for a while." Ben smiled and reached for the bottle of sparkling wine.

"I want to follow up on that GI who went missing too. My gut says it's not going to be more than a guy gone AWOL for a good reason. But still. We need to know." The dogged reporter was in the room.

"I think that can wait a day or two. Let's enjoy this moment of calm." Ben raised his glass.

"What would you say if I said my New Year's resolution was to get a dog?" Michelle grinned.

"Do we call her Traveler?" Ben had a conspiratorial grin.

They laughed and toasted to the uncertain adventures ahead of them.

EPILOGUE

JANUARY 1, 2009,
THE WEE HOURS OF THE MORNING

At a remote base near the mountains east of San Diego, soldiers were putting away gear from the strangest mission they had ever been assigned.

"Sir?" A weary officer turned to look at the man who had spoken. "Do think Colonel MacLane is crazy?"

Captain Jim Hayden stopped to consider the question. "Private, if he's *not* crazy, then the biggest doggone secret in the entire history of the US military is still a secret."

"Yes, but do you think there was anything to what he was ranting about?"

"He was talking about a time traveler in the helicopter. What do think, Private? Are there time travelers walking among us?" Jim Hayden needed to put an end to this conversation.

"I don't know, sir. But if there was, it would sure be something."

FAMILY TREES

Nishimura Family

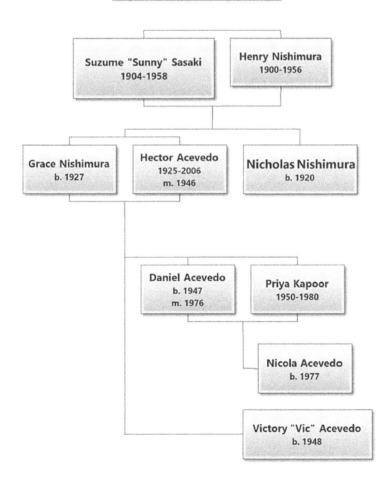

Grant Family

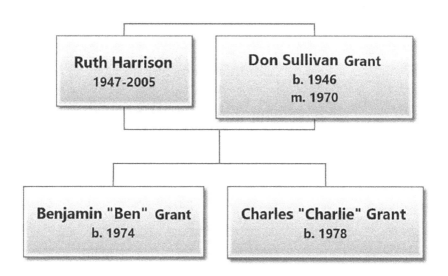

Stanton Family

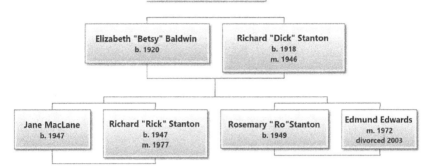

Cisneros Family

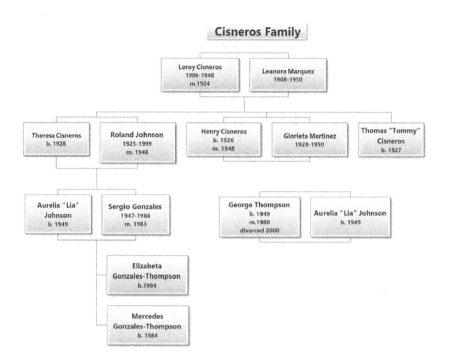

MacLane Family

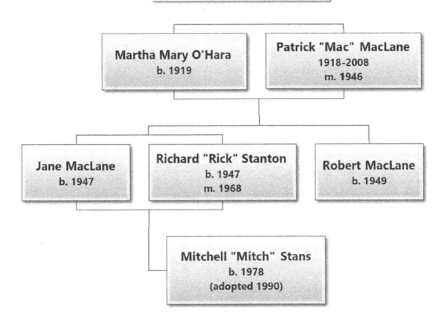

Gustafson-Hickson Family

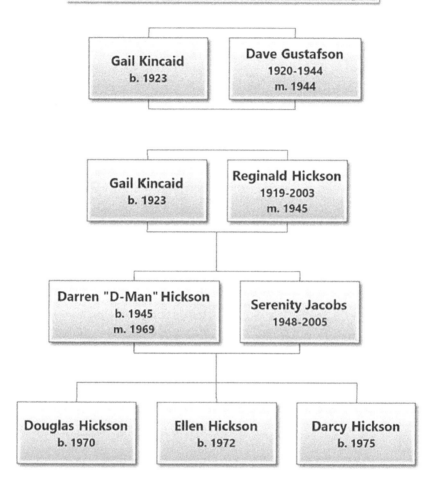

Gustafson - Hickson Family

Gail Kincaid
b. 1923

Dave Gustafson
1920-1944
m. 1944

Gail Kincaid
b. 1923

Reginald Hickson
1919-2003
m. 1945

Darren "D-Man" Hickson
b. 1945
m. 1969

Serenity Jacobs
1948-2005

Douglas Hickson
b. 1970

Ellen Hickson
b. 1972

Darcy Hickson
b. 1975

ACKNOWLEDGMENTS

If you are reading this, then you may well have plowed through the entirety of book 2 in the Measured Time Series, *Of Secrets and Spirits*. If you enjoyed it, then you, like I, owe a debt of gratitude to my early readers. If you read it and didn't enjoy it, that's all on me. The characters and story lines sprout from my imagination. What makes this book readable is, in large part, due to the skills and generous hearts of Linda Peterson, Peggy and Jim Halderman, and Dr. Marilyn Newsom. They have read more than one (maybe five) versions and revisions on the way to the final draft. Then the bulky Word file is sent to Nora Custead at Page Publishing. She is the publishing version of a midwife, a production coordinator. Together we birthed a book. Her skills, recipes, and sense of humor are boundless.

The momentum from Book One pushed me to finish Book Two. The encouragement of friends, readers, and booksellers has been a source of motivation when I question why I continue to do this. Diane Ventura-Goodyear in Tucson and her neighborhood book club were the first to read it as a group, followed by my Madison South Rotary book club. Then Rye Kimmet, owner of Kismet Books in Verona, Wisconsin, began to carry signed copies of my book on her shelves. In July, Other Worlds Books and More in Sturgeon Bay, Wisconsin, owned by David and Margaret Magle, offered me not one but two book signings.

First, last, and always is my husband, Diamond Jim. Ready to spar with a new idea for a character and offer suggestions. He reminds me that self-doubts are part of the process and come with the territory. Embrace them and move on. Thank you. It would be no fun without you.

ABOUT THE AUTHOR

Lynn Perez-Hewitt is an unlikely adventurer. A Catholic schoolgirl from Rockford, Illinois, a Bradley University graduate, and a PR professional with many traditional achievements, she nonetheless followed her heart and curiosity through six states and seven industries. She came to writing novels late, though words and language have been themes throughout her life. Whether giving speeches, performing on stage, or persuading an audience to adopt new ideas, her craft is language; her canvas is people. Constants in the mosaic of her life are her love of reading, music, pets, and people. Her adventures became focused and fine-tuned when she found a fellow adventurer. He plays music and loves dogs, cats, ferrets, and more. They live, play, write, and throw Frisbees in Wisconsin.

CPSIA information can be obtained
at www.ICGtesting.com
Printed in the USA
LVHW102320100922
728086LV00003B/7